JEWELS
BEYOND PRICE

JEWELS
BEYOND PRICE

WYVERN AND STAR 2

Sophy Boyle

First printed in this edition 2017

Published by Palestrina
First Floor Radius House
51 Clarendon Road
Watford
Hertfordshire, WD17 1HP

ISBN: 978-0-9956066-2-3

Book design: Dean Fetzer, GunBoss Books, www.gunboss.com.
Cover design: Mark Ecob, Mecob Design Ltd, www.mecob.co.uk
Cover image © DEA PICTURE LIBRARY / Getty Images © Shutterstock.com

For Edward

Contents

PART I

WOLVES

All those last days in Chepstow, while Robert Clifford's attention was occupied by that which he loved best in all the world – being soldiery – a different kind of adventure was playing out not ten miles distant and the mainspring of his heart was unwinding, inexorable and unobserved.

The man's ill luck played its customary part. If, on that fateful morning at Dyffryn Hall, Alice had chosen to come down to him, he would, doubtless, have forgotten Jasper Tudor; had the relics of Leonard Tailboys cried out from their concealment, the departure would have been deferred. A hundred other incidents or accidents might have conspired to keep Clifford from the Chepstow road and, when the pursuers descended the ridge towards Dyffryn Hall, the Wyverns – who were certainly spoiling for bloodshed – would have left them all for dead, no doubt.

But it was not to be. As the group of strangers made their wary way down the vertiginous bank towards the house at Dyffryn, the Wyverns were beyond reach and Sir Hugh Dacre was in command. He hurried out to the gates and threw them open. Poor Sir Lawrence looked on from the house, roundly failing Robert Clifford, his old companion-in-arms, for he was concerned only with the fate of his heir – a fate that was resting in the hands of King Edward.

At the first alarm, Alice had slipped Blanche's hand and run towards the house in high dread. She burst in upon her gentlewomen.

Cutting through the breathless tangle, Constance darted to the window. It faced south, the view as peaceful as ever. "We must get a message to Lord Clifford. I'll find the groom." It was not Lord Clifford she pictured then, but his steady and gallant son. She was down the stairs and into the bright yard before anyone could hinder her, heading, nothing daunted, for the ominous stable. But as she passed before the gatehouse, the doors swung open to admit the raiders and she halted in the shadow of the wall.

The leader dismounted and strode forward to meet Sir Hugh. Here was a man somewhere in his mid-thirties, of medium height and medium build, chestnut hair cropped short in the old style, a complexion of dusty tan, a long nose and broad, tapering brows. Shorter than Hugh Dacre, but shown to greater advantage, an impression of firm and quiet assurance. Sir Hugh's hair was more scarecrow than ever, standing quite on end. The two men embraced.

"By God, Simon! Jesu, but I'm glad it's you! Else I'd a deal of explaining to do."

"Some account will be needed." The newcomer's voice was self-consciously well-bred; cold and precise. "Is she here?"

"She's here. Clifford left for Chepstow at dawn."

"I see. Just now he'll be encountering a surprise in the shape of Roger Vaughan."

"Let's hope that's the end of him then. Dreadful fellow. Clifford, I mean." Dacre glanced around. "Come inside, Simon, and we'll talk."

"This is Lawrence Welford's house. Lead me first to him. You'll have your chance in due course."

Running a hand through his rumpled locks, Sir Hugh took his friend by the arm. The errant groom had appeared at his side, too late to be of any help, for Constance had already backed out of view.

* * *

Behind the door, the voices were shrill and anguished. If Constance were thunderstruck at the betrayal, how much worse for Alice? Elyn was incoherent, but it was the loss of Master Guy that was uppermost in her jumbled mind and she was abandoned to her pain.

"How could you, Blanche?" cried Alice, tears of fury trembling in her lashes. "When my husband said we harboured a spy in our midst, I did not believe it. Edmond did not know the half. After betraying me with Sir Loic, you have betrayed me to my enemies!"

"Lady Alice – no! Think on what I told you at Ledbury! As you had no proper care for yourself, another must bear that burden. Sir Hugh will watch over you, and Simon Loys is an old friend from our Middleham days. He will protect us." Tremulous, Blanche, too, was starting to cry.

"Sir Hugh played the traitor with anyone who cared to follow. When Robert Clifford returns he will slay your false Sir Hugh! I wish you joy of each other, while the man's head still tops his body."

Constance turned, addressing herself only to Alice. "No man shall force us to leave this place – isn't that what Lord Clifford said? Sir Simon can hardly drag you bodily from the house. Tell him you went willingly with Lord Clifford. Tell him you are lovers. Tell him you are married. Do not speak of the babe. *Blanche,*" she turned with sharp mistrust on the miserable gentlewoman, "say he knows nothing of the babe!"

Blanche's hands fluttered. "If he didn't know before, Sir Hugh will have told him by now."

"May God forgive you, Blanche, for I never shall."

There was a firm knock, startling all within. The catch clicked.

"Listening at doors," sneered Constance.

"I defy anyone who caught that tale not to hear it out," said Simon Loys from the depths of his bow. "It's pleasing to see you again after so long, my lady. You shall walk with me. We have much to discuss."

All the nausea returned at a rush. Silent with her desperate thoughts, Alice descended the stairs before the knight who clanked and scraped against the walls. She was keeping well ahead, upwind of the sour drift. As they neared the bridge,

Loys caught her hand, careless of the difference in rank, pinning it in his steel-clad elbow. The metal was very hot. She flinched away. He leaned against the parapet as she frowned into the shallow water – clear and speeding despite the spell of brilliant weather. After a moment, she breathed and turned back. He'd aged, perceptibly, in those few years since she saw him last at Middleham. There were lines about his face, new-grown, or perhaps not; this was always a man beneath her notice.

"Sir Simon, you're come with the best of intentions, but under a false premise." Her hands were earnestly clasped. "Since you overheard, I won't deceive you. It's true I carry the Duke of Somerset's child. I am under the protection of Lord Clifford, the only man I trust to protect my babe and its inheritance. So if you've followed us with any idea of rescue, I wish you will go away again before my protector returns and discovers you here. He is not a placid man."

He eyed her in his turn. "You speak of Robert Clifford as a champion. All know him to be a monster of depravity." No matter what the subject matter, Sir Simon's voice was always chilly and measured; she remembered it now. "In your innocence, he has deceived you. Lady Alice, consider: your guardian, Warwick, is dead; your brother is fled into exile. You are a widow, friendless and helpless. Yes: Edmond Beaufort was beheaded this Monday past, before my very eyes." He paused, but she was conspicuously still. "You have no protector. As I was of Warwick's council and have known you since you were a child, I shall take that role."

A tumult followed.

"Your surprise has betrayed you into foolishness, my lady. This is not of my making. I was so charged *by the King*."

"The King? I acknowledge only one king!"

"Try not to be *stupid*. You are fortunate to be offered a second chance: your freedom and a rich parcel of your brother's lands."

A calculating pause. "Then the price is too high. I know what Edward of York will demand: the surrender of my child."

"Don't call him *Edward of York*. King Edward does not require the surrender of your child, who shall remain beside you, in safety and comfort. It is promised."

She blinked at him, wondering if she'd misjudged.

He put her right. "So: I carry with me the licence for our marriage. We wed tomorrow." And then he shut his eyes and blew a great, bored sigh as she lashed him with her infantile fury and contempt. "No, I think you'll find that I *can*. An unpleasant fate awaits if you do not submit. Childhood accidents are common, are they not? Falls, fevers, poisonings. You wish to grow old, alone, in a nunnery, and never hear your child's last cries?"

"Robert will cut out your tongue when he hears of this wickedness!"

"A distasteful image; clearly you've spent too long in the man's company."

"And I hope I'm watching."

"You'll be disappointed. At this moment, Chepstow Castle is besieged by Sir Roger Vaughan and a force of several hundreds; Clifford will not trouble us again. Meanwhile, I've ridden hard in full harness for two days. I'm hot and soiled and weary. Dacre promised me a bath, and it is calling. I leave you to think on all I've said."

"No priest can marry me if I will not speak the words!"

"True, my lady. I cannot force you to the altar, but I have warned you of the consequences. Moreover, I *can* force myself into your chamber, and will do so tonight if you remain obstinate. You'll be glad enough to wed me, I think, with all the world conjecturing on your child's paternity."

As the man made his way back to the house, Alice fell to her knees in an agony of despair.

* * *

By candlelight Marjorie Verrier entered Lady Eleanor's chamber, the shutters fastened against the pleasant warmth of the morning. She expected to find her mistress abed; the bed to which she was carried, bodily, by the physician on the previous morning. But the bleeding had done its work, for the lady was kneeling now, in her bedgown, at the prie-dieu, saintly in the glimmer. The elderly chamberer slumbered on, stool tilted to a hazardous angle, shoulder braced against the panelled wall.

The new waiting woman should be in attendance. She was, again, elsewhere. Marjorie breathed a little snort. There was never so besotted a bride; a rich seam of ridicule. A month since the wedding, and still Mistress Anna had thoughts for nothing and no one but Master Waryn, her hulking young husband, the last Clifford in the castle. It was a diversion too amusing to pass up, that nightly stroll past the under-steward's chamber. In the evening hour after Anna was released from her duties, the stairwell outside the couple's room was a thronged highway, thrumming with smothered laughter.

Marjorie busied herself in silence until stilled by a movement in the shadows beyond the bed. Good God – it was the Earl himself, gnawing at his fingernail, motionless and unattended in the gloom. From what little she could see, Harry Percy did not look at all pleased.

"Forgive me for startling you, Mistress Verrier," he said crisply. "My sister has been at her prayers a long time, but I fear that if I don't disturb her with my presence, she will never rise again."

"I have more pressing concerns than to bandy words with you, Brother." And then Eleanor returned to her devotions.

"That's a start, I suppose. The first words I've had from you in hours. I thought you'd lost the power of speech."

The irascible tone was so unlike the Earl's usual measured courtesy that Marjorie halted and frowned at him.

"Perhaps I never mentioned it," he continued, to his sister's back, "but I have ever admired the lack of feminine weakness. You would have made a fine earl. Yet now, in the moment of triumph, when you should rejoice that our enemies are vanquished, you display less restraint than the silliest young maiden sighing over some pretty boy. It will not do, Eleanor; you must rouse yourself and look to the future. Your peculiar attachment to Robert Clifford has already been remarked all over the North Country; this behaviour will be added to the tally. Regulate your conduct, I beg you, or you will find a husband of any rank beyond you."

"What care I for the chatter of those whose minds are still and whose hearts are cold? If my betrothed is alive, I shall go to him, Harry, and there is nothing you or any man can do to prevent it."

"Jesu! Firstly, there was no betrothal, as you well know," interrupted her brother, exasperated now beyond endurance. "And secondly, you'll find I can most easily prevent it: a turn of the key would suffice. While I never question your intelligence, I'm starting to despair of your sanity."

"And if my love has fallen, I hold myself bound to him forever. I shall wed no other."

This was magnificent. Marjorie's lips were parted. Revolted, Percy kicked the lapdog and stalked out.

* * *

Loys did not take an axe to the lock, for by sunset Alice had made the inevitable submission. The message was conveyed by that guilty pair, Sir Hugh and poor Blanche, who'd been battling icy disdain since noon.

Simon Loys and Hugh Dacre were old allies, working hand-in-glove in Warwick's interest – while it held good. They would have termed each other *friend*, though Loys did not, in general, practise friendship. The two men were not born equal: Sir Hugh was the cadet of an ancient baronial family while Sir Simon was solid gentry. But Loys was a landed man, inheriting a wide, treeless tract choked with heather and bracken and a stark Norman castle, impressively comfortless. Sir Hugh, meanwhile, had nothing beyond his name and his wits and the goodwill of a dead traitor. And so the bond had grown in ways that did not conform to the pattern of their birth, but reflected their progress in life. Once the King dangled the lush de Vere lands before Loys's greedy gaze, Dacre dwindled a degree further in his friend's eyes – and at once adapted himself.

All respectful attention, Sir Hugh presented himself. In the low-ceilinged hall, Sir Simon had begun the evening meal without him, dining with his taciturn marshal, his foreign chamberlain and the distracted Sir Lawrence. After a moment, Loys put down his knife and frowned up at Dacre's bonnet. Pinned into the black felt was a badge in the form of a wyvern. The beast had once possessed paired eyes of pink glass, but – like its master – it had shed one along the way. Now it winked impertinently at him. Loys signalled it with a finger and, grimacing, Dacre plucked out the brooch and ground it beneath his heel, as he'd done so many times before.

"Good," said Loys, when his friend had conveyed the tidings of surrender. "The girl wants taming, but I'd struggle to muster the enthusiasm tonight. By the way, Hugh, I hear there is a dead man in the stables. A dead man with no eyes. See to it, if you will." He took up his spoon.

Sir Hugh was in the act of sitting. Weary and incredulous, he pushed to his feet and, bolstered by a lantern and the stolid presence of Andrew Chowne, he obeyed.

Forlorn, ashamed, Blanche Carbery was for the last hours possessed of a strong urge to renounce her betrothal, but Sir Simon's manner brought to mind the futility of abandoning the winners to rejoin the losers.

* * *

Blanche had been banished from the garbing of the bride. Wan and red-eyed, Alice showed no interest in the preparations. Each of the lady's few dresses was examined, and found to be draggled and travel-worn, her best gown worst of all.

"How came your grey velvet to be so grass-stained and grubby?" wondered Constance, unbuttoning the dress again; it was unwearable. Then she recalled Leonard Tailboys's terrible tale, and pictured the pollution of the gown.

"I was wearing it when I fainted in the woods," murmured her mistress. "And when I came to, I was sullied." Off came the garment and Constance's face was hidden in its folds. "Good Master Aymer had laid me down, I think. Probably he was trying to wake me."

"As gallant as his twin," added Elyn.

Constance bit her lip, wishing for the solace of Hal's broad shoulders in this swirl of trouble. When all was as ready as it would ever be, the gentlewomen kissed Alice with sorrowful tenderness.

"There is one blessing in all this," Constance remarked, loudly, as they led her from the chamber. "As you carry another man's child, that cur will not touch you. Impious as he is, he would not cross that line. And by the time the babe is born, who knows what shall be?"

"True," said Alice and the frown eased a little. "By then Robert will have sliced him up like …"

"I wouldn't wait for that," said the lionhearted girl. "I would do it myself."

* * *

Northumberland had no leisure for his sister's idiocy; he was readying his retinue to ride south. With news of York's triumph at Tewkesbury, the northern stirrings collapsed without a blow. Once there was no risk of military engagement, the Earl found himself eager to rendezvous with King Edward in the Midlands; to present his sovereign with the good news and assure him of Percy loyalty.

He could not depart before he'd permitted himself one delicious moment. Returning, after a day's absence, to his sister's room, Percy settled himself once more into the low chair and unrolled a sheaf of parchment.

Eleanor, regarding both the man and his tantalising letter from the corner of her eye, concluded her prayers with unhurriedly dignity and seated herself on the bed. "Well, Harry?"

"Well, Sister." How he relished it. Rising, he crossed to the window and flung wide the shutters, letting in the daylight to dazzle her unaccustomed eyes. "When last we spoke, I had no certain tidings of Robert Clifford. I thought you might care to hear the news, now that news is come."

Her lips trembled; her breathing too.

"Oh, he's not dead. No. Very much alive."

She was transfixed.

"As it turns out, Robert Clifford did not reach Tewkesbury. The man left Skipton, for sure, moving south with that rabble of his. But he never took the field. It seems he'd forsaken the cause, for he rode straight for the Priory at Little Malvern, where Edmond Beaufort's wife was hidden. Having abandoned his friends to their deaths, Clifford discarded his queen, and

Edward of Lancaster's widow – Warwick's daughter – and carried off the Lady Alice." Percy's voice, so quick and clipped, had turned to velvet. "And now, as Beaufort has gone to the block, we may be sure that Robert has wed the woman. For once, the truth has outdone the rumours."

His sister had ceased, some long moments before, to breathe, but he was caught in his own thoughts – or pretending so.

"How I wish I'd met the lady! Only think, Eleanor: there was once talk of marriage between us, before Jack de Vere went … wrong. Imagine what she must be! To have vanquished Black Clifford; bewitched him until he'd disown the cause for which he's striven these twenty years. Lady Alice must be beyond compare."

Eleanor went on staring, unblinking, into her brother's eyes until his gaze faltered.

* * *

Borne before the bridal party – a dismal herald – Sir Leonard Tailboys lay now beside them in the church, hymned to his rest by a chorus of conjecture. Like worms, the whispers must die off when they had nothing left to feed upon. But meanwhile, the wretched Hugh Dacre would keep watching Constance as if he'd caught her wielding the pitchfork.

All through the ceremony, Alice waited for the doors to crash on their hinges and Robert's huge voice to halt proceedings. Though she bent all her mind to reach him, he never came. Then her attention was recalled to the present: it was not a lightning strike to the tower, nor did Loys suffer a fatal stroke on the steps of the church: the pair were now husband and wife. At the last she had said the vows only to spare herself worse, for Sir Simon had hedged her in at every turn, until she relinquished the birthright to spare the babe.

The knight kissed his wife in the church and afterwards ignored her, walking back to the house between his marshal and the limping Sir Andrew. "Why is it that you have not opposed me, Chowne?"

"In truth, Sir Simon, my late master, *the Duke of Somerset*" – this last was barely beneath his breath, but Loys let it pass – "was no friend to Robert Clifford, and with good reason. I don't believe my mistress was safe in that devil's hands. Mistress Carbery thinks the same."

"So I'm the lesser evil?"

"If anyone deserves peace and prosperity, it is Lady Alice, and these you will provide, Sir Simon."

"And what are your own plans?"

"I'll go to my brother in Yeovil," said Sir Andrew, "and look about to see what I might do. I suppose I must sue for a pardon, now."

"Would you come to me, if I offered it?"

"To you? You have a chamberlain already, Sir Simon; Master Brini, is it not?"

"Indeed. But my household has no butler. We're coming up in the world, and I feel the lack. No doubt you could fill one role as well as the other."

"I would take the position with a right good will, sir. I thank you. I'd feel I was doing right by … *the Duke*; watching over his lady, now that he is gone."

"My wife requires no watching, I trust. Her adventuring days are done. Nevertheless, you may join my household if you will. Discuss the terms with Sir Hugh. And remember that from now on, your loyalties lie with me."

Chowne opened his fingers, inspecting the pewter badge that Loys had pressed in his palm, turning it about: a common bee, brisk and barbed. Here was the man's badge; and his very essence, captured neatly in his device – as was, so often, the case.

* * *

All through the wedding feast – quite as scant and plain as any other meal at the Hall – Alice watched her husband. Like Edmond, Simon was sparing with wine and meat and speech. But he was not like Edmond; not at all. By evening fall, she was exhausted. Wrung out and emptied, she longed for peace, and peace, at last, would be hers. The man would share the chamber –

that much was a given – but he was no stranger and doubtless she would grow used to his presence.

Her gentlewomen fluttered her upstairs, but she could not rise to their overwrought ado and sent them off, surrendering to Mitten's comfortable hands. He must have risen directly after, for she heard the murmurs behind the door as the little chamberlain undressed him.

Before he entered, Alice was beneath the sheets, nightcapped, gowned and sweltering. Loys slipped from his bedgown. He'd not suffer the heat to spare her blushes. Though she averted her face, she'd stolen a swift look; she could hardly help herself. His frame, too, was like Edmond's, though more dark; brownish rather than fair; muscled, but not unduly so, a body competent for the tasks required of it. He lay down at her side. Wordless, she turned her back and prepared for sleep.

Fingers jabbed her throat. The little linen cap spun across the floor. "Never wear that again. I bought you. I intend to see you."

The rebuke at her lips, she turned. He was on her like a beast, rending the bedgown, pulling her hard against him, greedy and rough. She protested in horror.

"Hold your tongue. You are *not* with child. The babe has not come into being; it is of *my* seed, gotten this night. As yet, it has no existence.

Then began the ugliest hours of her short life.

He was no stranger; that made it worse. A man who slunk at the lower limit of her world was now her lord, and lording it over her. How was it that none had seen the viciousness within? Her dear Richard Neville, seeking the knight's counsel, admitting Loys to his inmost plans, knowing nothing of his malice.

When the man began his study – candle so close it scorched the flesh – Alice covered her face with her hands and silent tears slid out. Never had she endured such handling: not as a child, nor as a woman, nor as a wife. Edmond was deeply reserved, and Robert's touch was beyond gentle and so very different, but she could not think of that.

As if in harmony with her fortunes, the glorious weather broke that night. First the shutters swung and creaked. Then the wind rose with a vengeance and flung its soaking gusts into the chamber until it extinguished the flame and he tore himself away to shut out the squall. By then, sporadic flashes at the window seemed to ignite the man, and Sir Simon, so frigid and calculating by daylight, was transmuted into some other being: cruel, sordid and grotesque.

Finally he had done and slumbered heavily while she, to whom sleep was always a sweet friend, lay broken in the dark hours.

Alice rose with the dawn, feeling silently for her bedgown. Now was the moment to smash the man's head as he slept – all tousled and harmless – and bolt for Chepstow; she went so far as to lift a stool by the legs, testing its weight but, instead of wielding it, carried it to the window and shivered at the sheets of rain. She gathered the fine linen into her lap. A faint wash of blood, marbled and sticky on her thighs. Self-pity flooded her.

"The babe has taken no hurt. You bleed easily because you are noble. Obey me as your husband, and I will be less stern with you." He pushed himself up. "Come here."

The man drew Alice into his lap and slipped the gown from her shoulders, starting again with his fingers. She turned her cheek from his breath, sharp and sour.

"Two years ago I asked the Earl of Warwick for your hand. My family is old and good, but the refusal wasn't courteous. Before the end, Richard Neville had need of friends and wished he'd been more civil."

Alice stared at the rough planks, some a foot wide, born of the vast old forest that encircled them.

"You were meant for Harry Percy, so Warwick said. Never mind. We've found each other in the end. A clutch of fine manors awaits us in your brother's country of Essex. So, little wife, I shall build us a great and beautiful house; I shall make you proud, if I can."

She lifted her eyes to his neck. She had bitten him, she was glad to see; he carried marks of his own. There was nothing fiendish in the morning light: a callous, striving man, like so many others.

Loys caught her wrist, turning it over where the great ruby was bound, and tugged at the thong. "Christ! By candlelight, I thought this a common garnet.

But no: a hundred times the worth! A wedding gift from my grateful bride."
With a fingernail he traced the engraving that proclaimed the ring's master.
The band was too large even for the middle finger, and it slid, heavy and
precarious, over his thumb. He pinched her chin and dragged it upwards.
"Was Clifford your lover? Rumour says he was."

She shook her head.

"A splendid token from one who asks nothing in return."

Her fingers crept to the hollow of her throat. Where did Edmond's emerald
lie now? Another splendid token – lost, seemingly, to the filth of the forest
floor. Wherever the gem rested, it was beyond the reach of this marauder.

The casement drew her eyes. The storm had blown itself out; the prospect
was lush and sodden. She could fancy the plash of distant hooves. "May I
dress, sir?" *I must be ready.* Surely, this day, Robert would make good his
promise and appear before her. Loys would be butchered as she watched; she
could well envisage Robert's rage. Beyond hope lay only fear. Of what use was
she? Her belly held the hope of Lancaster, sullied, now, beyond repair. After
Robert slaughtered the interloper: what then?

* * *

Unlike Loys, Dacre had not acquired a licence to marry outside his parish.
But – as he explained to the reluctant priest – Mistress Carbery and he would
be forced to gabble the words and hop into bed unblessed, if denied the
sanction of the church. And so this other marriage went on also, reverently if
defectively solemnized. In due course the priest was hauled before the bishop
to answer for his negligence, but that was none of their affair.

The second bride was attended only by little Cecily Welford, who did her
best to stem the running tears.

Though Fate had levelled the rank of Lady Loys and Lady Dacre, to all
intents nothing had changed and Blanche continued to attend on Alice,
alternately vituperated and ignored, her existence miserable indeed. Sir Hugh
was more fortunate. Blanche, at last, was his; no one subjected him to ill usage

and he'd accepted the post of steward in his old friend's rising household. Neither wife was consulted.

Through the trees, darkness was falling. Robert had not come. Not this day. It was vain to expect it: he was under siege.

"Sir Simon." Alice made her strike as they faced each other across the bed. "I demand that you respect my person and respect the strictures of the Church. I am with child, sir, and well you know it; you would not be here otherwise. You have carried your point, but from now on I share your bed, and that is all." Over the last hours she had steeled herself for this stately protest, but the words limped and the small hands trembled.

"You truly think I would heed either you, or the Church? It's hard to say which I reverence less. Remember that you're my third wife; I'm well practised at ignoring stupidity." His voice slowed. "And understand this: I shall do with you whatever I wish, whenever I wish, in whatever manner I wish. Master the urge to sink your teeth into any part of my anatomy, or it will go the worse for you."

"Then you, not I, shall answer for this sin at the Day of Judgment!"

"No doubt my immortal soul would be greatly in peril – if I had one."

* * *

On the day following, the residents of Dyffryn were roused, in differing ways, by news of the Wyverns' victory at Chepstow and the capture of Roger Vaughan. Alice strode in exultation through the muted gardens, skirts sweeping the mud, ear attuned for the galloping hooves.

Loys sat at the board in the low, damp hall, fingers steepled. To one side, John Twelvetrees, the marshal, who'd never instigated a conversation in his life. To the other, Leonardo Brini, chamberlain and confidant, a little Venetian eerily similar to Loic Moncler in any number of ways. As Sir Hugh was displaying his tendency to panic, they dispatched him on an errand to Newport, to learn how quickly the party might take ship for Bristol.

"You know him, this Clifford, mio signor? An old enemy?"

"I know him by repute, Leo; everyone does. We met only once, twenty years back, when he and his brother squired at Alnwick alongside my elder brother. What a vicious pair, heaping misery on poor Humphrey, who wouldn't acknowledge their lead. So we travelled north to Alnwick, my father and I: the beatings had been too brutal, and Father protested to the old Earl at the Cliffords' malice. But those boys were his pets, and Old Percy wouldn't lift a finger. And then, of course, the complaint came to be widely known and Humphrey's woes redoubled." Loys shifted in his seat. "I wasn't tall; my lungs were weak. I tried to keep out of their way, as one would. But on the day we left, I was making my way across the hall when Robert Clifford tripped me, deliberately, before the crowd of young men. You can imagine the scene. I was bleeding from the teeth, trying to pick myself up discreetly. Then Clifford kicked me like a cur, sending me headlong again. I can hear it now: the servile laughter of his tame dogs."

Brini rubbed his eyes with a knuckle, appalled that his master should suffer so; a man to whom dignity was all.

"Don't distress yourself. Life is full of such stings. And now I have wounded Robert Clifford more deeply than he ever hurt me; more deeply than he ever hurt Humphrey." At last Clifford was repaid, with interest, for the long-distant oppression. A ruinous rate of interest, compounding at a jaw-dropping rate. Sir Simon's thoughts ran on to the complacent letter he'd dispatched to Roger Vaughan, a man who hadn't the wit to keep it to himself. Boasting of his marriage at this juncture was an uncharacteristically reckless act, and one that was threatening to rebound on him. And so, when Dacre returned with news of a ship bound for Bristol that very evening, he was greeted with unusual warmth.

Loys climbed the stairs to his wife, dismissed the gentlewomen and broke the news of departure. Her composure deserted her. When Loys pushed her to the door, Alice braced herself against the frame, crying for her protector, refusing to be carried off – in just the way Lord Clifford had instructed. But Robert's promise proved as hollow in this regard as in every other. A sudden silence, pierced by pitiful sobbing, and then Loys appeared below, striding out through the hall, his wife cradled in his arms. The menfolk averted their eyes. The gentlewomen crowded in, crooning, protesting. Raising a hesitant hand to her master's back, Blanche tapped him with a finger, but he did not turn.

"Hold your imbecile tongues! Christ. What a pack of halfwits."

* * *

As both commanders had abandoned them, the men in Chepstow did as they pleased. Jasper Tudor had shipped enough wine to dull his injured ribs for a day and a night, possibly longer. Rowdy and discordant singing stumbled down the stairs from his chamber for some long while. Once it fell silent, his men broke open the cellars. Thus fortified, many of them – Tudor's household and the Wyverns, in noisy cheer – slipped from the fortress and descended to the town, disturbing its respectable inhabitants.

Of the senior men, only Loic and Bellingham and Reginald Grey remained to attend on their lord. Castor and Findern hovered briefly at the chamber door, anxious – and wearied also at the relentless onslaught of ill luck and ill news. Behind them on the stairs loitered a few of the FitzCliffords. George crept there on learning of his uncle's collapse. Failing to amend the situation, he sadly withdrew and hurried with Bede to the town below to commence the drinking. Aymer wouldn't suffer a rival to attend his father, but once George was gone he took himself off, seeking a gaming table. Omitting the drinking and the dicing, Guy stole the lead and by dawn he'd quite outdone George – ever the objective. Patrick Nield was nowhere to be seen.

As the muted commotion continued outside, Clifford lay motionless upon the bed, felled. His eye was closed. He hadn't troubled to remove the patch. From his breathing, it seemed he was slipping in and out of sleep.

Bellingham – reconquered, by now; easy within the walls, as though there'd never been a doubt over him – stared out into the twilight or paced quietly, watching over Lord Robert with all his fatherly tenderness. Kneeling at the prie-dieu, Sir Reginald was grim about the face; fierce, no doubt, for vengeance. Loic was perched at the edge of the bed, elbows on his knees. Now and again, when Monseigneur was sunk away, Loic took the heavy hand in his neat and slender fingers, stroking with the lightest touch.

All, now, was lost; all of it. If there were any feat the lad could perform to lessen this pain; to draw the poison; he – a willing martyr – would shoulder the suffering. If any prayer could conjure the girl, so fervently would he pray, and steal away, surrendering his master to the arms of another, yet know only the most perfect contentment. Or so, in that moment, he believed.

* * *

Hal was not within the chamber, nor loitering on the stairs, nor making mischief in the town. He had his own purpose. The cellars were plundered and puddled underfoot, but much of the choicest wine had been overlooked. Hal searched until he found the best of it, and drew two jugs.

Within the gatehouse, the jail cell was guarded by a single man, quick to surrender both the key and the guard room. Hal peered through the bars. Roger Vaughan's knees were as near to his chest as they would bend; hands behind his head, he was slumped in the darkness. Hal unlocked the door, drew out the blinking knight and brought up a chair, stoking the fire to thaw his stiff limbs.

Some of the bombast had leaked from Sir Roger since his brave performance in the great hall. The cell was a step closer to the scaffold; perhaps the thirst to wound was fading as he contemplated immortality.

"Releasing me, Master FitzClifford? A fair night for an escape, with your fellows disporting themselves in the town below."

Hal smiled. "I'm afraid not, Sir Roger. I'm come to show you a little courtesy and learn what you know." He poured a deep draught and handed it over; paused while the cup was drained; filled it again.

The prisoner smacked his lips. "Eh? Ask away. Keep it coming."

Hal steeled himself. "Sir Simon Loys …" he broke off. "Ah, I'm come on my own account, by the way, Sir Roger. My father knows nothing of this and I'd rather he didn't learn of it."

Vaughan winked. "Like that is it? I'll not breathe a word, then."

"Sir Simon Loys: I know the man a little, for his son's a page at Alnwick, where I was under-steward. The rumour there was that he proposed himself for the Lady Eleanor – Northumberland's sister. And now you say he's married Alice de Vere – or Beaufort, I suppose she is. Was. The Dowager Duchess of Somerset. Would you be so good as to tell me how this wedding came about? It's pure curiosity on my part, I'm afraid."

Vaughan was smiling on him. "I didn't know he was tilting at Eleanor Percy, but it's no surprise. He's a climber, is Simon Loys. Sharp elbows. High in Warwick's favour, at one point; in the Earl's northern council. But he chucked Warwick quick enough when the Earl started plotting against King Edward; brought him up like a bad whelk. So what now? Loys was fighting in the vanguard under Richard of Gloucester at Tewkesbury, the other day – seemed well in with the little lordling. But I suppose he'd known Gloucester since the Duke was a boy and living up at Warwick's household in Middleham. Loys will join Gloucester's affinity for sure, and up he'll go; sky high, mark my words. To my mind, a thoroughgoing arsehole."

Hal leaned over to refill the knight's cup. "And the Lady Alice?"

"It's true he knew her at Middleham. It's not that far from his lands in the East Riding. But a noble lady like her would never have paid Loys much heed. No – it's no love match. Of course it's not. The man's greedy; the girl's vulnerable. He can cure a headache for King Edward by claiming to have fathered her Beaufort whelp; Loys gets a noble wife and the promise of some of her brother's estates. Why not?"

"What's in it for her, Sir Roger?" Hal tipped the jug.

"How should I know? Why are you interested? Perhaps she's caught a fancy for him. Perhaps he forced her to it, though his letter says they wed in the parish church, all fair and square. Perhaps she's not exactly burning with desire for your hideous father and would rather live at ease on the de Vere estates than penniless in exile. Wouldn't you?"

The second jug stood empty. Queasy, Hal sloshed the contents of his cup into the other's.

"So, when will they come for me, Master Hal? It's mighty uncomfortable in that cell. I trust my stay will not be a long one."

"Not long now, Sir Roger. Tomorrow, I should think, once the Earl of Pembroke's recovered sufficiently from his damaged ribs."

Hal stood and, reluctant, the prisoner stood also. "Recovered from his hangover, you mean," commented Vaughan. "Jasper Tudor has a terrible singing voice for a Welshman. Thank God he's passed out."

* * *

Dyffryn Hall was all but emptied, Sir Lawrence accompanying the party in search of his son and Cecily Welford attending Lady Loys with tremulous excitement.

Through the half light, the shores of Monmouthshire slipped away. Leo Brini – rivalling Loic in depth of feeling for his master; all of the fervour and none of the undertow – would have sung for gladness in his smooth tenor, had not Sir Simon so disliked singing.

Alice stood on the aft deck, looking back towards Chepstow, of course. There was never a doubt that Robert would come, but when he came, now, he would come too late. At that very moment, perhaps, he wandered the empty and echoing chambers of Dyffryn Hall. She contemplated the cold plunge from the stern of the ship.

Surely her husband had not guessed it, or he would have stood guard. Sir Simon was snug in the captain's cabin, seated at the table, perusing a dog-eared volume by the dim and swinging light. Earlier, Sir Hugh had chanced to find that book beneath his hand. The illustrations were, to his wondering eye, pure sorcery. There was no word of English to render the meaning. As Dacre hugged his knees upon the cot, Brini was scribing for Loys, capturing the various utterances that fell from his master's lips. Some became letters and some became symbols. The flame fluttered as if touched by an incantation. Sir Hugh made his excuses and left.

A moment later, Blanche was joined by her husband at the fore of the ship. She could not see Alice, but she knew where the lady was standing, which way she was gazing and why and, despite the ill usage, her heart was wrung within her. "Did you direct Sir Simon, as I bade you?"

"Direct him where?"

Blanche made a peculiar noise, both quiet and shrill. "He has behaved ill, the girls say; he has been very rough. Lady Alice is a lost child and would cleave to him, if she could only recognise him as her protector. I thought he had more sense than this."

"I can't tell Simon how to handle his wife in bed!"

"Not in bed; in everything." Her voice was tart, as, seemingly, it always was. "He should soothe her; comfort her. Why are men such fools? And meanwhile, Constance is in her ear, no doubt whispering that Robert Clifford is the answer to her prayers."

"Wife, that girl is no proper company for Lady Alice. I shall have words with Simon about her."

"You'll have no words with Sir Simon except those I give you! You've already condemned me to great unhappiness in this household, when we'd agreed to seek service with George of Clarence." Constance was a thorn in her side, for sure, but evict Alice's niece from the household and Blanche might as well pitch herself into the Bristol Channel.

He frowned at the bow wave. "You don't understand me. Sir Leonard Tailboys …" he whispered. "I believe Mistress Constance is the guilty one."

She turned fully to face him. "What?"

"That night at Tintern Abbey, Tailboys was saying the most revolting things. Imaginings of what he would do to the girl. Why choose me to confide in, when there were far nastier men about him? I did pass one or two admiring comments on you, I suppose. Just for the sake of fellowship."

"How on *earth* do you leap from that to murder?"

Under the weight of her glare he brought it forth. "For sure, Constance was in the stable that night at Dyffryn; when she went up to bed, her hair was full of straw. At the time, I paid it no heed. But then Tailboys was discovered in the stable, and when his body was stripped for the shroud, we found it all mashed below. His bollocks, I mean. The man must have been in anguish. Easy prey for the pitchfork."

"*Pitchfork?*"

"The killer didn't trouble to hide the murder weapon. Its prongs were pointing straight at the corpse's crotch, as if to say – well – *serves you right*."

* * *

Unhappily for Roger Vaughan, Jasper Tudor did not appear the next morning, and neither did Clifford. The prisoner spent another miserable day crouched, famished, in the half-dark. But by late afternoon, Vaughan heard the saws and hammers at work upon his makeshift scaffold, and he rested easier that night. At daybreak, Hal was present in the yard to see him off, planted behind his father's chair. Clifford was impassive. Tudor wore an ugly leer. Faced with his father's killer, that was only to be expected.

The man made as good an end as one would expect from a lifelong soldier, Castor, as master-at-arms, doing the honours with swift proficiency. There was an air of glad satisfaction as the brushes got to work.

After the cathartic beheading, Robert Clifford abandoned his bedchamber to join the two Tudors in the day room.

Jasper had not worked through much of a plan, it seemed. He'd hold out in Chepstow, he said, and fall back to Harlech in the far West, if pushed. France was his ultimate refuge, of course, as it always was.

With no heir of Lancaster in his possession, Clifford was less sanguine of his welcome in Paris, and more pressed to retrieve his gold and wring every last penny from his tenants before he left England. Then on to Edinburgh, to gather Jack de Vere and William Beaumont, if rumours of their flight into Scotland proved correct. "Tomorrow I'll head north, but we'll meet in Paris by Christmastide. And there, we'll form a new court for your nephew, the undoubted heir of Lancaster." He bowed low, trusting young Tudor hadn't noted the abrupt change in his manner – now there was no rival claimant blossoming in Alice's belly. The lad pierced him with those penetrating hazel eyes.

His uncle – considerably less acute – clasped Clifford's wrist. "Henry and I will never forget your friendship, Robert. Without you, we should not have served Vaughan the reward he deserved; it would be my head decorating the gatehouse."

"Hardly, Jasper!" said Clifford. 'I doubt Vaughan's sorry force would have done more than trample the crops and annoy the townsfolk."

"It's good to see you smile again; you've put that silly girl behind you. What woman is worth a moment's pain?"

* * *

"He says he'll not come north with us, Lord Robert. Not another step."

Clifford glanced up. "Who, Bell? Who?"

"I told you, Lord Robert: Bertrand Jansen. He'll not come with us; not another step, he says. I'll summon him, shall I?"

"Summon him?" A long pause. "Ah, if you must."

At Clifford's side, Jasper Tudor was fixed in an attitude that resonated tragically in Hal's mind: his father's exact bearing as Roger Vaughan told the tale that crushed his heart. The Earl was bent over the great table, flattening the map, a finger tracing the Severn into the Bristol Channel. Then his eyes slid sideways and he broke the spell. "Look lively, man! Sounds like you're losing your best sword arm. Give you some time alone with him, shall we?"

"What? No, don't bother Jasper. If he's going, he's going."

Nothing loath, Tudor lowered himself, painfully, into one of the ancient, weighty chairs, motioned the page to fill his cup and rested expectant palms on the table.

As the huge Dane strode in to the great hall, Cuthbert Bellingham was trotting alongside, a look on his face as though he'd caught Jansen pilfering. They were tailed in by Castor and Walter Findern; cautious, watchful. The expression to be found everywhere, these days. Patrick Nield was nowhere to be seen.

"I was just coming to take my leave, Lord Robert. I didn't need *summoning*. I wouldn't *creep off*." Jansen's mother was a Yorkshire lass; his accent was Copenhagen but the English was perfect, the withering tone nicely judged. "So, I take my leave. I cannot stay with you, Lord Robert, though I was happy in the past. Things have not gone well of late."

Loic was cursing Bell with his eyes. What possessed the fellow to bring the deserter in here? Clearly, a tirade was boiling up. Just what wasn't wanted – before an audience of four dozen. Loic stood, abruptly, found he'd no notion how to prevent this, and slumped back. Clifford was gazing out of the window.

"No one could accuse you of cowardice, Lord Robert," Jansen continued, "for no bolder man ever lived. But you have disgraced your steadfast followers! At Tewkesbury: we might have made the difference. Probably we would. The Wyverns are the finest soldiers in England, few as we are. But you have shamed your men and squandered a kingdom, and all for a little…"

Jasper Tudor coughed forcefully at Clifford, and winced again. Clifford's eyes had flicked back to Bertrand, a look sufficient to quell the insult on his lips.

"Well, I've no need to voice it, Lord Robert. All the men think the same. Not that you give a toss what the men think."

All about the hall, wide eyes and little, scandalised gasps. The Clifford of old would have gutted Jansen by now.

"You expect them to follow for love alone. Which they won't. Not when you treat us all so ill. Just like when those knighthoods were bestowed, and my name alone went missing."

There was a muttering at that: not a respectable subject to raise before others, and Jansen was losing his audience.

"Your name was not missing," said Clifford, with weary patience. "I told you so at the time. Warwick struck it from the list. I would have pushed for you, but we were in Skipton by then, as you well know."

"And why would the Earl have struck only *my* name, Lord Robert, when he didn't know me from Adam?"

"How should I know? Perhaps because he didn't know you from Adam. In England, knighthood still requires a certain distinction."

Swiftly Sir Reginald intervened. "Go, Bertrand. Go quietly. We've lived without Leonard Tailboys; we shall live without you." The priest had managed to head the man off; not in the direction he expected.

"*Tailboys*? A further dishonour! I saw Tailboys's body for myself that morning at Dyffryn, though you bade me hold my tongue, Grey. One man here is a murderer!"

The hall breathed into perfect silence.

"Not a household man, no. None so base as to slay one of their own and conceal him beneath the hay. Your boy. Your boy has done it!"

Near on a hundred listeners, and every man among them shared the same querulous impatience: *which boy?*

Hal's face was as impassive as the muscles would permit. Behind the blank façade, his brain was whirring. Stuttering to a halt. Jerking to life again. Who could say why the sharing of Alice's part in this filled him with such horror, even now? He groped towards the truth. He could not endure the aftermath: the men taking Alice apart, appraising the episode in the woods; the whispers; the filthy jokes; the covert respect for Aymer – sure to emanate from some quarters of the household. Amid the flurry of dismay he was composing his confession. In the next moment, Jansen would accuse him to Lord Robert. The killing of a loyal gentleman would, no doubt, prove the final blow in their fragile connection. The Dane was not the only man to be leaving the household that day.

Robert Clifford's hands scrubbed his scalp; his voice, as one awakened from sleep. "I cannot believe any man here would slay Sir Leonard. But if it's so, he shall be banished, though he be the most beloved of all." There followed a silence – very brief – and then Clifford hurried on before the Dane was tempted. "And you, Jansen: you have chosen to leave my service, and I am sorry for it. Now go."

"Though I've long served you for nothing, I don't beg for gold, Lord Robert," pursued Jansen doggedly, "for you haven't any. You'll not deny me my horse, I hope."

"Your horse? It is my horse. You keep your possessions and I'll keep mine."

Jansen bowed as though a rope had wrenched his neck and, turning blindly, strode from the hall.

Hal was observing the twins, his vast relief veiled from view – or so he thought. Guy frowned at the floor. Aymer looked straight across; straight at Hal, and smiled. And then, lest Hal be left in any doubt, Aymer drove home the message with an exaggerated wink.

* * *

The day after Betrand Jansen's departure, the Wyverns bade the Welshmen farewell, set to commence the swift, uncomfortable rush for home.

As all was made ready, Hal tried to divert the cavalcade, a last, rash attempt. "I spoke to Roger Vaughan, my lord, about the Lady Alice. Someone had to!"

Those within hearing range exchanged glances and busied themselves, leaning in. Clifford had spun on his heel, face blackening.

"Loys has forced this marriage on the lady in return for a parcel of Jack de Vere's lands!"

"How could he force her to the altar?" murmured Loic. "No priest would permit it."

"He might have suborned a priest; easily done. Or perhaps there has been no wedding as yet," added Hal in wild, unlikely hope.

Reginald Grey elbowed in, eyeing the youth with glittering hostility. Marriage was his province and Lord Robert was his mission. For two long days the chaplain had been urging his master to race to Dyffryn. But he'd take no help from this Judas – one whose motives were all too offensively clear. "You speak of matters on which you have no knowledge and no authority. Hold your tongue."

In desperation, Hal turned to his father. Lord Robert was striding away with Grey at his shoulder. For a moment, the son considered – more seriously than he should – charging alone into the West. "This is *your* fault! She should never have been abandoned." But the cry was more of a croon, and couldn't be heard at a distance.

Loic laid a mild hand on his arm. "Come away. Whether she is married or no, that man is beside her and child's name is beyond redemption. It's your father who should be the object of your care: he has lost everything."

* * *

All the way north, Clifford brooded on Alice; cursing himself, even as he admitted her, again and again, to the sanctum of his mind. When Loic broached the subject, it was as much in support of Hal as with the wish to console. He was castigated for his pains.

"Mark my words: the little bitch has wounded me out of spite when I would not dance to her tune. Worse, she has wrecked the hopes of our royal house, all to take revenge for some hasty words of mine…"

"But Monseigneur! All a woman's care is for her babe. It makes no sense…"

"And this, from the woman I risked all our skins to save, who broke her solemn vow in Angers and now betrays me a second time. *Never speak of her again.*"

All of the way north, Hal brooded on Alice. In his father's place, he would have led the men at once to Dyffryn, slaughtered the interloper and discovered the truth. Married her on the spot, or carried her off. Never would he have allowed pride to master him, or submitted himself to the loss. Where was she now? Already crossing into the North Country, perhaps. Loys's estate lay west of Scarborough, amid the North York Moors, high, gusty and bleak.

None of the way north was spent in his father's company, for Hal could no longer bear to be near him, bitterness boiling up as caustic as heartburn. Instead, he was riding between George and Bede, the two lads singing across him. Not silly singing in imitation of Lord Clifford, but serious singing, seriously crude. He hardly heard them. His eyes were fixed on Aymer's back, thoughts revolving in slow circles like a spit: Aymer and Leonard Tailboys. How he loathed this brother; loathed him with unbridled force, as he'd never known loathing until now. But beneath the righteous disgust was the self-doubt; the twist of envy and shame. And so he rode on, with plans puffing up, insubstantial as clouds; trying – hopeless as ever – to dispel the images that Tailboys had planted in his brain.

Eventually the cavalcade entered the moorland, Skipton Moor, the skirt of Wharfedale. Stirring, so very dear and soon to be but a memory. They'd encountered no ambush en route; no army of York barring their path. And so they nested within the stout walls, and the Wyverns took up, again, their martial training, awaiting the quarter day when the rents were due, counting down to exile.

Spies – or assorted villagers, anyone with a nag to their name – enlisted in Clifford's service: one at every turn of the compass, ready to race to the castle, to forewarn of the force that must, some day soon, come against them. And, within days, dire news was carried up; news that should have come as no shock to anyone.

As Loic sauntered into the day room, Findern was tamping at a drum, adjusting the skin. Benet and Jem were about their duties, murmuring in Cornish. After years in close quarters, Loic could follow the gist of their speech, though it rarely repaid his trouble.

Perched on the table, swinging a leg, Clifford, in his hand a sheet of parchment. With a sudden gasp and an oath, he sprang to his feet. Findern started, knocking over the drum, sending it wheeling against the wall with a weighty and sonorous boom like a call to arms, a dramatic foretoken. Striding to the window, Clifford bent upon the sill, arms outstretched, head bowed. Loic crossed after him, a hand hovering at the broad back.

There came a low and wretched moan and a shudder, as if he were forcing down bile, and Clifford turned blindly from the window. "King Henry is dead. That murderous whoreson has slain our King."

* * *

It took a week to reach London by slow stages. Alice was grown ever more silent, her mind plodding only on Robert Clifford and his empty vow. For sure, she had not sent him word – but that was his own fault. For the very instant a message was needed was the very instant it could not be carried. A moment's thought, and he would have left her a boy expressly for the purpose. Worse, once he was free to come, he did not come. A revel in full spate at Chepstow, no doubt – girls and music and wine – and so he dismissed Alice and the babe without a thought.

By then it was a solace – a sour pleasure – to imagine him making his way at last to Dyffryn Hall. She tasted all his mounting dread as the still emptiness broke upon him and he knew that he had come too late. And so she left him further behind, choking on anger and pity and hurt.

The travellers made no merry party. Blanche, too, was heartsick and wretched. When they halted, the second night, at a small inn in Malmesbury, she begged a moment alone with her mistress. There was dumb silence in the mean chamber, both women seated on the bed, Alice staring at her hands, though she could hardly see them; the light was flattened by the heavy thatch. The gentlewoman lowered herself to her knees.

"Lady Alice … you blame me. I know you do. But there was never to be a safe and honourable outcome among those men. You feel that I've betrayed your child. But you must see we were in grave danger in such company. There's no man in England with a worse name than Robert Clifford. His household and those boys are no better."

"His only care was for the heir of Lancaster!" cried Alice, clinging to the old, uncertain faith. "Robert never touched me."

"If that's so, it was but a matter of time. And what of your gentlewomen? Would we have come through unscathed? Elyn? Constance? All at risk, for the remotest of chances. What? That you would bear a son, rear him in Paris and wait for England to rise in his cause, fifteen … twenty years from now? You must face the truth."

Alice laid her cheek in her gentlewoman's lap. When Blanche stroked the well-loved face, it was hot with tears. "I have lost everything, Blanche; everything. The Earl of Warwick, whom I reverenced, who took me in and raised me since Father's killing – he is dead, and John Neville is dead. Edmond is dead. Jonkin is dead. And those who have not gone in that way are gone from me in another. My son's as lost to our cause as if he were dead. I'm deserted by the Countess of Warwick – who is as a mother to me – by my brother, by Lady Ullerton, by Anne Neville. Lord Clifford has abandoned me, when I thought that he, above all others, would be my protector and the protector of my child. And now you, Blanche! Even you have betrayed me."

"I have not betrayed you, dearest one. I have saved you."

"Saved me for what?" Her voice was slow and wretched. "That man is a low and disgusting creature. When I said I wouldn't lie with him, he humiliated me; he hurt me, deliberately. What can I do? Nothing. Only avert my thoughts, for he doesn't merit my notice."

Tenderly Blanche raised Alice, undressed her and laid her down beneath the sheet, somewhat reluctant to leave, but it was too late for that. Blanche lifted the latch, and there he was at the threshhold, eavesdropping openly. She halted. "Sir Simon, it's a Christian duty to be forbearing, at such a time. Lady Alice has suffered grievously."

She didn't trouble to mute her tones. His were softer: "We've known each other through long years, you and I. Perhaps Lady Alice imagined I'd let her alone, but you had no such illusions." He tapped his neck – the scabrous ring of tooth marks, violet in the candlelight – as though Blanche might never have noticed. "Would I let a puppy cheek me so? Like all young creatures, my wife needs the reassurance of a strong hand. You saw me break her in: *I am your master now. Come to heel.* And she has come to heel."

Blanche twitched her skirts and swept away. Behind her, the faint click of the door. But by now Alice would be sleeping.

This night, as every night, while Loys listened and learned, his wife was visited by dreams vivid and disorderly. High in a tower, held captive by a necromancer: an unlikely beginning, but it was always, insistently, so. Robert Clifford was below – much too far below – urging her to the suicidal leap. Sometimes they made good an exhilarating escape, riding hard, she cradled in his lap. More than once she turned to find herself in Hal's embrace, his face running with blood. More than once she stepped from the window to float down, light and lightheaded, tumbling on her back beneath the canopy of leaves, gazing up into the beautiful, troubling face of Aymer FitzClifford, his breath boiling the sweat at her brow. As she twisted beneath the terrifying hands – barbed fingers, a foot long – the lost emerald swung against his throat.

* * *

In the tavern beneath the castle walls, the household men reverted to their favourite subject. And now they were driven to consult Arthur Castor, as so often, when intelligence was needful and they were flummoxed.

"Oh yes, I know the murderer," declared Castor, with quiet confidence.

A circle of faces, all agog.

He adopted his storytelling manner. "I grew tired of the speculating – on and on – so I asked Aymer, straight out.

'*Not me, friend Arthur,*' says he, '*and you know I love you well and would tell you true.*'

'*Who then?*' says I. '*Was it your twin?*'

'*You shall ask him yourself; it's not for me to answer.*'

So I asked Guy, straight out.

'*I don't wish to speak on this matter,*' says Guy.

So then I knew."

"Guy! It was Master Guy then," agreed the auditors.

"Not Guy," averred Castor. "Someone Guy was protecting. Richie." There was a bemused silence. Sir Arthur tallied the points on his fingers. "We know Tailboys lusted after Mistress Constance; he was stalking her that night at Tintern Abbey, as he let slip to Lewis Jolly. We know Richie couldn't take his eyes off the girl. We know Constance was not beside the Duchess during the evening at Dyffryn Hall. We know Constance had straw in her hair when she went up to bed, as Jem pointed out. We know Tailboys was hidden in the stable, for Bertrand told us he was buried in hay. We know Guy had no reason to kill the man. We know Guy doesn't wish to share his knowledge of the killer. So the killer is Richie."

"Except that Master Richie was lying in the garden with busted ribs and a broken nose, drinking himself into a stupor," objected Walter Grey. "We all saw him."

Castor didn't relish his deductions falling under fire from a man of Grey's mediocrity. "We weren't all watching him, all the evening! Most probably he shipped enough that his wounds no longer pained him. Jasper Tudor was in a like case after our little skirmish at Chepstow, and broken ribs didn't stop him singing from the depths of his lungs – more's the pity. So: Richie's drunk, he goes looking for Mistress Constance, finds Tailboys got there first and strangles him – for if blood were spilled, we'd have discovered the body. That's what happened. It's idle to discuss it further."

"But then, Master Bedivere never stopped gawking at Mistress Constance either. He could more easily have done the deed than Master Richie," suggested Bigod. "I saw him wandering that way myself."

Castor was growing fractious, as ever, when challenged. "That donkey Bede? He isn't capable." Someone added a quiet *hee-haw*.

Nield rolled his eyes. "If you think Bede isn't up to a bit of slaying, you weren't watching him at Barnet, Arthur."

"I didn't say he wasn't competent," snapped Castor, "for I trained the lad myself. I said he wasn't *capable*. You fellows asked my opinion: you should heed me when I speak."

"And do you know what that little shit Richie said to Master Guy – within my hearing?" demanded Findern. "He said: '*Walter Findern must be specially sore at Tailboys's death, for Tailboys was always known as the ugliest man in the household.*'" Then Findern looked about pugnaciously, as though Richie's guilt were proven.

A clamour of comment followed, none of it complimentary to the accused.

* * *

"What's that stench? There's a disgusting stench in here, again." Guy cast around with irritation and caught his brother's eye.

Richie was hunched over his saddlebag, strings of grey flesh dangling from an overstuffed mouth, festooning his chin; face like a guilty dog. He folded the leather flap on a priapic shankbone, shielding the bag with his arm.

"There are rats in here! We're sharing with rats, because of you. No wonder half the castle is sickening; you've fouled the air with your rotting meat."

"I'm almost done." The glossy knob resurfaced.

Giving up, Guy threw himself down on the wide bed and slept at once. Aymer looked on his peaceful features with wonder and affection and envy. An hour later, Aymer and Will were bent close in the blackness. On the near side of Aymer, pillow encircling his head like a bonnet, Guy breathed heavily. On the far side of Will, Richie was sprawled on his pallet, emitting little wheezes and snorts through his distorted nose. A slow slick of black blood oozed, unseen, from the left nostril, interesting a passing rodent. By morning, the seep would be gone.

"I have thought of something beautiful."

Will raised his head a little.

"That day in Alnwick," Aymer continued, "when you overheard Father raging at the Lady Eleanor about Hal, they two were alone. Father knows what Hal did with her and, doubtless, Moncler knows too. Guy and I, we know, thanks to you. There's someone who doesn't know, but certainly should. Someone who deserves to know."

Will lay still a moment, then turned his head in Richie's direction.

"Not Richie," said Aymer, dismissively. "*George.*"

There was a pause, and then Will must have smiled, for Aymer could see his teeth. Nodding, the elder boy flipped on to his back, hands behind his head. If Will had been quicker off the mark – if he'd shared the results of his eavesdropping while they were still at Alnwick – Aymer would, perhaps, have followed Hal's pernicious lead. Will too, perhaps. Together, perhaps. Their father must have had her as well. Aymer laughed quietly to himself. Eleanor Percy seemed game for anything, though surely even she had her limit. It would have been entertaining to test how many Cliffords she could manage;

how many was too many. He gave a little sigh of pleasure. This way was much more elegant.

* * *

It took Aymer a while to shepherd George on his own and, even when he'd accomplished it, Hal was surveying them closely. The pair idled in a corner of the yard while others practised shooting at targets. Aymer shifted a little so that George was standing with his back to the group. "We were talking, the other day," he began in his lazy tones, "about you; about what you said when we were coming away from Alnwick that first time. About the Lady Eleanor Percy. Richie and Guy reckon you made it up. They say it's a lie, all of it. They say the daughter of an earl would never have looked twice at you. I'm not so sure. You're a fine-looking fellow. Perhaps you took a kiss – but that's all, I daresay."

George was immediately a prey to emotions, strong and conflicting, which he struggled to articulate. "Piss off!"

"So they're right, then. Idle boasting." Aymer grinned. "No one believes a word you say."

"I did have the lady, though! My uncle doesn't wish it spoken of, that's all. Piss off, will you?"

"Come, George! Father didn't mean you to keep it from me, for I've heard it already. Besides, Eleanor Percy will never be Lady Clifford now."

George looked around uneasily. Robert Clifford's word was law. But Aymer was right: Percy would never give his sister to Lord Clifford. Not now.

"Go on, then," Aymer prompted. "An earl's daughter? I reckon we'd all like to have an earl's daughter, if we had the good fortune to just happen across one, let's say. Lying there on the ground. Out cold, let's say." He laughed softly to himself.

"What?" said George.

Hal was still watching with close attention. Aymer looked to be goading George into a fight; so wantonly provocative. The whole sorry story would come tumbling out at some point, Hal was certain of it. The episode in the woods, Tailboys, the lot. It shouldn't matter now. Alice was lost to all of them. He should let it lie. But it was still mattering, greatly. Yet as he read the language of their bodies, there was no tension; no hostility. George was miming, hips rocking suggestively. They were just speaking of some woman. Hal picked up the bow and took his turn.

"Just the one beautiful encounter, was it?"

"Well, yes. Lady Eleanor feared I'd get her with child. I told her: that can't happen. Not if you're standing up, or the man remembers to pull out, or you wear a King Solomon amulet – I bought her one at the fair – but she didn't believe me. And I said I'd marry her, if the worst came to the worst, but no. Later she yielded a bit. I was allowed to touch her again. Afterwards she let me finish myself off in her privy." He closed his eyes and smiled.

"In her privy, eh? Lucky you. But George, listen. How would it be, then, if I told you some wicked man had threatened to go to her brother, the Earl, and inform him of the love between you and the lady, unless she submitted to pleasure that man – with her mouth, let's say? And so it was that he blackmailed her to it, many times over. How would that be?"

George was staring, unable to grasp the sense. So Aymer repeated it, more slowly. "You see? How would it be, if someone had done that to your lady fair?"

Still the witless frown. "What are you saying? I don't understand. You forced Eleanor to do that? I'll kill you. I will kill you."

"Oh no, no. By God, no. You're misunderstanding me."

George looked cautiously relieved, swaying from foot to foot.

"I'm not telling you I did that; never fear. We've had our differences, you and I, but you're clearly in love with the lady. I wouldn't do something so cunning, so cruel. No, George, no. I'm telling you *Hal* did that."

* * *

They were nearing the capital now; one last night outside the walls. Loys settled on his back, staring at the whitewashed ceiling, ear cocked for another adventure; he was adjusting to sleeplessness. Where, he wondered, was Edmond Beaufort in all these escapades? Barely cold but never present. The fellow must surely have ill used Alice, for grief was a stranger to her. Meanwhile, a startling number of other men bestrode his wife's teeming mind. Robert Clifford, that great swaggering bully; in the daylight she denied him, but her sleeping self rebelled. And who were these others, with their odd and unappealing traits?

The next day, before Loys and his party had even reached the gates, astounding news reached them: Henry of Lancaster, the man who once was king, lay dead in the Tower; slain, so it was said, by Richard of Gloucester on the very night the forces of York made their triumphant return from Tewkesbury.

"I cannot believe this," whispered Alice. "I cannot credit this news. When we were young together at Middleham, I called Lord Richard my friend; a sweet and merry boy." Too queasy for the carriage, she was riding, now, behind her husband.

He turned his head, voice low. "The usual ludicrous conjecture. It cannot have been other than by order of the King, and Gloucester is not stupid enough to dirty his own hands in the business – why should he? So, Alice: you will doubtless reflect that the child in your belly is the rightful inheritor of the kingdom, but I caution you to keep the insanity to yourself, if you do not wish us all to end our days as Henry of Lancaster ended his."

By twilight, the party was installed in a small inn between the Bridge and the Tower, requisitioned by Loys, who'd no London house of his own. At this, a new sensation assailed Alice, at once novel and mundane: concern over the cost to him; to them. How well could they afford this sojourn, which he seemed to feel so necessary? All she'd heard of his lands of Avonby gave no cause for complacency. And then she understood that she had already identified his interests with her own, and she knew that the marriage had permeated through her, an accepted fact.

Sir Simon's purpose, of course, was to show himself promptly at court, to parade his wife – so grimly won – and contrive to thrust the King's promise of reward before him. At present, Loys was clinging to an elusive prospect: a grant of some imprecise scale and description at some unspecified future date.

Commitments of this nature were uncertain and unbankable. And who was to have the balance of Jack de Vere's manors? A man of power, no doubt, whose eyes might well slip sideways at his fellow beneficiary.

Such was his fear, though he entered the doors of the court as though most certain of his welcome. King Edward greeted Loys with his accustomed bonhomie. Gratifying as it was to be seen in conversation with the King, the knight's nerves were jangling. Adroitly he drew the conversation around, recalling King Edward's attention to that moment after the battle of Tewkesbury when the ladies of Lancaster were discovered at Little Malvern Priory; when Alice was first missed, and first marked as a threat; the moment when he and Gloucester – hatching the plot together – had gone, together, to the King, who at once dispatched Sir Simon in pursuit of the fugitive.

King Edward remembered it well, warmly commending Sir Simon's zeal in the cause of York. Naturally the King was somewhat less keen to address the quantum of the reward and the timing of its grant, but that was the way with kings.

Meanwhile, Alice was presented again to Elizabeth, the parvenu Woodville queen, haughty and stiff as ever, as though the last months had never been; as though the woman had not cowered in sanctuary while Warwick held the kingdom in his hand. Then Alice was shown off to the King, who behaved charmingly, admiring her new gown of sea-green silk; claiming, unconvincingly, to remember her from the last visit to court, some four or five years past; asking after her mother, whom he couldn't name and whom she hadn't seen in years; acting, for all the world, as though it were some other man who'd sent her father and Aubrey to the block. Perhaps he had forgotten: he seemed distracted and was addressing himself directly to her bosom.

* * *

George was fidgeting in their chamber when Hal and Bede came up for the night.

"Why weren't you at dinner? Are you sickening?" queried Bede. "George?"

George cleaned a fingernail with his teeth. "Be a good lad and take yourself off, will you? Go and sleep with the youngsters. I have to talk with … " He flapped a hand at Hal.

In silence Bede retrieved his blanket and backed out of the room.

"What's the matter?" said Hal, throwing himself down on their bed. "Was Aymer goading you?"

George turned his back, distress evident in every movement. Hal raised himself on one elbow. "Mother of God, George! What is it?"

The young man sat down, stood again and finally met his cousin's eyes. "Aymer says you used the Lady Eleanor. He says you threatened her. Tell me it's not true!"

Hal looked away a moment, marshalling his thoughts. The pause was fatal.

"You know I have always loved her!" cried George. "How could you do that to me, or to her? I don't want to fight you, so don't try to make me. I don't want to talk to you or look at you."

"Well, it was wrong of me, of course. But I didn't know you were in love with her. Ah, George – I do think you've forgotten how it was. And she'd already lost interest in you, I thought. In fact, you complained of it. No harm done, I thought."

"No wonder she did not wish for men around her, if you were forcing her with such a vile trick! That pure and gentle maiden. I can't bear to think on it." His fingers were curling into fists.

Hal's heart was truly wrung by the evil he had done poor George, but he couldn't let pass this unrecognisable description of the lady. "Really, George, it wasn't like that! The first time or two, I did blackmail her, I admit, but it was only to smooth my path. And meanwhile, she wasn't letting you touch her, so you see …"

"She *was* allowing me to touch her," insisted George, chin raised, voice stately with tragic dignity. "Many times, she permitted me that honour. The lady was gracious enough to let me complete in her privy."

Before he knew what was coming, before he could hope to prevent it, a great snort of laughter broke from Hal and, at that, despite the torrent of horrified apology, George was lost to him. Hal pleaded, and grew frantic in his attempts to be heard, and also to choke down the appalling snigger that would keep bubbling up, threatening to overwhelm him. His cousin soared from wounded to incendiary and eventually when Hal, in his anguish, tried to embrace him, George so far relented from his resolve as to strike him, very hard indeed, in the eye that had thus far escaped injury, felling him with the blow. On the way down, the other side of Hal's face – the side on which the bruising had mellowed – collided brutally with the corner of the table. Then no more was said and they lay together on their bed.

* * *

Richie was relieving himself when he was disturbed. He glanced over his shoulder and there was Bede, lounging against the wall with a bundle of bedding in his arms.

"For God's sake! Can't a man have some peace?"

"I know I said it before, Richie, but I cannot understand why you would spend all your time with the twins. Guy's bad enough, but Aymer … there's something actually wrong with him."

Richie busied himself with his laces.

"You know, like that man John Neville brought to the York assizes; the one who drowned those children. Richie?"

"If Aymer wants to spend all his time with me I can't help that," mumbled Richie, shirt tucked under his chin.

"Why don't you ride with me and George when we are back upon the road?"

Richie shook his head. "I hate George and Hal."

"But Hal rides with Father, doesn't he? George will be at peace with you if you'll only let the twins alone. And you and I have been fellows since we were boys. It pains me to be always apart from you now."

Richie turned, but wouldn't meet his eyes. "You wouldn't understand."

"Well then," said Bede with a sad shrug, "you'll go your own way, I suppose. Only ..." he rubbed an eye, "could you at least stop making those noises – you know what I mean – when I am near?"

Richie, who did know, shook his head, regretful this time. "No, I don't believe so, Bede. Sorry." He twisted past the boy and returned, with relief, to the room he shared with Will and the twins.

* * *

Wordless, Loys rocked back on his knees and lowered himself to the bed beside his wife.

Alice, too, lay silent, eyes closed, to close him out. As a rule, she would turn her back the instant he finished. Tonight, she opened her eyes and turned towards him. The voice was cold and brisk. "Sir Simon, have you yet made any provision for me as your wife? I believe you've settled nothing on me in the event of your death. Of course I brought no dowry to the marriage, but that is not my fault; you took me as you found me. I need to know what is to become of me if you should fall. Shall I be left to petition for my rights at law, when you are gone and I have no protector?"

He smiled, but her eyes were fixed on the corner of the room. "What, and sign my own death warrant? Well, Alice: if you lie in my arms as a living woman and not as a corpse; if you bear me sons; if the King makes good on his promise of your brother's lands – then I'll turn my thoughts to the matter. Until such time as I feel myself secure, I have no intention of making provision for you."

"It is no joking matter!"

"Nor is murder. Your gentlewoman Constance has already made away with one man within the last month, so I hear. She has been getting her practice in early."

"Sir Leonard Tailboys? Only Sir Hugh could have suggested something so absurd. None of us has any idea who killed the man; you know it. May we please discuss the matter at hand, Sir Simon? Can you not see how hatefully

40

unfair you are being? I have had to bear so much from you, while you withhold even those dues that common decency demands."

"My resolute little wife! On you plod, one foot after the other." He almost reached to stroke her cheek, but guessed she might savage him and stifled the urge. "God alone knows what you have suffered! Any creature who comes to see Robert Clifford in the light of a saviour must have sunk low indeed. Yet on you go, you poor, steadfast child."

At that, she pitched on to her chest and flung herself angrily at sleep, in a way he'd witnessed in none but she.

Loys lay at her side, eyes wandering the soot-dinged ceiling. Already his wife was snoring. These days he could not blame her for his wakefulness for she was at peace, the unruly companions forsaking her dreams. He eased her into the crook of his arm. The lovely hair tumbled through his fingers; not tugged in a tempest of mastery, but gently combed, releasing its soft scent.

* * *

The next morning, George refused to get up or speak to Hal at all, and his obstinacy was such that Hal eventually gave him up and went down to matins alone. The outward evidence of the evening's disturbance had slipped his mind.

Just inside the chapel, Hal encountered his father. "What is going on in my house?" roared Clifford, startling Reginald Grey at the altar, drawing the eyes of every man. Stragglers pushed forward hastily. "You are an *utter* disgrace! This is the very *opposite* of what I desired from you. And the other fellow: entirely unmarked, *again*?"

Hal's dismal gaze fell upon Aymer, in the midst of the kneeling crowd, eyes wide, a dark angel.

* * *

For Clifford, a full day lay in store: a visit to his brother's tomb – to take his leave – and to his mother – also to take his leave. John would wait an eternity for his return; Lady Clifford had not so long. The visit had a purpose beyond sentiment. Much of his gold lay at Bolton Priory and the remainder with his mother. He'd meant to take the two eldest FitzCliffords, but that was before he'd encountered Hal.

Shortly after matins, Bede came to him with a mumble that George was ill and could not rise. In point of fact, there was sickness rife within the castle, a number of the household vomiting rowdily – including Bellingham, his condition a source of deep concern on account of his advancing years. Nevertheless, Clifford sent back a sceptical and peremptory demand for George to present himself. He was fuming in his day room when George dragged his feet into the chamber. The youth looked in fine fettle. "Now, then!" shouted Clifford at his nephew. "Who has done this to Hal?"

"I believe I gave him an excellent clout, my lord." George's chin was tilted to a righteous and uncomfortable angle.

Clifford clenched his teeth. "Then how is it you look so pretty this morning, my lad?" He'd never fought his brothers as a boy; never, perhaps. But if he had, they wouldn't look as pristine as George. John's son gazed at the ceiling with a mulish expression that was pushing his uncle to the limits of endurance. "Ah, keep it to yourself then, you great mawk! You and Hal shall make up whatever fuckwit quarrel you're having, and escort me to Bolton Priory and thence to Lady Clifford's house. We'll return tomorrow."

"I beg you, my lord: if Hal is to ride with you, might I be excused? I cannot endure his company. I *cannot*."

Clifford was about to unfetter his temper again, when he thought better of it. "You may not be excused. It's only proper you bid farewell to your father's bones and to your grandmother. It is Hal who shall not ride with us. He is not fit to be seen."

He stalked to his bedchamber, where Loic was curled, a basin in the sweaty crook of his arm. "I'm just about well, Monseigneur. I shall be up and about shortly, when I've bathed. I'm rather rank, truth be told. Monseigneur … there's been a deal of shouting this morning." Arthur, Jem, Benet, Oliver and Walter Findern: they had, each of them, traipsed in at intervals to give Loic their versions and their views.

"I wasn't shouting."

"Ah. It was someone else, then."

Clifford slumped beside his chamberlain. He told a similar story; the interpretation wildly different.

"Monseigneur," said Loic, very earnest. "You've never looked with favour on Hal since you spoke with the Lady Eleanor this last time. You may feel he has injured you, but he is just a boy, and has done as boys do. Just as you would have done, I think."

"How dare you say it? I revered my father! Always the dutiful son. Always. Never would I disobey Lord Thomas or do anything of which I knew he would disapprove."

"Perhaps not," muttered Loic. In the heat of the moment, all the many disobediences – great and small; countless well known examples – had gone missing. "But it seems unfair that George, who knew the lady carnally, is so easily forgiven, Monseigneur, while Hal has been cast from your affection."

"Naturally I'm grateful to be honoured with your *unsought opinion*. You know that Hal deceived me deliberately, wishing to go on enjoying Lady Eleanor after she had become my wife, and his mother. It is this plotting behind my back that is so reprehensible and never once," his finger was raised now, of course, "has he admitted any of this, but laughed up his sleeve as I questioned him on George's misbehaviour. And then," Clifford was up and pacing now, and Loic winced, seeing that he had done Hal no very good turn, "then, I see in him signs of desire for the Duchess herself, whom God promised to me – to *me* – and I am forced to watch him take Lady Alice in his arms and clasp her against him and call her by name, wishing to make a conquest of her and, when I upbraid him for it, he is insolent and will not beg my forgiveness. And you ask why he has been cast from my affection!"

The account was so twisted that Loic threw up his hands in exasperation.

Clifford turned on him, malevolent, the finger finding a new target. "In truth, it's not hard to guess what has caused this outburst of undeserved sympathy. Your inclinations make you vulnerable to his wiles! Mark my words: you will get no more from Hal than from me, so mind your loyalties."

Loic threw him a savage look, his voice icy. "*Inclinations? My inclinations?* My inclinations are just as other men's; no different to yours, I assure you! Your imagination is fevered. I recommend a cold bath."

"*Loic!*" thundered Clifford. "*You forget yourself.*"

* * *

"Ah, come, mon petit. Don't scowl at me. I should not have spoken to you in that way; I own it."

"Indeed you should not. A poor return for my tireless service."

"It was unpardonably rude. Nevertheless, you shall pardon me, for I have much on my mind."

"And so clearly untrue that I cannot comprehend why you would hint such a preposterous thing. Have I not fathered a child? My golden Charles. That, you well know."

Clifford looked on his man with fondness. It was the proclivities, not the practices, that he questioned. But such nobility of feeling should never be sullied in gross words. "It was uncalled for," he temporised. "Now rest."

"I'm well enough to accompany you, Monseigneur. I can't stay in this room any longer. I, too, wish for Lady Clifford's blessing."

"And risk carrying the sickness to my poor mother? Your face is greasy. Go and wash. I will convey your regards."

* * *

A few days after her presentation at court, Alice faced another test. Sir Simon was keen to renew his acquaintance with George of Clarence, King Edward's capricious brother. This young man, who belonged to Warwick heart and soul for much of his life, had already defied King Edward to marry Warwick's daughter; betrayed the King in the vain fancy that the country itched to place the crown on his handsome head and, finally, turned on his father-in-law of Warwick when displaced by Prince Edward of Lancaster: a second and more promising son-in-law for Richard Neville.

44

These were no steady hands, but in the warm rush that greeted his latest treachery, Duke George was the richest, most powerful nobleman in the kingdom, a natural good lord for a lordless knight.

And so Alice and her husband rode the short distance to the Clarences' townhouse. The Duke greeted Alice with a marked lack of interest, and handed her on to his wife, keen to commence the dance that should end with Loys taking his badge, the Black Bull of Clarence.

Alice had known the Duchess Isabel half her life, though she was no easy woman to love and their fortunes had sent them in opposite directions. She had still to run the gauntlet of the younger sister – Anne; Anne Neville – her dearest friend in all the world, she who had done so much to shipwreck Alice's first marriage. When she entered, Anne came rather coldly to kiss her, but she did, at least, kiss her.

Tall and fair and lithe, with a low and mellifluous voice, Isabel should by rights have been creeping in corners after her husband's scandalous paradigm of treason, yet the woman was more composed and condescending than ever. By contrast, Anne seemed younger and scruffier than before, garbed in an over-large, buff-coloured gown that exaggerated her dull complexion and childish figure, her hair lank and unadorned; as a widow she should only have been seen in a headdress. Eyeing the Duchess Isabel, with her poise and her exquisite taste, Alice could not believe that Anne had been displayed this way by accident.

The friends and their gentlewomen sat an uncomfortable hour in the men's absence. Finally Isabel made her way around to the matter of interest. "They say you are with child, Lady Alice, though you've been wed only a month! Has our old friend Sir Simon been boasting too rashly of his powers, perhaps?"

No one had dared ask the question directly, and Alice had not framed an answer. "I think I may be with child, Lady Isabel. Certainly I hope so."

"Or … the child of your late husband, could it be?"

Time stuttered to a halt as Alice wrestled with herself. Of what use to stand defiant when nothing, now, could come to any good?

"Some even say," Isabel's eyes made mocking flight in Anne's direction, "that you took a lover and bear the man's child, though he has forsaken you."

Anne went on with her large and wobbly stitching, as if all this were nothing to her. Constance, Joanna and Blanche were effigies of marble, breathless and transfixed.

"If I am with child, the father is Sir Simon," declared Alice. "Such evil gossip cannot hurt me, when I have done nothing wrong."

If, in that moment, a cockerel had crowed thrice – proclaiming a betrayal of Biblical proportions – the listeners would not have been the least surprised.

"I thought so," said Lady Isabel, graciously. "And so say I, whenever others whisper it. The court is a wicked place, full of mischief-makers. You have an unswerving friend in me and the Duke of Clarence; never fear."

* * *

The departure of Robert Clifford with George riding at his side was salt in the wound, but it was also a chance too good to pass up, and he was, in any case, fully resolved by then.

The manservant's gloom was inauspicious. "Running away never solved anything, Master Hal."

"A foolish observation, Moppet. There are many occasions on which running away solved everything. Pack up your belongings, discreetly, and conceal them in the stable until later. My baggage is already under the hay at the far end: four bags; mind you bring them all. Meet me at the hour of vespers on the other side of the bridge with your horse, my horse and a strong spare. Ah, Bertrand's mount will do for that. Act confident, but if you're questioned, say that I've decided to join my father at Bolton for the night."

Moppet clicked his tongue in resentful assent.

* * *

When Loic turned in the shadow, he found Monseigneur's eldest blocking his path. The touch came, not unexpected. There was a still moment.

46

"Come away with me," urged Hal. "I value you as he never will. He is cruel, is he not? I would not be cruel." The hand moved on, until a finger slid down Loic's nape, light and slow, triggering a tiny shudder among the fine wisps beneath the hairline. Hal gazed down into the Frenchman's averted face, murmuring his traitorous persuasions.

Loic mastered the whisper of his body and measured his friend with detached interest. Hal was making a fair job of it; not shy in wielding the only weapon he possessed, in amusing contrast to that decent and steady reputation. There was, of course, not the smallest chance of surrender. The attempt was too naked, too desperate and, by now, Monseigneur's warning was whirring in the chamberlain's ear like a persistent wasp. Loic removed Hal's dangerous hand from his neck and squeezed it. "I'm truly sorry it has come to this. Monseigneur can indeed be cruel, but I love him nonetheless and he does nothing without a reason. I hope you can find it in your heart to return. You are dear to your father, whether you believe it or not."

At that, Hal abandoned all pretence and clasped Loic with simple and friendly affection, bidding him to carry all good wishes to Bellingham and Nield, to beware of Aymer and to look after George, none of which needed saying.

When Loic walked on and vanished into the gloom, Hal reached into an alcove behind an arras and retrieved the chest with the pointed lid; King Louis's chest. He paused, thinking, as usual, of Alice. Thinking of Alice made him think of Aymer. Thinking of Aymer made him think, for some recklessly long time, of his father: of failing income and relentless expenditure, of the wearying work in holding the household together; sustaining their spirits when hope was all but gone. Then he set his mouth, broke the lock with his knife and emptied half the jingling contents into a double twist of cloth and thence into his saddlebag, bearing away all he could swiftly and comfortably carry.

As Hal approached the bridge, he was relieved to see Moppet awaiting him with the horses, and not surprised to see Aymer's strapping figure also, lounging on the low wall, discomfiting the manservant with his knowing appraisal.

Hal drew level and halted. "Tell me: how did you learn of my trysts with the Lady Eleanor?"

Aymer folded his arms and smirked.

"Very well. So you told George. Did you tell Father also?"

Aymer bit his lip, apparently deep in thought. His tones were softer than ever; so soft that Hal had to lean in, uncomfortably close. "Tailboys must have told you of my tryst with the Lady Alice; he would not have died otherwise. That was harsh of you, Hal, when all the fellow did was watch: it was *my* fingers, *my* mouth, *my* pleasure." Now he was gazing into Hal's face, savouring the ragged breathing, the pent-up stance. "Her taste was sweet to my tongue. Ah, I tried so hard to wake her. What would you have done, I wonder, if the Queen of Heaven fainted in *your* arms? Envy is a slow poison. You're suffering the torments of the damned, are you not?"

Hal's hand was drifting inexorably to the knife at his hip.

The smile broadened. Slowly Aymer drew his own blade and spun it on his finger, a showy trick. "Try me if you will; I wouldn't advise it." There was a pause while each envisaged his next move. "Well now, Hal. You've obliged me by keeping my tale to yourself. So – in answer to your question – I have *not* told Father how you misused the Lady Eleanor." Aymer shook his head and sighed. "Farewell, Hal," said he, composedly. "I don't suppose we shall meet again."

Hal touched his brother's shoulder. "Farewell, Aymer. Farewell."

With an abrupt and forceful heave, Hal flipped the youth backward over the parapet and into the swift, treacherous stream below. Then he sauntered on – enjoying Moppet's face – mounted, and they were away.

* * *

Directly they returned to their own day room, Alice acknowledged her falsehood to Sir Simon; if she were to perjure herself, she may as well take credit for it. Though she waited in silence, he passed no comment, which left her scarlet-faced. "Shall you join the Duke of Clarence's affinity, sir?" she blurted.

"Clarence is keen to acquire me," he replied, after a pause. "He tried to pin the badge on me with his own hands, pursuing me round the chamber. A ludicrous scene. Before I commit myself, I must have a better sense of the King's intentions regarding your brother's estates. Clarence should be able to assist, but his influence, now, is untested. Nonetheless, the richest noble in the country, or soon to be. A vast swathe of estates."

"But surely the Earl of Warwick will be attainted for treason and his lands forfeit? The Duchess Isabel will inherit half her mother's estates one day, but nothing of her father's."

Loys was shaking his head.

"But this is what happened with my father," she insisted. "When Aubrey and Father were executed, the estates were forfeit. Edward of York bestowed the lands on Jack; York told my brother he was lucky to receive our own estates as a gift."

"Don't call him *Edward of York*. I'm sure even Clarence will prove himself more adept than your brother. In due course Clarence will come into the Warwick lands."

"Half only; Lady Anne would be co-heiress. And a great prize."

"*All* the Warwick lands. Lady Anne will be in a nunnery before she can wink at another man; I doubt you'll see her again."

"I should not care. It would serve … it would …"

"Would it? I seem to recall that when you and the lady were maidens at Middleham, you were inseparable. What can she have done to attract such malice?"

When she answered, it was very low. "Anne was one of they that spread lies against me. The last months of my marriage were truly wretched." She wouldn't meet his eyes.

The usual thirst had come upon him, but a direct approach would only serve to drive her away. Something in this woman was beginning to plague him; something hidden and slippery, something tantalising. With rather too great an effort, Loys dismissed her history, or at least those last years beyond his reach. "All that is behind you now, Alice."

With a tiny smile, his wife raised her chin. Though it was never safe to ascribe any words of his to kindness, she had chosen to do so. Inevitably, he rebelled. "Oh, I hold you guiltless – in deed, if not in thought. Too prudish to act the wanton and too stupid to evade the rumours."

The tremulous expression had settled into something more composed. "Perhaps, Sir Simon, we could dispense with all these *stupids*? Can we not take it as a thing understood that I am stupid, without you having to bring it up all the hours, tiresome as it must be?"

He grinned and stroked her cheek with a finger. "An excellent idea. I might say it now and again, just to keep in practice, but let it be as a thing understood."

* * *

On the day following, Alice was summoned with some urgency from her bedchamber. King Edward's youngest brother, the Duke of Gloucester, had deigned to visit their modest residence. Waving away her gentlewomen, Alice hurried to the narrow and airless day room, unsure of her welcome after all that had passed. Lord Richard embraced his childhood friend with warmth, greeting her in his harsh and high-pitched tones. She was coming to know Sir Simon better now, and could read the pleasure behind the parade of detachment. Both men were watching her closely.

"Lady Alice." The Duke perched on a corner of the table, hands clasped in his lap. "How greatly I feel for you, in all you've suffered. Thank Jesu our old friend Sir Simon was willing to rescue you from your troubles."

Her eyes met his and slid aside.

He continued in what passed, with him, for a smooth and gentle voice. "Listen. Listen well. I am too young to remember much of my brother, the Earl of Rutland." A lengthy silence. "Edmund was tall and handsome and brave; that much I recall, but he was taken from me before I had the chance to know him as I would have wished. King Edward feels his loss even now; they were close in age and greatly devoted. At the time he said he had lost his

50

right arm." Another pause. "Siblings die, of course. We must all accustom ourselves to loss. What made Edmund's death so especially dreadful was the manner of it: the disgusting depravity of his murder at the hands of the Clifford brothers. I ceased to be a child the day I learned of it." He stood, and walked forward, a few of his brief steps, then his hands were on her shoulders. "Lady Alice, I would do anything in my power to bring the culprits to justice. John Clifford, alas, is beyond any of us, but Robert Clifford lives yet, a free man; flaunting himself in Skipton. Shortly I go north to capture my brother's killer. Help me now: tell me what you know of his purpose."

She was trying to mute her breathing, and stared at his narrow chin, level with her eyes. "Lord Clifford did not tell me of his plans." She felt the two men exchange glances.

"Don't call him *Lord* Clifford. And you did not think to question the man's intentions, when he carried you off?" The voice had ruffled, but after a moment the Duke released her and lowered himself again to the table, hands on his knees, back to the familiar light-hearted tones. "Oh well. *Rarely does Vengeance, though lame, fail to catch the guilty man, though far in front.* Horace, Book Three, Ode Two," he added, at her blank look. "And I trust that vengeance shall, ultimately, be mine."

"Alas. It seems I have got there before you, my lord." Loys smirked.

Gloucester slapped him down; the only one who could. "I don't wish to disparage your wife, but I mean to do that villain a greater injury than the pilfering of Lady Loys."

Loys's expression did not change.

"So, my lady, you've been renewing old acquaintance?" Gloucester turned back to Alice. "My steadfast brother George and his sweet wife have been your hosts, I hear. But what of Margaret de Vere? No? Your brother's wife has taken sanctuary in the church of St Clement Danes. The King would quite like the lady to remove herself, I think. Her obstinacy implies that he intends some injury to her person."

Alice had turned deferentially to her husband.

"We may be in a position to assist Lady Margaret once we resettle in Essex," Loys said, pointedly. "There is no room at Avonby for any more great ladies; the place is an oubliette."

Gloucester laughed. "You are nudging me to speak to the King for you, Simon?" He paused. "I'm not sure there's much I can do. King Edward has not forgot the service you rendered, but perhaps it was rash to take your wife to court. Now he has looked her over, the King is saying that Lady Alice herself is a handsome reward, and some small manor or other will do for you. My brother sets great store by womanly charms, sometimes at the expense of more tangible advantages; the kingdom is already the poorer for it, as we all know."

Alice could feel the colour mounting to her cheeks. In this matter, she and Sir Simon were at one: without the de Vere lands, their marriage was a blind alley. She glanced sideways. Her husband's face was a frigid mask.

Gloucester was looking from one to the other, examining the effect. "Oh, Lady Alice: did your second husband mention that I met your first husband? I paid Sir Edmond a visit in his cell at Tewkesbury, the night before I condemned him to death."

She would not trust herself to speak.

"There was no message for you, I'm afraid, except obliquely, in that your husband assured me you are not carrying *his* child, which is good news for Sir Simon here, and good news for the royal house of York. Speaking of heirs, I hear our old friend Jasper is parading his Beaufort nephew, little Henry Tudor: an unlikely king, but beggars can't choose. Lancaster is a hydra. We keep lopping off heads, only for more to emerge. How I would hate for you to bring forth another."

Alice's gaze swept to the floor.

"Be that as it may. Your first husband was in good spirits, you'll be glad to hear, and faced the axe like a man."

"You think so, my lord?" said Loys, in a voice of smothered spite. "He seemed somewhat vacant to me. Was he known to be simple?"

"*Simon*! What a terrible fellow you are, to sneer at an innocent."

What could have happened? Though Simon Loys was never a likeable man, the Richard of her memories was a friendly, animated boy. A few years on, and he'd transmuted into one of Satan's imps, with skewers for teeth. But she was, after all, somewhat older herself; probably more perceptive. In the meanwhile, all the world had gone astray.

The Duke had kissed her and passed to the door before Loys turned. "My lord! Do you hear who is to have the bulk of Jack de Vere's lands? It seems I may have a fight on my hands, and should know my adversary."

Loys must surely have guessed the answer before it was given, for Gloucester had pivoted, a placid smile encompassing the couple. "Me, Simon. Jack de Vere's lands will go to me."

Then he was out of the door, amid a crowd of his gentlemen. Without a glance at Alice, Loys had started after him, shouting for Sir Hugh and his horse.

* * *

"And so, Monseigneur, he is gone, with his manservant and three of the horses."

Clifford turned about and examined the ceiling for a time. "Someone saw him go. You've questioned the men on the gate?"

"He left during vespers, but with so many absent at your side, and the castle disordered with the sickness, I did not learn of it for some hours. The sergeant said Master Hal went to join you."

"You knew it wasn't true, of course?"

"I suspected it wasn't true, Monseigneur, when Master Aymer returned. The lad had been wandering below the town when he came upon the runaway heading south, and Hal threw him from the bridge. Of course, there are great boulders along that stretch; it's a mercy the boy wasn't killed." Loic sounded ill content with Hal's parting gift. "Alas, poor Aymer; the episode has shamed him, I fear. He was trying to sneak back into the castle unobserved, but, as luck would have it, I was in company with all the youngsters when we

53

chanced upon him, dripping and shivering. So we carried him bodily to a hot bath and tried our best to cheer him."

Clifford scowled. "Aymer was out wandering alone, and just happened upon Hal? A likely story."

"Aymer is always out wandering alone," was Loic's retort. "A rash habit, for he's not popular, sad to say."

"If any harm were to befall Aymer, I would know exactly who was responsible, never fear. So: the lad went after Hal and they argued, of course. I cannot begin to understand Hal. He will not abide with his fellows, nor can he master them; better he is gone. We shall all live more peaceably without him."

Clifford stalked away, ordering the additional gold to be unloaded and borne to his chamber, to be added to that small existing hoard. When it was discovered that the small existing hoard had absconded along with his son, the promised peace was deferred, and any covert mourning scorched away as Clifford's curses blackened the air and the doors rattled in their frames.

The eventual discovery of King Louis's chest – broken, half-empty and concealed behind a tapestry – did little to mollify the irate parent and, by then, Loic had abandoned all hope of a speedy reconciliation.

"He has gone to London, Lord Robert, for sure," ventured Castor, later, when the temper had blown itself out. "He'll be needing to exchange that French gold; he has little enough of his own."

"Perhaps I should go after him?" suggested Nield. "He'd be easy to track."

"Let him go. Henceforth he is not my son; he is dead to me now. Even before this last outrage, Hal had sins on his conscience of which you know nothing."

As soon as they decently could, Castor and Nield excused themselves, scuttling in haste to reach their master's chamber and interrogate the chamberlain, who was proving oddly and most irksomely discreet. As they strolled back, empty-handed, Nield was drawing his own conclusions. "Well, Arthur: not so sure of yourself now, I reckon! Master Hal flown, and Lord Robert himself remarking the sins on his son's conscience."

"If you're bringing up Tailboys again, you needn't bother," said Castor. "Whatever Lord Robert holds against Hal, it's sure to concern the Lady Alice. The lad's no murderer – unless it's possible to question a man to death."

* * *

There was a destination in Hal's mind, but its exact location was hazy and, meanwhile, King Louis's gold was heavy in his bags and on his mind. And thus the pair made first for London. The ride was swift and uncomfortable; Hal had too little English coin and was stretching it to last until he could offload his foreign booty.

That first night, they slept a few hours in the lee of a wall near Ilkley, and swam the next morning in the river to cleanse themselves, emerging chilled and wide-awake and, in Hal's case, full of cheery optimism.

When he'd travelled to London in company with his father, the route had taken them close to Wakefield, but not close enough. Now Hal was his own man, he meant to walk the infamous bridge and confront for himself – if it were willing – the spectre that dogged his father's steps. Moppet was Alnwick-born and bred, but he knew enough of Robert Clifford's history to guess their destination as they turned aside from the accustomed road.

The bridge was swiftly located: an unremarkable crossing point, bustling and thronged at the end of market day. Leaving Moppet with the horses, Hal paced back and forth, head down, examining the pitted roadway, but there was not so much as the hint of a bloodstain. At last he pounced on a splinter of bone, a gleaming and silvery beacon amid the litter. It was a chicken wing. Hal wondered where York buried his dead: where Edmund of Rutland lay now. Not, it was clear, scattered over Wakefield Bridge where the Clifford brothers left the boy.

There was a perfect little chapel upon the bridge, overhanging the water and, naturally, in went Hal, the door swinging easily before him, but the place was deserted and the priest nowhere to be seen. It was pledged to St Mary the Virgin, which, to Hal's excited wits, seemed a wondrous sign, for his father venerated the Virgin most particularly. Hal prayed awhile, and made an offering, and then hovered on the bridge a while longer, but still Edmund of Rutland's phantom had not appeared, so they headed on into Wakefield for a hot meal and a cheap bed.

The two men found themselves a snug inn and ate fervently, the first substantial fare of the day. At once there sparked up a muttering and a nodding in Hal's direction.

"They think you your father, Master Hal," opined Moppet. "You're the living image of the man at your age, when he wrought such havoc here."

Hal stared at Moppet and put down his cup. "Ah, I forgot. You knew Lord Clifford when he was a lad."

"I did. He lived among us for many years at Alnwick, squiring for Old Percy."

"Like me all ways round, was he?"

"Oh no, Master Hal. Hardly. Much more fearsome and way more trouble. He and John Clifford bullied the other young henchmen something terrible. Girls and fighting: there was nothing else on his mind, I suppose."

Hal gave a short, affronted laugh. "Well! What's on my mind, then, do you suppose?"

Moppet eyed him, lugubrious as ever. "Poetry, I reckon, Master."

"You have forgotten my father's music-making, Moppet," Hal objected. "He is always composing and playing and singing. I have little of his talent. Music is always on his mind, is it not?"

"That, and other things."

"And, Moppet, he's constantly thinking on his devotion to God, and how best he can please the Lord; praying all the day long, denying himself meat, and so forth. I'm hardly known for that, am I?"

"Very well, Master Hal. Have it your own way: excepting only your looks, you are nothing like your father."

* * *

Sir Simon had accompanied Duke Richard, uninvited, to his mother's house and followed him inside; deep inside, leaving Sir Hugh kicking his heels an hour or two in the great hall. What transpired within was as yet unknown; Loys was silent the short ride home and Dacre's courage failed him again.

The Duke's departing words had sparked a dread in Alice. Seeking comfort, she spent those hours seated on the bed, Constance clasping one hand and Blanche the other, stroking her palm with a thumb. "If Richard of Gloucester is contesting the grant, my husband stands no chance. The Duke said that Edward of York is already minded to renege on his promise to Sir Simon."

Constance stared at her aunt as though she were deranged. "Why would you speak in this way? Let Sir Simon be disenchanted with his bargain; he deserves far worse, as we all know."

"If he gains nothing from all this, Constance, he'll reject me! Of course he will. He'll find a way to annul the marriage. I am carrying a child, and have no other protector." Alice began to cry. "What is to become of me?" It was noisy crying, that wanted sympathy.

Elyn, seated at her feet, chafed her half-sister's knee with helpless compassion, glaring at Constance.

Joanna caught Blanche's eye before speaking. "Lady Alice, he will not discard you. Sir Simon is a landed knight; he does not need the estate. You may call every noble in the land *cousin*; you may call the king *cousin*. You are worth more than an estate to him."

"For sure! Nothing is less likely, Lady Alice." Blanche was shy of speaking before them, and cleared her throat. "Joanna is right, there. Even if his hopes are disappointed, Sir Simon has married an earl's daughter and rises accordingly. Plenty are pleased to wed for less."

Alice closed her eyes. Soon she slept. When Elyn and Joanna crept away, Blanche and Constance lingered on in the dim room with its heavy air, hunched over their mistress like dogs coveting a bone. At last Blanche caught the younger girl's eye. "At least let me explain myself, Constance," she murmured, "for it hurts me to be at odds with you, when I love her as you love her, and only ever wished for what is best." It was so great a release to speak of it that the tears welled up as Blanche told her tale, and Constance heard her out, and tried to be just. "I did believe Sir Simon would show himself more respectful. He is coming to care for her, I think, though he has not been as gentle as he ought. And yet," Blanche concluded, "I cannot be sorry that Lord Clifford never returned. None of those men could be trusted."

Constance was honest enough to admit the truth of this, at least to herself. Robert Clifford was no flower of chivalry and some of the company he kept was even uglier. Blanche had been spared the worst of it. Constance had not. "My aunt shouldn't have to lower herself to such a one as Simon Loys; she has no choice now, for sure. But that is your fault. It is the treachery that's so hard to bear, Blanche. How could you take it on yourself to decide our path? A terrible betrayal, when we should be as one."

"Constance, I'm truly sorry for it." Blanche didn't sound sorry; she sounded as if it were hard to sustain the tone of humility. "And yet, as you say, the marriage is made now, for good or ill. She has begun well, and we must help her. We do her no kindness by fostering a spirit of rebellion."

While Alice was sleeping, Sir Simon returned. He closeted himself in the upper chamber with Master Leo Brini, as he was wont to do, often for hours at a stretch. At Avonby there was a small room dedicated to their mysterious purpose, from which reeking smokes and strange sounds would often emanate. When they were away from home they confined themselves to reading and writing and talking.

Loys did not appear at dinner, by which time Alice had whipped herself into a dreadful certainty. She meant to tackle her husband that night; prudent enough to wait until he'd obtained his pleasure, when he would be at his most amenable. Resting then at her side, he drew her close. "What is it, little wife? You've not been giving me the usual ardent attention. What weighty matter occupies your mind?"

How she'd loathed him for the sarcasm, in the early days. Now she barely heard it. "Sir Simon. Husband. What did the Duke of Gloucester say? Please tell me."

"Why? My troubles are my own. I don't expect you to suffer with them."

"Is Duke Richard striving after all the de Vere lands? Is the King to give us nothing?"

He laughed quietly, a rusty sound. "It will serve me right, you think? How you would enjoy that."

"I would not."

He smoothed her hair with his fingers. "Don't tell me you have come to care for me? Life would lose its seasoning if you stopped wishing me dead."

She feared to put escape into his head, but he would surely get there without her help. "Will you seek an annulment, sir?" she asked, at last.

"An annulment? You won't evade me that easily! Even were there to be no material profit, I have taken an earl's daughter to wife. To me, a prize well worth a few days' weary ride into Wales. It seems you have deluded yourself with false hopes. Now hold that foolish tongue."

She stretched and turned away, surrendering herself to sleep. A moment later, she turned back. "But what did the Duke say?"

He had turned away also, his voice muffled. "Gloucester said there was enough to go around, and King Edward would compensate him in any event. I should consult you as to the de Vere manors and he would handle matters with the King."

"I mistook him then! I thought he would take all for himself."

"Very likely he would. Why not? But every man has his price."

"What price?"

He clicked his tongue. "You are stupidly unobservant, Alice. Did you not mark the badge on my bonnet, as I came in? The White Boar of Gloucester; I have joined his retinue."

* * *

Hal's disappearance added greatly to the joy of the twins' little faction, an entirely splendid outcome. Aymer reckoned it well worth the ducking he'd endured; for, if he took credit for vanquishing the enemy, Hal's valedictory assault was, undeniably, Aymer's own fault. A valuable lesson: let the enemy retreat unmolested. That, or kill him.

George seemed presently unwilling, or unable, to fill Hal's shoes and while Lord Clifford made desultory efforts to raise up his nephew, there was now plenty of clear air for Aymer to flourish. Mindful that he'd failed to grasp the chance when first it presented itself, he seized it now with both hands. To finish his preparations, Aymer took himself off to George's chamber. Bede had already disposed of his old pallet and promoted himself to Hal's place in the great bed. Both lads were lying upon it, Bede looking pensive, George with a face most dismally morose.

"May I speak in front of Bede?" said Aymer, gently.

They both nodded.

"Ah, George. I'm grieved the news had to come from me, but what was I to do, when Hal refused to tell you himself?"

George's brows sagged at him.

"I was urging Hal for weeks to confess to you, ever since he first boasted of his abuse of the Lady Eleanor."

"Boasted of it!" muttered Bede.

"Guy and I were so disgusted, we beat him for his duplicity. That was when we were in the Forest of Dean. We gave him a good drubbing, as you saw. And still he said nothing."

"Sickening," muttered Bede.

"Does everyone know?" George whispered.

"Of course not! I wouldn't do that to you. Only Guy and me; we told none of the others. Richie joined us in dealing out the punishment, but he doesn't know the reason for it."

"My Uncle Robert?"

"No, no. I've left that to you – if you wish to tell Father. But probably you would prefer to forget the whole sorry affair."

"I think so, Aymer, yes."

Aymer turned to the door, then turned back. "George … where is he?"

"Who?"

"*Hal*, George. He must have said something. What are his plans?"

"How should I know? I couldn't care less."

Aymer sighed. "Soldiery, I suppose. Somewhere." It was not quite the resolution he'd sought; an unnerving want of finality.

"I'm grateful for what you've done, Aymer. You're a good fellow."

* * *

Hating Hal most particularly, Richie found that his cup of happiness could not be said to overflow while he was as yet reliant on the unspeakable Pleydell for his comfort and ease; Pleydell, who served Bede with prompt devotion, ready to attend to any of the youngsters before he would obey Richie. The youth reverted to the matter so often that the others could bear it no longer.

"Richie, you must go to Father if you will not assert yourself. Put the problem in his lap, for he holds the purse strings. Aymer and I, we speak with Father all the time. Yet you're afraid to approach him. It's not the mark of a man."

Certainly Richie was afraid of Robert Clifford and would avoid this if he could. By now the others were watching to see if he would rise to it. And so, as loath as if he were marching to the block, he made his way alone to his father's day room, and knocked on the door.

Jem opened up with the usual irritating pantomime of wonder, staring and open-mouthed. Richie hovered at the threshold. There was a map spread upon the table; a map of what, Richie did not know. If only the music makers were within, he might stand a chance. But it was not to be. The mood in the room was grave and sombre. Around Lord Clifford sat his most senior intimates: Loic, Castor, Findern, Reginald Grey, Patrick Nield and Bellingham. But no George, Richie noted happily, whereas Hal would certainly have been among them.

Clifford raised a staying finger to mute the visitor, and stabbed at the map. "James Thwaite?" – an utterance enigmatic to Richie, though it sparked a general nodding and some dissenting murmurs.

61

Clifford gave a sudden laugh and clicked his fingers. "Fetch the letter, Jem! Gentlemen, this arrived for Hal the day after he left me. Don't bother reading it; my son Waryn is no stimulating correspondent. Just the last paragraph, concerning his marriage to Anna Thwaite." He laughed again. "Let's arrive at Belforth unannounced, shall we? I don't want to give James time to revenge himself on my family."

The letter passed from hand to hand, evading Richie's twitching fingers, each of the men falling prey to the mirth until Sir Reginald took it up and scanned the page. "This marriage will infuriate Sir James. Resist the urge to taunt the man, Lord Robert."

Clifford waved a dismissive hand and turned to Richie. "Ah, what is it, then?"

"Oh! Your pardon, Father. I hoped to catch you a moment alone. I will try another time." He bowed and would have withdrawn, willingly defeated, but Clifford had pushed himself up and crossed to the window.

"We'll take a moment, gentlemen. My son must be in some distress, to have disturbed us. Return when you've stretched your legs."

They all stood then, talking, shuffling off, Patrick Nield sending the boy a disparaging glance; Loic, halted by a hand on his sleeve, reseating himself. The matter which had dominated Richie's thinking for months seemed at the vital moment to dwindle, inconveniently, into pettiness. "I'm ashamed to bother you now, Father. It's not so very important."

"Important to you, surely, or you would not have come."

So Richie plunged in. "Well, it's about our service, my lord. George has Taffy all to himself, and Aymer and Guy have a manservant between them, but the other seven of us are all sharing one man. One man – for *seven*! I did mention it to Sir Patrick Nield, but he seemed to feel nothing could be done. That is, he walked off without venturing an answer; perhaps he is puzzling on it still."

The household servants were not the steward's province. Loic rolled his eyes.

"Anyway, what I was thinking, Father, is that possibly Will and I might share a man?" Richie was speeding up. "You may probably be concerned about the money, but perhaps you have forgot that Moppet saved you the cost of his wages by running off."

"*Mon Dieu.*"

Richie continued, now, at a sprint. "And perhaps if Will and I didn't ask for new clothes or boots or harness – say for a twelvemonth – would that pay for a manservant? So, even if our boots grew holes: no new boots? I just thought I'd ask …"

"Look at my doublet, Richie," instructed his father. "It shows my buttocks, does it not? Sir Loic here tells me it's the height of elegance to show one's buttocks in this way. And of course, they're a fine pair. Next year, no doubt, the skirts will be lower, and my buttocks will look most odd, standing proud for all to see. Women will look at me askance. Men will talk. I shall still be wearing this doublet then and doubtless many years after, though skirts may fall and rise and fall again. I shall take good care of it and not wear the elbows or spill my wine. And so must you. Take good care of your clothes, your boots and your harness, for they will need to last you now. You may ask for new boots if yours grow holes; it does not mean that you will get new boots. Does that answer your question?"

"Yes, my lord," said Richie mournfully. "But my lord, perhaps there could be a reshuffling, if we cannot have another manservant? For George having Taffy to himself, and the twins sharing Notch and then all *seven* of us. Seven! And Pleydell won't do for me, my lord. He runs to Bede's side but I seem to come last, though I am senior among the younger men."

Clifford perched on the edge of the table. "Well, Richie, you must learn to inspire loyalty; isn't that the lesson? I'm a poor man and, very shortly, I'll have no income at all. Many of my men will serve for nothing. I do not expect them to abandon me, for they love me. I am a good lord to them, and they follow for love alone."

Also, they have nowhere to go, thought Richie. *Where would they go?*

"Then again, perhaps you've irked Pleydell with those infernal noises. You've certainly irked the rest of us."

"Oh. But Bede has pestered me in his turn, Father."

"He has. He is full of advice for you, is he not? In truth, it's in adversity that one sees a man's mettle. What matters is not whether a companion is the very devil himself, but whether he will back you, when the time comes. Bede has not learned this yet."

The boy looked up, wary of another sermon on his treachery; he could not expect their lord to approve a shift in allegiance. Never had his father talked like this in his hearing, and certainly not to him. But perhaps he was drunk.

"So, have you asked the twins if you may share Notch? No?" Clifford grinned at Loic, but the Frenchman was gazing away. "You come to interrupt me as I plan our future path, yet you've not the courage for that? Clearly there is one among your fellows who is a natural-born leader: he has conquered you with ease! Ah, young Richie, I can do little in this very desperate case, but Sir Loic here shall ask George if he would agree to share his man Taffy with Bede. There. Now I have done my best by you. But answer me this: how *is* Aymer? Is he more content than he was?"

"Yes, my lord," said Richie, puzzled. "Much happier, now that …"

"Quite," said Clifford, drily. "Off you go then, my son," and interrupted his thanks, waving him away through the door via which the other men were entering.

As the door closed behind him, Richie stood a moment, eyes shut. It had gone so much better than expected, and Lord Clifford had been so genial and forthcoming – with none of the accustomed rough-handing – that Richie fairly swanned back to his chamber, sauntering in on the little group. They fell upon him.

"So Father dismissed the senior men just to have speech with me alone, for all that there was no music in the room, just the busy map. He understood my problem *exactly*. He was very good to me, but he says, well, all our buttocks are on show – now and for many a long year; they may be seen by any who care to look, so that fellows shall follow for love alone. Oh, and he wishes you to share Notch with me." Smiling, Richie held up a hand to silence the furious outburst. "Don't fret! I told him I'd rather George shared Taffy with Bede, and Father has agreed to ask him. He was most sympathetic, I must say, and spoke with me man to man."

The three of them were gazing at him, Will shaking his head in wonderment. "You poor fool!" said Guy, at last. "So George shall not share Taffy unless he chooses, eh? And if he deigns to do it, he'll not share with you, but with a younger boy, while you – who are senior – must go on trying to bend Pleydell to your will, wresting him from that nest of youngsters every time you need to shave or have something fetched. Father must think you're insane. Donkey will kill himself laughing."

Richie shot him a venomous look. "Not at all, *actually*, Guy. I would not share Taffy with George, not for all my weight in gold. This way, Bede is off my hands and Pleydell shall have no choice but to serve me. And you should know that Father said some other things too, especially about Aymer and the devil, but I seem to have *forgotten* them now. Maybe I'll recall his words in a day or two, if certain fellows can bring themselves to stop behaving like *turds*."

He was out of the room rather smartly, for he suspected they were about to start jeering and he didn't choose to hear it. Which indeed they were, and for rather a long stretch, the laughter pursuing him down the stairs.

"Will someone please alert me," cried Guy, "if there are fellows creeping up on my buttocks with love in their eyes? I'd like some warning!"

Will gasped, helpless, from the bed.

"By God," drawled Aymer. "Remind me never to put my affairs in Richie's hands."

* * *

Between Wakefield and London the journey was companionable and without incident. When Hal and Moppet fell in with a rowdy group of pilgrims, Hal FitzClifford became *Hal Prynne; Prynne* being on the tip of his tongue, his mother's name. He was now a merchant's son from Newcastle, off to seek his fortune. His story was requested time and again, and no one listened to the tale. But he learned something in return: where to change his French gold unhindered, where to find work, where to disappear.

Southwark, of course. Dangerous, interesting Southwark – he might have riddled the location unaided – and off he went, at once, on entering London by Bishopsgate. In the warm, drizzling evening he wandered the lanes, pondering which inn to broach. He'd got as far as stabling his horses, when he beheld a woman resting by the entrance to a narrow house opposite, wiping her brow. As he watched, she recommenced: a little run up and a shoulder-barge upon the door, which failed, again, to give. Hal grinned, and strolled up. "May I be of assistance, mistress?"

The woman stood back and breathed, hands on hips. Too strapping and full-figured for him, and she might be twice his age, but handsome nonetheless, with an expression of frank interest. "A young ox!" She gestured at the door. "Assuredly, sir, you shall be of assistance."

He barely had to lean upon it.

"Well, now. One good turn deserves another."

They were within, and drinking with the household, and supping with the household, before too many words were exchanged. There were two sons present, silent, solemn fellows, who ate quickly and retired quickly, for they were bakers, up before the dawn.

And then this Mistress Tilney sat back and questioned him, just as the pilgrims had done, but she listened to his answers and she smiled. When she rose and locked up for the night, Hal stalked after her, expectant. The woman tossed a blanket to Moppet, waving him down in an alcove by the chimney. There was no alcove for Hal. He waited outside her chamber as he counted, slowly, to a hundred. The little room contained one sturdy bed, and a pallet for the maid, a deaf girl who didn't turn at his entrance. Resolute, Hal shrugged the doublet over his head. As Mistress Tilney watched, he unbuttoned his shirt and peeled it from his body, slow, deliberate, making a play of shadow about the carven forms of chest and shoulder. There he stood, in only his hose, head cocked to the side.

"Well, Master Prynne, shortly my sons must be up, and so must I. You're a fine young fellow, but the posturing has gone on long enough."

He knelt on the bed and tugged the motheaten curtains about them. Only a moment later – he was barely into his stride – she pressed her hands to his chest, halting him.

"What is it?"

She patted his arm. "Go to sleep, Master Prynne. When you have yourself better in hand, you may approach me." Her head was a black ball, featureless in the gloom.

Hal lurched face-first into the mattress. His hose were tangled around his knees where they'd rolled in his urgency. Pulling them up or pushing them off: either would attract further comment, so he let them be, tightly furled and pinching at his veins. Then he felt cautiously about for a pillow, but as there was none, he cradled his head in his elbow and tried, perplexed and thwarted as he was, to go to sleep.

* * *

When the others could finally bring themselves to stop behaving like turds, Richie consented to recall the rest of Robert Clifford's words, producing further puzzlement.

"Why Aymer?" wondered Guy, aloud. "Did he not ask also after my happiness? You have forgot it on purpose!"

Richie shook his head, slow and happy.

Aymer tilted his neck, first one way and then the other, accepting his dues. "He fears I shall leave him, of course. You saw his anger toward Hal, when that knave had so disrespected me as to strike me unprovoked. Father has driven Hal away, rather than risk losing his favourite."

Which served only to increase Guy's irritation. "That is such utter bollocks, and well you know it."

"Riddle it another way, then Guy – *if you can*. You may see yourself the same as Aymer; Father does not." Probably it was beyond Richie's power to drive a wedge between the twins, but he could hardly stop from trying.

"More likely you've muddled his speech again, for nothing is straight in your head. You are a foolish fellow and it's barely worth talking to you. I shall see you all in the morning." Guy tipped his bonnet to a jaunty angle and then halted in the doorway, backing a few steps into the room, his smug leer levelled only at

Richie. "Brothers, I'm off to put a gingerbread man in the oven. The baker of Carleton's away at Knaresborough, and his wife cannot get enough of me. I've the sturdiest prick in the North Country, so she says; she's never seen the like."

"She *has* seen the like, *actually*, Guy," Richie flashed back. "Hal, George, Donkey, Moncler *and* Father. The little whore probably says it to all the fellows who use her."

"But never – my poor Richie – to you." They heard Guy's retreating voice, on the hunt for Notch.

"Ah, don't take it to heart," said Aymer carelessly. "I've not had the baker of Carleton's wife either, and nor has Will, I warrant. Eh, Will? Oh, well, it seems he has, then."

* * *

Hal's residence in Southwark must be the briefest of excursions. How easy, how perilously easy, to start to sink and, once the waters had closed over his head, to find himself but a poor journeyman. No one had expectations of him now. Liberating, to a point, but he knew himself to be better than this. Unaccustomed to labour – aside from fighting – he found the work rather satisfying, the first few mornings. Then it began to disgust him and, though he'd given over the oldest of his few shirts to the task, he was soon concerned at the wear to the precious garment.

By night, Mistress Tilney made herself his tutor, and there was more of vinegar than honey in her methods. The skill of pleasing a woman, like the skill of baking, intrigued him at the outset but tried his patience before long.

And Moppet was most unhappy. "They cannot understand a word I say. Three times I'm accused of being a Scot. At least, I think that was the charge. I can't abide this for long, Master Hal. Surely we'll be changing your money and moving on?"

"I'll be the judge of that, Moppet." But the manservant was right.

Richenda Tilney had a circle of noisy and disreputable friends, in the habit of visiting at all hours for a drink and a gossip, making altogether too much of the great young buck now in residence. Hal was plagued with such winking, leering and laboured humour that he took to pre-emptive innuendo himself, absurdly crude; bitingly sarcastic. He found he couldn't shame them into silence, for only Mistress Tilney comprehended him, gleaming her amusement.

Among the reprobates haunting the house was a moneychanger, taken aside for confidential speech on Hal's pressing matter. Leaping Abel seemed so improbably dishonest that Hal went through the motions only to avoid angering his hostess. The old man eased his wooden leg before him and fingered the fine gold, sniffing, biting, licking at assorted pieces. It would all need a good scrub after he'd gone.

It was, in truth, most unlikely that the imaginary merchant father would endow him with foreign treasure and, for that matter, Hal was growing exasperated at his real father, who could so easily have changed the gold himself when last in London. In a stilted voice, he relayed again his doubtful tale.

Leaping Abel shouted with laughter and enveloped Hal in a smelly fug. Did Master Prynne think he was born yesterday? The only men trying to trade hoards of louis in London were rebels against King Edward, lately come over from France, now looking to bury themselves. "Your head will end up on the Bridge if you stay here! Take my advice, young master: gather your louis and scamper back to Paris where you'll be safe among your friends."

For a brief moment, Hal considered whether Leaping Abel had the right of it. The gold would go further if no changer took a cut; thanks to Loic, he now spoke passable French and he was indeed – implausible as it seemed – a rebel with no prospect of a pardon. But he'd never been abroad and he couldn't go alone. He smiled. "I'm no rebel, Master Abel. Just a plain man from up north. Your best price, if you will?"

The moneychanger spat and rubbed his chin, leaving an eggy smear. "Here's what I'll do. As you're a particular friend of Mistress Tilney's, I'll take just one third as my fee. You'll not do better than that anywhere in the city. Poor Abel shall take all the risk for little enough reward."

Hal's smile broadened. "You impudent wretch! I'm not quite so green as you imagine. We've wasted each other's time."

"Well, well, Master Prynne. We'll see about that. You'll be seeking me out soon enough, I reckon, and I'll not give you such a civil price, next time. That is – unless I pass you first, looking down over London from a spike upon the Bridge. They'll mount your noggin next to Robert Clifford's, and a pretty matched pair you'll make."

Hal turned away so the man wouldn't see his expression. It was clear he'd tarried too long.

* * *

For the first time, Alice was admitted to the bright little upper chamber. Though her eyes pounced into every corner, she uncovered no wand, no pentacle; only Sir Simon, reading her with his penetrating eye. Hands on her shoulders, he guided her to the chair beside Master Brini, who smiled through his eyeglasses. Before them lay a map of the county of Essex. Her gaze wandered over the ancient names that once had meant so much.

"The Duke wishes my lands to lie toward the south west of the county, that I may be close to London and so better serve his interests. I expect often to be absent and my brother, Sir Nicholas, will oversee the estates in my absence. His manor is Danehill, *here*. So tell me of these manors *here*."

And so she told him: every small detail that she could recall. Sevenhill, he settled on, as the core of the estate, cheek-by-jowl with his brother's little patch. There was a house already on the site: a good house, built by her grandfather, the eleventh earl, when he was a young man. It would require alterations, perhaps; a frontage, even, to bring it up to date, but a lesser drain on his purse than a new dwelling.

"You bear a heavy responsibility, little wife." His finger stroked her hand and Brini followed its iterations with interest. "I should not like to find Sevenhill stony and infertile, with a crumbling and comfortless house. I possess just such a property already, as you'll shortly discover. We'll break our journey to Avonby by visiting my brother in Essex and taking a look about us; too late to do any good if it's not to my taste, of course." He was in a high humour; about him hung an ill suppressed exhilaration.

She struck swiftly. "Sir, may I call on my sister-in-law Margaret before we leave London? The lady is abandoned and friendless in sanctuary at St Clement Danes. A visit would cheer her, I know." She was desperate to explain herself to Jack; since that was, for the foreseeable future, impossible, his wife must stand proxy.

His hands were clasped behind his head. "We'll see."

She waited, but he only lounged and surveyed her. Perhaps if she pushed for more she would secure her aim. "And Queen Margaret, sir: do you think Duke Richard would let me pay her a visit before she's moved elsewhere?

"Don't call her *Queen* Margaret." He was smiling.

"The Tower being but a few minutes' walk from here. Another poor lady, alone and filled with grief."

"That grief she brought on herself. And she is not alone. In point of fact, the Duke has appointed my cousin among her attendant gentlewomen."

"Oh? Who is this?" His connections were nothing to boast of.

"Elizabeth, Lady Ullerton. Formerly your senior gentlewoman."

In truth, she'd no great longing to see the Queen and she certainly lost all desire at that news. Alice was ambushed by a sudden vision of the Prior's chamber at Little Malvern, her last sight of Elizabeth Ullerton. Less than three months had passed, but a yawning chasm divided her from the scene. In her mind's eye, Elizabeth stood motionless in the window embrasure, eyelids pink and swollen in the warm sunlight. Robert was thundering at the woman. Alice tried, rather feebly, to hush his voice, disturbing and distracting. Lady Ullerton's tears were for her betrothed, Edmond's steward. For the first time Alice brought the man to mind. "Do you know what became of Sir Gabriel Appledore, Duke Edmond's steward?"

He yawned. "*Duke* Edmond? If calling oneself a duke makes it so, we'd all be ennobled. *Sir Edmond Beaufort,* child. Do try to remember – it's growing tiresome. I believe Appledore was one of the traitors dragged out of

Tewkesbury Abbey with Sir Edmond. And met the same end, no doubt. There was such a queue of them at the axe. Torrents of blood, tedious to watch. Lord Hastings fell asleep and rolled off his chair. At least the prisoners appeared to be attending. All but your husband, of course, who was nodding along to some inaudible celestial choir. The man had taken leave of his wits."

In some desperation she summoned Robert back; anything to close out this cruelty. "May I see the … lady, sir? May I go to the Tower before we leave London?"

"Of course not. How would that look? And don't assume that because I've denied one devious request I'll agree to the other." He was still smiling. "I'm not minded to allow you a visit to Margaret de Vere either: sister to one traitor, married to another. If your brother Jack had any care for his wife, he would have carried her into exile with him. I am not accountable for the lady. She may starve in sanctuary for all I care."

* * *

Richard of Gloucester had sounded out the King already; later, with Loys at his side, he perused the map and pronounced himself satisfied. "Leave this in my hands. Go home, Simon. You've been too long from the delights of Avonby. Make yourself useful in the North Country. Robert Clifford is surely plotting to join Jack de Vere in Scotland. You can intercept him."

Loys nodded thoughtfully. At once he doubled the planned sojourn in Essex.

"And Simon – your wife must let slip what she knows. Lady Loys plays the innocent very well; I'm not a buyer."

"At first I thought as you did, but she's reconciled to our marriage by now and would help me if she could, my lord. She knows nothing of value."

Gloucester raised a sceptical brow.

"Already she tells your sister-in-law of Clarence that the child is mine, then boasts to me of the lie."

"Excellent! She's in capable hands. As I said, I'll stand godfather to the child. Let me know if you meet obstacles in raising a loan for the work on

Sevenhill; my name can unlock doors." Gloucester sat back and they eyed each other a moment in silence. Quietly Loys cleared his throat. The Duke gave him a small smile. "No, my friend; not I. Go to Sir John Howard; tell him I sent you. Ralph Jocelyn also – former mayor. They will do for you if money is at issue."

Loys nodded, a tiny movement.

"You'll be relieved to hear the King suffered another attack of clemency and pardoned those turncoats you took into your service. Not that you waited for it; everyone's seen Dacre and Chowne strutting about in your wake when they should have been keeping their heads down. You want a great house and fine household – who doesn't? But don't let ambition outstrip your caution."

Loys nodded again, attentive to the pipsqueak. He'd bitten his tongue and an ulcer would blossom. "Indeed, my lord. But Andrew Chowne is guilty of nothing more than keeping ill advised company. The man's lame: he wasn't present at either battle. And, of course, Dacre is the very one who delivered Lady Alice into our hands. In point of fact, he deserves our gratitude."

"Careful, Simon! Dacre took up arms against the King at Barnet. If that's not treason, I don't know what is."

"Hugh was certainly present at Barnet. He may even have been bearing arms, if only for the sake of appearances. If you knew this knight as well as I do, my lord, you'd know that was the sum of it. I once watched him wield a mace by the wrong end."

Gloucester grinned. "I didn't say we were at any risk, did I? Good Sir Hugh used to joust at Middleham, and very wary he was too; the only man I've known to charge his opponent at a trot. Though I can't say I've seen you in the lists even once, my friend. You're more wary still."

"Bold enough in the service of the King, my lord; ready enough with a sword. Wearing a pretty ribbon and cavorting for the crowd? Not if I can help it."

"There's no pastime so excellent as jousting. None. It demands of a man every fine quality." Gloucester waited for the gracious compliment. It didn't come. "Well. Tell Sir Lawrence Welford the King has released his heir. In point of fact, no one thought to tell the boy his father was hanging about the court, and he has flitted off already to Monmouthshire. Never mind."

* * *

A fortnight after Clifford's return from his mother's house, Roger came to him at Skipton. Lady Joan's grief over her brother, the well-beloved Courtenay, was too raw to permit Clifford entry to her house, when Robert might have swayed the outcome at Tewkesbury had he stifled his pride, had he hastened to the side of his fellows rather than hastening to Somerset's wife.

"Why am I blamed for this, when you never stirred from home?"

"You're expendable," said Roger. "I am not." He followed his brother up to the day room.

Clifford had turned with a retort when his attention was caught by the tall and willowy child peeping around Roger's arm. "What have we here?"

"Your son Peter, as you very well know. Thirteen years old. It's high time he joined your household."

Clifford blinked at his brother. "You cannot be serious! In a day or so we'll be on the road. Look at him, you mawk! Can this child wield a sword against a full-grown man? You'd condemn him to death."

Roger made suppressing movements with his hands. "He is slight, but he will grow. The lad's been training hard. He's not unhandy, even now."

"You're better placed to have him than I, and well you know it. If it's money you want, I'll spare you a little for his keep."

"The cost was never at issue, Robert. Joan is wearied with caring for your bastards; five of them, she's nurtured." Roger could see his brother frowning over the figure, and clicked his tongue in irritation. "John the Younger perished of the measles at Pentecost. I wrote to you, for God's sake – not that you troubled to reply. And you can guess what Joan endured with the twins, those last few years."

Clifford was reminded of Aymer's disgraceful aside on the subject of his aunt. He grunted. "Excellent soldiers, though."

Roger raised his brows, deflected. "And how is young Robbie shaping up?"

"Hopeless," said Clifford, spitefully. "Anyone would think he were *not my son*, so incompetent is he." He folded his arms. "That lad will fall before long, mark my words. And this one will go the same way if he rides with us. Mother of God, Roger, show some sense!"

"If you won't take him, I'll send him to Triston. Not over-tolerant of a man's slips, is our little brother, but I'm sure he can find employment for the boy."

After that, there could be no more debate over Peter's future, and his father unbent so far as to give the lad a playful cuff to the head as he called in his younger boys. Since George had proved less than adept in imparting his martial skills to Robbie, Clifford consigned Peter to Oliver's care. Then he ejected them all from the room. "Ah, our household has lately lost a man, as it happens." He'd reverted to the subject at the vanguard of his mind. "Hal, my eldest, my firstborn. He has left me. I didn't see it coming. He gave no warning. He took leave of no one. He left no message."

"There you are then!" said Roger, jauntily. "Lose one, and replace him at once. God is smiling on you."

Clifford had planted himself before his brother and stood gazing down, a degree, into his face. "This is the end, Roger, I know it. We part now, never more to meet in this world."

Roger examined Clifford's feet. "Don't say it," he murmured. "You and your bloody visions. Has any one of them ever come to pass?"

"That depends on when you judge the outcome. Until I die, my story is unfinished. Ah, Brother, you may have my hounds. They're a fine pack, as you know. Take them with you. I've no use for them, where I'm going."

* * *

On the ride back to the inn, Loys was thinking aloud. He could conceive of few exploits he'd relish less than an assault on the Wyverns as they moved north to Scotland.

"I should say not! Jesu! Does the Duke wish you dead, Simon? Sir Simon, rather. Clifford would dismember you for the trick you served him."

"Hold your tongue, Hugh. I'm quite capable of envisaging the outcome for myself. Which is why I intend to throw another man into his path. You'll not be attending us to Essex; make ready to depart for the North. This afternoon."

"What, me?"

"You'll travel to Londesborough, to my neighbour Threlkeld."

"Sir Lancelot?"

"The same. There's a man who has good reason to wish Robert Clifford ill, and may actually jump at the chance of revenge. And you shall offer your services on this occasion."

"Me? But Simon – Sir Simon, rather – surely the better choice for this mission would be Sir Andrew here?"

"Who is lame."

"Or Master Twelvetrees, as your marshal. Please. For Lady Blanche believes that she's with child. Of course she needs me constantly beside her. You know how women are!"

"Regrettably, I do. From my observations, though, Lady Blanche manages admirably without you."

"But she's rather late in years to begin childbearing, and somewhat frightened."

"You are confused again, Hugh. It is not Lady Blanche who is frightened. Remember that I have demoted a perfectly competent steward to make way for you."

Sir Hugh looked round bitterly at Leo Brini, who was choking into his doublet. The Venetian pulled down his upper lip. "Who is this Threlkeld who burns with vengeance, Sir Hugh?"

"What?" The knight clicked his tongue. "His wife is the widow of Clifford's elder brother. Clifford murdered her son, the heir to the barony."

"Gesù! The more I hear of this devil, the less I understand why you were in his service, Sir Hugh."

"What? I did not serve him, of course! Of course I did not. I was his prisoner. You know that."

Loys sliced across the petulance. "The child disappeared some years ago, Leo, during one of Clifford's periodic invasions of the North Country. No one knows what became of young Henry, but Threlkeld and his wife believe Clifford killed him, and that's what matters now."

* * *

To preserve the smoothness at his jaw, Hal would, in less slovenly times, submit to a twice-daily shearing. Abandoning his razor three days since, he'd a good, dark growth to hide behind. The bruising masked the rest. When he'd found himself a peaked crimson cap, he felt he more closely resembled one of the Three Wise Men than Robert Clifford.

Inspiration had struck, and he made his way to the docks in the Pool of London below the Tower, where the tall cranes swung, the air of industrious bustle contrasting markedly with his last visit. During Warwick's ill fated attempt to change London's mercantile allegiance, the place was paralysed.

Hal sat on a low wall with Moppet perched alongside, and waited for his instinct to guide him. Predictably, his instinct guided him towards the doxies who haunted the place; towards one in particular, younger, cleaner and smaller than the rest, with pale skin and a pointed chin. "Wait here, Moppet. I shan't be a moment. I'm fair desperate and I find it's disordering my wits." He pushed to his feet.

"Desperate? You, Master Hal, with that buxom finch in your bed every night?"

"You have no idea," muttered Hal.

"I got one stroke of her maidservant before I was bit by the little cat. The whole while I've been in this benighted city …"

"The girl's deaf, Moppet. You startled her. Approach head-on, next time, and she may keep her teeth to herself."

He wouldn't spare the coin for Moppet's purposes. Ignoring the man's sour face, he strolled over to the women. The girl of his choice turned out to be considerably less fragrant than he'd imagined, but he was committed by then. She led him into a filthy alley and he had her against the wall, beautifully swift, with no endless, wearying preamble or pretence of interest in her pleasure, and he called her *Alice*.

Then he resumed his seat and waited.

Hal's eyes wandered again: over a fair ship, mid-sized, standing out in the river; wandered over other ships, and returned to the beauty that had caught his eye. On her decks he picked out a tall and well dressed fellow: the master. A little boat rowed the man to the wharf. Up and down strode the object of his gaze, directing his men, chatting, hailing others, alert and good-humoured. Hal liked him on sight. Eventually, noting his interest, the man approached and struck up a conversation. He was Richard Carling of Hull, plying mostly to Antwerp, but sometimes Calais, sometimes Bordeaux, sometimes Lisbon.

"You've come looking for work, Master Prynne? A young fellow like you – lofty and strong – you'll be most welcome."

It was another snare, of course, like bed and board and baking in Southwark. Hal shook his head. "Not on this occasion, sir, though I'll give it some thought. Ah, I suppose a gentleman such as yourself would be in a position to exchange foreign gold, if you'd the inclination?"

Master Carling studied his face. "Yes, I could do so, at the proper rate. Would you care to step aboard, Master Prynne, and we'll discuss the matter privately?"

Moppet rested his elbows on his knees and lowered his head into the cradle of his arms. Hal followed Master Carling into a small craft and across to the ship. Among the seamen were two fellows with the most astounding skin, burnished quite black by the sun. Hal craned over his shoulder, tripping on a coil of rope as he wandered after the captain. Everything seemed to be handsomely made, fashioned with more than necessary care. But these were inexpert eyes: he'd never been aboard a ship. At once he fancied himself riding the decks amid the storms and serpents of the high and rolling seas.

"Is she not a beauty? *God's Gift*. Taut and weatherly. A fine seabird. Come within." The master produced a small and marvellously wrought key, inlaid with a pretty and superfluous curlicue. They entered his little cabin, with its low window angled towards the river. Carling seated himself in a low chair at a small oak table and gestured Hal to a stool opposite. Out came the gold, glinting in the dapples of sunlight reflected off the water, and out came the story, somewhat less polished. The captain laughed, though less raucously than Leaping Abel. "Come, Master Prynne. Come now. Your father a merchant at Newcastle and yet when I tell you to look to starboard, your eyes shift about. What does he trade in, your father?"

"Many things. Jet?" suggested Hal, hopelessly. *Fur*. He should have said *fur*. He knew about fur.

"Jet from Whitby? Whitby's a seaport. What's the jet doing at Newcastle? Have you been to Whitby? Have you even been to Newcastle?"

A foolish smile, and it was all over.

"Let's start again. Either you're fresh out of France in the train of Margaret, our would-be queen, or you're a common thief who's robbed such a man. Either way, my price won't be to your liking. I'll take two thirds of your louis, and you can count yourself lucky if your head doesn't end up impaled upon the Bridge."

Head bowed, Hal rewrapped the gold, tying it carefully. "I'm sorry to have troubled you, sir."

Carling shrugged, his eyes roving Hal's face. "Whoever says they'll do better means only to cheat you. Don't touch the Jews, even if you're desperate; they'll sell you out." Hand on the door, Carling had opened his mouth again, when something in Hal's face halted the man. Hal paused also, dropping his eyes.

"My God," breathed Carling. "I know who you are! It was your youth that threw me, but put that aside and you're the very man himself, in the flesh." For a moment the balance swung in thunderous silence, and then Carling made an error. "Well, well. Forget the Jews; I'll sell you out myself. My God. I've waited years for this!"

Hal clicked his tongue, as aggrieved as Moppet. Then he punched Carling with full force in the jaw, and the man went down. At once he feared he'd cracked a knuckle, but he always feared that, and he never had. Cocking an ear, he hastened to the table, breaking open the drawer with his knife. It was stuffed with sheaf upon sheaf of parchment covered in a scratchy script. He dithered about the cabin for a moment until his eyes alighted on a long wooden box tucked behind the curtain that hung across the cot. The box proved to contain just what one would wish it to contain.

Returning to the prone man, he purloined the intriguing key and suspended it by its silver chain about his own neck. Then he secured his adversary with strips of the man's shirt and doublet. It took far longer than expected, but he remained calm. Tucking the box under his arm – beneath the roll of cloth that contained his father's gold – Hal exited the cabin, locking it behind him. He sauntered across the deck, smiling and touching his cap at every seaman he passed. "He's a good fellow, your master," he remarked to those about him, as he sat, coolly awaiting the return of the waterman and his craft.

There was common assent. "That he is."

Reaching the north bank, Hal sprang on to the quay, collected Moppet and vanished into the crowd.

* * *

Sir Lawrence left their party at once upon the news of young Edward Welford's release, brimming with thanks at Sir Simon's tireless efforts on behalf of the family. Loys swallowed the wholly unwarranted praise and banked the gratitude, bidding Sir Lawrence to pass to Richard of Gloucester all news of Jasper Tudor's doings in South Wales.

Cecily Welford was given into Alice's care, to join her gentlewomen, and very happy were both at the prospect. It behoved Sir Simon to provide his wife with a suitable entourage, of course, but Alice welcomed his particular kindness in the choice of companion, and surprised her husband with a kiss, chaste and happy.

She was riding behind him as they passed out of the inn towards Aldersgate in the direction of Essex. "I'm so grateful, sir, for your thoughtfulness. Elyn and Joanna may probably marry in due course, and then I should find myself searching for new companions. I don't know how easy that would prove at Avonby."

"Not easy, unless you're content to be attended by rabbits, who may after all prove less dim-witted that Mistress Elyn. Certainly less interested in mating."

He was awkward at accepting compliments, she saw, taking refuge in sarcasm, so Alice pressed on. "I'm glad of these beautiful new gowns. You've been generous to me, sir. The old ones were sadly worn and stained."

"Indeed. Your appearance on our wedding day was shocking enough, with only slow Sir Hugh and dead Sir Leonard as witnesses. I could not allow myself to be shamed before the sharp eyes of the court."

"And I thank you also for the gift of little Tamlin..."

"Tamlin?"

"The kitten."

"*Christ*, woman. Enough."

She smiled to herself. His left hand had covered hers, clasped in his lap. Her hand slipped free and wandered lightly about the great cushion-shaped ruby, circling with a finger. He shook her off. Alice peered around his shoulder at the carriage. Constance was craning from the rear after the departing backs of a couple of men, but Alice was facing the wrong way, and the men were vanishing around a corner.

"Since I took the White Boar of Gloucester, George of Clarence has cut me twice at court," remarked Loys. "Clearly he regards me as a defector. There is bad blood between those two royal dukes, and it will grow worse, now."

"How so?"

"Gloucester intends to wed the Lady Anne Neville. There will be a storm when Clarence finds out."

* * *

Peter settled quickly and easily among the boys, keen to prove his father wrong; eager to be out training with Oliver, all the hours.

"Are you happy, Oliver, to be among so large a household? You were living meanly when my father came for you, were you not?"

"We'll soon be living more meanly than this, believe me. Hand-to-mouth," said Oliver, as they circled and clashed in the yard, as the blunted axes jarred and rasped. "Yes, they're easy fellows, most of them. You should beware of Aymer, though. There's something wrong with him. Don't be holding the poleaxe so straight. Force yourself to swipe diagonally; in time it'll feel less clumsy."

"I've known Aymer nigh on all my life."

"That's right. Then you know it already. Peter, if the pole is too long for you, ask Rawn to cut it down."

"Robbie, and John the Younger and I; we always avoided him; him and Guy. Guy's as bad. Worse, in his way. He can turn himself ... he does this horrible trick with his face – have you seen it?" A pause, but no kindling of interest, so Peter passed on. "Father seems well content with them though. Not like our Uncle Roger!"

"Careful. So flat as that, and your head is at risk – see? Lord Robert values their soldiery. And he's not that bothered about any of us. You may do as you will, so long as you're brave and strong; that's all he wants."

"But what happened with Hal, Oliver? Hal was the golden boy, the last I knew, when you lot visited Sir Roger a few months back."

Then Peter stumbled heavily from a crack to the neck, and Oliver laid down his weapon to help him up. "I don't mind you talking, Cousin, provided you concentrate. Otherwise you must be silent."

"Your pardon. I was distracted about Hal."

Oliver kicked the shaft between his feet and paused to catch his breath. "Honestly, I don't know. When he left us, they say he robbed my uncle, which I cannot believe, for Hal is a grand fellow. But there was a young girl travelled with us from Malvern to Chepstow – not a girl; a duchess, rather. Lord Robert and Hal were both of them smitten, it's said, and fell out over her. I think trouble was brewing before that, even. And George has some rage against Hal. He won't speak of it. Not to us, anyway. Aymer's pretending to know it all, as usual. Probably he doesn't. Although," Oliver added, thoughtfully, "he has been a good deal less spiteful and difficult since Hal left us, and that is certainly a blessing."

* * *

"My good man, you must learn to curb your sulking; that face would curdle milk. Now, I have business back at the house, but as I love you so well, I give you this coin to go and disport yourself with as many whores as it'll buy. Three, I'd say, unless you're fussy about quality. Then hurry back. We leave London tomorrow."

Dazzled and speechless, Moppet disappeared before his luck could change. Hal headed for home, dispatching a boy to seek out Leaping Abel; setting the pointed, foreign cap upon the messenger's head before he departed. By the time Abel limped up, Hal had completed the shaving, slicing his chin in diverse places, relieving himself of a disguise that had proved dangerously ineffective. "Well, Master Abel, it seems you were right about the rate you offered, and I beg your pardon most humbly. If you're still prepared to trade, I'll trade with you."

"I told you I'd not do it again at that price," scoffed Abel. "My cut was three tenths when you thought yourself so wise. It'll be four tenths now!"

"You're a good fellow, Master Abel. You did offer me three tenths, and I was too green to take so generous a price. But let's agree now on one third, and we'll shake hands on it at once. You'll have had a bargain and I'll have learned a valuable lesson." Hal held out a hand.

Abel paused, then put his hand in Hal's. "Very well, young master. Take heed, for I have been soft with you." He called in his boy and the exchange was made, to the satisfaction of each.

That night, Hal treated the party to jugs of ale. When he carried Mistress Tilney off to bed, she scolded and mocked as sharply as ever, but he'd had a good day and he took it well. Had he known of events unfolding a mile away, he might have tempered his joy. By this time, the report of the assault on Richard Carling – and the identity of his assailant – was making its way up the ranks to the Constable of England, King Edward's brother, Richard of Gloucester.

* * *

With Bede steadfast against Findern in the yard, George took the chance to slip away to their room, dispatching Taffy, the manservant, to find Peter.

"My lad," George's arm was heavy across the boy's wiry shoulders, "if you're in any difficulty, you may turn to me, you know, for I am the master among the FitzCliffords. I am the eldest, you know. I've always been the eldest, even before Hal left."

"That's very good of you, sir."

"Only, I see Aymer about you and I wonder if he's teasing you. He can be like that."

"He's been teaching me a few tricks, sir: how to unbalance a taller opponent; also an easier sword grip."

"I was master-at-arms to the Earl of Northumberland."

"The grip has made a great difference. Already my wrist aches less."

"Oh. Sometimes Aymer does a fellow a good turn, but generally, no."

"I've known Aymer near all my life, sir. It's Guy I really try to avoid."

"Yes, I know what you mean. What a fool. He thinks everyone's looking at him. No one's looking at him."

"He's always boasting he's lain with my mother. I hate to hear it."

"I should say so! Nobody would wish to hear that. In fact, I don't wish to hear it and she's not my mother. Is she pretty?"

The boy looked so downcast that George suspected she wasn't, and hurried on to the reason for his summons. "Now, Peter, what I was meaning to ask: can you read your letters, and write them, also? For real, I mean – not just guessing?"

"I can read and write, sir, yes."

"Excellent. I have need of a scribe for some private business. And you don't have to call me *sir*." He paused. "Actually you can, if you want."

Some while later, the pair had struggled on together, each coming to a lesser view of the other than before they started. "That will do, I think. Recite it back to me."

In spite of Peter's subtle direction, the letter read very ill. "Sir, I'm not sure your cousin will understand it."

"Well, that's where you're wrong, young Peter, for Waryn is a particularly cunning fellow, and will easily tease out my meaning. But I cannot be too open, you see, for if this letter were to fall into the wrong hands, every man-jack in Alnwick would chatter over the evil Hal has done, and that would be demeaning for … a start."

* * *

The missive was the literary equivalent of a wink: signifying *something*, no doubt; not sufficient to dispel the fog of bafflement that descended on Waryn as he sat hunched over the table in his room at Alnwick, cheek resting in his palm. Among the maladroit hints were two certainties: the Wyverns were shortly to quit Skipton for Sir James Thwaite's house of Belforth and there was *something* troubling George.

A rustle behind him and Waryn started up, flipping the letter on its face. It was only the manservant Mayhew, discreet about his duties. Waryn locked the parchment away in a drawer and left the room, deep in thought, shepherding the man before him.

A few moments later his bride entered, seeking her new husband. Anna's sharp eyes found the key lying careless in the lock. She was on it at once. The letter that presented itself was swiftly opened. Then she seated herself and studied carefully, following with a finger. The handwriting was childish and painstaking, more probably that of a woman than a man, the writer making familiar use of Waryn's name, and signing herself only *Your own, G,* which was troubling in itself. Of the contents, nothing could be gleaned, other than an arresting reference to Anna's own brother James, with what might perhaps be construed as a suggestion that Waryn meet the author at Belforth, James's house, in a few days' time. Perplexed and indignant, Anna slipped the letter into the sleeve of her gown and made her way to Lady Eleanor's chamber.

Eleanor was not in the room. There sat the chamberwoman, repairing some of the lady's linen. Anna settled herself in the window seat, ostensibly to supervise the work, in fact to ponder the disconcerting discovery.

Could it be that her young husband had a mistress of whom she knew nothing? Perhaps Waryn was attempting a rapprochement with her brother, Sir James, who'd taken the news of her marriage so nastily. She searched her sleeve to take a second look. The letter was gone.

* * *

"I cannot understand why we're leaving." Not the first time Loic had said it, and still there was no ready answer.

Across Clifford's estates, sour little insurrections were breaking out and so, as steward, Nield made his rounds among the recalcitrant tenants, leading a train of men to labour the point. Bellingham hadn't dismounted at any of these frequent stops, his horse ambling him away; then the marshal would dawdle out of earshot and out of sight, though generally the violence stayed within doors. That way, Nield didn't have to witness his friend's wincing face.

Now they were homeward-bound. Their last call, the local mill. The beef-cheeked miller knocked a few men into the millstream by way of greeting.

"I cannot understand it at all." Loic had pursued Bellingham up the hill.

The commotion followed them both: "Tell Lord Robert from me just how disgusted folks is hereabouts with his broad thievery!" roared the miller. "To pretend to stand in judgment over felons? Not his place to do so. Taking bribes to let ruffians go free? Lord Thomas will be turning in his grave. You know it, Sir Patrick! You, who served the Cliffords so long."

"We were besieged at Chepstow; we saw them off," persisted Loic. "Why can we not hold out in our own home?"

"My dear boy, not a man of us would survive it. York would make sure of that."

"There are worse ways to go."

"Speak for yourself!"

The miller was trussed, bellowing, at his own millwheel and Patrick Nield led off, wiping his hands.

At last the quarter day arrived; the day of departure. The rents, bribes and backhanders so ruthlessly harvested from manors and tenants were secured on the pack animals as the Wyverns made ready to leave.

Clifford summoned his men to the hall. The boys assembled promptly, in good order, for the next episode in the adventure; the only FitzClifford with more considered ambitions had already departed. Behind the boys, the junior men. Clifford cast around for his intimates. Arthur Castor and Walter Findern, side by side, as ever; Bellingham, his creased eyes rather pink; Loic and Reginald Grey, whispering together. Patrick Nield was nowhere to be seen.

"Gentlemen!" Clifford's great, deep voice filled the cavernous space with ease. "Those many of you who served loyally for years will know this as the third time we've left our home without certainty of seeing its walls again. Ten years ago our king was dethroned by Edward of York; we lost the kingdom; in '64 we were back, before misfortune overtook us. And now we must leave Skipton once more. But I promise you this: we will return. Ah, we lost many a dear companion and tasted defeat many times, but our spirits are undimmed; our sword arms as strong as ever they were. As Sir Reginald has warned, God tests those he loves again and again before the ultimate reward is bestowed. It will come, if we keep faith. The house of Lancaster will rise once more, in the figure of our young king, Henry Tudor."

No! Not Henry Tudor. Reginald Grey was swinging his head in brazen dissent. *Not Tudor. The true heir of Lancaster: Alice's child.*

Clifford looked away and strove to continue. He'd lost his rhythm. "And we shall be there at his shoulder. At Henry Tudor's shoulder. And... I mean to give that whoreson of York the roughest of rides. Come, my brave Wyverns: onwards to Scotland!"

Grey was still mouthing at him. But from the younger men, a storm of roaring and stamping.

As the cavalcade passed out beneath the massive barbican, Clifford's fingers trailed the smooth masonry. He raised his head. He did not turn. With one accord, the men followed his lead, resolved to face only onward; to take no leave of the fortress, their grim, beloved home. All save George, who hung in the saddle and gazed, mournful, craning round, jostling at Oliver and Bede until the castle passed from view.

The day was warm and low with cloud and all was quiet as the party left the purple moors and descended, by the gorge of Knaresborough, into the Vale of York. Nield, Castor and Findern had forged ahead with a small band to the village of Thirsk, arranging the billet for the night, commandeering chambers in the better houses, grudging with the recompense if not with the threats. After a dejected day in the saddle, the men were ready for their beds, mean and lumpy as they might probably be.

It was one of those disconcerting moments in which George was abruptly promoted, this time to the flattering distinction of sharing Lord Clifford's borrowed bed. Loic lurched crossly down the centre of the mattress, wedging himself between George and his master. Adding insult to insult, the youth slept at once, snoring into his face, wallowing, elbowing and spreading about. The Frenchman vented his irritation, pinching the unconscious George with exasperated spite. And then, of course, there was no remedy but to turn his back on the interloper, yielding his body to the slumbering curves of Monseigneur's muscled back and heavy thighs.

In the throes of such intimacy, sleep was elusive. Songbirds struck up, and his eyes were still open as the rosy rays of dawn broke over the village. Then a different sound obtruded itself: a drumming of quiet feet, a scurrying, muffled alarum. Loic extricated his hands and shuffled rapidly down the coarse mattress, crushing George's feet, darting to the little window, cracking open the shutters. Armed men were dispersing themselves amongst the houses, weapons at the ready.

"Monseigneur! Monseigneur! Master George!"

The Wyverns were swiftly roused and up, bracing doors, harnessing each other with sweating efficiency, Clifford bellowing a warning from the window before a flurry of arrows chased him inside. He took up his mace, weighing it in his hand, dropping to one impatient knee as Loic set the helmet on his head, stately as a coronation. Standing by, George was frowning at his uncle, who seemed different in some indefinable way.

"Monseigneur!" Loic snatched up the eyepatch from the bedpost, but Clifford was gone, thundering down the rickety staircase, giving many of his boys their first impromptu glimpse of the naked socket.

Weapons aloft, clusters of Clifford's men sprang from their several quarters almost upon the instant, and at once began the savage brawl across backyard and vegetable patch, smashing through fences and panicking animals, steering the struggle towards the inn where many of their fellows had bedded down; where the mounts were stabled. The Wyverns had trained together, fought together, lived together so long that they would muster deftly, apparently by instinct, waiting neither on plan nor command. As if to demonstrate, a knot of the boys darted past in the direction of the stables. For a moment, Clifford caught his breath and watched them go: Bede, Peter, Richie, with the twins bringing up the rear: petty squabbles forgotten, a united band.

The exception that proved the rule, Robbie appeared alone in a doorway, yawning, shivering, clad only in shirt and hose, unshod, unharnessed, unfocused in the midst of the running battle.

"Arm yourself!" roared Clifford, jolted back to the danger. Dazed, inert and soft, the lad was a conspicuous target. Then one man found the target with a backhand slash and Robbie sank to his knees, frowning.

Clifford slammed in, one moment too late, pulping the assailant's head like a baked apple. Bent double, he rammed a steel shoulder into the boy's crumpling form and hoisted. Then he was staggering under Robbie's weight, wandering somewhat, and tripped over a man who seemed to be backing into him deliberately.

"What in Christ's name are you doing, George? George!"

"He's coming apart! For God's sake, Father, he's trailing behind you!"

The Wyverns were now hammering the foe and a dozen bodies littered the side streets, the enemy collapsing in disarray despite their greater numbers.

"Get to the horses," Clifford grunted, through his teeth.

The lad was vast and slack, body tilting as wildly as a waterlogged boat in a heavy swell. Then George hefted Robbie's legs onto his shoulders while Clifford manhandled the torso, and that was better. When they reached the stables, Clifford swung up and the other men wrestled to lift Robbie before him in the saddle. It simply couldn't be done, armfuls of jellied bowel slipping off in all directions like hatching serpents and, by then, the entrails were so mired underfoot that the battle was well and truly lost.

With one accord, they gave up the struggle and laid the youth gently on his back in the churned yard. Someone caught up the absconding guts and strewed them on him, softly, like flowers. Someone shrouded him with a cloak.

"You there!" shouted Clifford to a well dressed fellow craning from the gallery above. The man vanished. He tried again, and an elderly woman approached, sideways, blenching at the stink. "See this boy decently buried, of your charity, mistress."

Walter Grey pressed a coin into her hand. The woman eyed Robbie's twitching feet, and everyone busied themselves. Clifford wheeled impatiently while the baggage was retrieved, while others mounted, then he led them off at speed.

Charging away at the head of his men, he was surprised to feel little more than a sombre relief, and swiftly concluded that the twins had the right of it: the boy was not, after all, his get, but Roger's. And – a further poignancy – he now recalled that in the confusion, George had called him *Father*.

* * *

Before sunrise, Hal was up and at the baking. When he'd finished his duties, he bundled together his belongings, fingering Richard Carling's key that lay against the sapphire ring concealed at his breast, another token in his small and interesting collection. Swiftly and surreptitiously he counted his staggering wealth. Then he took affectionate leave of Richenda Tilney and her sons, and set out.

By then, Gloucester and the sheriffs had heard the report.

Hal and Moppet called at the local inn to retrieve the horses and, since they'd a long ride ahead, Hal treated them both to good meal.

Meanwhile, the sergeant led his men southward towards the Bridge, bearing a warrant for the arrest of Henry, natural son of Robert Clifford.

On a whim, Hal hired the boy who minded their horses, thinking to arrive at his destination in greater style. Then he bethought himself that he owned no gloves, and turned in to a shop below the Bridge, spending some time in choosing a handsome pair.

While he was within, the sergeant's party passed the shop, scattering bystanders in the street outside.

Hal and his attendants were, as yet, within a hundred yards of Richenda's house. As they crossed the Bridge into the city, Hal eyed the shrunken and blackened heads clustered on poles: Warwick's riotous Kentishmen, who were plundering Southwark at the very moment that Hal and his father were missing the battle of Tewkesbury. Hal was, indeed, conscious that he'd pushed his luck to the limit; glad that he would be clear of London by evening.

There came a hammering on Mistress Tilney's door – which had stuck again – and only with difficulty did she open up to the sergeant and his constables. Ale flowed as the men questioned the household. Mistress Tilney was intrigued at their news. Robert Clifford? Of course she knew of the man. His sons? She'd heard he had a dozen. Henry, son of Clifford, who went by the name *FitzClifford*? She knew nothing of him, but if Henry FitzClifford and Hal Prynne were the same man, you could knock her down with a feather.

Alas, said she, Master Prynne had left the house a few hours since; probably well beyond the walls by now. He must have quit the city by one of the north western gates, avoiding the main roads, for he was heading for the

North Country to join his father – apparently still making merry in his ancestral home; besieged, it was said, by no man. Robert Clifford was a notorious scoundrel. Why was no one pursuing *him*?

The sergeant shrugged. Robert Clifford was none of his concern.

By this time, Hal was possessed of a pair of fine gloves: kid trimmed with winter beaver. Naturally, the merchant tried to con him, but Grandfather Prynne was a trapper; Hal had spent his infant years cocooned in cheap pelts and could spot one when he saw one. How he wished his grandfather were there to see the array: a man who'd never entered a furrier's shop; a man who'd never ventured so far as Newcastle. Now Hal felt the lack of other ornament, and detoured into Cheapside, wandering among the jeweller's workshops, eventually selecting a heavy chain with which to adorn his doublet. Here, he was well out of his depth, and made a bad bargain.

By now the sergeant and his men were out and searching, pursuing various trails, the usual mishmash of eager recollection and mischievous suggestion. One fellow swore that Master Prynne had passed him not one hour before upon the Bridge, but when the men doubled back, the unlikely trace was cold.

Skirting his pursuers, several times over, by a hair's breadth, Hal by this time was south of the Bridge once more: he'd recalled with a pang that among his belongings one significant item was missing, forsaken amid Mistress Tilney's sheets: the bloodstained handkerchief purloined before the gates of Goodrich, his only relic of Alice.

* * *

The Wyverns pressed swiftly northward, skirting the steep ridge that rose to the uplands of the North York Moors. Somewhere high above them lay Loys's fortress of Avonby, but Clifford knew nothing of it, his mind pounding not on his lost love but on the identity of the assailants. He cursed aloud, startling Cuthbert Bellingham. "Threlkeld. Lancelot Threlkeld! I thought it would be Richard of Gloucester. As did we all."

"As did we all," agreed Bellingham, though Clifford was arguing with himself.

"That shifty turd, Stanley. Or Parr, FitzHugh's arsehole of a son-in-law. He has men sufficient for a siege. Ah, by now I thought we'd got away with it."

"I did think of Sir Lancelot's brother, Gawain, but we had nothing to fear there," interrupted Bellingham.

Clifford's voice turned black. "Gawain Threlkeld raids Wharfedale at his pleasure. The Priory will have lost all its flock by now."

"But it's not so! I hear that since we fired his house, Gawain Threlkeld cannot hold his men; the bulk of his household has shunned him. You know how fellows flee from ill luck, Lord Robert." And then Sir Cuthbert was rocked by a most clumsy confusion and, glancing sideways, noticed Castor peeping through his fingers in mock horror.

Clifford ploughed through the awkward hush. "I wasn't thinking of either of them. For once. For years it's been nothing but Lancelot Threlkeld, with me, and now this!"

"Lancelot Threlkeld, Monseigneur? The knight who wed your brother John's widow, is it not?"

"That's not all he did with her!"

"No. I know that, Monseigneur. I know all about the child…" He tailed off.

Bellingham shook his head. Lord Robert mustn't blame himself; not when they'd all overlooked an older foe. Sir Lancelot Threlkeld, swooping in from his wife's lands of Londesborough; his wife Margaret, widow of Lord Robert's beloved elder brother, she who'd beslimed the Clifford name with a bastard whelp, a little golden-haired cuckoo. The cuckoo had flown, and Threlkeld would not pass up the chance to kill Robert Clifford. Despite Cuthbert Bellingham's assurance, nothing was, in truth, more predictable.

Then Bellingham mused on to a detail no one else had noticed: the presence among the assailants of their old friend, Sir Hugh Dacre. Wending his way through Thirsk's narrow lanes, weapon poised, Bellingham had chanced upon the man squatting behind a barrel. Dacre had recoiled with a start, careering backwards into a wall, brandishing his mace at arm's length, as if it were a cudgel; *as if I were a feral dog*, thought the marshal. Bellingham had done no more than frown into his friend's face – staying his arm – when Sir Hugh broke the impasse by sprinting off with a surprising turn of speed. More charitable not to mention it, and Bellingham spent the next while pondering the badge upon the man's surcoat: a bee, the motif unfamiliar and ominous.

Some time later, the party reined in under a clump of trees to rest the horses. Gingerly, Clifford swung down and lowered himself to his back. He'd wrenched his left knee manhandling the boy. If more fighting were needful, he'd be limping and slow. More troubling was the failure to maintain his focus: loitering in Thirsk's highroad, thinking on Aymer and his other lads, on the absent Hal, while Robbie was cut down only feet away. As his men crowded in, he interrupted the expressions of sympathy. "It was waiting for him, and well you know it. He was hopeless; beyond help, poor child." He frowned up at Bellingham and Nield. "And very heavy. Which made me wonder: how was it that you carried me away, when I was brought down by the arrow at Ferrybridge?"

The two men breathed at each other, ten years gone in a twink, the awful day opening before them. "We tried it the same way, Lord Robert, and we couldn't lift you either. We hauled you over the horse on your belly. But the arrow was catching against its legs, so we pulled you down and Sir Roger cut the shaft, and we heaved you back up."

"Wasting time, Bell. You should have pulled out the arrow when I was on the horse. The eye couldn't be saved."

Nield shrugged. "Well, we weren't so sure at the time. A headless arrow, and the shaft gone in so neat with your eye open. We didn't want to cause more damage, Lord Robert, or make a mess."

"I thank you for your efforts to preserve my beauty. I'm not sure it was worth risking everyone's life over, but I do thank you. Whose horse was it? Not mine. I slit the poor beast's throat a while earlier."

"That's right," recalled Nield. "Yours was maddened by arrows. It was Miles Randall's horse, Lord Robert. Miles shared mine."

As ever, Randall's name triggered a general forlorn murmuring. On Loic's face, an expression at once bored and mutinous. He twitched aside, busying himself at a saddle bag. Bellingham's arms were folded as he stared away, stiff-jawed, across the hills. Drawing out a new patch of black leather, Loic waved it rudely in Clifford's face. Hal's inquisitive eyes would have been busy.

"Who is Miles Randall, gentlemen?" queried Aymer.

Much of the household turned his way. "Lord Robert's chamberlain," said they, with one voice.

* * *

"Waryn was always a sly one. Now he's plotting with a traitor and he shall suffer for it, unless he throws himself on my mercy. It's a fortunate thing Harry is away; he's too timid for this work. Kit, my imp, run and fetch Master Waryn to me."

Eleanor folded George's letter to a fat square and dropped it into a coffer. Marjorie watched, hands clasped. There was a suppressed savagery about her mistress, a whiff of vindictive thrill. The lady strode to the window, gazing northwards, tossing her hair over one shoulder and then the other until the under-steward presented himself.

Waryn cleared his throat. "What do you require of me, my lady? Do you have questions on the accounts?"

"Not the accounts. I'm sure the accounts are in painstaking order; they always are. No, Master Waryn. You have an accusation to answer." This was a very tall youth, of course, but the woman herself seemed suddenly to have grown; even to loom over him as he waited, ill at ease. "Treason, Master Waryn! I accuse you of treason! A man who has covert dealings with a traitor is a traitor himself. You obtained news of Robert Clifford's movements and instead of divulging it to your betters, you concealed the information. I could, and should, clap you in irons for this."

His mind was reeling. "Then I imagine you've somehow found the letter from my cousin George. If you can decipher it, my lady, your wits are quicker than mine. As usual, I cannot make head nor tail of what he says."

"Your cousin is certainly an imbecile, but it's perfectly clear that Clifford is leading his men to Belforth. Why would you not declare it at once? You are shielding them, of course!"

"I received that letter only yesterday, and I've been puzzling over it ever since. The Earl would not condemn a man on so flimsy a hint, Madam. If it please you, we'll defer this matter until his return."

"If it please me? It would please you, for sure! By the time my brother reaches Alnwick, your father will be taking his ease in Edinburgh, and well you know it. I am chatelaine, and my word is law. Unless I have more from you than this, the Earl will return to find you tallying your accounts in a cell."

He brushed aside the idle threat, all his thoughts for his kin; headlong into danger. "Madam, forgive me, for I mean no impertinence, but the Earl would wish you to take no rash step in this matter. I know it."

By now he should be on his knees. "Master Waryn," said she, very slow, as if she were addressing an imbecile – her mind was still on George – "*Clifford is coming.* My brother is hundreds of miles away and knows nothing of it. In his absence, I am lord of the North. It is my duty to capture the rebel and deliver him up to King Edward, and that is what I shall do. What *we* shall do. The Earl may overlook your doubtful loyalties; he will not forgive you if fail to protect his sister. Now you understand how to redeem yourself."

* * *

Hal dismounted at the corner of Mistress Tilney's lane, leaving the horses in the care of Barnaby, his new boy. He was now striding rather briskly for, in his mind's eye, the woman was already feeding the handkerchief to the flames or washing it clear of its faint but bewitching scent.

As he approached the house, a familiar scene was playing out. Richenda leaned against the door, panting. Hal grinned. Then his view of the woman was obscured by a gaggle of passers-by and, as he drew level, one among them paused to offer help. The door was charged inwards. The new champion was a very tall man, florid and stout, with a shock of yellow hair. He righted himself and turned back to the street, smiling. It was Bertrand Jansen.

There was an explosion of indignation. What was the fellow doing there, his puffy mitt upon Richenda? And now her hand was upon him, and they had disappeared within. Disgusted, Hal passed on, circled back and mounted his horse; Bertrand's horse. The woman was nothing to him. He'd no desire ever to cross her path again. Jansen himself was a large and conspicuous fellow, sure to run into his own perils, as Hal informed Moppet.

The Dane bore no awkward resemblance to a widely reviled traitor, was the gist of Moppet's discourteous reply. Eyes were now following them everywhere; had Master Hal not noticed? Enough of this – this browsing for geegaws and chasing after dirty napkins.

By now, their small band was north of the Bridge again – entirely unhindered, despite the attention they were attracting – and heading for Aldersgate, the easternmost passage out of the city. They passed the boundary without question, the sergeant's men supposing this particular felon to be long gone, in a contrary direction.

That evening the little party rested deep into Essex, taking the last room at a bustling inn; a room vacated only that morning by Brini, Chowne and John Twelvetrees, but the new occupants never knew of it. Hal's final stroke of luck on this fortunate day fell out when Moppet attended his master to the privy. Rolled in the rear of Hal's waistband he found Alice's handkerchief. Jubilant, Hal pressed it to his face, breathing the girl's delicious perfume. When the master had gone down alone to dine, Moppet and Barnaby took turns in sniffing the rag, no longer a bold white and scarlet but a grubby greyish-brown. Nothing was discernable beyond a stale and wholly masculine odour of sweat.

* * *

Two days later, the cavalcade had been feasted and fêted and soothed and rested at the old Clifford port of Hartlepool. No deed was too wicked to ascribe to the natives of Thirsk and Londesborough; Hartlepool bristled with outrage.

Back to discomfort the next night, when the party bedded down at little Blythe within the sound of the sea and the rampant clench of herring stink, and Clifford fancied it was clinging still and wafting behind as they rode on toward the Scots border. Harry Percy was known to be licking York's arse in faraway London. Nevertheless the party skirted Alnwick widely and passed north without challenge.

Just as they moved beyond the castle, the manservant Mayhew was returning to its precincts. Waryn's answer to George's letter – an emphatic, frantic warning – lay undelivered in Mayhew's saddlebag. For the serving man had reached Skipton three hours too late, to find the quarry gone and the fortress deserted. Disconsolate, Mayhew had meandered his way back to Alnwick, missing the Wyverns on several occasions by the slimmest of margins.

Among the boys, George's sporadic preferment was prickling his rival like nettles. The eldest FitzClifford looked around to find he'd acquired a shadow. "You're very glum, George," drawled Aymer in his ear, "and I think I may guess the reason. You were wishing to see my brother Waryn up at Alnwick, were you not? Speak to my father," he urged. "He may permit you a detour, perhaps."

Aymer hadn't long to wait. The reprimand could be heard from halfway back and must have deafened those at the head. By the time George reappeared, scarlet and panting, Clifford found himself joined by Aymer. Over Loic, the clouds piled up. Riding through the silence, Clifford was revolving George's latest idiocy in his mind, reaching, at last, the inevitable conclusion. Sighing, he called for Castor, and the man diverted them awhile with his fund of rascally local gossip.

After a time, Aymer ventured gently upon a fresh subject. "Father, the lads have taken Robbie's death very hard. So last night I called them together and spoke to them." If only Lord Robert had noticed.

Clifford grunted. "Then I trust they drew the proper lesson."

"The paramount importance of training? I mean always to set an excellent example in that regard. '*This is no game*,' said I, '*and loss is part of life. Never let it be you.*'"

Loic snorted. "What would you know of loss, Master Aymer?"

"The boy lost his mother." A gruff defence, but a defence nonetheless.

Aymer had, indeed, lost his mother; lost her face, her voice, lost even her name. Much of his early life was shrouded from him, the first ten years distilled into that hellish journey, when, alone and penniless, the girl had led her small sons north from the soft verdancy of Kenilworth to Roger Clifford's moorland home. No more than a hundred and fifty miles, but the trudge took weeks through cruel weather. Sleeping in barns where they could, and stealing food where they could. Once, he and Guy had trapped a rabbit. When they couldn't set a fire, the pair refused to give it up, but tore into the flesh, raw and slimy. So they lost a day, coiled, griped and shivering on the sodden ground. All the while the cough racked their mother's wasting frame until the fever took hold and she burned up.

"What was my mam's name, Father? Do you recall?"

"How the devil should I know? There were a lot of girls in those years."

Aymer cast the memory adrift. "Ah, I suppose someone should inform Sir Roger of Robbie's death. You're occupied with more weighty matters, Father. I'll take that task, shall I? You – or Sir Loic, of course – may wish to look over the letter to ensure I haven't said something I oughtn't."

Clifford gazed at Aymer with some interest. "Well said, my son. Certainly you may take that chore from me."

The early wariness between Loic and Hal was as nothing to this. "It's your mother who wrings my heart, Monseigneur! Elderly, abandoned and beset with misfortune. Of course, I shall write to Lady Clifford myself and break the tragic news, since I don't imagine you'll find the time."

Clifford clicked his tongue at the malapert chamberlain.

"And speaking of *never* finding the time," continued Loic, "you'll be relieved to hear I've already written to Madame Babette Delaurin in Flanders, telling her not to expect further gold, for none will be forthcoming. I suppose she must find herself a new protector now, Monseigneur, or your favourite son will run short of food. But then, she's a good-looking woman; there'll be no shortage of offers."

Clifford turned the reins smartly and rode back to join Bellingham, leaving Aymer and Loic to single combat.

"Are you sure we can't press on to Lindisfarne, Lord Robert? It's not so much further and my son Maurice would give us a warm welcome."

"No, Bell. Too far tonight. We'll be safe enough at Belforth; James has no notice of our coming and, in any case, I shan't be caught napping a second time. We must be close by; we're just about in the Cheviots. Isn't that it now? There, on that scar of land, with the village below."

The square and buttressed tower was ancient and very dark, having a grim appearance beneath the grey and lowering skies, like a man in war-torn harness. And its owner belonged to the stone; spare and unsmiling even as he grasped his old companion to him. "Robert! Why didn't you warn me of your coming? My God, but it's been a long time! Seven years, at least, since you took refuge at Belforth on your last adventure. You know I've lost my father since then? It's to my own home that I welcome you."

"We're all poorer for the loss, James. Your father was a brave man, sheltering me at no small risk to himself back in '64."

James Thwaite looked beyond his boyhood friend. "My God! Are these your sons, then?"

"Most of them. George, the eldest: he is John's boy, born at Alnwick. Do you recall Elizabeth, the daughter of Master Richard, Percy's huntsman? She was his mother."

"Elizabeth Almond? How could I not? We all wanted her, but John must have her, of course."

"These two are my eldest." He hung an arm about the shoulder of each twin. "Oliver, there, is also John's. The rest are mine." He might have mentioned Robbie, but he let the boy's shade depart.

"Well," Thwaite rubbed his mouth. "It's a large retinue you have, for a man on the run. You gave me no warning, and there's little room for guests; Belforth's an old-fashioned fortress, not like your soft southern castles. The three eldest may share a small chamber and we've room for a manservant and two of your men to attend on you. There's the inn for the others and those left over must billet in the village."

"A moment, James, while I see to my men." Clifford turned, his hand on Nield's arm.

"Leave it to me, Lord Robert. I assume Masters George, Guy and Aymer will sleep up there with you?"

George was already attempting to express dissatisfaction with the arrangements.

"They will. Ah, take Loic away with you, Patrick." *Before I box his ears.* "And send Castor and Findern to attend on me tonight."

Castor and Findern? These two were the tallest, the best sword arms in the household – now they'd lost Jansen. Beneath Thwaite's sharp eyes, Nield gazed silently into his master's face. Clifford trusted Nield would also enlighten the chamberlain, or tomorrow he'd suffer a fresh wave of Loic's intolerable sulking.

An hour later, Clifford was drinking in Thwaite's day room, as dark and inhospitable as the rest of the house. Drinking steadily; he'd rather his friend were a little incapacitated. All the while, as he pondered on their welcome, there was an ominous tingling at his nape. Thwaite had made a competent effort at surprise, but Clifford wasn't convinced.

"So, Robert, Percy double-crossed you, eh?"

"No! He said he'd sit tight when York invaded. He kept his word."

"You'd been promised his sister, had you not?" Thwaite leaned back, hands behind his head. "What a fine young woman little Eleanor has grown into, eh? I wrote to Percy offering myself, but your star was in the ascendant then. I might try again now."

Clifford snorted with laughter. "Northumberland will not give his sister to you, James. Don't set yourself up for a fall."

"He could do worse! The Thwaites of Belforth have the Conqueror's blood in their veins, even as you do, Robert; even as Percy does. A man must have ambition. Let's not quibble."

"Indeed. It's hardly worth it. I wish you luck, for I've an idea the lady has her own views on the subject."

"You think she's pining for you?" It was Thwaite's turn to laugh.

101

In present circumstances, gratitude should be uppermost in Clifford's mind, but in truth he'd never much warmed to James Thwaite. This one had always a resentful temper; no merry company, even as a lad when they squired together at Alnwick. Hard and slim, with hollow eyes the colour of piss in snow. Clifford felt he was conversing with the skull beneath the skin. Malice bubbled up. "And you and I are now related by marriage, James! Your sister has wed one of my bastard boys, so I hear … and just how is that supposed to enhance your standing in the Earl's eyes?" He sat back, gleeful.

The man made some wretched attempt at nonchalance. "Of course I'd nothing to do with that. Anna's a widow. She did her duty the first time; now she has taken her pick. Your Waryn is younger than she, and a rising man in Percy's household. You know how it is."

"No, I can't say I do, James, my own sisters being somewhat less …" *mortifying* "… headstrong. Still – no doubt Eleanor permits your sister to wait on her?"

Dinner was served, a dismal affair, the two of them still alone in the day room; Walter Findern, Arthur and the boys to dine in the hall with Thwaite's taciturn sons and his household.

"Ah, I must speak with my boys before they go to eat. They don't agree well together."

"Of course. I'll have them summoned." Though Thwaite gave him no privacy when they came.

Trying to convey a covert message to George was a futile undertaking. The lad was openly moping at the separation from his fellows – no doubt enjoying a jolly time at the inn – while he'd spent the afternoon arm-wrestling Thwaite's bastard sons or slumped, sullen, beside his cousins. Between themselves, the twins would tend to converse in garbled half-phrases and significant looks. George couldn't follow, and wouldn't give the satisfaction of asking.

Clifford looked them over. George could never take Hal's place. That much was now clear. Aymer, though: he was a good deal quicker on the uptake, and the lightest of gestures towards Clifford's knife was sufficient to alert him. The pale eyes studied Clifford, unsmiling. Guy was regarding his father also, features impassive. Aymer bowed and led the others back to the echoing hall.

James Thwaite grunted at the retreating backs. "Where d'you get those two pretty boys?"

Clifford shook his head, mouth full. "My brother's house. Roger told me their mother turned up at his door in the last stage of consumption, naming me as the father. They're from Warwickshire – that's all I know."

"You've very trusting," sneered Thwaite.

"What? Clearly they're mine! I know I was at Kenilworth with my father in the Christmas of '50, which would be the right time. And the twins are excellent soldiers. And, of course, they have my look."

"Eh? *You wish.*"

The meal continued in silence. When the commotion finally began, it was something of a relief.

* * *

One day more, and the small party came to Crawshay Hall. They were preceded by a letter, and the response was favourable, but there was a persistent catch in Hal's throat as they descended the gentle valley to the edge of the walled park. There was the house, and it was simply beautiful, looped by the placid river that fed a slender moat; bowed windows and turrets reflected in waters strewn with faded petals. Hal approached the gatehouse, his easy demeanour belying the inner feelings.

He was admitted with prompt courtesy, nerves somewhat soothed by the servant's deference. A page had run on to the house, and Hal was escorted by the elderly steward through the hall to a panelled parlour beyond, and there he found the whole family assembled.

Before him, at last, stood his father's youngest brother: the traitor, the turncoat, the detested, contemptible Triston Clifford. The man stepped forward with an engaging smile. He did not greatly resemble Robert: tall –

not tall for a Clifford – well formed and slender, with a long, dark face and bright eyes. "Henry! You are welcome! Most welcome at Crawshay. I'm truly glad you are come to us."

"Sir Triston, I thank you from the bottom of my heart for your greeting and your generosity. Please call me *Hal*, sir. None but my mother ever called me *Henry*."

The knight smiled at him; in fact, he had not ceased to smile all the while. Triston turned to his wife. Lady Honor was as dark, and almost as tall as her husband, pretty, merry and vapid. Up stepped his sons – or rather, up stepped Stephen, the elder, a few years Hal's junior. He was lighter-toned, resembling Bede, not only in colouring but in a certain sweetness of expression. The boy embraced Hal with a frank and pleasing openness. The younger one, who was darker and very like his father, looked up from his chair, a ready grin upon his face.

"Gregory cannot not rise to greet you," remarked Triston and, after an awkward pause in which Hal tried not to stare at his cousin's warped ankles, he stooped to clasp the boy about the shoulders.

Behind the boys was a bevy of daughters; he counted six in all. Beatrice was perhaps sixteen years of age, also tall and dark, also pretty, very like her mother in looks, though her eyes glittered with wit. The younger girls were all copies, of varying heights and ages, boasting among them some most peculiar names: Idonia; Radegund. He muddled them at once.

* * *

A second ambush, but this time he was ready. Clifford seized his knife and sprang to his feet in one swift movement, the formidable impression marred somewhat when his left knee gave way beneath him, causing him to stagger against the table, elbow in his dinner.

Thwaite didn't rise. "Skittish."

Wiping irritably at his sleeve, Clifford limped from the room and down the few steps to the hall, where the uproar was intensifying. Sir James strolled after.

George was standing off to the side, mouth gaping like a trout, silvery and moist, right wrist clasped gingerly against his chest. Two of Thwaite's sons had pounded faces. Guy, his cheek slit from brow to chin, was pinned in Findern's sympathetic arms, roaring. In Castor's hands, a cluster of confiscated blades.

As his heart steadied, Clifford sheathed his own knife and turned to the bloodied youth. "What is going on here, my son?"

Shouting broke out again. Clifford cuffed Guy smartly on the back of the head, spattering crimson droplets across his gravy-stained doublet. He cast around for some sense.

Aymer's voice was so soft it stilled the room. "This brave boy," a lazy finger signalling one of the unrecognisable Thwaites, "who could not fairly defeat us at the wrestling, has broken my cousin's wrist against the table."

Clifford turned to his host, arms folded, head back. "Not greatly hospitable, James. No doubt they'll be beaten soundly for this lapse in manners."

"Your pardon," answered Thwaite coolly. "None of them should have been fighting at the board." He motioned his three lads away.

Clifford eyed his nephew, shoulders sagging. George being young and fit, the wrist should heal well, but it would be long before he were truly comfortable in his swordplay. Jansen, Hal and now George: three of his finest lost to him. At least Robbie, the millstone, was gone.

* * *

In his uncle's airy and pleasant day room, Hal stood, hands clasped behind his back.

"You may sit, Hal. You had better sit, I think."

Hal sat down, and lost the lush view.

"We must establish whether you have need of a pardon. So, the engagement at Barnet, this last spring: my brother led the left wing for Warwick, did he not? The usual guileless charge, as I recall. Oh yes – I was there," he added, at Hal's look of surprise. "On the other side, naturally! And you fought under Robert? Against King Edward?" But the accustomed smile did not waiver.

"I'm afraid I did, sir. As did we all – sons and nephews."

"All of you, eh? And what of the battle at Tewkesbury? Or had you left Robert by then?"

Hal shook his head. "We arrived too late for the engagement at Tewkesbury."

"Truly? How humiliating for all concerned!" Triston pursed his lips and wrinkled his nose. It was clear he knew of the mishap.

"My father had quarrelled with the Duke of Somerset. I don't think he was hurrying."

"Don't call him *Duke of Somerset*! That man was plain *Sir Edmund Beaufort*, and you'd do well to remember it. So, tell me if I have it right: before all this, you held the position of under-steward to the Earl of Northumberland, an honour indeed for so young a man and a baseborn son of an attainted traitor. And yet you were enticed to leave this worthy position to join a notorious malefactor and criminal?"

Hal rose above the insults to his father. He had himself well in hand, for he suspected there was more where this came from.

"Hardly a wise choice," Triston continued, "but then, you do not know the man as I know him. So, led astray by my brother, you took up arms against King Edward. Then, repenting the course your life had taken, you resolved to leave Robert, penniless and friendless though you were, and seek the King's peace. Yes, that will do, I think. Shortly I'll go to court and seek a pardon, Hal. The King is not a vengeful man. He has not held my connection with Robert against me; I trust it will be the same for you."

"Words cannot express my thanks, Uncle, for your goodness to me."

"Truth be told, I'm astonished to hear you've been living in London for weeks, a wanted man. You might have been apprehended at any moment!"

Possibly, thought Hal. *Possibly*. But his father lingered, unmolested, in Skipton; if Edward of York couldn't be bothered with Black Clifford, he was unlikely to trouble himself over Hal. He envisioned York as a younger, larger, stupider version of Cuthbert Bellingham; a thoroughgoing soldier, bluff and jovial.

Triston folded his hands. "Now, listen well: Crawshay is a quiet house, Hal, and I intend it to remain that way. My wife and daughters are virtuous women; my sons are decent and respectful; the household is well-ordered and peaceable. No doubt you'll find our ways strange after Robert's style of life, but you must conform yourself if you wish to remain among us. Cruelty and depravity have no place here."

The good intentions faltered somewhat. "I won't try to defend my father to you, sir, for you know him well. For sure he's a rough man, and a bawdy one. But his bravery and devotion to his cause are legend, though they have brought him to ruin." His eyes had slunk to his lap, for he may very well have gone too far. When at last he looked up, the smile had turned pitying. His uncle shook his head.

"Oh no, Hal. No, no. Greed and wilfulness, not courage and loyalty; I trust you understand the difference. But now, indulge my curiosity, for there's something I don't understand. All his life, my brother has, as you say, shown singular devotion to his cause. Henry of Lancaster made an abysmal king, as everyone knows; weak and feeble-minded, with a termagant for a wife. His son and heir, Edward of Lancaster, was the best hope of their house. But the boy fell at Tewkesbury and, with him, Sir Edmund Beaufort, the next heir. And now Henry of Lancaster himself has died. Of displeasure, so they say. There is, to all intents and purposes, no heir of Lancaster. So: who is Robert to follow now? What is his purpose?"

Hal clasped his hands in his lap and frowned. Slowly he answered. "The Duke of Somerset's wife is carrying her husband's child, the heir of Lancaster. It is this unborn infant that my father was guarding when he carried off the lady from Little Malvern Priory."

"Don't call him *Duke of Somerset*. Beaufort's wife? Are you sure that was Robert's purpose?"

"Entirely sure. Father intended to bear her to safety – out of the reach of Edward of York. He made sure not to lay a finger on Lady Alice."

"Don't call him *Edward of York*! He is your king! So Robert didn't soil her? Well, she must be the first young woman one could say that of. What's wrong with the lady?"

"Ah, there is nothing wrong with Lady Alice, sir. "

"Nothing wrong with her judgment, at least, for they say she has escaped his clutches. So the child is lost to him. What now?"

"Now he hails Henry Tudor as his king, Uncle."

"Little Henry Tudor?" Triston's brows had shot up, and he laughed with true incredulity. "Scraping the barrel there! Tudor's royal blood – dilute as it is – comes through a woman, his Beaufort mother. If Tudor has any claim, then King Edward's claim is clearly superior; it derives via a more senior line. This is arrant nonsense even by Robert's standards!" He clapped his hands and laughed again, then rubbed at his eyes with the backs of his fingers. "Forgive me, Hal, if I'm causing you distress. There's no love lost, as you may have guessed. Truly, your father is a vile man, a disgrace to a proud family. You have left him just in time, I think, before he could taint you."

Perhaps Hal had eluded the taint. Perhaps it was present already. Certainly he'd contrived to use and misuse a fair few who'd crossed his path.

Triston was leaning in the chair, still smiling at him, and abruptly changed the subject. "My steward, Cardingham, is growing old. He has his wits still, but he's slow and stubbornly. I'd like to put him out to pasture. So: how would it be if he handed the reins to you?"

Hal trusted Fortune to tap his shoulder, and here was the touch. He gazed soberly across the table. "I wish above all things to serve you, Uncle, and will do so to the best of my ability. I believe the Earl of Northumberland was well satisfied with my work."

The smile broadened. In the hours Hal had so far spent with his uncle, it had never quite left his face. "Good. I'll speak with Cardingham, and you must be gentle, for he's an old mule. Early next month we shall all travel to London and seek that pardon. In the meantime, you'll not stray from my lands."

* * *

The evening wound down from that point. There was no entertainment, the wine was sour and Robert had lost his appetite.

Excusing himself, he hobbled off to his chamber in the building's stubby turret, past the boys' adjoining room, its door ajar. Someone had fashioned George a sling and he was, of course, supine and snoring. Beside him sat the twins, one dabbing salve on the other's open cheek. The lads rose and made their bow. As Clifford waited on his sons' report he glanced beyond Aymer's shoulder, his gaze climbing the hillock of familiar armour and, stacked to the side, the weaponry. A great quantity; more than they'd arrived with. He cracked a grin at that. "Where d'you get the key?"

Aymer answered. "The armoury guard gave it up."

"And the guard?"

Aymer grinned back. "And I have sheered off the key in the lock, Father. Now they must break down the door, and that may be beyond them."

Clifford pulled the young man into a rough, one-armed embrace.

A similar pile of steel decorated his own chamber. Findern and Castor were smiling their relief, sufficiently reassured to strip for sleep, Findern climbing beside him into the musty bed. Arthur Castor, to the far side of his master, sank alone on the pallet, low and damp. The man was said to scorn all bodily contact, but Clifford had known Arthur Castor for thirty years, and he conjectured otherwise.

As he reached to quench the candles, he saw Castor stiffen, gasping into the dimness beneath the bed. Chary, Clifford leaned over until his head was upturned beside Castor's pillow, hair dangling in the dust. There, directly below his side of the mattress, lay the guard's corpse, gaping upwards as if staring, avid, at his body.

"Walter!" He shook the sleepy Findern. "Change places with me, will you? Castor's been eating garlic. I can't abide it over here."

Findern gave a grunt of assent and rolled sidewards as Clifford crawled across him. That was better. Castor's gaze was still roving the corpse at his side. Across the purple throat, the unambiguous fingermarks; by now he was somewhat less certain it was Richie who'd murdered Tailboys.

* * *

John Cardingham was exactly the man Hal had envisaged and, with the young man's accustomed skills, he set about his task. Hands quiet in his lap, he sat some hours with the old steward, listening and learning his methods, though there was, in truth, nothing to learn. Cardingham was using the same ledgers, the same conventions, as Hal had employed at Alnwick; appropriate for the control of a vast household; nonsensical for Sir Triston's modest arrangements. At first Hal scented fraud, uncovering codes and columns denoting imaginary under-butlers; cellarers; masters of the wardrobe. It was soon clear that intransigence, not deception, was at work. The man couldn't bring himself to simplify his practices even to exorcise a horde of phantom servants.

"You're so quick, Master Cardingham! I hope one day to approach your speed and skill. But tell me: where did you get such thorough training? It must have been a great house." With half an ear to the steward, he quickly reckoned the primary accounts. Almost all the running tallies were wrong. At first sight the final balance was only a little way out, but this small discrepancy resulted, it was clear, from the netting off of giant errors in both columns. Hal closed his eyes, then resumed the look of enthusiastic interest.

"Well, young master, you have the right of it there! I am the son of the under-steward to none other than John, Duke of Bedford, brother of King Henry the Fifth of glorious memory. My father taught me all he knew in the hope that I would follow him in due course. Alas, the Duke of Bedford had no son, and the household broke up at his death. I took a position with the Duke of Suffolk for a time, and came at last into your uncle's service."

Triston Clifford would have been a bitter come-down for the man, then. Though Suffolk himself was a notorious old horror. It must have been an uncomfortable time. "I take it you served in France, Master Cardingham? Yes? Would you tell me a little of your adventures? It's exciting to meet a veteran of the great war in the flesh." He'd encountered so many of the poor old fellows, lurking, hopeful, with their long-winded tales. Readily the man began, and Hal returned to the tangle before him, shepherding the figures in his mind. Eventually he was roused by the mention of his grandfather.

"… so, yes, I knew Lord Thomas Clifford in his heyday; your grandfather served in Normandy under the Duke of Bedford. It was Lord Thomas who famously besieged Pontoise and captured the town in a driving snowstorm. Well, you've heard all the stories, I don't doubt. A formidable soldier, very stern and silent; not a man you'd wish to cross. Sir Triston doesn't greatly resemble his father." He sounded regretful.

Hal wasn't feigning his interest by this point. "Master Cardingham, were you acquainted with the household of Lord John Clifford, Sir Triston's eldest brother?"

"Not so well, except the older ones. The marshal, now – I have forgot his name."

"Sir Cuthbert Bellingham."

"Bellingham; that's it. A good fellow. Why do you ask?"

"Ah, I'm curious about one man in particular: Sir Miles Randall, Lord John's chamberlain."

Cardingham puffed. "A sordid wretch! Airs above his station. Some say he led John and Robert Clifford into wickedness, but those two were well wicked enough without help from Randall. Lord Thomas would have turned in his grave." There was a long and awkward pause. "Oh. Begging your pardon, Master FitzClifford."

"Do you know what befell Miles Randall?

"No, I do not. Probably God struck him down."

* * *

Just before dawn came the muted beat of hooves on grass. The sleep-skimming Loic would have woken at once, but the Frenchman was sharing his bed with Reginald Grey, out of earshot in the village below. Castor stirred at last and shook Findern, shuffling to the pinprick window, but it gave on to the woods. They roused the others.

"That whoreson has summoned men from somewhere. Let's give Sir James a little surprise."

Off they went, down the spiral stairs, led by Clifford, who began the descent at a trot and ended at a wincing hobble, holding everyone up. Bringing up the rear, George, fretful and clammy with pain, wrist braced by his gauntlet and fastened across his breastplate in a careful sling; an incongruous sight.

As they approached the dim foot of the stairwell, the uproar was audible below. Sir James's voice had lost its snide undertone; hoarse, now, with vexation. The armoury door was, apparently, immovable.

"They can't get a run-up," murmured Aymer, filling his father's ear with hot breath. "A heavy door and side-on to a steep stair." He made a sharp right-angle with his hand. Clifford snorted with laughter.

Of a sudden and close by: a woman's voice. "You *fool*. You *dolt*. You'll be the laughing stock of the North Country when this comes out."

"*Eleanor!*" breathed Clifford and George together.

"*You*, Madam. *You* will be the laughing stock." Thwaite's manners had deserted him. "This was *your* idea. *Your* vanity. If you'd left him to me, we'd be well rid of a traitor by now, but no – you must take the glory to yourself and this is the result. Look at you!" The sneer had returned. "*What were you thinking?*"

"How dare you disparage me, you low minikin? I've done my part: gathered my men; armed myself; ridden through the night to seize Clifford and take him into custody. More than can be said for you, you upjumped cur! A skinny runt, squealing in your underclothes."

The men squirmed with suppressed mirth – all but George, queasy on the bitter taste of her treachery. In that moment of perfect pride, Clifford had forgiven Eleanor everything; he could not have loved her more.

"Where is he sleeping?" she snapped. "I'll take him myself." And following Thwaite's inadvertent glance in the direction of the stairwell, Eleanor swept into the gloom, snapping her fingers at the sergeant. She rounded the corner. In an instant she was pinioned, her back against Clifford's steel breast, his gauntlet brutal at her mouth.

* * *

"Cardingham has adopted you as a long lost son, Master FitzClifford! You must be a cunning fellow indeed; a smiling executioner."

"Not at all, Master Petyfer. His quiet and honourable discharge is as much in Cardingham's interests as my own."

"If you say so. Accounts all over the place, were they? I saw you unpicking them. You've bored Sir Triston good and proper."

"No, I haven't. He must understand why I've made these changes, and now he does. I know what I'm about. And so did Cardingham, once, but his eyesight is no longer up to the task. At first I thought his wits were sliding, but now I know he cannot see the figures he's written." Hal pushed back from the small table. He tipped his chair and stretched. "How about you, Master Petyfer? Have you served as chamberlain elsewhere?"

"Not I. My father was chamberlain to Lady Honor's uncle, but I've been nowhere else. Nor would I wish it. Our Triston's of noble family, not like the Thorogoods – Honor's kin; parvenu upstarts. And he's a good master, when you're used to his quirks."

Hal turned in his chair to examine Clement Petyfer, a sharp fellow with a gargoyle face, who was reclining on Hal's bed, strumming affectedly at Hal's lute. A compulsion for the instrument: was it a qualification for office? All the chamberlains he'd known were proficient, or thought themselves so. "Quirks?"

"Well, he's an odd fish. I've never known Triston lose his temper, even when sorely pressed … though he won't forget a slight. That *smile*. And of course: no women. Don't let him catch you with a woman. Don't be looking at Mistress Beatrice. If you're needing female company, go to Colchester. Yes? Then come with me and Boulter next time. We'll show you what's what. But you must be careful."

How he thanked God for his failure to entice Loic along. The man would be a veritable fish out of water, all those talents gone to waste. "I reckon I know what's what, but I'll tag along if you allow it. Thanks."

"Oh, and mind how you treat Master Gregory, his father's pet. Don't overlook him or speak of him as simple, or you'll regret it. Any other man would have banished the little cripple to a monastery, but not our Triston." There was a long and awkward pause. "Master FitzClifford, I was forgetting Sir Triston's your uncle and his children are your cousins. Don't be taking any of it to heart; I'm just jawing. I don't mean it. I do mean it, but I don't mean any offence by it."

Hal laughed. "I'd rather you spoke as you thought. The hints are helpful. And Sir Triston may be my uncle, but I've never met him before and to be honest it's rather different from life in my father's household."

"Jesu, yes! It would be." And then Petyfer wanted to hear all about it.

* * *

Eleanor had drawn a knife before he could secure her, slipping at once for the vulnerable quarter: the hamstrings.

"Well tried, sweetheart!" He crushed her wrist until the blade fell, kicking it into the shadows. Then he'd just time to loose her sword belt and toss it to the grinning Findern before a handful of Percy's men jogged around the corner after their lady. Clifford thrust Eleanor towards George, who dragged her in, circling her neck with his good arm, her throat tucked in his elbow, his lips in her hair.

A flurry of blows and the men-at-arms were floored.

Then they were faced by a tall man in full harness. Clifford began to laugh. Guy was too tardy with his mace, and the fellow blocked the strike. "For Christ's sake, Guy!" He lifted his visor. It was Waryn.

"Well met, my son. Come!" Hobbling, Clifford led them to the day room just as a further troupe pounded up the short flight from the hall. For a moment, there was stillness, every man measuring the state of play, all eyes on Eleanor. Over the lady's gown she wore an ornate breastplate – no doubt her brother's. As she'd no arming doublet beneath, it was rocking and clanking as she moved. George's knife was at her neck, though he didn't look capable of wielding it. Findern stepped up to assist, twisting Eleanor's hair in his gauntlet, tugging to expose her throat. Waryn looked on in miserable indecision.

Thwaite and his three bastard sons were in the opposite state, clothed only in their arming doublets and hose, a sword apiece. Guy broke the stalemate, launching himself through the silence on to the back of eldest Thwaite boy, unbalancing him. In a swift moment, the lad was weaponless in Guy's arms.

"Be still, all of you," ordered Sir James through his teeth, just as Eleanor countermanded him.

"Take them!" she shouted at her paralysed men.

There was a half-hearted shuffling in the Wyverns' direction until Findern halted them again. Hand on George's hand, he forced the blade down the lady's throat, leaving a weep of blood.

At that moment, the rest of Clifford's men burst in, pounding, heedless, past poor Mistress Verrier – curled in a corner of the hall, face in her hands, moaning.

"What took you so long?" demanded Clifford of the room in general, plucking Thwaite's second son by the scruff of the neck while the youth was distracted, wringing the sword from his grip.

"Not Lyall," said Thwaite, faintly.

"Ah! He has a favourite! Now: which is Lyall?" wondered Clifford. "This one?" With a thumb he tilted the captive's chin to the rafters and opened the lad's throat, pulling back to avoid the arc of blood.

"Or this one?" countered Guy, imitating his father.

Thwaite's face shuddered to a strange contortion, teeth like daggers. Behind his head floated Waryn's dumb hand, wavering and hopeless. He let it fall.

The youngest son – about Robbie's age – quaked until his knees buckled. His sword splashed across the spreading crimson slick. Aymer hauled him up and Clifford gave him a casual kick toward the door. "Go and shit yourself somewhere else."

"Forgive me, Lord Robert." Bellingham was still panting. "We had to burn the gate, and it wouldn't catch. Oh! Master Waryn! And Lady Eleanor!" He bowed courteously. "What now?"

PART II

EMERALD AND RUBY

While Hal was greeting his new relations in Essex, Alice was no great distance away at Danehill, greeting hers: Sir Simon's half-brother Nicholas and his wife Petronilla, a childless couple whose modest lands adjoined the much larger manor of Sevenhill.

These two made the most beautiful pair Alice had ever seen, and she found herself frankly staring as introductions were made. Nicholas did not in the least resemble his brother. Much younger, some good way taller and more slender, he'd eyes of deep blue, curls of dark gold and a cleft to the chin. His voice was not the least attractive feature: clear and crisp, with a rasping undertone. Petronilla, Alice found enchantingly pretty: very fair, with eyes a true sky blue and perfect rosy skin. Her voice, too, was arresting, much deeper and more sardonic than the angelic face would lead one to expect, as if she were mimicking Sir Simon.

Whenever Simon had spoken of this brother, he called him *Sir Nicholas*, so that Alice followed suit as a matter of course. Now she perceived the cruelty, for Petronilla was quick to correct her. "Oh, my husband is no knight but a plain esquire, Lady Alice. He was honoured last year through Jack de Vere's influence and, of course, Nick repaid your brother by fighting under his banner at the field of Barnet. But since my husband chose the losing side, his knighthood has, naturally, been disregarded by King Edward. He'll be lucky to escape with a pardon, and it will cost us deep. But that's the Wheel of Fortune at work, is it not? Up we go, and down we go."

Alice blinked at them, glad to find in the husband an adherent of her brother – where she feared only hostile ground – and hoping very much that she'd not unearthed another Isabeau Woodhuysen.

Nicholas looked on, deaf to his wife's scorn. He turned his back on Petronilla and extended a silent arm, leading Alice to a heavy chair in the window embrasure.

"Have you any news of my brother Jack, sir? At court they say he is in Scotland."

He nodded. "So I hear. Did you see the Countess while you were in London?"

It was Alice's turn to shake her head. "Sir Simon preferred that I didn't visit my sister-in-law in sanctuary. I'm hoping he'll permit Lady Margaret to join us when we move to Essex."

"A more gracious lady one could not wish to know, and she, too, has suffered greatly."

Alice looked on him with warm approval; a sympathetic and courteous man. Then she noticed the absence of her husband, and looked about. Her gentlewomen were grouped around the other casement, where Blanche was seated in state, her hands on her slender midriff, holding forth.

Master Loys was gazing through the glass. Beside the house lay a small, crowded orchard, its trees chalky with lichen. Petronilla lolled with her back to the window, one hand on a branch above her head, swaying a little on her heel as the breeze licked the folds of linen about her throat. Standing a respectable distance beyond his sister-in-law was Simon. On his face, a look of avid interest, uncomfortable to witness.

* * *

Clifford stepped back to admire his handiwork. Sir James certainly drew the eye.

The arrow had slipped in smoothly. Deeply buried, it would not be retrieved with such ease, but that was the way with arrows. Though Thwaite was shivering in the blusters of rain, he'd played the man; the bony face impassive as he was disrobed and hauled across the saddle, as his wrists and ankles were bound together, as the captor busied himself. Perhaps Thwaite had got off lightly; when Robert Clifford last stripped a lone adversary, it had not ended in such merriment. The lewd jokes reached their peak, and several hands reached to joggle the flight of feathers. There was a groan then.

"Soft!" exclaimed Clifford. "The head's a good way up, gentlemen. You're giving our friend no pleasure."

Mounting in the yard, they led the quiet mare to the blackened gatehouse, where the great doors once stood, and tethered her to the hinges. Sir James made not a sound. There was a fresh round of ribaldry and then the Wyverns were done.

Behind them, hands bound, a file of men plodded off in the direction of Alnwick. Gusts of rain doused every inch of naked flesh, chilling and pitiless. Waryn turned away, sank his spurs and then wrenched back on the reins, unsettling his horse. "I regret that you were forced to witness this disgusting spectacle, my lady. I'm ashamed of my father."

Clifford laughed.

Her arms about Clifford's waist, Eleanor was gazing around his shoulder at the horizon. They were heading not north to Scotland but east, towards the sea. She lifted a hand to smooth her hair, tucking the mantle more tightly about herself, frowning into Waryn's thunderous face. "Why? Your father is well-practised in the art of the disgusting spectacle. It was deplorable, of course, but no more than Sir James could have expected. A coward and, worse, a halfwit."

Waryn stared at her with ill concealed dislike.

She leaned forward and said in a light, cold voice, "I presume there is some degradation in store for me, my lord?"

"I've something in mind," agreed Clifford.

After a brief struggle, the under-steward's habitual deference to the Percy family reasserted itself. "While I live, no man shall sully you, my lady."

Clifford laughed again.

"Waryn!" George was impatient to share his burdens. His cousin fell back with some reluctance, overtaken by Mistress Verrier, that pout-lipped trull, riding pillion behind Guy. Somehow, Waryn should put a stop to that, but his impotence was all too plain. He scowled across at Aymer, cantering beside his twin, standing bolt-upright in the stirrups like a tumbler – God knows why – a hand at his eyes as he squinted towards the sea.

George's gaze slid down Waryn's armour. The fit was awry, the greaves perceptibly too short, inviting a swipe to the ankle. "That's my harness, Waryn!"

"The Earl won't stretch to a suit for me. It's too small and pinching like the devil. You must have toothpick legs." There was silence. "My God, this is a disaster. Where is he taking her?"

"What? I don't know. Scotland, of course. I suppose I shall let him have her, though it pains me so. Anyway, as I revealed in my letter, Hal has fled. Now let me tell you why. It is the most astonishing wickedness."

George's tale did nothing to improve Waryn's mood. Foolish, perhaps, but he'd expected better of Hal. And Eleanor sank even a degree lower in his estimation. Slinking away from his cousin, he fell in beside Cuthbert Bellingham, most respectable of his father's adherents. "Surely you can't approve Lord Clifford's actions of this morning, Sir Cuthbert? You, who fought with such honour in France."

"Oh well, Master Waryn. The Thwaites … they would have killed him if they could, you know."

"The slaughter and torment of unarmed prisoners? I thought he'd put such deeds behind him. Where is he taking the Lady Eleanor? The Earl will not sit idly by; this abduction is reckless even by Clifford standards. And I will lose my position, of course," he finished, with gloomy candour.

"But I thought you were joining us, Master Waryn? Don't be going back to Alnwick now; we're off adventuring! Lord Robert can't mean to take the lady with him. It would slow us down. Moreover, she's rather overbearing as a companion."

"Yes, she is," said Waryn, with feeling. "This was all her doing, and look where it's led. Now men will say she fled with him on purpose, when she intended to bring him back in chains to Alnwick, and so take her revenge."

"Revenge is it?" Bellingham laughed knowingly. "If she has any sense she won't reproach him over the Lady Alice: that affair did not end well."

* * *

The Wyverns crossed the causeway to find themselves blessed with a rare stroke of luck: the Prior of Lindisfarne was away at York, and Maurice, Bellingham's son, had the rule of the place. Clifford, more boisterous than anyone could remember, was pounding Reginald Grey repeatedly on the back, as if it were a touching surprise arranged between God and his priest.

So it was a raucous gathering that night, and Eleanor and Marjorie, who should have been eating apart in their chamber, were muddled in with the other guests. Abandoning her mistress at the door, Marjorie manoeuvred herself again between the twins and, before long, she'd swilled sufficient wine for the habitual preoccupation to come to the fore. "Gentlemen, did you ever hear tell of Sir Miles Randall, your father's chamberlain?"

Bewildered, Guy cast round at Loic, but Aymer was well ahead. "The men still speak of Randall. He was your lover," he hazarded.

When her expression affirmed it, he leaned in, searing her with the unaccountable heat of his skin, even as the slow harbingers of dread were reaching his heart. *"But why would you speak of this now?"* The words were forced out against his will. Somehow, before the ominous rejoinder, he already knew. On her other side, Guy was fidgeting.

"Because you two are so like Sir Miles! In looks and voice and form; in every way. Exactly so." Her tones had dropped away to match his own.

The woman was far too close: her skin, a coarse terrain; oily waterfalls of hair pooling in his lap. His voice was a nasty, frightened hiss. *"Never speak of this again."* Aymer rose and stalked away to Lord Clifford's side.

121

Marjorie blinked after him, then Guy's fingers walked over her own and she turned away.

* * *

At Marjorie's pleading, Eleanor had discarded the deplorable breastplate before her stately progress to the guest refectory. She paused at the door, then took her place beside Lord Clifford. He looked her over with insolent slowness before returning to the uproar around him.

All about her were drink-soaked men and drink-sodden banter. It was too dark; the crowd had blotted the light. Along the table, George was sprawled, chin sunk on his breast, morose amid the clamour; beside him, Waryn, silent and dismal. Eleanor searched, again, for Hal, her gaze probing the disorder. A dubious champion, for sure, though at least she had his measure. But she'd not seen Hal all that day and could only conclude that he had left his father. And then she was wondering if she, herself, were the cause of the rift, and that brought to mind the terrible confrontation in the small chamber at Alnwick, when Robert lashed her with his contempt and left her pleading on her knees. How she wished, now, that she'd laughed in his face.

Across the room, the day's events were related and retold and fashioned into the foundations of future legend. Everywhere, Aymer was toasted for his wit in putting the Belforth armoury beyond use; there were a hundred ugly jests on the fate of Sir James. "*Ah*, which is Lyall? *This* one? Or *this* one?" The cheap quip was repeated, over and over, as they relived the slaughter of the Thwaite boys.

Then Walter Findern strutted up, unsteady on his feet, drawing hoots and shouts. Clifford raised a hand for silence. The ruffian knelt heavily on Eleanor's skirts, articulating his apologies with drunken care, pressing an impudent fingertip to her throat, the sweat stinging the wound. Furious, she slapped his hand away. Laughing until he was overcome, Clifford sloshed wine into her lap. His hands followed, rubbing at the puddle, spreading it about. Eleanor stood abruptly, with an exclamation of disgust; looked, in vain, for Marjorie and swept out on another gust of vulgar mirth. In the cool of the evening she paused with her back to the stone, listening to the sea. She half expected Robert to come after her, but he was glorying in the obscene triumph and did not trouble himself. The true Lord Clifford, it turned out, was none of the dark and intriguing adventurer of her imaginings, but a soused and swaggering fool.

Up the cold stairs and hopeful to the bedchamber; it was empty. She knew then that Marjorie would not return. Eleanor paced the room, swinging her arms. The chamber was no prison; she could reach the stables and she had the spirit for it. But the tide was high, the causeway under a fathom of water. To take a boat, alone, into the darkening sea: it was beyond even she. There was no hope now but to wait out the night.

* * *

While Findern was drawing every eye, Guy slipped Marjorie away, leading her to his guest chamber with its row of beds, bolting the door. Wordless, he bundled her skirts. She smoothed them down. His fingers tangled with hers, rending the fabric. He ripped free and the skirts were around her waist again.

How she longed to speak of Miles Randall; to explain herself; to tell him of that lost love, at this, moment of all moments, when God had granted her a second coming. "Guy, listen a moment!" The boy was deaf and hungry and Aymer had unsettled her. "You're the first man to touch me since my one and only lover, all those years ago. It was the bad winter. It was '59."

The skirts unfurled, sliding down. *Jesu – how old was this woman?* In '59, Guy was eight years old.

"Christmas Eve. My twelfth birthday. The others were hawking. *'I've a gift for you,'* he said. *'Follow me'.* He was so beautiful. I did not understand until it was too late."

Then the fellow was clearly a scoundrel. Not all men were made so, and Guy would prove it, if she would only be silent. He reached down and gathered her up.

* * *

Loic spent the evening on the margins. As Eleanor stalked away, Aymer slid into the vacant chair, exerting himself, absorbing his father's attention. Loic slipped from the dining chamber, circled the Priory and then he was back, pacing to his master's side, flourishing a heavy iron key; a clear invitation for Monseigneur to take himself off. Clifford dropped it on the table, pulling Loic into his lap with careless affection, his attention on Aymer and on Castor also, now perched on the arm of Aymer's chair. Then he was idly jogging his chamberlain like an infant on his knee. Aymer's eyes flicked from his father to the Frenchman. Loic was gulping, his palms braced against Monseigneur's thigh, the tears not so far off. Beyond them was Patrick Nield's empty seat. Aymer dragged up the chair, handing the ungrateful Loic back to a place of dignity.

* * *

Eleanor locked the door and checked the latch, twice. With some difficulty, she unbuttoned her gown and set it aside, bedding down in her chemise, drawing up a blanket. After an angry while, her thoughts drifted, swimming to the brink of sleep.

A heavy step; a flurry of rising nerves. She half rose, and stilled herself. "Marjorie?"

A pause, a faint click, a key turned and he was within. She measured the drinking hours, presaging violence. There he lounged in the doorway and bent his shadow towards her: vast, dark and outlandish, the demon lover of the song.

"Eleanor."

"You have killed whatever care I once had for you. Do not dare approach me!"

"What is it? I am the same."

Pride was all that remained; it should have curbed her. But there he was, and out it came in a headlong rush. "I held myself betrothed to you, my lord, until you abandoned your friends to their deaths at Tewkesbury to abduct another man's wife; that very woman whom all past rumour has linked with you; the rumour you expressly denied! Do not trouble me with your lies. It's been a gruelling day. Leave me."

Clifford had no more desire to speak of this than she; Alice de Vere being secured in some far distant quarter of his mind, her recall was inexpressibly painful. Limping across, he flung himself on his back beside Eleanor. His ways were so familiar, so self-assured that she made not a sound of protest. When he turned his head, the glittering eye belied the steady voice.

"Then I'll tell it all, thought it's agony for me; I hardly know how to begin. Well, we came too late to the field of Tewkesbury. It was no fault of mine. Of course it wasn't. Who ever knew Robert Clifford to tarry, when battle lay in prospect? By then the Prince was dead and Edmond of Somerset was trapped in the Abbey. My life's cause fell that day. I went at once to the rescue of Queen Margaret and Prince Edward's widow, and neither would come away. So when I learned that Lady Alice carried Somerset's child, my hope breathed again. She offered to come with me. Not as lovers," he touched her lips with his knuckles; she was not breathing, "but, I trusted, as allies; travelling south, seeking Jasper Tudor, the Earl of Pembroke. In the house of a friend I left the lady and went on to meet Tudor at Chepstow. There, we were encircled by thousands of besiegers. As I was leading our men to victory over the enemy, the lady was wooed and won by another man, spurning all chance to raise an heir for Lancaster; turning her back on our hopes and plans, and crushing my spirit."

The tale was both glib and stilted – disgracing his usual ready style – but Eleanor's judgment had wheeled out of her control. All the weathervane anger swung round on Alice de Vere. She was startled, truly; appalled at the cold wickedness of the woman, and gazed, heartsick and stricken, into his face.

"Ah, sweetheart, I thought that of all the world, you at least would not forsake me. And when I heard your voice at Belforth, I gave thanks to God. But you had come not to my succour in the hour of need, but to take the last boon left to me: my liberty." He was surely overdoing it now, and would have been lighter of touch were he not weighted with a tun of wine.

125

She was all eagerness. "But you must see that from my point of view, it was you who'd abandoned me, Robert! And when I'd so committed myself to your cause that I risked everything to send false reports under my brother's seal to Ki … to Edward of York."

He laughed then, and pinched her chin, and she laughed too. "*How* I love you, Eleanor! Ah, my spirited Eleanor. There was never another woman like you." Lie one moment longer and he must surely pass out. He levered himself over, propped on his elbow, and stroked her hair. Solemnly she looked on him. He touched his lips to her brow, nose, mouth, and rested his cheek against hers.

A shy touch to the eye patch. With hesitant fingers – he could stop her if he chose – she untied the ribbon. When Robert met her curious gaze, she took his face in her graceful hands, conferring the lightest kiss upon the blank socket, like a blessing.

If he'd a penny for every unsolicited, unwanted and unnecessary reassurance of that sort, he could hire a private army on the profits. And then he started to think about private armies, and he livened up a little.

Robert traced the scratch at her throat with his tongue. He was trying not to dwell on the two eldest FitzCliffords; on what they might have taught her. In truth, Eleanor had no more than a meagre grounding, her history more sorry than glorious: Hal's cynical self-gratification, which both was and wasn't forced upon her; George's heedless stampede.

By the first caress, the girl was trembling; by the first kiss – tender, soft and deep – she was lost. One hand had slipped the laces of her chemise. The folds of fine linen glided down, settling in clouds about her elbows. One knee was sliding the blanket from her legs. When he rose to tug off his boots, she reached with shy hands to free him from doublet, shirt and hose. There was never a man stripped to her view, neither of her lovers having given it a thought. Drinking him in, the sight and the scent, she traced his skin, with reverence, first, and then with a callow ardour. Every inch of him had the power to fascinate. He stood and allowed it for a time, twirling her locks in his fingers, though she was hurrying him on.

"Slowly, sweetheart."

But his form was the most captivating thing Eleanor had ever seen, and she could not command herself, so he lowered himself back to the bed and took up the reins.

With half a mind on the task it was likely he would enchant her. He'd well more than half a mind to it by the eventual culmination; greatly roused and keenly sobered. Robert showed Eleanor how love could be and, when she woke with the dawn and woke him also – rather green around the gills – he showed her again.

* * *

Alice was wise to be wary of Petronilla – so beautiful and self-assured a trespasser – but perhaps she wronged the gentlewoman in assuming the antipathy was mutual.

"Come and walk with me in the grounds, Lady Alice. If we climb this track towards the woods, we have a fine view of the house at Sevenhill."

Obedient, Alice followed. "I am not sure I wish to look, Mistress Loys. I've not seen Sevenhill since I was a small child. It would be too great a blow were my husband not to be granted the estate."

"Have no fear on that score. Whatever Simon wants, Simon takes." A peculiar statement, and not one to probe. "How do you find married life, Lady Alice?"

This was tending somewhere. Alice cleared her throat. "I'm a widow, Mistress Loys. I was married some time since."

"How do you find marriage with this particular husband?"

"Sir Simon … has given me fine gowns. A lute. Also a cat."

Petronilla raised her pale brows.

"Have you been married long to Master Nicholas?"

The woman sighed. "Let me tell you the story. It's sure to amuse you." The trap had been sprung; Alice would have blundered in whichever way she turned. "Some years back, his father, Sir Christopher, was looking about for a wife for his son. Here, in Essex, for Nicholas's mother was local-born. Poor Nicholas. He was suffering an unlucky passion for another girl, whose dowry wasn't sufficient. So he was ill disposed when he was brought before me. He was very young and gauche, and all spotty and sulky; refusing to look me in the eye. I was rather conscious of my good looks – I was much sought-after – and I was offended. But it didn't matter, because it was the elder brother who caught my eye. And since Nicholas wouldn't open his mouth, it was Simon with whom I spoke. We walked here in these gardens, and we talked and we talked. I've never known anyone like him. Before or since. When they'd all gone away, I told my father I'd have the elder son or none. Well, Father was willing, and put it to Sir Christopher. I've no idea what was Sir Christopher's view of the match, for Simon came to me in person, alone, to give me his answer."

She had turned on Alice with an arch smile, and Alice found she didn't want to hear it. There was Sevenhill before her, serene and long familiar; there was the great oak tree, framing the house, spreading wider than ever; and there were Aubrey, Jack and her father before her mind's eye. She wished these others at the bottom of the sea.

"Simon said that if I were the last maiden on earth, he would not have me. I was a spoiled hussy, he said; impertinent, presumptuous and brazen, and a great deal more of similar flattery."

Alice turned at that, the menfolk vanishing in a flicker.

"He told me to wed his younger brother and be glad of it. And so, not for the last time, I found myself doing just as he bade me, and Nicholas and I have been making each other miserable ever since, as Simon no doubt intended."

* * *

The night had blossomed with a charm Clifford neither expected nor, probably, deserved; too lovely, in fact, despite a slight inebriated haze. Now it was hard to part. He feared that she would break the spell. Dreamy and tranquil, Eleanor surprised him. There he sat, an imposing trespasser in the

Prior's high-backed chair, the others arrayed before him: Waryn, staring fiercely at the wall; the lady; Bellingham; a grey-faced Mistress Verrier.

"Well now, Waryn. Your sergeant's dead and it's a long trudge back to Alnwick for the rest of your men – if they survive the chill." Clifford rubbed his hands and grinned. He was picturing those pasty figures trooping glumly past Belforth's market cross, hands bound at their backs, privates jiggling, looking about in despair. "You'll be ahead of the news and have the advantage. So, here's the tale: I took the womenfolk as hostage against an attack; you followed us only to guard their virtue, in which you were bravely victorious, spending the night in full harness outside their chamber. If I know Harry Percy, he'll take a pragmatic view: it will suit him to swallow the story. You'll keep your position and the ladies shall not end their days in a nunnery. Let's pray there's no little FitzClifford to give the lie to this fable!"

Waryn's disdainful eyes flicked up, and down again.

"Bell," Clifford continued, "your son must be persuaded to give up some of his lay brothers as escort. Four should do it."

Bellingham hurried off. Maurice would probably be reluctant, but this was entirely necessary if he were ever to rid himself of his dangerous guests. The sub-prior rose at once and led his father out of his snug lodgings, down the squally steps beneath the Priory church, and out among the lay brothers' graves before the strand. The dead were gifted with a chilly outlook: grey acres of saltwater below a sky of scudding gulls. Attending the sub-prior was a young servant, a tall, dark youth who followed their steps with silent eyes when his master bade him halt.

Bellingham made his request and, with a weary shrug, Maurice assented. He was marvelling, again, that Sir Cuthbert, whose instincts were decent, could live among these impious men. "Father, I brought you down here for a reason: there's something I would show you before you leave. Last night, I was listening when your fellows spoke of an old companion." And then he told Sir Cuthbert the strangest of tales.

* * *

By now the homeward party was hurried on by the turning tide. Clifford led Eleanor to Waryn's horse. "My heart is yours." He said it openly, easily and, disconcerting those present, kissed her with ardour, clinging to his lover and all she signified; that which was fading away as he readied himself for the border. At last he stepped back, folded her mantle around her and lifted Eleanor onto the pillion saddle behind his son. "I do not ask you to wait for me, my lady, for probably you would wait in vain. But remember me in your prayers, as I shall remember you."

Across the blustery causeway they cantered. Eleanor had twisted in the saddle, gazing until the watchers vanished behind the walls. There was a strong sense that she would never see her lodestar again. Through the pensive quiet she was borne away.

The man in the saddle was most profoundly unhappy. His father and the FitzCliffords were alive and at liberty, which was proving a poor consolation. How Waryn had dreaded the confrontation at Belforth – and how differently it had fallen out. Now it was the Earl, and poor Anna, whom he must face. Some called Robert Clifford the most evil man in England and, just then, he could not hit upon a worse.

Shortly before nightfall the little party entered the castle precincts. The men who came to assist were looking in vain for their fellows, eyeing Waryn with dread. His stern face brooked no inquisition.

"Tomorrow we'll speak. Remember your loyalties, Master Waryn," said the intolerable harpy as she swept away. He bowed. He was permitting himself a dizzying vision: his hands closing, relentless, on the lady's white and yielding throat.

At the sound of his heavy tread, his wife bounded from the bedchamber and enfolded him, crooning and crying. He hushed her as best he could. Ushering Anna gently to the bed, he knelt at her knee and clasped her hands between his own. Then, full of woe, Waryn brought forth the grisly tale, addressing himself to her lap.

"My brother was alive when you left him?"

"He was, Wife, but he cannot last. They will kill him in extracting the arrow. No one could be sorrier than I! Please believe that there was nothing I could do to prevent it."

"Hush, I know. And his two elder boys: they are dead for sure?"

"For sure they are dead, alas."

"Only Lyall left alive?"

"Only the youngest."

"He's not more than thirteen years, a mere lad. Waryn, think on it: when I chose to wed you, James swore we'd not have Belforth …"

Thwaite had, indeed, written to his sister, giving her his unfettered opinion, for Anna had debased herself to take the Earl's baseborn servant at the very moment that Sir James was burnishing his hopes of the Earl's sister. *I have drawn up a new will. You shall have Belforth over my dead body.* Now the words hung, prophetic. Neither chose to give them voice. She continued, "He named his bastard sons as heirs, in order of their birth. This new will must lie in the armoury with the charters and, for now, the armoury cannot be entered; your brother Aymer has seen to that. We should send a man north to enquire after my brother's health."

He gazed at her, full of misgiving. "My family has wrought such harm upon yours; I cannot, in all conscience, seek to profit from this evil work."

"*Waryn*," said she, and her large, hazel eyes brimmed with reproach, "Lyall had never a hope of Belforth until my brother chose to handle me so unjustly. It was devotion to you that first brought harm upon *me*, and it is *I* who has lost a brother and two nephews at your father's hands. *I* am the rightful heiress. Surely it is your duty to amend this wrong?"

He turned away, ransacked by doubt.

In another part of the castle, Eleanor lay upon her bed, thrumming with life. "Oh Marjorie – why can't I die now? So perfect that I cannot begin to describe it! Robert made love to me in the dark hours and again at the dawn."

The gentlewoman was giving off a baleful air. "It was seven times, with Master Guy. And all the while, men cursing and hammering at the door. Seven times. I'm limping."

Eleanor's eyes flew open. Lifting her head, she frowned at her friend. "Robert was slow and tender, and most concerned for my pleasure."

"Guy wasn't." Marjorie took a listless turn about the room. "How could I have been so rash? But then, he is so beautiful and so like Sir Miles. How could I resist?"

"I thought it was Aymer FitzClifford whom you preferred."

"Master Aymer puts me more in mind of Sir Miles, for sure, but when I said as much, he grew agitated and left me to his twin."

"He did not care to hear you speak of another man, I suppose."

That wasn't it. There had been fear writ across Aymer's face – dread, not jealousy – but Marjorie could make nothing of it, and a more immediate problem obtruded itself. "My God. I must surely be with child after all that, and the Earl will pack me off if I have fallen. They say there is a midwife in the town who can make such troubles disappear."

"Mistress Grosse? I thought of summoning her after George FitzClifford forced me to submit to him. As it turned out, I had no need of her arts. You must wait a little and, if you begin to fear it, you must see the woman."

"But what of you, Lady Eleanor? Should you not see her also?"

"I've thought on it all the way home. The matter lies in God's hands. If I carry Robert's child, it is a blessing and a sign. I would tell my brother I've wed Lord Clifford; it is so near-enough the truth. It is the truth in my heart. I held myself betrothed to him, and we have consummated our love; we are as good as married." She felt with a certainty that Robert had sown himself within her. How fervently she would love his child: a pretext, if any were needed, to surrender her fate to the man.

"No one would believe the same of me," said Marjorie, dismally.

"No. Nor would it assist you if they did. Which is why you must prepare yourself."

* * *

The marvellous weather rekindled and the land roasted in late summer heat. Hal joined his cousins, as so often, in the bathing place the boys had taken for their own: a loop of the languid river, secluded and tranquil and draped with willows. Within the limpid current, Gregory was a bright fish, darting and frisking, but Hal was shy with his gaze as the boy levered himself on to the bank. From the knees up, a slim and handsome youth; below the knee, something had gone badly wrong.

The three of them draped their hips in linen and lounged on the warm grass. The Clifford boys had begged Hal to bring his lute; to play and sing for them, and this he did, rather self-consciously.

"That is a most beautiful, heart-rending song. What's it called?"

"*Farewell*, Stephen. It's a composition of my father, who's an exceptional musician in singing, playing the lute, the pipes, the shawm, and writing the most exquisite melodies."

Stephen was determined to praise his cousin. "But you have a fair voice yourself, and play well."

"If you'd heard Lord Robert, you would not think so. He has surrounded himself with talented men, and there is music always to be heard in the household. And Loic is more skilled even than he on the lute."

"Who's Loic, Hal? I've heard his name before, I think," said Gregory.

At once the young Frenchman materialised before his mind's eye, accompanied by an unexpectedly violent spasm of homesickness. A longing not for any particular place, but for *his* place, in the midst of his father's household; at the head of the FitzCliffords. "Sir Loic Moncler is my father's chamberlain. Ah, a little Frenchman, not so much older than I. Domineering, prideful and scheming; good, true, wise."

They blinked at him. Hal realised he didn't much like himself when in the company of his trueborn cousins. Somehow he sounded, to his own ears, both whimsical and self-important. But these boys were so diffident, so inquisitive, that it was hard to speak with them as equals.

"He sounds a strange fellow?"

133

"A strange fellow," agreed Hal. "I love him well, as he loves me. But it's my father he adores, body and soul. He shares Lord Robert's bed – those hours when there's no woman in it – for my father cannot bear to be alone. The most uneasy sleeper you could imagine."

His cousins laughed, a little uncertainly.

Mastering the temptation to shock them, deliberately, with the lopsided essence of that entanglement, he shocked them by accident. "My father's steward is a competent man, but," he added with a meaningful look, "it's Loic's task to supply the other necessaries."

The boys digested this. "And your father: he doesn't forbid you to avail yourself? He is not disgusted …" Stephen's voice was hushed.

Hal cast about for an illustration. "Last Christmastide, when Lord Robert first mustered his sons and nephews, Robbie was barely thirteen years; Oliver and Tom were fourteen or fifteen; Edwin a year older, but then, he'd been at the Abbey since he was seven, and blubbed all the time. Father brought us lads to a whorehouse, paid for all, and tutored the untried – in some detail, apparently. A revel, you see, to mark the gathering of his boys about him. I believe he'd be disgusted if we didn't consort with women."

The cousins were gazing at him, slack-jawed. It was fair to say that in that moment, Hal was deeply pining.

* * *

Anna held her husband guiltless, of course. His prompt and dolorous contrition was evidence of nothing more than the man's decency. But when the gentlewoman awaited the contrition of others, she waited in vain. Eleanor would rarely question her own impulse or conviction; she was now more defiant than ever; she did not hold herself accountable for the atrocities at Belforth – quite the contrary: she'd done her best to capture the outlaw, and was a victim herself, forced to witness the vile conclusion and carried off against her will. In short, remorse was not appropriate and Eleanor did not show remorse.

Over the next days, Waryn was pursued and hectored by Eleanor. In her presence it grew painful to breathe, his hands twitching convulsively – that long white throat exercising its awful fascination. Quitting Alnwick was become a seductive whisper.

All the while, Anna nudged him on, plaintive and ingenuous. "Surely we shouldn't neglect my wretched brother at such a time? He must be wondering why we've not sent to ask after his health."

Sir James was wondering nothing of the sort; an envoy from Anna and Waryn might very probably finish him off. But the courtesies should, doubtless, be observed and Waryn was bending. Eventually he dispatched his man Mayhew to ride the twenty miles north.

By nightfall of the next day, the manservant was back at Alnwick with a ghoulish report. Belforth was still roiled in Robert Clifford's bloody wake; the residents talked of nothing else. As yet, Sir James clung to life; the knight had been offered an extraction but chose, instead, to let nature take its course. With sluggish tenacity, nature was doing just that, ripping his guts en route. To the couple's surprise, Mayhew carried a letter from Thwaite's steward, begging Waryn, as Sir James's brother-in-law, to hasten to the castle and take charge. What had it cost the man to make such a plea? When Waryn escorted Eleanor Percy to Belforth, it was with the greatest reluctance and no unlawful purpose, but the household could hardly exonerate him of the savage aftermath.

In fact, Thwaite's man had little choice. Young Lyall had taken himself off, just as the marauder directed. He'd not yet returned, his whereabouts unknown. Thwaite's only other kin was an elderly uncle with whom Sir James had been feuding this past decade, and his steward knew it.

* * *

"So the plan has failed. I'm not in the least surprised." Loys laid down the letter and went on with his dinner.

"Oh?" said Petronilla. "What plan is this, Simon?"

Nicholas clicked his tongue at his obliging wife, his eyes on his meat.

"The plan to kill Robert Clifford on his way north to Scotland."

Carefully Alice rested her spoon.

"I sent Dacre up to Londesborough to incite Lancelot Threlkeld."

"Did you? I'm sure Blanche said your steward had gone to Avonby to make ready for your arrival."

"Do try to keep up, Petronilla," said Loys. "Hugh didn't tell his wife the true purpose, lest anxiety for him imperil her health. If only every wife were so devoted. Anyway, we may console ourselves with the news that Dacre has acquitted himself bravely, wounding Clifford's marshal."

"Sir Cuthbert Bellingham?" cried Alice. "But he's a veteran of the French wars and on friendly terms with Sir Hugh! Surely not?"

"I quite agree with you. *Surely not.*" Simon tossed the letter before Nicholas, who went on eating. "So, our bold Sir Hugh made it through unscathed. Threlkeld lost a number of men and the quarry escaped, though Clifford left behind a mangled son. Careless, but then he has so many. I don't suppose he noticed."

Alice was swallowing air. When Nicholas frowned, she closed her lips.

Simon captured her gaze with his kestrel eyes. "And the lad was, in fact, alive."

The back of her hand slid over her mouth.

"But not any more."

* * *

They were over the border now, England slipping away. Clifford was difficult company: at times elated; otherwise contrary to suggestion; squabblesome with Loic; finding fault with every word that fell from George's wretched mouth. It was wiser to absent oneself just at present. So Aymer's campaign entered its off-season and he hunkered down, out of harm's way.

"Turns out gentlewomen are different," declared Guy, educating a broad mid-section of the column. "Just as I suspected. Finer and more …

pleasurable. Did I mention I rode her seven times? By morning my bedfellow was limping." He lounged in the saddle and smirked into Richie's scowl.

"So you keep saying, you braggart, as if anyone gives a shit. The rest of us were locked out and had to bunk up. Tom farting on me all the night long."

"I would say you'll have your fun when we reach Edinburgh, but probably you won't. What you need, young Richie, is a wife. Only way a woman will smile on you."

Once more, Aymer was staring away, scanning the skyline for that spellbinding wonder, but the sea had disappeared beneath low heathland hillocks. He turned to his twin. *Seven times?* It was an age since Aymer had a woman. He doubted he could bring himself to it, now, even the once. Heavy on his heart was the unfinished venture with Alice de Vere, the Queen of Heaven. The Queen of Heaven had laid him low, alas. He shook his head and steered his mount a little closer to Castor's. "Did you ever think to marry, Sir Arthur?"

Though Aymer's face reposed at its most angelic, Castor recognised the mischief for what it was, and his smile had an edge of flint. "Few of us, Master Aymer, have had the good fortune. Nield and Eglantine are widowers; Tailboys abandoned a wife somewhere; Jolly's lady abandoned him for someone else; Osbert Dormer was married, and brought his wife away the last time we fled into Scotland, and thence to France and on to Flanders. The poor woman lived among us, cheek by jowl. When Dormer fell, at Montlhéry, Lord Robert managed to shrug her off. Not much use any of us thinking of marriage now, is it?"

"We may very well become richer outside the King's peace than within it," pronounced Richie. "Actually, I shall like nothing better than to wed, and have a woman always at the ready."

"What an undaunted fellow you are, Master Richie!" said Findern, his eyes seeking Castor's. "With those dark good looks, there will be quite a queue forming, no doubt."

"No such thing," said Richie coldly. "I was speaking of the future, of course, when we have settled ourselves."

* * *

Alice had flurried the gentlewomen into the orchard before she began her fearful tale. "Please don't be frightened, Blanche: we know for sure that Sir Hugh has taken no hurt, for it was he who wrote the letter. He says he has wounded Sir Cuthbert Bellingham."

Constance snorted.

"Sir Hugh also says that one of the FitzCliffords was wounded and left for dead."

"I suppose *that* could be true," said Blanche.

Elyn's hand was pressed to her heart. "Which FitzClifford?"

Miserable, Alice shook her head. "He didn't say. Perhaps he cannot tell one from another."

"My husband rode among them for weeks and knows them all. In fact, Hugh knew Master George and Master Hal even before he fell in with the Wyverns. If either of those two were slain, Hugh would have remarked it."

Alice turned. There stood Sir Simon at the window, hands at his hips, following an exchange he couldn't hear.

* * *

Harry Percy wasn't surprised to learn that his sister had taken matters into her own hands; she always was taking matters into her own hands.

Eleanor had forbidden Waryn to write to the Earl, and with good reason, for when he disobeyed her to tell the faltering lie, their stories didn't quite tally. Leaning at the great table in his London house, Percy flattened both letters side by side, scanning with a forefinger. Every chink in the story was a narrow window through which a wide world could be glimpsed. He tapped his teeth. There was a midwife in Alnwick, it was said, a wise woman who could dispatch an unborn child with the aid of a herb and hook. *Only let Eleanor be spared such dishonour*, he prayed. Marjorie Verrier, he could and would cut adrift.

To Waryn, the Earl dispatched a nasty letter filled with careful hints. To Eleanor, a careful letter filled with nasty hints. Then he turned his thoughts to the matters that had called him south and tried to give them his full attention.

A week later, Waryn scanned the Earl's response with a sour and mounting resentment. It was all too possible that Robert Clifford had imparted his customary gift, an injurious legacy poised to unfold; the danger his father had acknowledged as Waryn and Eleanor stood before him in the Priory. Indeed, he made a crude jest of it. This, from a man who claimed to love the lady. He may very well have ruined her. And still the harlot had kissed him and clung to him.

There were always the dark arts of Mistress Grosse, as the Earl's letter made less than plain, in its circuitous style. Waryn might have prompted his wife to whisper such a remedy, but Anna had quit the castle. A week ago he'd sent her north to Belforth, his prudent answer to the steward's prayer. Now he was pulled in contrary directions. He dreaded his master's return, yet if Eleanor's shame assumed physical form, she had none to blame but herself; he almost craved it. By now his heart had slipped the bonds of its accustomed loyalties. In his imaginings, he was twenty miles north, reclining at his ease in what he suspected would shortly become his own stronghold.

Had his wife been present, Waryn would have learned that there was, in fact, nothing to fear from this quarter, for neither woman would bear a Clifford child. Marjorie greeted the reprieve with elation and relief. Eleanor wept bitter tears. She had no cause, now, to wait for Robert, and he had not asked it of her. But she could do little else; the man who ruled her stars.

* * *

"Blackfriars, Patrick?" remarked Clifford, when Nield returned to meet them at the gates of Edinburgh. "Strange, as I recall ordering you to billet us anywhere but the Blackfriars. We've been here twice already. We always end up at the pissing Blackfriars when we're kicked out of England. I hate the place. It's ill fated."

"Or could you view it the other way round, Lord Robert?" Bellingham was becoming ever more nervous when that surly look settled over Nield.

"Actually, when we go to the Blackfriars, we always end up back in England. Perhaps the place is a good luck charm!"

"Well, Lord Robert," said Nield, and the others could hear the tension in his jaw, "I had my reasons. Jack de Vere is here. William Beaumont is here. They're away hunting with Lord Hamilton, but they're staying at the Blackfriars. And my brother says King James is most concerned that the English don't spread themselves too much about the city. It may cause trouble, he thinks."

"How absurd. You'd better speak to the men, Arthur."

"I shall, Lord Robert. And your boys?"

"That's what I meant, you mawk. Where the hell is Davy? Why isn't he here to greet me, Patrick? Send for him at once! In one hour we're away up to the castle. I shall see King James without Jack de Vere clinging to my cloak. I shall tell him how things really stand."

Muttering savagely, Nield rode away. His brother Davy served the Abbot of Holyrood; he wasn't some manservant to come running at the call of an impecunious and exiled Englishman.

"I thought it would be hovels," remarked Loic, as they rode up the rise of the Canongate.

Clifford turned with a disbelieving smile.

"The town's quite grand. I thought it would be dirt poor and filthy."

"It is filthy," came Clifford's loud whisper. "It's full of filthy Scots."

Bellingham coughed.

Clifford raised his voice. "Good thing we'll be gone by winter. It never grows light and the cold shrivels your bollocks. Why do you think Nield has fathered no children?"

Patrick and Davy Nield were awaiting them at the castle, and Lord Clifford was admitted at once to the presence of James, the young King of Scotland.

* * *

On reaching the unexceptional rented house, Triston gathered a few of his men and went on at once to the imposing residence of the Duke of Buckingham, brother-in-law to King Edward's Woodville queen. The knight had been cultivating this young man for quite some time; the assiduous attentions were beginning to repay him.

"I was of the Archbishop of York's council, in the old days – Warwick's brother." Triston had fleshed out his history for Hal's benefit during the ride into London. "And once I settled in Lady Honor's lands in Essex, I'd often act as his confidential man of business at court. Then Warwick and Jack de Vere turned traitor, fleeing to France and after that, of course, I quickly turned my back on the Neville interest. I could see which way the wind was blowing, even if others couldn't. The Archbishop was bound to follow his brother into treason before too long. I wanted no part in it."

Which was all very interesting, but Hal wished his uncle had started the story some years before, when his path first diverged from the rest of the Cliffords.

"You'll meet the Duke of Buckingham in due course. But not this time; not until we procure that pardon. For now, it's head down, go directly within, do not leave the house."

Directly Triston had departed, Hal gathered Moppet and Barnaby and left the house, crossing the river in the direction of Southwark. There were fresh heads now upon the Bridge, just as black, but fleshy and less gorged-upon. One day, perhaps, Hal would blink upward against the sun and behold his father's grinning skull. Amid a forest, perhaps: George, Bellingham, Loic, Aymer.

Hal dismounted at the corner of Richenda Tilney's lane. As he approached the house, a familiar scene was playing out. There was Mistress Tilney, leaning against the door, panting. Hal grinned. Then his view of the woman was obscured by a gaggle of passers-by and, as he drew level, one amongst them had paused to offer help. While Hal watched, the door was charged inwards. The new champion was a slim man in early middle age, with a tanned face and receding brown hair. He righted himself, and turned back to the street, smiling. It was the master of *God's Gift*, Richard Carling.

This time, Hal cursed aloud, startling the oncoming foot-traffic. His thoughts were not of the danger to himself – for he was quite in ignorance of the fortuitous escape on the last occasion – but only of his overwhelming and thwarted need. Certainly he'd never gone so long without the comforts of the flesh, not since he was a youngster. Still cursing, Hal passed on, circled back and remounted.

An hour later he was lounging in the boys' chamber, strumming idly, until Stephen took the lute from him and set it aside.

"What is it, Hal? What are you thinking on?"

"Nothing. Well, I'm thinking on women."

"Any woman in particular?"

"Always."

There was a pause while the boys digested the melodramatic utterance, a clear invitation to probe further. "You're in love, Hal?" said Stephen. "You hope to marry?"

Hal examined his hands in self-conscious silence, yearning to speak of the beloved but having so little to offer up. "I am in love with a most perfect woman, Cousin, but she is married already and so far above me that I never had any true hope of her."

The brothers exchanged glances. "Please, tell us, Hal!" Gregory lived through the heart; he was delighted to unearth a lover in his strong and confident cousin.

Hal shrugged. "There's nothing to tell. I think on the lady without ceasing, but perhaps I may never see her again, and there it is."

"And does this lady have feelings for you also?"

Hal conjured, with familiar ease, the few, precious moments in which he'd held her full attention: the time he'd knelt before her in the house at Ledbury, when they'd laughed over his little brother's loose tongue; she had looked so intently into his face, then, as if learning him. And more – much more – that moment before the barbican at Goodrich, when he'd caught her in his arms, when she wiped the blood from his face as they held each other close, oblivious of the world. Not truly oblivious, or he would have kissed her.

Restrained by his father's rampant jealousy: Robert Clifford would, verily, have slain him for that. "Does she? Perhaps she does; I hope it's so." And because he was young, thinking about one woman led him back to thinking about women in general. "But it is impossible, living like a monk! The stews of Southwark are so close by, I cannot help myself. Stephen, come with me."

He could see that Stephen was tempted. The lad turned to Gregory and raised his brows.

Hal was appalled. Appalled at his own boorish manners – for ignoring Gregory as though he were a piece of furniture – and appalled too at the prospect before him. It was one thing to slip quietly away for a brief recreation in Triston's absence; quite another to organise an expedition to a brothel for a cripple.

He stammered: "And are you …? Is it …?

"Oh, yes." Stephen glanced at Gregory. "Apparently it's all in working order. You just have to tell him what to do with it."

Gregory grinned at Hal, whose face was eloquent of his dismay. "He is teasing you, of course, Cousin! Let us be quick. Dove will help. Dove is as silent as the grave."

Once they were saddled and Gregory had been levered into Stephen's arms by the manservant, Hal's confidence began to return and, likewise, his pride as the veteran. Their business was completed smoothly and most satisfactorily; a pleasant, easy transaction. Soon his cousins wore the same expression as the youngest FitzCliffords after the detour to Newcastle: an angelic naughtiness; a blissful shame.

Alas, they re-entered the courtyard not a moment after Sir Triston's untimely return and, as it turned out, Hal's uncle had enough of the Clifford way about him to know immediately – instinctively, it seemed – what had occurred. Without a word, Triston strode out of the yard and, in a voice of doom, eyes fixed above their heads, Dove instructed them to abide in their chamber and await the master's pleasure.

For an hour or so, Triston left them like pricked bladders. When he sent his man, it was for Hal alone. Hal, who'd packed his bags and mapped his entire future during the walk from the boys' chamber to his uncle's.

The smile was slighter than usual and more saintly. "Hal." Triston gestured him down.

"Sir Triston," interrupted Hal. "It was my doing. Your sons are as innocent as babes. I compelled them to it. I shall be clear of your house by evening." His face bore the hallmarks of martyrdom, spoiling the generous impulse.

"We both know that you were the leader of this expedition, though I'm not convinced there was any coercion involved. The boys are old enough to understand their wrongdoing. And I, myself: I am not blameless. I'm a great advocate of early marriage as a remedy against evil, yet the years have passed in the blink of an eye and it seems I've been remiss with both my sons in this regard. As soon as we return home, I shall consider a remedy. Now, Hal, you are older than they and still unmarried. Greatly at risk, unless we also find you a wife, and soon."

Hal tried to smile, but could force only a ghastly contortion.

"Surely you do not wish to repeat this sin? In this moment, you must repent of what you have done?"

The voice sounded earnest: "Of course, Uncle, of course. I regret it deeply." Try as he might, Hal knew he was turning into his father. "But I am not inclined to marriage just at present. I believe God will send me a sign when the time has come." There was a strange sort of confusion in his mind. On the one side, if he could not have his true love, he wanted no one. Equally, and at the same time, he had ambitions to make his fortune with a splendid match.

Triston's smile had turned dubious. "You are not my son, Hal. I cannot have you remain within my household if you fall again into error. You do understand that? For now, you shall wear a hair shirt as a constant reminder of this dangerous proclivity."

Unsure, Hal gave him a sickly grin.

"I am serious, my boy! Queen Elizabeth's brother wears such a garment at all times to ensure he never slips to those vices to which the flesh is heir. What is good enough for Anthony Woodville, that peerless knight, is good enough

for you. And Hal – you should know that you have gravely disappointed me."
He didn't look disappointed, but that was the peculiarity of the man. "Not
only in relation to the sin you've committed; in relation also to your
disobedience of my instructions; your flagrant disregard for your own safety,
at the precise moment I was labouring for you on this very point."

Hal was inducted, then, into a strange and interesting emotion: shame. He
examined himself from all angles, fascinated.

That evening, the chaplain came to Hal's room with the dread object
dangling between finger and thumb. Hal took it gingerly and held it to the
window. It was dense and heavy. Plainly too small, the garment would nuzzle
him closely.

"It's got beings in it," cried Hal piteously.

The priest bent close. There were, indeed, tiny creatures wending their way
among the hairs. "I can't see them," he said, firmly. "Master FitzClifford, your
uncle wishes only what is best for you. You should incline yourself to his
counsel."

After a few insufferable days, Hal submitted to the shaving of his upper
body in a fruitless attempt to mitigate his distress. When the hair started to
regrow, which it did, at once, it prickled worse than ever. By now, marriage
and the disgusting vestment were irretrievably connected in his mind.
Marriage was a hair shirt. He desired it less than ever.

* * *

With a jouncing step Loic returned to the Friary, utterly delighted with
Edinburgh, admiring its dramatic setting, its solemn stone. Ensconced in
Monseigneur's high-backed chair, he gathered about him the junior men and
the FitzCliffords – all but Guy and Richie – to describe the reception at court.

The young King was most eager to prove himself a leader of men, Loic
related; most eager to prick Edward of York in the backside and renew the
Auld Alliance with France. On hearing that the Wyverns carried a highborn
Frenchman among their number, King James had clapped his hands, rising at

once for private speech with Loic, an arm about his shoulder. The chamberlain's feet were jigging as he told them of his welcome.

Just as the youths were applauding the honour done to Moncler, Patrick Nield passed through the chamber. Rigid, he paused. Davy Nield was a well-known man about the court, yet the eyes of the King had slid straight over Davy's brother – for all that Patrick, himself, was a Scotsman born, a countryman of the King. Nield's expression was quite thunderous as the door banged in his wake.

Castor pushed himself up from the wall where he'd been lounging beside Aymer, lending an indulgent ear to the excited Frenchman. With a deep sigh, he followed Patrick Nield from the room and into the antechamber where Findern was already in the act of pouring the steward a drink.

"What is it, Patrick?"

"What is it? Oh, it's bad news, my friends. Oddly enough, bad news. Thought matters had gone a tad awry, did you? Thought we weren't having the best of luck? Wait till you hear this: turns out we'll not be spending Christmastide in Paris at the court of our little King, for Jasper and Henry Tudor have been blown off course en route to France and seized by the Duke of Brittany. The fucker has clapped them up, primed to sell to the highest bidder. And that, lads, means the whoreson of fucking York. Someone else can tell Lord Robert – I'm damned if I'll suffer any more of that filthy temper. God has chosen to punish him again and, given the follies of these last fucking months, I'm not in the least surprised."

The dismay on the faces of Castor and Findern was aimed not at Nield but over his shoulder. The steward spun around to find his master filling the doorway. There, before him, was Reginald Grey, reaching up to clasp Clifford's face between his bony palms, quelling him with a stern and steady stare, as though Lord Robert were a startled horse. After a moment, the priest nodded, once, and released him, taking Clifford's hand; leading him away, dazed and docile.

* * *

As Clifford and Loys were no more a danger to each other, there was little excuse to postpone the journey to Avonby, and Sir Simon had long outstayed his welcome in Essex. For days, Nicholas was dropping naked hints as to the expense and disruption of the prolonged sojourn in his modest home.

"If you'd any sense, Nick, you'd welcome me with open arms. Can't you be glad one of us has come through victorious? How much did that pardon cost you? You should have the crumbs from my table if you'd but humble yourself to ask."

The cavalcade was arrayed before the front gate at the foot of the hill, preparing to depart. Petronilla had been making her farewells; when Loys spoke, she fell silent. Nicholas turned his back, but the utter rigidity of his posture conveyed its own message.

The brothers didn't trouble to embrace. As Alice was enfolded by her sister-in-law, she sensed the honest goodwill.

"If Nicholas would permit it, I'd accompany you north. As it is, I can only wish you a speedy labour and a safe delivery. And look forward to the time when you return to live among us in Essex."

A good portion of that first day on the road, Alice was ruminating on Petronilla, a gentlewoman clever, amusing – even kindly. True, she was in love with Sir Simon, but that was a misfortune that deserved nothing but pity. Alice had watched as her husband exerted himself to hold the woman's interest, to rule her; intriguing and nasty in equal measure. And yet Alice sensed no carnal liaison. And so, for the pair of them, that itch went unscratched, bothersome and badly behaved. It put her in mind of another predicament observed at close quarters, but she couldn't remember whose.

The journey stretched on for days. Simon was a stimulating companion when he chose to engage, but Alice could not take to horseback now and so spoke little with him. Her gentlewomen read poetry aloud or played at cards, but the nausea would return if Alice did not sit at the window, the kitten in her lap, and study the harvest scenes through which they passed. Blanche was in good spirits, her own belly beginning to swell, while Elyn bore herself with the tragic dignity of a widow; it was beyond the others to sympathise, given the clear odds that Guy FitzClifford was alive and unbridled in Edinburgh. Cecily was merry and sweet, an instrument with only one string. Constance was calm and settled in the privacy of her own contemplations. As ever, no one troubled to enquire into Joanna's inner workings, as though the girl were destined always to be overlooked.

* * *

There was no response to the Earl's bad-tempered directives and, a fortnight later, Percy rode into Alnwick in grim humour. He spent all the first day tailing his sister, affording the lady ample chance to confess the dreadful burden she might be carrying, but Eleanor went undaunted about her business and so, as usual, he took the easy way out.

Meanwhile, twenty miles north and with Anna kneeling at his side, James Thwaite received the last rites. Beneath the bed stood a pail for those dark fluids that bubbled, unceasing, from his bowels; dribbling down the arrow shaft and seeping out through the mattress.

Just as life was guttering out, Waryn's faithful Mayhew was taking an axe to the armoury door. Once within, the manservant examined the document chest and swung his weapon, splintering the lock. The heavy box was filled with rolls of yellowing parchment that he rummaged with brusque effrontery, tearing three ancient charters and a letter from King Edward the First. Since he couldn't read a word, Mayhew drew from the depths the only manuscript untouched by mildew and cantered down the spiral stairway, past the locked door to the guest chamber with its putrefying contents. He crossed the day room – the parchment poking and rustling under his doublet – then up another flight to Sir James's room, where the knight's manservant opened at his quiet knock.

"Clear that pail." Anna watched her brother's man exchange the brimming vessel for an empty one, and glide slowly to the door, lips clamped. Mayhew unburdened himself. At once she knelt in the firelight and smoothed the manuscript, following the text with a finger. Here was the reference to her three nephews; not only they, but also one Henry Clifford, and Sir Miles Randall, who was, she seemed to recall, a childhood friend of her brother's. She could make neither head nor tail of it – not any of it – but since this seemed to be the pernicious will, she thrust it into the flames, where it crackled and flared and gave a fleeting glow to the gloomy chamber. Anna returned to the bedside where, within the hour, she closed her brother's eyes with a gentle hand.

Returning to Alnwick, Mayhew found his master and presented Anna's letter. Tremulous, Waryn hastened to his room. After moments of fevered scrutiny, at last he could draw breath. Waryn reached for a candle and offered this parchment, also, to the flame. A soft knock. He jumped, violently, billowing charred embers across the room. When Mayhew cracked open the door, they found little Kit Loys with the expected summons. Heart surging with elation and remorse, Waryn made his way to the Earl's apartments.

Percy examined his servant as he'd examined his sister. In his absence, it seemed, their two stories had bred and brought forth a third, subtly different from both its parents and complete in all its parts. Relieved, Percy was minded to be magnanimous and turned to other matters, but Waryn halted him. "My lord, there's been a further, shocking consequence of my father's brutality. My wife's brother, Sir James Thwaite, has, this last night, gone to his rest. Mistress Anna was beside him at the end. As my brother-in-law was never married, my wife is now the inheritor of Belforth." He fully expected to be struck down as he gave voice to it.

"Good God, Waryn." The Earl steepled his fingers, then the tips slipped, inevitably, into his mouth. He was still a moment, gnawing. "Knowing you as I do, I hold you guiltless of all evil intention. But you were certainly present when your father tortured the man and, if I'm forbearing, I'll be among the few. Your name will be trampled, and well you know it."

Waryn swallowed. "As master of Belforth, I shall be as much your man as ever I was, my lord."

Percy shrugged. "As was Thwaite. That's no advantage to me and adds nothing to my retinue."

"But my lord, I trust that if evil is spoken in your presence, you will stand by me?"

"And this is damned inconvenient. First your brother Hal, and now you. Where to find an under-steward so steadfast and able? I must poach from another man, and that causes ill feeling."

"There must surely be plenty of masterless men about, my lord – so many nobles lately fallen. What became of the Earl of Warwick's under-steward, I wonder."

"Slain at Barnet, I imagine, along with the rest of Neville's household. Aha!" Percy raised a finger, shifted as though he might stand and decided against it. "Edmond Beaufort's steward is going begging. And I mean that literally, for the fellow accosted me in London, practically ragged. I'll send for him. What was his name?"

* * *

Triston had not achieved the pardon on that visit, but then, as he explained to Hal on the ride back to Crawshay, he had not expected it. He had sown the seed, and Buckingham had promised to speak to King Edward on Hal's behalf. Triston was confident of a satisfactory outcome, if his nephew would only be patient.

Eventually, his faith was rewarded, and Hal was a free man within the King's peace. His uncle summoned him to the day room to break the news. "And then I heard of other charges laid against you, Hal, by the master of a trading vessel." A rattle of the head, as though Triston had water in the ears. "Theft and common assault! If I thought there were truth in it, I'd turn you out. But this Carling fellow hails from Hull, of all God-forsaken places, and has some spite against my family, so we'll treat his tales with the contempt they deserve. Shall we, Hal?"

In the silence that followed, his uncle had never seemed more strange; more, as Petyfer had it, of an *odd fish*. Triston was smiling, of course. Not a knowing twinkle; it was one of his slighter smiles. A little stretched. A little thin. Hal opened his mouth and closed it again.

"It cost me more, Hal. It cost me more." Another pause, then Triston rose, strolled to the leaded casement and leaned on the sill. In the low west light, the prospect was soft and fruitful. "Be that as it may, King Edward must be in good humour, for I hear that pardons have come through for all who took up arms against him."

"*All*, sir?" *Surely not.*

"I mean all my neighbours who chose wrongly: Piers Brixhemar, for one. Mark Rohips's nephew. We'll ask them to dine with us, now Brixhemar can hold up his head again. Don't mention the subject of knighthood. Piers gained the honour, briefly, at Jack de Vere's prompting and now, of course, he's lost it again. What was I saying? Pardons: Fabyan, Fulk Demayne, Gilbert Sheringham and his brother-in-law, Nick Loys, who was also honoured and then dishonoured rather promptly ..."

"*Loys?*"

"Loys. What of him?"

"Is he kin to Simon Loys, Uncle?"

"They're half-brothers. Why do you ask?"

Hal's heart began to drum. "Ah, I know Sir Simon a little, for his son Kit is a page at Alnwick."

"Indeed. Nicholas has land hereabouts from his mother, and married a local gentlewoman, Petronilla Doune. The couple lives at Danehill. It's odd you mention Simon though, for Buckingham says the King has granted Loys a parcel of lands that belonged to Jack de Vere, one-time Earl of Oxford. Sevenhill lies close by, some fifteen or so miles. Shortly he'll be our neighbour."

Hal stood dumbstruck.

Triston continued, "I've known Simon for years, of course, through the Neville connection. They say he's ordered the building of a great new house. Thousands of blue and golden tiles being fired, so they say; thousands of panes of glass. There's a perfectly good house on the site already. No doubt we'll see it all in due course. Glad enough to leave the North York Moors and abide in Essex, and I should know – I've stayed at his castle of Avonby: ancient, incommodious and blasted by gales."

Hal wondered what hue his face might be by now, though Triston noticed nothing amiss. His palms were running with sweat. Once released, Hal stumbled off to collapse in the orchard. It was possible he might vomit, for it seemed a grasshopper had lodged in his stomach. Rolling back on the baked earth, he took to rocking to and fro in an itchy ferment of exultation. *She*, near at hand, and Hal free to act, while hundreds of miles separated his father from the lady.

In a small upper chamber, Clement Petyfer, the chamberlain, and Adam Boulter, the marshal, were whiling their hours with a game of cards. Play halted as the two men leaned on the sill of the open casement, observing their fellow servant. Eventually Hal noticed their interest and stilled himself. He vanished and, a moment later, sprang into the room. "My pardon has come through, gentlemen, and I'm free to wander. How soon might you be going to Colchester? I have a vast and sudden appetite that only oysters can satisfy."

"I wondered what you were doing down there." Petyfer snorted with laughter. "I find I'm grown hungry too, friend Boulter. How is your ancient aunt, whom we are wont to visit on such occasions?"

"My aunt is ill again," said the blank-faced Boulter, "and writes begging me to pay her a visit. She begs you to pay her a visit too, friend Petyfer, for you were ever a favourite of hers. No doubt she could come to depend on Master FitzClifford also, if he feels moved to join us."

* * *

No man at the Friary was long in ignorance of Jack de Vere's return.

"Clifford? Here? My God! Why was no one sent to fetch me?" His boyish tones rang in the stone archway as he vaulted from his mount. "He's here, William! Well, follow when you're done, then."

In the panelled guest chamber directly above the gate, Clifford lounged in his chair, feet propped against the hearth. Loic signalled Jem to stoke the fire and Benet to pour the wine as Castor, Reginald Grey, Bellingham and Findern, alerted by the merry voice, shuffled in from the next room. A moment later the footfalls bounded on the stair, the door swung and Jack de Vere announced his arrival with a hunting cry. Clifford pushed up and turned, as if for the embrace. His men bowed low.

De Vere's arms were outstretched as Clifford stepped in and punched him full in the face. Jack reeled backwards, collided with the door and stumbled heavily to his knees.

Each of the Wyverns started, hands reaching; checked himself and stepped back in dismay. It was an image that would linger: slumped on his heels, the Earl made no move to rise, a blood-stained handkerchief pressed to his face – and above it, the shocked gooseberry eyes.

Clifford perched himself against the arm of the chair, hands on his thighs – the better to observe Jack – just as William Beaumont rounded the threshold and halted, aghast. "What is the meaning of this?" Beaumont's hand found the hilt of his knife. He strode in.

"What indeed? Some explanation is owing. Will you oblige, Beaumont?"

Findern helped Jack de Vere to his feet. Castor pulled up a chair and Bellingham helped de Vere into it.

Lord Beaumont was still gazing at Clifford. "God in Heaven, man! Have you lost your reason? Why would you strike him?"

"Tell me, Beaumont: was it cowardice or treason? Our Queen expected any day; our Prince sailing to join us; the Earl of Devon and the Duke of Somerset awaiting you with frantic hope … and you two abandon your fellows to their deaths, and flee for the Scots border!"

Tremulous, Jack lowered his hand. The nose was puce and swollen. Both lips were torn. The young man turned in distress to his friend, and Beaumont looked him over with a brief, exasperated shake of the head. "Not broken," he muttered.

"Hark at you, Robert!" Jack was aiming for authority, but his mouth slapped wetly and his voice had thickened. "This is beyond anything. None of that is our fault." When Jack saw Clifford inspecting his nose, he swathed it again. "Somerset wouldn't see us by the end. He was sending jibing messages via Lord Devon, threatening to put aside my sister. Warwick realised

Somerset was aiming at the throne. I know! We couldn't credit it either, but then the Duke didn't join us at Barnet. After that, we knew we couldn't trust him."

"Oh, this is much better, then," snarled Clifford, gesturing at their hospitable surroundings. "I can see why you'd rather crawl into this hole to die."

"No one knew when, or even whether, the Queen would come." William Beaumont's voice was grave and stern, as though he were older by far. "With Edward of York holding London, we couldn't lie safe in Jack's lands, and we couldn't go into the West Country; we'd have been in the Duke's power. Of course we meant to return if the Queen took London, but she went straight to Duke Edmond and by the time we heard, it was all over."

Jack gave a great sigh and a shrug and, crossing the room, laid a tentative hand on Clifford's wrist. "God in Heaven. Let's not fight amongst ourselves. We know how desperately you feel it; we feel it too. But we must stand united."

Arthur Castor was shaking his head as if stunned. Fairmindedness was never among Lord Robert's strong points and, oftentimes, self-deception shaded into the deception of others. But there was something awe-inspiring in this bare-faced onslaught of duplicity. It was all so spectacularly false; almost beguilingly warped.

Bellingham grimaced at Findern, who turned to pass the grimace along to Castor, but Castor was still examining their master – that displeasing and well-beloved countenance. His thoughts were just as they always were, of late. Robert Clifford: a great hunk of granite in a stormy sea; adamantine. *Nothing will ever change him; he cannot learn.* Lord Robert was fated always to follow the same path, making the same mistakes, like the poor condemned sinners in mythic Hades: Tantalus with his low-hanging fruit, perhaps, or that fellow cursed with the uncooperative boulder.

"How did you escape the field of Tewkesbury? No one else managed it." Beaumont accepted a cup of wine and leaned against the wall. His voice was quieting to its habitual sleepy burr.

"Mother of God, but that was some battle!" Clifford's glance flicked to his men, silencing them. "When we were spent from the fighting we had the good fortune to find ourselves in a far quarter of the field. We headed northwards to rescue the Queen and the Prince's widow, but the Queen was a broken woman and Lady Anne returned to her family's former habits. So we pressed on to the aid of Jasper Tudor in Chepstow. Drained as we were by then, we rescued him from a vast and superior force." His voice roughened and he pointed, accusingly, at Jack. "Your sister is carrying the Duke of Somerset's child; the heir of Lancaster. I brought her away with us."

Jack dropped the linen square, mouth agape, but Clifford stayed him. His teeth were clenched, and not only for effect. "No. She has abandoned our cause. She has wed another."

"Wed? Who has she wed?"

"Simon Loys. A knight of Warwick's affinity, in days past. A lapdog of York."

"Simon Loys?" Jack was peering at him in disbelief. "*Why?* A bare knight, a nobody … and Alice carrying the heir of Lancaster? That makes no sense. That makes no sense at all."

"Just what I said," mouthed Loic to Castor.

"Nonetheless, the lady has done it. And so I turned north and left her to enjoy her new husband."

* * *

Passing out of the low-lying Vale of York, Loys's small company began the toil up the vertiginous Sutton Bank to the moors beyond. Blanche and Alice were deserted in the carriage, the others riding pillion to lighten the load.

"Lady Alice, you're not still thinking on Lord Clifford, are you?" said Blanche, triggering a long and fidgety silence.

"You did what you thought was best, Blanche. I'm prepared to accept that. Sir Hugh probably did what he thought was best. Even Sir Simon, harsh as he was, perhaps did what he thought was best. And now the heir of Lancaster will be brought up the son of a bare knight. But nobody can control my thoughts, and nobody has the right to try." She rifled among the caskets and drew from its case her lute, inlaid with scrolls of coloured woods, filling the carriage with a wonderful scent, pristine as it was; another of her husband's many presents. He was unstinting – one could at least say that for the man; very ready to stuff her mouth with gold, as if any gift could smooth the scar of that first encounter.

"You seem to have settled with Sir Simon, though," continued Blanche, in a pleading tone. "I see you talking pleasantly together, sometimes. He shows you affection, I think?"

"He hasn't hurt me since the early days," replied Alice, coldly. "But nor will he let me alone. He flouts the prohibitions of the church; it's nothing to him that I'm heavy with child."

"I don't think that's a particular failing in Sir Simon," said Blanche, after pause. "But rather, of men in general."

"And Sir Simon is not a good Christian. I believe he has unnatural interests – and you believe it too; I know you do. At least we won't be reunited in Paradise at the Last Judgment: my husband will spend all eternity in Hell, tormented by devils."

"Company for Lord Clifford, then."

Alice gave a snort of laughter. To answer Blanche's original question, she took up the lute and played *Farewell*, Robert Clifford's haunting melody. She handled the instrument very ill indeed; so badly that – had she not begun to sing – the significance would have been lost on her audience in a jumble of discordant noises.

An outraged exclamation from outside on the windy hill: "Christ! Is it the cat or my wife? Lady Blanche, I order you to throttle whichever creature is inflicting this obscene cacophony on our helpless ears."

Lightheaded, on account of their condition, probably, the women in the carriage smothered their giggles until tears ran down their cheeks.

* * *

Reckless and spoiling, Clifford had squared for the clash and Jack hadn't risen to it. It reminded him unpleasantly of Somerset; the way exile had leached the man's spirit until only a dry husk remained. You had to guard against that. You had to keep your blood up and your sword sharp. He said as much to William Beaumont.

"You're an odd fellow, Robert. There's no excuse for what you did. Jack has ample fire in the belly – don't you worry about that. He's more than capable of defending himself."

Clifford turned on him with a belligerent shrug.

"Well – yes," Beaumont conceded. "His first thought does tend to be for his looks."

The squabble was primed to continue at a favourite tavern in the Canongate, but Jack refused to leave the Friary and so they lounged all the evening in Clifford's chambers, away from the city's interested eyes.

"You may delude yourself over your sister if it pleases you, but she did not go with that man against her will. Every woman I've ever carried off has connived at the deed. There is so much bollocks talked about this sort of thing. If the girl says different afterwards, it's just buyer's regret." Clifford realised he was jabbing his knife towards de Vere's face and laid it down.

"Mm, just so with all the women I carry off," agreed Beaumont. "Buyer's regret!" He grinned at Jack but, as so often, the younger man had lost focus.

"You cannot be right there. Alice knows Loys, of course, but that makes it even less likely." Jack's mind had jumped backwards; back to the early days, when first he fell under Warwick's spell. "Every time I was at Middleham, Loys was there. Always hanging about. Richard Neville valued his counsel; I doubt he liked him much. There wasn't much likeable about the man. Not even pleasing to look upon."

"Never met him." The black cloud settled. *He* wasn't accountable for Alice de Vere. She was nothing to him. Where were these heroes when the lady bartered her child's birthright in exchange for her own comfort? Cowering at the arse end of the earth.

"Actually, you have, Lord Robert. Met him. Simon Loys was knighted with us at St Albans, back in '55. But we'd run across him before that, even –

at Alnwick." For Castor was present, one among many, a lounging youth, laughing and jeering as Robert Clifford sent the pitiful boy sprawling in the dust. No surprise that his master had lost the puerile episode after the passage of twenty years, but Arthur Castor was cursed: he never could forget anything, when there was so much he would like to forget.

Clifford, too, had been transported back in time, though Simon Loys was still beneath his notice. "I say not! That was his brother: the whey-faced turd, prancing about Alnwick like a Knight of the Round Table. Sanctimonious little shit. Not so cocky once I knocked seven bells out of him."

"No," Castor said, crossly. "I'm not talking about Humphrey Loys."

"Anyway," said Beaumont, swilling his cup. "Whether Robert could or should have obliged Lady Alice by killing her bridegroom, the damage was already done. That babe is a lost cause."

* * *

A third of the way across the moor, the party joined the road from Pickering to Whitby and, as afternoon was closing, sighted Avonby. The place was just as Alice envisaged: the tower of those dreams that visited in the nights after her marriage. The keep was not large; unadorned and bleak, a louring black silhouette against the dimming light, it seemed over-tall and top-heavy. Crouching near its foot was a sad huddle of a hamlet. The castle stood at one end of a high valley where the land rose to a presiding peak, on an island of sorts, with narrow streams falling below at either side, the flow nearest the village half-damned by a dead sheep.

Nothing stirred as they approached, but when the gate swung inwards there was life within the bailey. Sir Hugh was waiting on the steps amid a small group of servants. A step higher, a middle-aged gentlewoman. Above them all, a girl a little younger than Alice, her dark locks loosed to the wind, proclaiming her unwed state.

"Who is this?" wondered Alice, aloud.

Blanche craned round. Sir Simon had dismounted and was beside Hugh at the stairs; no warm words of greeting, but displaying offence at the presence of the sheep. Hugh turned on Peter Considine, the man he'd displaced as steward, and repeated Sir Simon's complaint word-for-word, directing him to remove the rotting carcass. Alice was waiting for her husband to return when Sir Hugh's head appeared in the window.

"Who is that young woman?" muttered Blanche in his ear.

Sir Simon was already behind them, leading forward the girl. "Wife, this is my daughter Catharine, only child of my first marriage. Catharine, greet your new mother, Lady Alice."

The girl made a decent obeisance, though her face was cheerless. "I would have written to you, Lady Alice, had my father told me he'd married again. I learned of the wedding only when Sir Hugh arrived all of a sudden."

Loys dropped his daughter's hand. "It's none of your affair." He gave Alice his arm and escorted her within.

You have the advantage of me, thought Alice, *for I have never heard of you.*

Inside, Avonby was exactly as promised; Loys had shown no false modesty. The apartments were cramped and close, except the hall, which boasted its own weather: a squalling wind and fogs of choking smoke. There was no separate parlour; they must all dine together in a noisy and old-fashioned huddle. Alice stared at the floor.

"It's horrible, isn't it, Mother?" said Catharine Loys, in her ear. "Sir Hugh says you were raised at Middleham, enjoying every luxury. I expect you're disappointed. May I call you *Mother*?"

Alice took a step back. "*Madam* is suitable."

"Go away, Catharine; Lady Alice is heavy with our child, and weary, no doubt. Don't settle over her like a black cloud." He helped his wife to a chair and clicked his fingers in the air, summoning wine and wafers. Clearly as offhand with his daughter as with all those within his orbit, but on this occasion, Alice was grateful. The others had already abandoned her, besieging Sir Hugh for news of the ambush at Thirsk.

"Go on, Hugh." Sir Simon's voice rose above the buzzing. "By now, even I'm intrigued. Which of those most interesting Fitz-fellows has been lost to womankind?"

159

"Well, I don't know his name. There were so many of them, I never could tell one from another. It wasn't Hal or George FitzClifford. That's all I know for sure."

Elyn swayed dramatically, a hand to her temple. "Please, Sir Hugh – not one of the twins? The beautiful ones?"

"Was there something amiss with his fingers?" prompted Sir Simon, baffling his audience. "Did he sport an emerald, perhaps? Face running with blood?"

Alice looked up sharply. Everyone was staring at Loys.

Sir Hugh faltered out, "I don't believe so. Honestly, I'm not sure. Not one of the twins, though; I'd know them anywhere, they were so ghastly. No, the one who died was very young and fat. Or he would have been fat, if there were anything left inside him."

"Oh!" A gust of merry relief. "It was Robbie, then!" and "Only Robbie!" and "We should have guessed!"

* * *

Lady Honor was quite the stupidest person Hal had ever met, but she was good-natured and unobservant, permitting the household to make its way more easily than otherwise it would. Two gentlewomen attended her. The elder was Mistress Sibel, middle-aged and motherly. He would have thought her foolish, were she not shown to such constant advantage by her mistress.

Grace, the other, was no older than Hal. She was colourless and round-shouldered; she couldn't help that. But the girl was also somewhat heavy, with splayed feet and a mannish tread and, in repose, her mouth dangled open. These attributes were self-inflicted. It made him indignant to have such wanton unprettiness always before his eyes. The household men made sport of Grace behind her back, Petyfer – who'd no pretentions to beauty – the quickest with the wit.

Before too long, Hal had seen beyond the unprepossessing veneer and discerned her worth; a little later and he could, for the first time, truly call a woman *friend*. He would take Grace into his confidence more readily than any man he'd ever known. "My uncle has been plaguing me this morning on the subject of marriage, Mistress Grace." She was stitching in Lady Honor's chamber as he lounged in the window seat, biting the dead skin at his nails, blocking the autumn sun. Mistress Sibel had fallen asleep over a shirt of Sir Triston's.

"And he has good reason, sir, as I understand it."

He fidgeted. "He's turned on me because of his failures with his own sons … hounding Buckingham, who clearly never meant to give his sister to Stephen."

"Aunt, not sister. The Duke's aunt."

"And poor Gregory, whom no one will take, though it's all in sound working order, as confirmed by a good-natured red-head in Southwark. I don't wish to marry at all, but if I must, I think I know who it shall be."

"And who is that?" She frowned over her needle.

"My cousin Beatrice. Wed her, and I shall truly belong here. Sir Triston will give her what he can, and she's a clever girl, which matters more to me than prettiness, of course. Though she is pretty. Very pretty."

"Will it serve, do you think?"

"Why not? Lady Honor says he praises me without ceasing. I am his nephew and I shall rise, given a chance."

"There's a difference, perhaps, between giving you his esteem and giving you his eldest daughter. And your birth is a particular obstacle to a man of Sir Triston's principles."

"Not an obstacle; an offence. And not my fault."

"Not your fault," she agreed. "But a fact, nonetheless. Perhaps you will not understand, but it irks me when men praise a woman's beauty. Or perplexes me, rather. As if those of us who aren't blessed in that way are lesser in virtue, or intelligence, or as if the favoured girl is somehow responsible for her own looks."

Hal was thinking just as he always thought when he looked upon his friend. And then out it came: "I do understand, and not everyone can be fair to look upon. I am a case in point, a great, rough fellow as I am. Yet I keep myself strong and hard and lean: that much I can do. It is the same with a maiden, I suppose. She cannot help how God makes her, but she may choose to smile with her mouth closed, to eat fewer cakes and to walk lightly on her feet."

And then Grace bit her lip and looked at her lap, and he looked at his lap also.

* * *

"Since Warwick's death, Jack de Vere is a hound without a master. A fine, vigorous, lively hound. Like all such beasts, he needs the reassurance of a strong hand. Ah, you saw me break him in: *I am your master now. Come to heel*. And he has come to heel." Clifford threw himself back on the bed. It was an odd thing about beds: he had only to see one to wish to be in it.

"It was a strong hand, Monseigneur, for sure. I'm less certain the blow served as a reassurance."

Cuthbert Bellingham shook his head. "I really don't know why I was surprised, Lord Robert. After all these years I should know better!"

Unbidden, Loic had levered off his master's boots. Perched on his ankle, he carried one long, sallow foot into his lap. Then both hands were busy upon it, thumbs working the arch; fingers delicate at the instep, the springy black hairs rolling beneath his fingertips.

"Ah, harder," grunted Clifford, writhing somewhat. Bellingham strolled away to the window to gaze, unseeing, over the thoroughfare. Findern clasped his hands behind his back and rocked back and forth, whistling silently at the wall, rolling his eyes in Arthur Castor's direction. But his friend was slumped in a chair, lids half-closed, captivated by the actors on the bed.

Jem Bodrugan knocked and fell into the room all at once. "Lord Oxford and Lord Beaumont, my lord!"

Clifford pressed a heel into Loic's thigh, keeping him from rising. The other men stood ready.

"A good day to all." Jack de Vere swept in. "Actually, not such a good day, my friends. Terrible news: I see you haven't heard. Warwick's cousin has been executed. It's said his skull is set upon the Bridge facing into Kent, where he's been stirring for us just lately."

Clifford sat up, shaking his head. "So dies our last friend in England with any belly to continue the fight. The sooner we leave this benighted place and get to France, the better. Patrick and Davy Nield are supposed to be hiring ships." He frowned at Loic. "Where is Davy? Where is Patrick, again? He's never around when I want him. Why must you all be so wayward?"

"You exaggerate, as usual," said Beaumont. "We've plenty of friends in England. Jack has any number of supporters – among the Essex gentry, especially. All of them up and rallying on our behalf."

Jack patted his doublet, which rustled suggestively. "And Clarence and I are in constant contact. The Duke waits only on my signal to raise his men. Once we've the support of France, England will have a new king before twelve months have passed; of that I'm certain."

But Clifford had swept Loic out of the way and was on his feet by now, a look of appalled incredulity across his heavy features. "George of Clarence? George of *fucking* Clarence? Is this a jest? You cannot, surely, be serious. You cannot!"

Jack looked both puzzled and crestfallen. He glanced at Beaumont, who was frowning at Clifford. "Well, we are serious, of course. Clarence has the strongest claim to the throne, Robert, if his elder brother is a bastard – which he is."

"What? Edward of York isn't a bastard. Not that I have a good word to say of his mother, but the stupid bitch is renowned for her piety. Who invented this wagonload of bollocks?"

"Everyone knows it," said Beaumont trenchantly. "Duchess Cecily cuckolded the old Duke of York with an archer when they were stationed in Calais in '41. So Clarence is her eldest trueborn son. We didn't make it up! Warwick put it about when he was thinking of Clarence for the throne. Before he changed his mind and gave his allegiance to Prince Edward of Lancaster, may God rest his soul."

"Then at least Warwick had the sense to see that none would swallow such horseshit; he gave up on Clarence. And so shall you!"

"Isabel of Clarence is my wife's niece. There are strong bonds between our families." The mulish look was settling on Jack's face.

Clifford's voice was withering. "There are no strong bonds between Clarence and me, I assure you – unless one counts the slaughter of Edmund of Rutland as a bond. Which, somehow, I doubt he does. Somehow I doubt he harbours any particularly warm feelings towards his brother's killer. Put Clarence on the throne? I'd be dead in a week."

"Actually I don't believe George of Clarence is overburdened with family feeling. If he shows any such loyalty, it's for his wife's family, the Nevilles …" They watched as the betrayal of Warwick obtruded itself on Beaumont's memory. "No. I don't believe he's inconvenienced there either. I don't foresee any difficulty. And we won't proceed without his promise to pardon you... of course we won't."

"You won't proceed at all! Clarence has changed sides twice already and looks primed to do it again: not a man I'd trust in a dark alley."

"It happens all the time. Your own brother fights for York, does he not?"

"To be fair to Triston – not that I'm suggesting anyone should be fair to that little twerp – he never betrayed us. He was strong for York from the off. '*The house of York has the better claim to the throne,*' says the stupid turd, '*and in the end, that's what matters.*'"

"And he has a point," said Beaumont.

"My God!" interrupted Jack, diverted. "But what did your father say?"

"My father? Lord Thomas was dead by then, thank God. My brother John locked Triston in the castle undercroft and he languished there three weeks until someone let him out. Threlkeld let him out." He smashed his wine cup down on a chest; it bounced to the floor and spattered his calves with crimson.

"Wait on." It was always like this, arguing with Clifford. William Beaumont hauled the conversation around as if it were a great, unwieldy cart. "Before we waste any more time, perhaps you'd care to tell us who you are following."

"I'm following the *King*, Beaumont. King Henry. Henry, whose claim comes through his Beaufort mother, Somerset's cousin. The heir of Lancaster. *Lancaster*."

Then came the derisive snorts – Clifford expected no less. He folded his arms and looked down on Beaumont and de Vere from a commanding height. "*Lancaster*."

"*Tudor*, you mean." Jack was openly laughing. "Might as well follow me as Henry Tudor! I'm descended from the second King Edward."

Henry Tudor. Many of the Wyverns were looking around the room with surreptitious eyes; checking for the presence of Reginald Grey, no doubt; the priest would not quietly let go Alice's child, the true heir of Lancaster. But Clifford was exploiting Grey's absence to secure his will. "So you have royal blood in your veins. Who doesn't? But you are not of the house of Lancaster – and that is where my allegiance lies."

"Neither Jack nor I have even met Henry Tudor. He's just a child."

"Not so. A very wise and subtle young man." An odd little homunculus, but then, Henry the Sixth wasn't exactly Charlemagne, and Clifford would have given his life for him.

"No," said Jack. "And that's my final word. I'll not risk my life for some Welsh brat I've never met."

"And I've never met George of Clarence," snarled Clifford. "If I do, I'll butcher him as I butchered his brother Rutland, and piss on the pieces." Now he was scowling at his household, a most unwelcome audience as this fine, vigorous and lively hound failed – utterly and publicly – to come to heel. "France is mustering already for an assault on Brittany. The Tudors will be in friendly hands before Easter, the country will rise and you will eat your words, my lords."

Jack was shaking his head with a smirk.

"We can at least agree on one point," said Beaumont the Peaceable. The point was so self-evident he need not have troubled to voice it. "We all want to kill Edward of York. We'll cross the other bridge when we come to it."

* * *

165

"Hal! Let me go at once. At once."

Hal had joined a game of shuffleboard with Sir Triston's daughters, instructing them how to play better. He shouldn't have been in their chamber at all; it was an excuse to look at Beatrice, just as he'd been warned not to by Clement Petyfer, who was no fool. And then, more than looking. To demonstrate aright, he found he had to stand hard behind the girl and guide her wrists. Which became an embrace when she'd mastered the trick, then tickling, until he pulled her onto his knee and nuzzled her neck.

Her sisters bridled, heads swivelling like geese.

"I mean it, Hal! Stop at once or I'll tell my father. He warned us of your ways."

Hal took his lips from her throat and frowned at her.

"He said you'd spent time with wicked Uncle Robert and should not be trusted. It seems he was right." She stood and shook out her skirts.

"No, truly, Beatrice, I'm not like my father at all. Sir Triston has directed me to marry, and I'm thinking on it."

"Then think on it in private, please."

"You'd like to wed me, wouldn't you, lass? A fine, strapping fellow as I am?"

"Not particularly, Hal. You're well enough in your way, but any maiden must prefer a man born in wedlock. And I like my husbands mortal-sized and a little better endowed with means."

She shooed him away and, roused to action, he strode at once to his uncle without nearly sufficient pause for reflection.

Triston heard him out in silence, though Hal should have noted that the smile – which had phases like the moon – was at its weakest; waned to the barest sliver. "Have you finished? The answer is no. It's my intention that Beatrice go to Gilbert Sheringham's eldest. The negotiations have been interminable, but finally we seem to be moving forward. If I can get this agreed they'll wed next year, as soon as Hugo turns fourteen."

"Oh, I see, sir. I didn't know. Never mind."

"But I do mind, Hal. On several counts. Let me make myself clear. First, you are baseborn; conceived in shame. There is no point not stating it baldly. Your birth would be against you, even if all else were in your favour. Second, you are a servant. A senior servant, clever and diligent: as your uncle, I am proud of you, and as your master, I prize you, greatly. But beneath my daughter in station. Third, you have no means and would marry in the expectation of what little I can give Beatrice. Gilbert Sheringham has property to settle on the couple."

"Forgive me, Uncle. I should have mentioned that I do have coin laid by." He named his treasure.

"Now you alarm me! I dare not enquire how you came by so large a sum. Why did not buy your own pardon, then, rather than keep quiet and rely on me to do it for you? The gold does not in the least change my opinion; quite the contrary, in fact. The last point on which I object is this: we have already discussed the expedition to Southwark by which you led the boys astray, and I made my views clear, I think. Yet despite this, and with no encouragement from me, you have raised your eyes to my daughter in a way that cannot be proper. It is a betrayal of trust. Again."

"I've never thought of your daughter as a woman," protested Hal, attempting to ward off the inevitable, and there was silence as the arrant lie lay between them, naked and squirming.

The smile barely glimmered now; all but eclipsed. "You know the remedy."

Hal's expression took a ludicrous tumble. Triston set his jaw and summoned Dove to fetch Mistress Beatrice while Hal fidgeted, morose, before him; when the girl appeared, Hal refused to meet her eyes. Then he was dismissed, dragging his feet to the chaplain to retrieve the instrument of torture.

"What is it, Father?" asked Beatrice, her face a comforting picture of perfect composure. "Hal looks very glum – as so often, these days. I fear my cousin is planning to leave us. I was wondering if we could find him a wife, but as far as I can tell, he has no interest in marriage."

* * *

"Sir Loic, may I speak with you a moment?" Aymer slid into his father's chamber without knocking.

With a curt nod, the chamberlain released Jem and Benet from their duties. As they filed out – Jem shuffling backwards, mouth ajar – Loic turned on the youth, wordless; the arms crossed themselves and up came the chin. Despite the challenging attitude, the Frenchman's eyes were near-on half a foot below Aymer's. When Loic took a step back and sprawled into one of the heavy chairs, Aymer pulled up the other chair, lowering himself into it, leaning in. Loic stood again.

Aymer smiled. This pretty fellow was the gatekeeper to his father. Unlock this door, and he was well within. The key was comfortable in his hand. "We have got off on the wrong foot, Sir Loic. It is my fault, for sure. I was raised to believe that men of your country are cowards prone to all manner of vice. And then again, I was unsettled within the household. Now that Hal is gone I mean to make myself a better man, if I can."

"So deeply does Monseigneur regret the parting with his eldest, Master Aymer!" Loic's smile was like a painting of a fire; alluding to comfort, but shedding no warmth. "You should understand that his place cannot be filled."

"Ah, I am not aiming to fill his place. Hal was uniquely worthy."

Loic cocked a sceptical brow. Aymer made one of his rapid changes of bearing. "Sir, it won't have escaped your notice that Patrick Nield is a discontented man. Is it not likely that he'll remain with his brother in Edinburgh? A new steward will be needed. George is the natural choice, perhaps, being the eldest, but my father has come to see poor George for what he is."

Loic's smile had a seasoning of sneer. "You are way off. Master George is far from the natural choice. He may be the eldest of you boys, but that means nothing. No, you'll find that Castor or Findern takes the post if Patrick deserts it, and a creditable steward either would make, for they are men grown: wise and steady. And, of course, popular figures, with whom I'd peacefully work. And that is what your father will require. He wishes no quarrel among the men that is not of his own making."

The look of pleasant interest had frozen somewhat; the only sign that the shaft had struck home.

"Since you *are* here, Master Aymer …" Loic altered his own trajectory. "Why Tailboys?"

"Tailboys?"

"Even Sir Arthur's defence has fallen silent. Not that Castor is gifted with insight in this case, for he has a blind spot where you're concerned. I knew the culprit from the first. Did Sir Leonard insult you? You quarrelled? Over a woman, perhaps."

"Women bore me. I have never fought over a woman, nor ever would." The pale eyes roamed Loic's face. "Tailboys's killer is out of range; we can all of us sleep easy."

A preposterous mischief. Loic laughed, allowing free rein to the scorn. "You wish to make yourself a better man? Casting aspersions on Hal is not the way to do it. Hal had no reason to injure Tailboys."

"Sir Loic … you're a clever man. No one doubts it. But even you do not know everything."

"Master Aymer … I've duties to attend to. Arthur is well disposed towards you and, where he leads, Walter Findern follows. Go and pay court to the next steward, if you think Patrick a lost cause."

"But then," Aymer continued, as if he hadn't heard, "my father is a law unto himself. Your youth and inexperience didn't prevent him making you his chamberlain; neither did he consult the senior men, so I hear. But his faith has been rewarded. I know how well you love him. And I am just the same as he. Don't keep me at arm's length, Loic." Still the smile was sardonic, but Aymer chose to take its presence as a spur. "Come, friend, let there be good fellowship between us. Give me the kiss of peace."

Before Loic could protest the touch or flinch away, Aymer was on his feet, fingers hooked at the Frenchman's neck, lips scalding Loic's mouth. Aymer's eyes were open; Loic's eyes were wide. "I thank you," said Aymer evenly, and sauntered out.

Loic wiped his mouth with the back of his hand.

* * *

169

The reappearance of the hair shirt was a source of interest in that placid household, and of some consternation also. It seemed that Dove had held his peace, for Dicken Boulter and Clement Petyfer cornered Hal as soon as the news spread, interrogating him with urgency. *Was it Colchester?* He must say it wasn't Colchester! God forbid Sir Triston had discovered the true purpose of those visits.

"Of course not." Hal elbowed past them, crossly. "Otherwise you two would be wearing one of these." He tugged the collar of the hated vestment, triggering a ripple of itches down his back.

"What, then?"

"Never you mind."

Grace was full of soothing pity. She and Hal were seated in their accustomed places in Lady Honor's chamber. Honor and Sibel were sorting yarn, chattering together in their usual mindless fashion. In the early days, Hal was circumspect in his aunt's presence, but there was truly no need to censor one's words, for she comprehended nothing beyond the most commonplace of utterances. Hal wondered, again, how his uncle tolerated the lady with such patience and good humour. *Intelligence*, he thought, *must surely be foremost among a wife's desirable qualities.*

"For what it's worth, you have my sympathy, Master Hal." Grace interrupted, at last, the aggrieved rant. "Your choice was misguided, but you were trying, after your own fashion, to obey Sir Triston. How is any man to begin to think of a potential wife without thinking of her first as a woman? It does seem harsh. He is brooding on the Pastons, no doubt. There was a recent scandal, hereabouts."

"And I suppose I should shun your company," he grumbled, "or I shall be hauled up over this also!"

"Not so," said she, lightly. "Our master is delighted if the servants make a match among themselves. He says it steadies the household. Master Cardingham's second wife was a gentlewoman of Lady Honor's. Sir Triston tried to foist Mistress Sibel on Master Boulter, with what result you may imagine."

Hal snorted with laughter. "A stout widow, ten years his senior!"

"Quite. And, of course, he is forever pushing Master Petyfer into my path."

Hal laughed again. "Nothing less likely, eh?"

She tilted her face to his. "Oh, I don't know. Clement Petyfer never did require much pushing. I may take him in the end. Probably I shall."

It was rather horrible: clearly the poor girl had no notion of the banter that went on behind her back.

She read his face with ease. "Don't trouble yourself, my friend. I don't want your pity. Clement has a sharp tongue and an urge to amuse his fellows, but it's a different story when we're alone. He trots after me; he can't keep his hands to himself. No one else will have me and I don't want to die unwed."

Embarrassed and sorry, he turned the subject. "In truth, Mistress Grace, all of this has led me to question my position here at Crawshay. I held a more prestigious place at Alnwick Castle when I was barely out of my boyhood. I'm growing older, and yet I'm sinking. And Sir Triston being so overbearing, and this torment ever against my skin ..."

Her brow puckered. "Where would you go, Master Hal? You've no money, I warrant. Your father's in exile. Surely you won't go back to the Earl of Northumberland?"

He thought of Harry Percy, who had been so good to him, and he thought of the wide emptiness of Northumberland. He thought of Waryn, of Grandfather Prynne, of poor Dorcas, whom he had, frankly, ruined, and he thought of his small sons. He'd return and gather them to him, one day, when the saplings were become tall trees. "No. I won't go back to Alnwick. And I don't feel I can return to my father, either." There was an alternative, of course. He could offer his service elsewhere. Not necessarily a greater household, just one with greater potential: he could offer his service to Simon Loys. The impulse had come to him that past night, in a dream; he woke with a shout of laughter. Parley his way within the house – that fine new house of Sevenhill – and wreak his promised havoc. "I must find something purposeful to do with my life, for nothing will ever happen here at Crawshay. It's so pleasant and dreary. No quarrels, or rivalries, even, among the men. Do you think me ungrateful?"

"Hatefully so! This world is perilous and full of woe. If you have found peace, you should thank God for His singular favour."

She had never asked his story but, finding him in a reflective mood, Grace did so now. He told it all, confessing adventures and misdemeanours alike in a fine frenzy of honesty: the blackmail of Lady Eleanor; his pusillanimous desertion of Dorcas and their boys, without provision or farewell; the house-wrecking and the proud soldiery; his love for Alice and the painful rivalry with his father – a self-inflicted wound; the killing of Tailboys; the catastrophe that was Aymer; the theft from Lord Clifford and the theft from Captain Carling. It was half-dark in the chamber by the time he had done, the two others long gone.

"Good God, Hal," said Grace, quietly, when silence had settled. She moved to touch his cheek with her fingers, but didn't quite reach. "What an awful inventory, and you so young! You'd need to battle the Moors to atone for those sins, I don't doubt. For now, the best you can do is lie quiet in this backwater; try not to add to the burdens on your conscience."

For a few moments, they sat in the gloom, engulfed in their separate thoughts – hers full of good sense and his, not – until Dove appeared in the doorway. Sir Triston wished to see Hal.

"Ledgers?"

Dove shook his head. "On a private matter, says the master."

"What have I done this time?" demanded Hal, omitting to thank the manservant for his discretion on the last occasion.

He returned from his uncle's chamber in very different spirits, joining Stephen and Gregory in the parlour before a merry fire. When Lady Clifford entered with Grace in tow, Hal favoured his friend with a broad grin, unbuttoning the neck of his undershirt, flashing her a glimpse of the dark curls licking his collarbones – his own soft pelt; no loathsome penitential scourge. Beatrice caught his glance across the room, and he closed his eyes: a slow blink of gratitude.

* * *

"Don't you dare! Don't even think of it." No *Monseigneur*, and the tone was irritable.

Surreptitiously, Castor was watching Loic; when was he ever not? Lord Robert, though, was barely attending, roaring encouragement at the juniors – his boys and the household men; delighted laughter or howls of disappointment.

"What did you say?" asked Clifford eventually, evenly, when the players paused to rest.

"The knee must be allowed to heal. How would we manage if you did some permanent damage? It is a selfish impulse."

"Ah, I'm on the mend. You play for me, then."

"Shall I?"

Clifford smirked. "I'll watch you."

At once, Loic was eagerness personified, beckoning Benet to unlace his boots. Arthur Castor turned sourly from the gratified grin. Loic wriggled his toes – none of them had any suitable footwear – and then, wretchedly self-conscious, he jogged on to the field of play, a patch of undulating, mole-hillocked meadow at the foot of Salisbury Crags. He wasn't too bad: swift and bold, and helped to appear effortless by Aymer, who would keep passing the ball, feeding him easy shots, charging down any Scot who looked likely to tackle the Frenchman.

Castor frowned at the pair. Others may be content to live in a fog of confusion, but he was unused to the sensation.

"Watch Aymer," Clifford directed. The lad jabbed a spindly opponent in the eye. There was a spout of blood. "He does everything excellently well. A son to be proud of."

"I am watching, Lord Robert. I am. I wasn't aware there was such fellowship between the two."

"You mean Loic and he? Just so, for Aymer is grown into a man, Arthur, is he not? I cannot regret Hal's departure. Not at all."

Castor clicked his tongue and pondered the odd pairing in silence. He favoured Loic and Aymer both, in different ways, to different degrees and for different reasons; he wasn't keen for the three to become a triangle. Under a barrage of misfortunes, the household was breaking down and reforming itself in ways that were strange and disconcerting. Probably Arthur would find himself promoted, shortly, to steward. Once, the pinnacle of his ambition. Now he prayed merely for the world to stop spinning and, if Patrick Nield would only rest easy in his allotted place, that would be an auspicious start.

Eventually, purple clouds billowed up from the West; harbingers of a ferocious rainstorm. The light began to fade. The Scots players acknowledged themselves defeated and the young Englishmen trooped from the field, Aymer's arm draped about Loic's neck, triumphant.

* * *

Her belly was huge now, filled to bursting, the child clambering to turn in laboured toil. Simon was very gentle. Not in words, of course, but betraying himself by his touch. And then, just when Alice felt her time must surely be upon her, he made ready to leave for London. She was restless and fretful; she did not wish him to go, and so far forgot herself as to tell him so.

"This female hubbub is beyond anything endurable. You'd not find my presence in the house alleviates any of your trouble." He pressed the small hands to his lips. "The Duke of Gloucester requires my attendance; I have the building work at Sevenhill to oversee and, when you send word of the child's safe arrival, I'll secure the Duke as godfather. Others will follow him, I've no doubt, and we shall do well for the little one."

When he kissed her brow, she clung to him. "Could you not conjure me some remedy for the pain before you go? I am so small in stature and the babe is enormous. You must know of some charm that can help me, sir!"

He looked quite unusually startled, then incredulous and then he began to laugh. "Sometimes I have thought you are wiser, but no – I see I'm misled by chance words. You are quite as stupid as my other wives. There is no charm that can help you, you foolish girl! Drink a great draft of wine is my advice, and that is all the magic any man can offer. Wait till I tell Brini of this latest idiocy!" And then he left her, still laughing.

174

"He'll be sorry if I die in childbed!" said Alice to her gentlewomen.

"What makes you think so?" demanded Sir Simon's daughter, before the others could answer. "Master Considine says Father wasn't sorry when his other wives died; not in the least. And besides, Madam, if you do your sums you'll see that Father must certainly be back before the child comes: you were not married until May and so you cannot be brought to bed before the end of winter." As ever, Catharine disregarded the array of looks, hostile or incredulous. She clung close to Alice, always, careless of the lady's impatient ill will.

The girl was still dogging her stepmother's footsteps when the babe announced its intention to appear, several weeks late, casting further confusion over its own paternity.

"Get out!" shrieked Alice, between grunts. Catharine was staring in horror at the noblewoman – sweating and purple and beyond common courtesy.

Joanna had began to push the girl bodily from the room, when they were interrupted by a bad-tempered wailing, and turned to find that the heir of Lancaster had made his way into the world: a fine boy, just as Aymer had not, in fact, predicted.

Peter Considine dispatched the news to London, where Sir Simon recruited the Duke of Gloucester as godparent. The child was christened in the tiny church of Avonby with proxies standing in for the illustrious sponsors. He was named *Edward*, like so many thousands of others, in honour of the King, though his mother had wished for *Henry*. But by this time, Alice knew nothing of the world beyond her bed, for she had fallen gravely ill, the village midwife bearing death into the bedchamber on her dirty hands.

The days dragged on. By the time Loys appeared at the bedside, Alice was out of danger. He cradled the frail body in his arms and carried his wife to the window where she was dazzled by the light, and winced and blinked and struggled even to see the snow which lay thigh-deep across the brown moors, transforming the country into a treacherous paradise.

Loys returned her to the comfort of the bed and peered into the cradle. There lay the infant, widely alert. Edward's hair was unusually light for a newborn, his eyes an indeterminate colour, though certainly not black or chestnut. And if he looked nothing like Robert Clifford, neither did he resemble Simon Loys – another putative father – except, perhaps, for a certain sardonic cast to his expression. The babe eyed the standing man, sidelong and measuring. "I am the King of England," he seemed to say. "*Grovel.*"

Loys clicked his tongue and turned away. Waving the gentlewomen from the room, he stripped and climbed between the sheets where he tried his best to warm the lean and chilly girl within, who closed her eyes, exhausted.

* * *

Hal rode out from Crawshay through the light snow, attended by Moppet and Barnaby, heading west on an interesting errand. His cousin Beatrice was betrothed at last, and letters must be dispatched about the neighbourhood, proclaiming the good news. Most were borne by messengers, but Hal had offered to carry one particular message himself, for its recipient was Nicholas Loys, and the destination was Danehill, which stood, so Hal understood, within sight of Simon Loys's new edifice of Sevenhill.

An interest in building was Hal's excuse which, though it satisfied Sir Triston, didn't satisfy Grace. "You're the strangest creature, Master Hal. Your manner is so steady and sensible that you wrong-foot all who think they know you. The truth is quite the opposite: a very reckless fellow. You're set upon a path towards danger. I can sense it."

"My mother died when I was nine years old, but I'm lucky to have acquired another in you, Mistress Grace. No harm can come while you watch over me." He raised her hand to his lips with breezy affection.

After several hours' riding, they came upon Danehill. It could fairly be termed a manor house, though its origins were clearly as a prosperous farmhouse, extended at various times, giving it a haphazard appearance. The setting was very fine, upon a good hill, in fertile land, with a commanding southerly view. Hal was shown to the parlour, which was low and not grand, with windows on two sides. There, at the table sat two men, playing at dice.

One was young, tall and fair; the other, short and dark and fleshy, with protuberant eyes and a roguish face.

Hal bowed and introduced himself. "Which of you gentlemen might be Master Loys, if you please? I bear a letter."

Nicholas rose. "I am he." He broke the seal and scanned Sir Triston's words. "The betrothal of Mistress Beatrice to my sister Jane's son, Hugo Sheringham. I knew of this already; it's been in the offing for months. Why has Triston bothered to tell me again? There will be a letter for you also, Piers, I would think, bearing this stale news."

"It's obvious, isn't it? Since he can't get the two boys decently wed, he must proclaim a minor triumph." The other man raised his heavy, half-moon brows at Hal. "Piers Brixhemar," he pronounced. "Where's mine?"

"Ah, I believe there is a letter for you, sir, but it's been taken by separate messenger."

He examined their faces and he recalled his uncle's words. These two had fought alongside him at Barnet, but in the retinue of Jack de Vere, Alice's brother. And gained knighthoods, only to lose them again at the triumphant return of Edward of York. Nicholas Loys looked nothing like Simon Loys. Nothing at all, and Hal liked him the better for it.

"Oh yes? So what brings you here, Master FitzClifford?" demanded Brixhemar. "You come to spy on Nick Loys, yet you don't deign to visit me and my uncle Rohips?"

"Nothing of the sort, sir. I have an interest in building work, and the whole neighbourhood is talking of the great new house of Sevenhill. I thought I might take a look and deliver the letter while I'm out this way."

"It's not a new house," said Nicholas, reflexively, as if he'd made the correction many times over. "There's a perfectly good house on the site already. My brother is remodelling and extending. I shan't tell him the neighbourhood's talking of it. He'd enjoy that."

No love lost there, thought Hal, with sharp interest.

"Neighbourhood?" repeated Brixhemar. "The whole county is talking of it. Not so much admiring its beauty as wondering how an impecunious northern knight has raised the funds, and from whom. No doubt your brother puts on a fine show before others; they dine on bread and water when no one's watching."

Nicholas smiled and shook his head.

"Shall we walk up, then, and introduce Master FitzClifford to this folly?" suggested Brixhemar. "They say the front is finished."

Hal retrieved his cloak and followed the two men on the crunching path that led to the peak of the hill behind the house.

"FitzClifford." Piers Brixhemar was walking backwards up the track. "A baseborn son of Robert Clifford, then? You certainly resemble the man. Possessed of both eyes, of course, and not nearly so pretty. Then again … who is? One of his army of brave boys. And a turncoat, abandoning your father to join the only Clifford who backed the right king."

"I'm his eldest son, sir," Hal said, a little stiff. "I'd no wish to spend the rest of my life in exile, so we parted company."

The other two exchanged glances.

"Here it is, then," said Nicholas, gesturing to the west.

The snow had petered out and the house stood plain before them, set upon a matching rise. It was large and handsome, and quite of the moment. If there were older parts, they were buried deep. Not all the frontage could be seen from this vantage, for a giant oak draped the house with black and spidery branches.

"They say there's a contraption to pump water uphill for Simon's bath," remarked Brixhemar. "Newfangled stuff." He nudged his friend. "Or sorcery, possibly …"

Nicholas clicked his tongue.

"Cauldron. Wand. Newt."

Hal shot a sideways glance at Piers Brixhemar; words were still sloshing out, though Nicholas had turned from the flow, facing Hal with his back to the house.

"What are those odd hillocks to the side, Master Loys?"

"The barrows? The seven hills for which it's named. There are ancient warriors buried beneath – so they say – and golden grave goods. If Simon hears the rumours, he'll dig it all up, curse or no curse. So hold your tongue, Piers, if you please." Nicholas glanced eastwards, behind the visitors. "We have a mound of our own, of course: the *Danehill*. Only the one. It is larger and more shallow and I have left it well alone."

"And when will all be ready, Master Loys? When does your brother mean to settle in Essex?" Hal waited, breathless.

"Soon, I fear. He's driving the craftsmen mercilessly. My sister-in-law fell gravely ill, but now out of danger, thanks be to God. When every possible comfort has been installed, and Lady Alice is strong enough to make the journey, then I suppose he will come."

Hal wiped his palms on his cloak. The beloved had lain at the threshold of death while he knew nothing of it. Life was short and uncertain, and he must seize his chance.

* * *

Alice was young and her health rebounded, though she was as yet too thin for comfort. Casting about for a remedy, Loys ran through physician after physician, finally dismissing his cook; bringing another up from York. For weeks after, every meal was a succession of her favourite dishes, tedious to others and alarming to the chaplain, for the household seemed to have abandoned fish entirely, and even Fridays saw an impious parade of succulent meats.

In due course, Blanche, too, was brought to bed, and delivered of a healthy son, and Sir Hugh was drowned in happiness. Alice and her husband were godparents, and the child was named *Simon*, of course. The two infants shared a wet-nurse: foster brothers, destined, surely, to grow together as lifelong friends.

The building work at Sevenhill continued apace. When the house was but a month from completion, Simon surprised his wife by bidding her make ready for a journey, not south to Essex but north to Alnwick.

"My son is page to the Earl, as I probably told you. I mean to fetch him away: I'll place him in Gloucester's household, if I can. And you must accompany me to Alnwick. Percy once scorned me as a suitor for his sister. I want to show you off."

"Lady Eleanor Percy? I did not know you'd sought her hand, sir."

"Oh, I know why you're interested, child: you're as transparent as a pane of glass. She was intended for Robert Clifford just lately, and they say she made a great fool of herself over him. You'd like to take a look at the lady, would you not?"

Alice could not control the blood that heated her cheeks, mortifying her.

"Perhaps you've not heard," he continued, slick as oil, "but there's a strange tale doing the rounds in London."

She shook her head and studied the floor.

"They say that when Clifford travelled north, he seized the lady and carried her off to Lindisfarne, delivering her back to Alnwick when he'd had his fill of her."

Alice had turned on him in dismay.

"No doubt you'll be keen to question Lady Eleanor, and discover all you can." He remained motionless for some time in his chair before the window, hands clasped, watching as she wandered, aimless, about their chamber, plucking up objects and setting them down, unseeing. When, finally, he spoke, his voice was quiet and hoarse. "You told me once that he was not your lover, yet I sense that you dwell constantly on Robert Clifford. This is neither wise nor healthy. By now you should be reconciled to our marriage, thinking only of me in that light. You could take pleasure in my arms if you would but allow yourself: there is no shame in it. There's little I would not do towards your happiness. Believe me when I tell you that Robert Clifford is not thinking of you, and cares nothing for the misery he causes."

Such speech had cost him dear. Were she older and wiser, she would acknowledge it. "You presume to know what is in my mind, and in his, but you know nothing of it! True, I am your wife. I have submitted my body to you. You cannot control my thoughts and you should not try."

"Very well, you little fool. You deserve no hand of friendship from me, and you shall have none." He pushed himself up as if to quit the room but stopped, with an ugly smile, on the threshold. "There is something you should know. When Sir Lawrence Welford last wrote, he corrected a certain misapprehension of mine. Let me share this with you. Last year, when we heard news of the defeat of Roger Vaughan, I was hurrying us away from Dyffryn Hall. I expected, as you did, that Clifford would come for you. The man burned with jealousy and rage; I was sure of it. No such thing! We needn't have hastened, for Clifford never came to Dyffryn. He drunkenly despoiled the town of Chepstow, beheaded Vaughan and then rode away, directly north, heading for Skipton with no hint of a detour. You were utterly forgotten: out of sight and out of mind. For Eleanor Percy he turned aside – but not, little wife, for you."

* * *

As Piers Brixhemar lived at Roliford, in the direction of Crawshay, he chose to ride home in Hal's company. "Come back with me and meet my uncle, Sir Mark Rohips. Nigh on sixty years old and a childless widower. I've been his heir for ever, until last year, when his wife ups and dies. Now I spend all my time trying to stop him breeding just to spite me. He's a cantankerous old shit."

Hal laughed. "Is your uncle likely to marry again, Master Brixhemar?"

"Most probably. Perhaps he can't get it up, though, so I live in hope. Now tell me, young Hal, what caused the breach with your father, that gentle giant. I'm most discreet."

Hal laughed again, with no intention of testing him. "Do you know my father, sir?"

Piers raised his chin and folded his arms. "Ah, here am I, Black Clifford: the most dangerous man in England. I swear Piers Brixhemar shat himself when Jack de Vere introduced us in London last spring."

Hal's mouth fell open. It was the most unexpected, unlikely, astonishingly accurate imitation of Robert Clifford. For one terrifying moment, the man himself rode beside him, in the flesh. "My God, Master Brixhemar – you're quite the mimic! I've never witnessed anything like it!"

"I have some small talent in that direction. My only talent, in truth, but it does make me popular. And who is this?" Now he became Sir Triston for Hal's amusement, every foible nicely observed.

"The only man I ever saw do anything alike is my brother Guy, who can transform himself at will into his twin, Aymer."

"Twins? Identical twins? Forgive me, but that doesn't sound greatly challenging."

"Perhaps not, Master Brixhemar, but somehow they don't resemble each other at all – not until Guy decides that they shall."

"Call me *Piers*. A mere steward, like yourself – at least for now. Don't be misled by my grand manner. I have a feeling we'll be great friends."

"You're a steward? Trueborn, and your uncle's heir? That's unusual."

"Well … my mother's marriage didn't delight her kin, shall we say? Father was a Fleming; a cloth merchant and, as Uncle Rohips constantly reminds me, not a prosperous one. Mercifully, they died when I was an infant. Enough about me. You were telling me *your* history."

"Little to tell. I served Old Percy as a lad and, afterwards, John Neville. When Neville lost Alnwick, I became under-steward to the Earl of Northumberland until last year, when I joined my father's household. I took the field at Barnet like yourself, but Lord Clifford's a difficult man to live with, and I didn't want to follow him into exile. Sir Triston was willing to take me in." He shrugged.

"That's three times you've changed sides already, and you can't be more than twenty!"

"Changed sides? Oh!" Hal laughed, a mite offended. "I don't think of it like that. I stay the same, and the world changes around me."

"Is that so? Very well. Don't think I shall let up. I'll find out where your loyalties lie, if it's the last thing I do." Brixhemar smirked. "So, you've heard the latest news of your father? No? Clifford's ardent admirer Lancelot Threlkeld ambushed him at Thirsk. A miserable failure. And then your father popped up at Belforth near the Scots border, tortured James Thwaite to death and slew his young sons. For some reason I don't understand, Northumberland's sister was there also. They say he carried the lady off to an abbey and ravished her on the altar. What a busy man your father is. Perhaps you couldn't keep up?"

"Very possibly."

"Why are you so interested in Simon Loys? Is he an enemy of yours?"

Holy Mother of God, thought Hal. *And they say I'm curious. This one, so sharp he may do himself an injury.* "Ah, no. I just wanted to see his house."

"Oh – I have it! The man has married Alice de Vere, hasn't he? Stole her away from your father. That lady is lighter of a bonny son, so they say. A brother of yours, no?"

"No!" shouted Hal, before he had a grip on himself. "That child is the heir of Lancaster." Beads of sweat sprang out on his forehead. Just here the road wound through a shady copse, the trees bending to meet above their heads. In one nervy moment, every whorl and knothole became an ear. He could, and should, and would, be more careful in future. Much more careful.

Brixhemar was beaming. "Is he indeed? I'm not so sure he's Somerset's son. I was watching Lady Alice and your father at Jack de Vere's house last Spring. Whispering together; creeping off into corners concealing themselves. Then the Duke turns up, all shouty. Next we hear, daggers drawn in the street. Thrilling. We'll contain our impatience until Sir Simon arrives at Sevenhill and then we shall delve in, eh? Find out why the lady abandoned her lover."

Hal stared straight ahead between his horse's ears. *Oh God.*

* * *

Alice had long forgiven Robert Clifford for failing to prevent her marriage, besieged at Chepstow as he was. But it was impossible to forgive him now; now that she knew the truth: he had never come for her, for all that she'd lingered so over his imagined heartbreak. She felt as though the ground had collapsed beneath her feet, and she was falling.

Simon was right, of course. Of course he was. Robert Clifford was not thinking of her, not ever, and did not deserve that she should think of him either and so, sickened, she ceased to do so.

For much of the way up to Alnwick, Alice rode behind her husband, relishing the freedom of movement, the return of health and strength. Loys was as sardonic as ever, belittling her just as usual, but here too the ground had shifted and, if his touches were as frequent, they were not as warm.

"This is the second marriage in which my husband has turned from me," said she in a low voice to Constance, as her niece undressed her that evening in a guest room of a little inn. "I feel I have hurt him, something I did not believe possible."

Constance pursed her lips. She might venture to advise her aunt – if the lady's feelings were not so utterly opaque. One fact, though, was certain: clinging to Robert Clifford was a vain exercise even before this latest blow. What matter whether the man had or had not wandered the empty and echoing hall at Dyffryn, searching, forlorn, for his lost love? None of them would ever see his face again. And Sir Simon: very probably his pride had been wounded, stiff-necked as he was; he would recover. He could hardly help himself.

* * *

Aymer and his faction had spent the evening plying Peter, youngest and greenest of the FitzCliffords, with ale until the lad could barely stand. Though quiet and awkward beneath his father's eye, once he'd sunk sufficient liquor a thought had but to signal its distant approach and the words were already out of his mouth, brave, blithe and offensive.

There they were, Peter and his four companions, extravagantly loud in their corner of the tavern in this alien city, attracting a great deal of notice. By now it was only the richness of their clothes and their formidable size that shielded them. Had they been less intoxicated, the hostility would have obtruded itself as more than a low background hum. Eventually the lads prepared to move on. Richie was seeking after challenges to set before Peter sobered, keen to play the puppet-master for once, and not the puppet.

They were followed into the street. A crowd of young men tramped close behind, and now jostled among them with broad curses. The speech they barely followed, but the intent was plain enough and Richie and Guy felled four without hesitation. Though a few others drew blades, it seemed the natives had lost any serious will to engage and, backing away, took off up the Grassmarket towards the yawning blackness of the castle, careering into the dark mouth of a wynd. Bonnets trampled underfoot, hair salted with sleet, Richie and Guy were all grim swagger. Two of the Scots lads pushed to their feet and were knocked down again.

Contained behind Will and Peter, senses dulled, Aymer had not felt the knife at his belt. Of a sudden, he was gone, sprinting after the departing footsteps; a wild burst of speed from a standing start. The wynd plunged sharply away and Aymer vanished into its stinking belly with his companions bawling after. Guy leading, they slipped and scurried down the echoing sandstone alley. At last they found him, astride the thief's limp body, the head gushing into a black gutter dammed with rubbish. In Aymer's hand, his purse, brandished aloft in triumph.

There followed one of those scenes that Richie so hated.

"*What is it*? What the *fuck* have you there? Oh no, *no…*" Guy hauled his twin to his feet and shook him with violence, one hand grasping for Aymer's purse. The twins strove together a frantic moment until the leather pouch spun from their clutches, spewing its contents across the cobbles.

Richie crouched at once, sourly alert to this latest mystery. He ran his fingers about in the half-dark. Several mean coins; in a matter of hours, they'd run through the month's tiny allowance. Nothing there to spark such fury. He looked up in bafflement. Peter was vomiting with gloomy patience against a wall. The three others had fixed on a glint of metal beside Richie's toe and the twins sprang for it at once. Richie swooped down: it was a chain and some kind of pendant, set with a good and glittering stone. He dangled the dainty piece and laid it in his thick palm.

Wondering, he raised his eyes to Aymer as vast swathes of the story fell into place. Richie knew the jewel at once. Its colour – when viewed in full sun – was a clear and conspicuous green, a little bluish, perhaps; a little greyish; more sage than grass; a striking memento of its owner's emerald eyes.

At the foot of the alley, echoes chimed against stone. Aymer snatched the pendant from Richie's hand.

"Go!" Guy hurried them all before him, back to the entryway, where whorls of snowfeathers fluttered in a crescent of lantern light. Shadows pressed forward. They were trapped.

* * *

When the party reached Alnwick, there was no Earl at the barbican to greet them; it was not to be expected. Little Kit Loys could be seen from a distance, hopping on the wall, waiting to embrace his father. Touched by the child's unaffected joy, Alice paused to watch as Loys lifted him, and held him close a moment, then brought him forward. Kit took her hand, calling her *Mother*, earning no reprimand. He was a handsome boy, small and slight, with soft eyes.

She turned away, smiling, to find a ghost at her elbow. It was Edmond Beaufort's steward, Sir Gabriel Appledore.

"My lady." The man bowed very low, as he would bow to a duchess and not the wife of a fellow knight. Loys smirked, gratified. "Sir Simon. In the name of the Earl, I welcome you to Alnwick. I'll conduct you to your chambers."

Loys turned to follow Appledore but, as Alice had not moved, he strode into her. When he motioned with impatient hands, his wife ignored him, gazing after the servant's retreating back. The man had turned a corner. Loys pushed her on. Behind, among the gentlewomen, a low hubbub.

When they were shown within, Sir Gabriel bowed again and left the guests. The door closed and he paused a moment outside, pressing his quaking fingers to his face. The Earl had given him not nearly sufficient warning of her coming, and he could not compose himself. In truth there was no warning that would have paved the way. Soon he must face her again, but he had a little time in hand. As he walked to his chamber, the familiar feelings were creeping upon him, threatening and unmanly, and his pace quickened.

Sweating, Appledore reached the sanctuary of his room, and pulled out the chamber pot just as the retching overcame him. He lowered himself to the bed, muffled his clammy face in a pillow and – loosing his desperate grip – began to cry.

Within the guest chamber, Loys clapped his hands for attention. "Enough! What are you hens fluttering about?"

"Sir Gabriel Appledore, husband. He was the Duke's steward. I can't guess what he is doing here."

Loys closed his eyes. "The *Duke*? I've warned you often enough, you little fool. Call Beaufort by that false title *one more time*, and I shall be forced to drive the message home. Gabriel Appledore is now Northumberland's under-steward; you'd have heard it, had you been listening."

"The Earl's under-steward? Lord Clifford's son Waryn was under-steward here. So what has become of him?"

"*Woman.*" He enunciated it with icy slowness. "I confess it would give me enormous satisfaction to strike you, just at present. This is your final warning."

Alice gazed at her husband, unhearing, while the unknown and absent FitzClifford took up residence in her mind. She was far from Alnwick by now, through sunlit woods toward Tintern Abbey; cradled in the crook of Robert's arm, her ears filled with the man's rumbling voice: "*I have other sons than these; Waryn is now under-steward at Alnwick in Hal's stead; the rest are too young to ride with me.*"

The gentlewomen shuffled. "Lady Alice," said Blanche, "the households of many a noble must lately have broken up; just as we have Sir Hugh and Sir Andrew among us, Sir Gabriel likewise will have sought a position. Now he'll be looking in vain for Lady Ullerton, I suppose. Sir Gabriel was betrothed to your cousin Elizabeth, sir," she said, to Loys. "But God has divided them, alas."

"He isn't looking for Lady Ullerton," murmured Constance to Blanche. "He's just trying to avoid us."

"Hugh! If this Appledore harbours any notion of marriage with Elizabeth Ullerton, put him right at once. My cousin is suitably employed with the

Lady Margaret of Anjou in the Tower of London; make him understand that I would view any such union as a personal affront."

In due course Sir Gabriel returned to conduct the party to the great chamber. Constance was right: the man was behaving oddly, moving with an awkward rigidity as though he'd been left too long in the rain. He would not look beyond Sir Simon, let alone greet the gentlewomen with whom he'd lived for months. Common courtesy demanded more.

Into the wide apartment: the Earl was there with a number of his gentlemen. His greeting was courteous and inquisitive. Loys watched Harry Percy's eyes flick to his bonnet; just as quick, they twitched away, but not quick enough: Percy had taken in the White Boar of Gloucester at a glance, and turned aside, brimming with thought.

Then the moment so long anticipated: the door swung and admitted Eleanor Percy. Alice knew she had herself well in hand and she knew that the other lady had not. Northumberland's sister was quite breathless and agitated; it was pitiable. Lady Eleanor believed precisely the same of Lady Alice. Neither recalled anything of the conversation, and then it was time for the guests to go and rest before dinner. Alice lay down upon the bed, closed her eyes and contemplated her adversary. Some inches taller than she; thin, with a gamine and confident grace; large blue-grey eyes in a long face; lovely hands; clear skin; crooked teeth; lank hair. Alice wished that her own hair were on display, in all its lustrous array.

Sir Simon lowered himself beside her on to the bed, reading her. There was a hint of the earlier strain in his voice. "No, she is not as beautiful as you; but why – *why* – does it still matter?"

Alice opened her eyes. "Forgive me, Simon. It does not matter."

* * *

"Well now. The lady is not as I expected; not at all."

"Indeed no, Harry!" His sister turned on him with alacrity, undoing all her good work. "A dab of a thing, not worth a second glance. It just shows how little one can trust the report of others."

188

Of course his provocation was deliberate, to test if she would rise to it. Eleanor hadn't risen; she had leapt. In rushed all his angry misgivings. "Pretty," Percy continued, "and no man would fail to mark it."

"You think so? I'm astonished."

"But a child, nonetheless; gentle and quiet. Now I come to think on it, it's not so strange. If any creature would tame a great brute like Robert Clifford, it would probably be just such a one as Lady Alice – all delicate fragility."

"What an absurd thought! They were never lovers. Lord Clifford avowed it himself." Her voice had escaped her control.

Eleanor was contemplating her brother's dry and powdery scalp. He was seated, as usual, with what began as a disguise against a want of inches and gradually became his habitual preference. As yet, the man was slight and sinewy. In her imaginings, though, his habits left him sluggish, his shoulders spindling, a soft bulk settling about his hips like a pear. Perhaps his sister could sense somewhere within the Earl the beginnings of the end; his heart would give out, if only he were let to live long enough.

Eleanor was standing – contrariwise. He glanced up through his brows. The tell-tale stain in the sheer skin of her cheeks; the fervid breathing. She would make herself dramatically, wretchedly ill – again. Not so long ago his sister was an ally; a quick and daring accomplice. She had become a wasting asset.

* * *

On the next day, the two ladies advanced upon the field to commence the ordeal by combat. Eleanor was fully conscious of the desire to crush and vanquish; Alice, less so, for she could boast nothing of the other's honesty and she was hobbled before the start.

"Do you hear any news of your brother, Lady Alice? Is he in Scotland, still?"

A conventional opening thrust; she might have expected something more original. "I believe so, Lady Eleanor."

189

"How Jack de Vere must thank God for Robert Clifford's arrival. And the FitzCliffords also; a veritable army of virile men."

Elyn shifted in her seat, as did Marjorie Verrier.

"Lord Robert told me of the escape after Tewkesbury. He told me everything, though he confessed it was agony to speak of it."

Silence.

"He was greatly shocked when he heard you had married, of course – your unborn child being lost to the cause; that babe whom Robert held to be the heir of Lancaster."

Constance and Blanche were staring at Eleanor as though she had lost her reason and Blanche coughed, forcefully, jolting Alice to her senses.

"My husband would prefer me not to speak of this, I'm sure," Alice murmured. "Forgive me, Lady Eleanor."

Eleanor tossed a withering glance in Blanche's direction, returned to Alice and then turned slowly back. There was no mistaking it: at the gentlewoman's breast lay a crucifix set with seed pearls, an unusual piece and plainly, inexcusably, a twin to the one at her own throat. Her first, inconsequential grief was not that Robert should have seduced this woman – as he clearly had – but that he should not have bothered to distinguish the rank of his lovers. Oh, this was Robert, in all his glory. Arrogant and infuriating.

Her voice sharpened irritably as she groped to conceal her own cross beneath the neck of her gown. The chain was too short; it kept peeping out. "But perhaps you had not wished to be rescued, Lady Alice? Perhaps your loyalties lay only with the house of York? There can be no other explanation for this astonishing behaviour."

A full frontal assault, now; offensive in every sense. "Oh?" Alice stood, colour kindling, and walked to the window. She swept the dust from the sill. "You are mistaken, my lady. Lord Clifford knew nothing of my marriage when he rode for the North Country. It is he who abandoned my child." She had trespassed into fiercely dangerous ground. Joanna and Blanche glanced at the door. Constance half rose and sank again.

Eleanor tittered angrily. "Hardly! He knew full well of your betrayal. He, of all men, to be misused in such a way! All his life dedicated to this cause, and then to be served such a trick. He told me that you crushed his spirit. It has devastated him."

Alice stood for quite a time, regarding the rolling hills of Northumberland – or not regarding them. When she turned back, her eyes had filled with tears.

"Oh. Come, Lady Alice, into my chamber where we can speak alone."

* * *

"Forgive me. I did not intend to distress you, but I have witnessed his pain at first hand; it's unbearable to see a strong man so broken." Eleanor had contrived to remove the cross during the walk to her chamber and now laid it on the table, covering it first with her hand, and then with a small coffer to weight the mischievous object.

There was further silence. The lack of curiosity – or the abundant self-restraint – was beginning to smart against Eleanor's nerves. "At one time I thought it was love for you that had left him wounded and wretched, but he said not; his only care was for the heir of Lancaster. When he learned of your marriage and understood that the child was lost to him, he had no further concern for you, and rode away from Chepstow."

"I am glad you have told me this," said Alice slowly. "For until now I believed that Lord Clifford had abandoned my child without good reason, and that caused me so much pain."

Eleanor sat down before her. "Why should it cause you pain? You chose to sacrifice the child's birthright for your own comfort, did you not? No? Then what are you saying? That Sir Simon forced you into marriage against your will?"

There had been far too much of her strength expended on a man who was barely more than a phantom. "It was none of my doing. Lord Clifford was besieged at Chepstow when Sir Simon arrived at Dyffryn Hall – I was offered no choice."

Eleanor seized her hand. "But this is terrible! What an impious man. Did Loys threaten you with violence? I would have killed him rather than submit."

"What would that have availed me?" cried Alice. "I was with child and had nowhere to turn!"

"Well, I'm not surprised to find Loys a villain. Such a supercilious air, and yet his family are nothing. Some say he killed his last wife. Others say he practises the black arts. There's no smoke without fire. He petitioned for my hand, you know. Of course, Harry sent him about his business. But you had no protector! It was wicked of Robert to forsake you like that, helpless as you were. He might at least have slaughtered Loys for you, even if it was too late to safeguard the heir."

"As you say," answered Alice, bleakly, "once Lord Clifford knew the child was lost to him, he had no more concern for me."

"A remarkably careless man." Eleanor was thinking again of the necklace. "But there's no reason for us not to be friends, is there? You've probably been wondering how I have come to know so much of this story. I shall tell you, if you promise to keep it to yourself. When Robert rode north after Tewkesbury, he sought me out at the house of his friend Sir James Thwaite, where I was conducting a little business in my brother's absence. And what do you think he did then?"

"Tortured Sir James to death and slew his sons."

"Oh yes – which he forced me to watch. But after that?"

Alice sat, motionless, on Eleanor's bed, hands pressed in her lap.

"He carried me off! Against my will, naturally."

"That must have been very frightening." The tone was not confrontational but bemused. By now Alice had looked upon Robert from a bewildering succession of windows; at every vantage, the view altered.

"Oh, of course. He rode with me to Lindisfarne. While he caroused with his men, I was pacing my chamber, searching for a means of escape. But the man had found a key to the room, and during the night he came to me."

Alice rubbed her forehead and then stuffed her hands into her armpits, for the urge to cover her ears was well-nigh irresistible.

"Alas, his reputation is so well-known that I abandoned hope."

To display the doubt so plainly was not courteous, perhaps, but Alice had good evidence that the man's notoriety was – in that particular, at least – unfounded. She had too many memories of her own; now ambushed by a groundswell of rebellion. "Did he threaten you with violence, Lady Eleanor? Surely you would have killed him rather than submit?"

"You should not judge Robert so harshly." Eleanor's eyes were downcast, but her teeth were glinting. "In fairness to the man, my brother had already given consent for our marriage before changing his mind to forbid it. So it was not … not the first time Lord Clifford had touched me. There had been a moment – it was in the darkness, I recall – when I allowed Robert to kiss me. After that, he surely felt that I belonged to him, for he told me that his heart was mine."

Alice stood, abruptly, and leaned against the panelling. "I've not been well, Lady Eleanor, and I feel rather faint. Would you be so good as to summon my gentlewomen?"

* * *

When Alice was helped to her chamber, Loys was already within, hunched at the table, following a text with his finger. He sprang up. "What is it? Has she been taken ill?"

"Lady Alice is worn out, sir," said Constance, "and must rest. Alone, I suggest, would be better."

Elyn was hopping about, news threatening to spill from her.

"Alone? No. You shall leave us. All of you." Ignoring the mutinous looks, he carried Alice to the bed and lowered himself to her side, one knee pinning her skirts. He murmured into his wife's ear, "I should not have brought you so far, evidently; you are not strong enough." One by one he slid the pins from her hair. "Lady Eleanor has wrung you out, I see. Now, I've also had an interesting afternoon. Shall I tell you about it?"

* * *

Loys and the Earl had spent an hour or two hawking together. The discourse flowed better on horseback: the men could speak without their eyes meeting.

After a longish period of small talk, the preparatory silence had fallen, broken by Percy. "So you've joined Gloucester's affinity, Simon? I'm surprised you didn't discuss it with me first." When Loys remained silent, he continued. "I suppose the reason for your visit is not to see little Kit, but to retrieve him. It's over-hasty. There's no harm in your son remaining at Alnwick. Think on it: I'm fond of the boy, and you would be wise to spread your risk. Gloucester is young, after all, and an unknown quantity, while there's a long connection between our families: your father once squired at Alnwick; your brother Humphrey, in his turn. I remember him well. As a lad I looked up to him. It was Humphrey who showed me that honour and courage can defeat oppression and violence."

Loys turned away to hide his expression. If Humphrey's lonely stand showed anything, it was precisely the opposite.

"Your marriage has caused plenty of talk, Simon. A considerable step up."

"I was resolved not to wed again unless I could better myself in that way."

Percy eyed him beneath those sparse brows. "Come on then: out with it. You're still smarting that I refused you my sister? It cannot have been a surprise."

"It concerns value, my lord. The value that one man places on another, on his wits and on his service, rather than his birth. Gloucester values me greatly, as the Earl of Warwick valued me."

"As Warwick denied you Alice de Vere, don't forget."

"Hard to forget, my lord. I left his affinity after that slight."

"As you have turned against me, also? To hold grudges … it poisons the blood. It will shorten your life."

"Failing to heed an injury is likely to do the same."

"No. You would have left Warwick either way, for there were rumblings of treason by then. The timing was little more than incidental."

Both men shook their heads. They'd returned to the outskirts of Alnwick by now, passing Grandfather Prynne's little dwelling and Hal's three infants, larking in the mud as their mother swept the doorstep. Like the other townsfolk, Dorcas had paused in her chores to watch the Earl pass. Everywhere were the deferential motions, but few tossed their bonnets or cried "God bless you!" How different to the days of Percy's father and grandfather: men just as small, just as unprepossessing, but far from bloodless, with their ferocity and their fierce drive.

Percy rode on, serene in the silence; perhaps he knew no better. "I can't guess what Gloucester's giving you. I'm generous to my affinity."

"Very little, in point of fact, though I expect the sum to rise over time. Just at present, my lord, the Duke's influence is worth so much more than his gold."

"Sevenhill?"

"Sevenhill."

"So you and Gloucester cooked up that little scheme between you, and vanquished the unborn heir of Lancaster? Brave warriors. The King must be grateful."

"We did, my lord. He is."

"It seems I can't compete. But leave Kit with me and I'll take that as a sign that you are well-disposed."

"And shall you, sir? Leave Kit with the Earl?" asked Alice, engrossed, when he'd recounted the conversation.

"I haven't decided." Loys licked his lips. "Northumberland has a point. Sending Kit to the Duke of Gloucester is to put all my eggs in one basket and risk offending a powerful man into the bargain."

"And your son is happy here."

"A point of very little importance."

* * *

"Lady Alice! The most horrible thing! You will not credit this. I must speak with you." Elyn was clamouring; so distressed that Alice at once turned about and led her back to the chamber. Fortunately, Sir Simon was gone.

"What is it, Sister?"

'There is a wicked woman here – Marjorie Verrier by name. She says Guy has lain with her!" She raised a hand as though Alice would deny it. "*My* true love! The man I trust one day to come for me."

"He will never come for you."

"She said he carried her off to Lindisfarne. She says he ravished her! She as much as says it."

Alice lowered herself to the bed and pulled Elyn down beside her. "I don't believe any female was ravished on Lindisfarne. Whatever happened there was, surely, the desire of all concerned. Lady Eleanor went willingly with Lord Clifford, who – whatever else his crimes – has always a tender way with women. Her gentlewoman must probably have gone willingly also. Guy FitzClifford is one of those men who are always around women. With their cunning, they flatter and snare the vain and heedless. Such men should be avoided."

"Oh no! Not he! It is a rare love and it will endure. As you'll see when he comes for me. That Verrier woman lies, or perhaps she confuses Guy with the other twin who is so much less gallant."

"He will never come for you, Elyn. Nor should you wish it. Such men are dangerous; such adventures bring nothing but pain and shame. Our future lies in quiet comfort in Essex. In due course, Sir Simon and I will find you a good, steady husband, and you shall be the mistress of a household, and a mother. You should let go – as have we all let go."

Elyn, who was so much slower to accommodate herself to realities, or perhaps so much more steadfast, burst into tears upon her half-sister's breast, and would not cease until the others had swarmed in, scolding, kissing and contradicting each other.

* * *

Aymer was in rather a wretched state – dirty, hungry and hirsute – when the jailer released him into his brothers' care. "Has Father not come for me himself?"

The tone of surprise grated intolerably on Guy's nerves, rubbed raw all over again. "No, he has not! You're bloody lucky he bought you out at all;

Castor had to twist his arm. He's most sore about the gold. He says he'll reclaim it through your allowance though it take a hundred years. So you know what you'll do now? Hawk that fucking jewel and repay Father at once, before he catches sight of it and wallows in your guts." Guy no longer troubled to speak in riddles before Richie. "Hard to credit, even in you, that you'd keep it as a token. What a *fucking imbecile.*"

He pushed his brother out into the low afternoon light. Aymer patted his twin's neck, sniffing at a hunk of meat proffered silently by Richie; palming it away.

"The cutpurse survived your attempt on his skull," Guy prompted, when Aymer didn't ask. "Thank God, or the price would have soared beyond Father's means. Turns out he's a bastard son of some great man hereabouts."

His twin passed on, brazenly stroking the guilty purse. "A jewel beyond price, and it shall never leave me. Father may deny me as he pleases. Richie will keep me in ale, will you not, Brother?"

* * *

With dragging steps, Sir Hugh went in search of Gabriel Appledore. He looked about the great hall and the kitchens and peeped into various chambers, large and small – aiming not so much to succeed in his quest as to garner a long and useful list of places where the quarry wasn't. By then he'd received so many directions to the under-steward's room that he had no choice but to slink at last to the small chamber that once was Waryn's.

Dacre had the good fortune to meet with Sir Andrew Chowne along the way, and strong-armed his colleague along, for Chowne and Appledore were old friends; fellow servants in the household of Edmond Beaufort. This task rightly belonged with him.

"Forgive us for disturbing you, Sir Gabriel. You know Andrew Chowne, of course, and you may remember me, Hugh Dacre? I was a household knight of the late Earl of Warwick." Dacre halted a moment, suddenly unsure that it was permissible to refer to Richard Neville by his title. Yes. Yes, it was.

Everyone was doing it. He resumed. "We met in Angers, a couple of years back, and again in London last spring."

Chowne had limped forward, embracing Gabriel Appledore, and now held him at arm's length. "I say, Gabriel – are you quite well? You don't look it."

Appledore touched his throat and waved Sir Hugh within. He sat on the bed a lengthy while, hands clenching and unclenching, until his voice returned. "Forgive me, friends. I am afflicted by an ague. I was having an attack just now when you knocked. How can I help you?"

Dacre's embarrassment was displaced only briefly by his confusion, and soon returned. There was no way of conveying Loys's warning without offence, and this man looked like he'd suffered enough. Chowne folded his arms. He hadn't been tasked with the awkward duty and he wasn't going to help. After another lengthy silence. Dacre ventured, "You may know that I lately married Blanche Carbery, gentlewoman to Lady Loys – as she now is."

The intelligence triggered another round of twitches.

"Lady Blanche was telling me, Sir Gabriel, that at one time you considered marriage with Elizabeth Ullerton. But Blanche supposes nothing shall come of it now."

"Elizabeth Ullerton?" He failed to suppress a shudder. "There was some talk … we were never formally betrothed. No – no. I am so grateful to the Earl of Northumberland for my position as under-steward. I must stay just where I am. I cannot think of marriage now. I am not well. I hope the gentlewoman does not expect it of me?"

With alacrity Sir Hugh rose from the bed. "Oh no, no. Nothing of the sort! Forget I mentioned it. It was good to speak with you, Sir Gabriel. I hope your health improves." And then he rushed away in triumph to his master, leaving Chowne to his old friend.

"You seem truly unwell, Gabriel. You must have suffered greatly from this … ague. It has been a difficult time, hasn't it? You were with the Duke at the end, I think."

And then Chowne was trapped in the chamber a long while by the laments of a thoroughly broken man. "Lady Alice is a most gracious and kindly mistress," Sir Andrew protested, patiently, many times over. "All of this was Lord Clifford's fault." Not all Lord Clifford's fault; just most of it. That awful Ullerton woman had aggravated matters, perhaps intentionally, and – dare he think it? – even the Duke himself was not blameless.

Sir Gabriel's eyes were bulging. "The Duchess Alice is a terrible woman, an evil woman. She shamed the Duke, may God rest his soul" – tears had begun to course down his cheeks – "and absconded with that devil Clifford while our master was still living."

"It wasn't like that, Appledore! Your loyalty to the Duke has clouded your judgment."

"Parading a new husband, strong for York, now that she is abandoned by her wicked paramour."

"It certainly wasn't like that, and I was there." But Chowne found he could do nothing with the man; nothing at all.

* * *

By the time Aymer reached the Friary, the evening was drawing in and a deep bath was waiting, with its scents of mallow and camomile.

"Shall I rub your back, Aymer? I reckon you're that stiff and sore from sleeping on a board."

"I slept as well in the jail as any bedchamber."

"Not well, then?"

"There was this little thief beside me all the while, eyeing my purse. To whet his appetite I showed him what I had."

Richie's appetite was whetted, too, by the contents of that purse. For days, he'd thought of little else.

"So to pass the time we laid wagers of all sorts: where the sparrow would next land, let's say; whom the rat would next bite. Over time I won all his ill gotten gains. But we'll not tell Guy, eh? Or the old biddy will set on me again. Where is Guy?"

"I won some coin also." Richie had been battling all-comers with a grim intensity of purpose. "To pay for this bath. Which wasn't cheap." The winnings were enough for a bath, only enough for a bath and now they were gone.

"Then you may get in after me. No, not yet. You'll soil the water."

"I'm not wishing to bathe again just now. If a man loses his natural essence it leaches his strength."

"Ah, water is healthful. Your natural essence smells of wild beast."

Enough. "So tell me of the emerald, Aymer. What did you do?" But as so often, Richie had trouble meeting his brother's eyes: pale points of light piercing the shadow beneath the canopy. The great tented hood drew up swirls of vapour like a chimney, though the water was no more than tepid. Richie traced the steam to its source: it was rising from Aymer's skin.

"You know what I did."

* * *

Loys had resolved to leave his son at Alnwick. The more he thought on it, the more prudent it seemed. One day only of the sojourn remained, and none of the guests was sorry. Alice felt perpetually queasy, as though she'd eaten too much rich food.

Before dinner, Eleanor chivvied Alice into the kitchen garden, arm-in-rigid-arm. The gentlewomen were crowding some way behind; all but Elyn, shut in the chamber, mourning the defection of Master Guy, refusing to emerge. "Did you come to know the FitzCliffords, Lady Alice," said Eleanor, "when you travelled from Tewkesbury?"

Hal – his face running with blood, clasping Alice against him. Her dreams were before her once more. And Aymer – the curious way in which her mind chose to present him: the fingers; the emerald. She sighed. Why could Lady Eleanor not discuss the latest fashions at court? Her favourite ballad? Her patron saint? "Not really."

"Shall you hear the most shocking tale, Lady Alice? You'll not believe it, I daresay. But I shall tell you something I have told no one else, if you promise to keep it to yourself."

What more? thought Alice, grimly. *Truly, these women are beyond anything.*

Eleanor squeezed her arm. "Do you recall one amongst Robert Clifford's sons: Hal FitzClifford?"

"No."

"The eldest son, who resembles his father so precisely?"

"No. Possibly."

"And what do you make of him?"

"He always seemed to me a good man."

"He is not a good man. Far from it."

"Oh. Alas." *Alas*

Eleanor walked on in silence for a time, shaking her head.

"Well, what has he done, then?" ventured Alice, who was only human.

Eleanor's voice dropped away, a thrilling whisper. "When he lived among us here – he was our under-steward – Hal FitzClifford learned a certain secret of mine, and threatened to go to my brother the Earl and inform Harry of this secret, unless I submitted to pleasure the man – *in an unnatural manner.* And so it was that he blackmailed me to it, many times over."

"Good God! How appalling! If this is the truth, he must burn in Hell through all eternity."

"*If this is the truth?* Surely you acknowledge the innocence of the victim? I, an Earl's daughter, like yourself? We do not give ourselves so easily!" Eleanor had halted, turning on Alice with cold hauteur.

"No, indeed!"

"Or would you exonerate, rather, this brigand, who takes what he can?"

"I did not mean to offend you." Alice was profoundly unhappy by now. "Those FitzCliffords; they are baseborn, of course, and so probably do not comprehend … they are low fellows."

"You are quite right! Lord John Clifford's eldest, Master George, might be a fine-looking man, but he's also exceptionally wicked, with all the same tendencies. He forced himself on me when I was a maiden. I did not even understand what he was doing until it was too late. Alas for the disgusting depravity of such men." She had set off again and Alice trailed after, wishing herself anywhere but here. "*That* was the secret shame that Hal used against me. I bore no blame, and yet I was punished – again and again."

"I am most profoundly shocked. Truly, I don't know what to say, Lady Eleanor. Why did you not go straight to your brother and have these men flogged?"

"You must know little of the world, to think I could solve my predicament so easily. In such a case, the woman is always blamed. You, yourself: we all heard the rumours coming out of Flanders and London; you are held to be a great Jezebel, wed to a duke of the royal house, yet whoring yourself with Lord Clifford – the two nobles striving together in the street over you; a vulgar, public brawl."

Alice bared her teeth. The effect was not in the least menacing, and Eleanor threw her arms around her guest. "It is a base lie; I know it! Do you not see? We have suffered alike, and through no fault of our own."

* * *

Thus far, Sir Simon had shown no curiosity concerning the time spent in Eleanor's company. Alice knew his ways by now: the questioning would be acute, but it would come later; possibly much later. Even as she longed to be away from this terrible place, she suspected that half the ordeal was yet to come.

Northumberland was an empty county. It was hard to roust up much company at short notice, though the Earl had done what he could among the neighbouring gentlefolk. His sister had a small but interested audience when, boiling with indignation at the misconduct of Sir Simon, she chose to give the knight a public reprimand. Or made the attempt; he was a difficult man to best.

Perhaps she had not noted the Clifford ruby, or perhaps she had put the detail aside for later. If so, the moment had arrived. "How came you by that great stone, Sir Simon? There can be few rubies so magnificent."

If Percy recognised the ring, he gave no sign and continued at his dinner. Loys raised his eyes, regarding Eleanor through those straight brows. "Indeed. I prize it most particularly, as you will perfectly comprehend. A jewel beyond price, and it shall never leave me."

"Surely it cannot be a family piece? I think I have seen it on the hand of another."

"Perhaps you have, Lady Eleanor. Perhaps you have. If anyone would have taken a close interest, it would be you. But tell me this: how came you by the fine crucifix you were wearing the day we arrived? An unusual design and hard to miss. Surely it cannot be a family piece? I think I have seen it at the throat of another."

Both Percy and Alice looked at him, bemused. Blanche was seated in the antechamber with the other attendants, beyond the reach of the voices.

Eleanor folded her lips in a slight smile. "You are mistaken." Loys smiled also, but the lady was not so easily discomfited. "How does your son, Lady Alice? It's a shame he's too small to travel with you."

Alice cleared her throat. "My little Ned is well, I trust, Lady Eleanor. I look forward to seeing him again."

"How fervently I would love a child of my own. You are blessed."

"I don't doubt God will favour you with just such a gift before long, Lady Eleanor," commented Loys. "In fact, He's been surprisingly remiss, thus far."

The Earl looked up sharply.

"For you shall soon be married, I don't doubt."

The last of the dishes were cleared.

"Sir Simon, I congratulate you on the godparents you procured. How did you persuade the Duke of Gloucester to sponsor the little scion of a rival house?"

"For God's sake, Eleanor!" exclaimed the Earl, banging down his cup. "Forgive my sister, Lady Alice! Everyone knows your child was born early; undoubtedly the son of Sir Simon, here. Lady Eleanor has confused herself." He raised his voice. "Sister, favour us with some music, if you please. At once."

"Of course, Brother, if you wish it."

Kit Loys knelt and presented a lute to the lady, who ruffled his hair and whispered in his ear. With an eager smile, the boy brought up a drum for himself, settling at her feet. His father hunkered down as if anticipating something painful.

Eleanor sang well and played better, but the choice of song was unhappy and felt, somehow, inevitable. Loys and Alice suffered through a heartfelt and word-perfect rendition of *Farewell.*

* * *

"You were abysmally rude to Loys and before all our guests. You embarrassed me, and his wife also. The man is a climber of the worst kind; you shall not lower yourself to his level."

"He forced that sad, helpless girl into marriage; threatened her child with violence. Did you know that, Brother?"

"Of course. I would have expected no less, especially of him. A chance too good to pass up, on many counts. I hope you didn't tell her the man poisoned his last wife. I see from your face that you did. But attend: Loys said one thing that was to the point: it's high time you are married, Eleanor. The matter has now become pressing."

"You know I have no wish to marry! On that, my mind is made up. I shall live out my days quietly at Alnwick, assisting you in the management of the household, chatelaine of the castle. It suits me to devote myself to your interests."

"Well. I cannot force you to the altar, though you must know you are being perverse. I can tell you, however, that you cannot remain as chatelaine of Alnwick."

"If you are speaking of a convent, you might as well kill me! Nothing will induce me to the take the veil. You can force me to that less easily than you can force me to the altar."

"Why must you be so histrionic? You are growing ever less sensible as you grow older, when usually it is the other way around. I am speaking of something much more commonplace. You cannot remain as chatelaine of Alnwick for the simple reason that the place will be filled by another. For I must marry, even if you are not inclined."

She was looking out of the window. "Oh? It sounds as if you have given this much thought already, though you've not mentioned it to me."

"I've done more than think about it: I've concluded it. Maud Herbert is to be my wife. Her brother and I agreed the terms when I was last in London, and now the King has given his approval. I'm fortunate in knowing her so much better than most men know their wives-to-be, for we were playmates at Raglan when I was the ward of her father. Maud is a delight: prudent; sensible; virtuous. She'll make a most admirable countess. I know you'll welcome her and submit to her as you should."

"I bless you, Harry, with all my heart. I could not wish for happier news."

He had not looked at Eleanor once, slouching in his high-backed chair at the great table, trimming his nails with his teeth. *Sit up straight!* Silently she scolded him, with fretful petulance. *You are puddling.* She bent in for the dutiful kiss. A new Countess of Northumberland: a possibility Eleanor dimly believed she could frustrate, possibly for years. "When do we welcome the lady?"

"Before too long has passed, I trust. I'm overwhelmed with impatience."

* * *

King James led the hunt, Clifford to his right and de Vere to his left, Beaumont riding at Jack's side. Some way further back were Clifford's men, craning to watch as the young King of Scots turned first one way and then the other, laughing, nodding, gesturing.

"The King was only a child when Lord Robert last led us to Edinburgh," remarked Cuthbert Bellingham to Loic. "His mother was regent of Scotland at the time. A firm friend to the house of Lancaster."

"How greatly does King James admire Monseigneur! All his heart is bent on becoming a fearsome warrior, joining with King Louis and taking the fight to Edward of York. Our coming could not be better timed. Perhaps you noticed how excited he was to find a Frenchman of noble birth amongst the Wyverns? His attentions were rather flattering."

"I know. My dear fellow, I saw it all."

The pair ambled on in companionable silence until pleasant contemplations were skewered by Walter Grey's intrusive tones. "Where's Davy today? He comes and goes like a will-o'-the-wisp. You're mighty glum again, Patrick. Smile, for God's sake! Face on you like someone died."

No, Walter, no! Could Sir Reginald not control his imbecile brother? Loic grimaced at the priest, but Reginald Grey rode on, chewing his lip.

"Smile? There's precious little to smile about! And if he orders my brother to attend on him one more time, I swear Davy will draw steel."

Loic sighed. *Unlikely*. Davy Nield was rather a testy individual; not noticeably suicidal.

"My brother serves the Abbot of Holyrood; why cannot Lord Robert get it into his head? The Abbot wrote a most discreet letter, a mannerly protest, and he tossed it on the fire. Lord Robert thinks more of his horse than of any Scotsman. He'll barely notice if I leave him. Has anyone heard him mention Bertrand? Because I haven't. Jansen served loyally a good five, six years, paid not a penny and away he goes, forgotten, a creature of no account."

Tailboys next, predicted several of the listeners, settling in.

"And most shameful of all: Leonard Tailboys. That man was devoted to Lord Robert, as he was devoted to Lord John and Lord Thomas before him. Faultless in service. Foully slain by one of those miscreant boys, and Lord Robert looks the other way. That I should live to see the Wyverns at such a pass!"

"For Christ's sake, Patrick – not Tailboys again!" Findern spoke for the first time. "It's such idle speculation. I, for one, don't mourn the man. There – I've said it. Whoever killed him probably had good reason. Tailboys had a vicious way about him. We all know it; we all saw what he was capable of."

"Says one whose own hands are none too clean!" hissed Nield. "Who among us shall cast the first stone?"

"Well, then, let us speak plain," said Bellingham, quietly. "Sir Leonard was a bold soldier and we honour him as such. And doubtless we've all done evil when the blood is up. But you know as well as I, Patrick, that Tailboys gave his impulses free rein, in peacetime as in war, at home as abroad, long after he'd outgrown his hothead years. We'll not applaud the man for that."

"And this, from one who served the Cliffords, father and sons! You craven. I'll not stay, and I shall tell Lord Robert why to his face."

"Have a care," said Castor. "Once spoken, words cannot be recalled. Wound him now and you'll get no second chance."

"He has wounded me, greatly; if the rest of you had any backbone, you'd feel the same. The author of his own misfortune and everyone else's into the bargain. Yet never a whiff of shame or apology. A whining, self-pitying child. Bertrand was right: Lord Robert has lost us the kingdom. Had he and de Vere backed Edmond of Somerset at Tewkesbury, York would have stood no chance." Many voices were trying to break in. Nield silenced them with an impatient gesture. "A fine pair to keep the flame alight. They can't even agree who to fight for."

"Who cares? We're so far from striking any real blow against York, it hardly matters!"

"*Helpful as ever, Walter.*" Reginald Grey rolled satirical eyes at his brother. "Though quite inaccurate, as you'll shortly discover." All faces turned on the priest. "We're about to give that whoreson of York a right sharp sting. Patrick – you may wish to wait awhile."

* * *

"Mistress Elyn?" Loys was leaning from the doorway of the small and sinister chamber at the tip of the turret. "Spare me a moment of your time."

They were back in Avonby, reverting to accustomed routines. Still Sir Simon had idled in obtaining his information. Wary, probably, after his wife's cruelty of a month back.

Elyn turned on the stair below and mounted a step towards him, her eyes slipping past, testing the door. He reached behind and pulled it close. "You're very quiet, these days. Not your usual merry self. Have you had bad news, perhaps? I am your brother now: you may confide in me."

She hovered, uncertain. She could not recall when, if ever, she'd had speech with the knight alone.

"So, I ride south today. My son's grandfather, who was once mayor of York, is very ill, and I fear death approaching. Is there anything you wish for, from the city? But you must tell me if there's anything you need. We'll charge Brini with the task, for Master Leo will be choosing little tokens for his lady-love, I don't doubt. Watch to see who is sporting a new adornment on his return and then you'll learn the secret of his heart!"

It was so wholly unlike Sir Simon – this sportive trifling – that Elyn took a further step upwards, then immediately dreaded lest he were luring her towards the wicked room, and stepped down again. She was envisaging limbs melting into the cauldron, hair crackling in the flames. In point of fact, it smelled already of burnt hair in the stairwell.

He leaned upon the sill a moment, biting back the smile, then turned to her. "What do you think, Mistress Elyn: is little Kit well-kept at Alnwick? Is Lady Eleanor all that she should be? Are her gentlewomen properly behaved?"

Solemnly she shook her head. "They are not, sir. They are not. We learned some unpleasant particulars. Mistress Marjorie Verrier, the chief gentlewoman, is a strong liar, for she accused Guy FitzClifford of carrying her off to Lindisfarne and ravishing her, when he is my love. *Mine.* That gentlewoman has seduced him and then lied to conceal her shame!"

"That is certainly shameful," said he, gravely. "Not to mention eye-wateringly indiscreet. There can be nothing more, though?"

"Oh, yes! There is more, Sir Simon. Worse, even. But I cannot say it."

He opened his hands. "For the sake of little Kit, though?"

Elyn had approached much nearer, forgetful of the danger, and propped her back against the wall. "Well, sir, Lady Eleanor went willingly to Lindisfarne with Lord Clifford – so Lady Alice says. Lady Alice says that Lord

Clifford is a most tender lover, and never would have ravished any lady. And then I heard Lady Alice telling Constance that Lady Eleanor confessed to relations with George FitzClifford, Lord Clifford's nephew – also not ravishing – when I thought all great ladies would be pure of heart like Lady Alice and the Countess of Warwick! What is the world coming to? It is coming to an end, probably. So they say. And this is surely one of the signs."

"Well, well," said Loys. "You have given me much to think upon, and no mistake. And I believe Lady Alice mentioned that one of these Fitz-fellows suffered some injury to his face. Who was that, do you recall? For these names mean nothing to me."

"I know who that would be, sir! Hal FitzClifford, Lord Clifford's eldest. Lady Alice and Constance were speaking of him, also, after the shocking tale of Lady Eleanor and Master George, but I don't know what they were saying, for by then they noticed me and told me to go away."

"Don't call him *Lord* Clifford. But how did this Hal FitzClifford came to be running with blood?"

"Oh, in the forest. For Lady Alice was falling from the horse, and Master Hal sprang to catch her up in his arms; her teeth caught him and his face was running with blood, but he would not let her go. We all thought he would kiss her. Lord Clifford was wild with jealousy, of course, for he loves Lady Alice like the hero of a song. And not long after, when Lady Alice fainted in the woods, Master Hal and Master Aymer came to blows: Master Hal's face was marred again."

"Don't call him *Lord* Clifford. And who is this Aymer? Another son? Is there aught amiss with his fingers? Does he wear an emerald?"

She tilted her chin at him. "Master Aymer is as beautiful as a star, for he is Guy's twin. His hands are much as another man's, I suppose. I did not see any jewels and, in any case, sir, these are poor men. Lady Alice lost an emerald though: it was the day she fainted in the woods and Master Aymer saw to her. When he brought her back in his arms, the emerald pendant was gone, though we did not notice at the time, she was that dishevelled. The gem never was seen again. A fair stone: a gift from Duke Edmond. It is a shame."

"Don't call him *Duke* Edmond. Yes, a shame indeed, though I've no doubt someone has it in his safekeeping. Well, Mistress Elyn: you are the veritable Tree of Knowledge. The others do not understand your value. If you think of any present I can procure, be sure to let me know."

"Yes, Sir Simon, but I have been thinking of it all the while. Ribbons would be welcome, for mine are old and tousled. Long ones, if you please, assuming there is a choice of length, which there usually is. Some have tiny knots at the end, which is better, as they don't unravel. Lilac is nicest, but if it cannot be lilac, then let it be pink, but not deep pink. Finding the right colour is more important than chasing after the ones with knots, though, because I can always tie the knots myself, if I must, with the help of a needle. Oh – and I wouldn't wear cream or yellow. It simply amazes me that anyone would choose to, when those colours always look dirty. And never brown, of course!"

"Oh – of course. Only a fool would choose brown."

He'd descended a few steps and his scent was sinking over her; metallic and damp, as though he'd been exerting himself. One hand grazed her breast on its way to her waist. He kissed the corner of her mouth. His breath smelled of pepper. "So be it. In lilac, then, to suit your pretty colouring. Lilac and a pale pink."

* * *

And so the journey to Sevenhill was deferred again, while Loys and his men rode through the wild wind to York, where one of his fathers-in-law lay dying. Loys was rather fond of this one, a deferential fellow who lingered appropriately, took appropriate instruction and signed his name to a new and more appropriate will that disinherited all his anxious relatives and left every penny of a respectable merchant fortune to his grandson Kit. Sir Simon was one trustee; Hugh Dacre, the other.

After an interval, barely decent, the men quit the hushed house. They passed a church and Sir Hugh turned in, unthinking, and promptly turned out again when he found himself alone. The pair walked on to a local tavern where they joined Sir Andrew Chowne and John Twelvetrees in a toast to the dead man.

There were girls circling the tables. The other men sipped their drinks, pensive. Loys had produced a ream of figures and was tallying with urgency, lips moving, when he was interrupted. "Take your hand from me, woman. Christ! Vulgar *and* dirty."

The others exchanged glances and went back to their silent ale.

"So here we are!" Leo Brini puffed up. He raised a quizzical brow at his master. Sir Simon folded away the parchment, nodding. Soon the table was arrayed as a haberdasher's stall; a pretty tangle of ribbons.

"Very good. Take the short, the unknotted, the cream, the yellow and the brown and throw them away."

"I'll gift them to the girls hereabouts?" suggested Sir Andrew.

"No. What have you there, Leo?"

All the party craned in as Brini untied two boxes for their inspection.

"Delicate, and most suitable for a maiden. And what have you chosen for my wife? Yes. The emerald's a good size and a clear colour. It doesn't match her eyes, which are a grey-green rather than a true green, but everyone will say that it does. This workmanship is surprisingly fine. You have done well, as ever, my friend."

"Oh!" cried Sir Hugh, vexed. "Then I must buy some trinket for Lady Blanche. Come, Master Leo. Show me where to go before they shut up shop."

* * *

The brief and nasty spat between France and Burgundy – which Lord Clifford had done so much to foster – had petered out. Now, across the narrow sea, the French crown was once more mustering its restless might, brooding westwards toward its little cousin, the Duchy of Brittany. Brittany turned anxiously for English help; York's help. The young King of Scots was itching to muddle his fingers in that pie, but he was impoverished and distant and couldn't tempt his canny councillors along. Their verdict: let the English exiles earn their keep.

A few weeks later, the exiles had begun to earn their keep. So here they were, ploughing south through the deep and freezing North Sea and, at last, Patrick Nield was smiling, or perhaps it was a grimace, his eyes smarting with salt as the gusts lashed his sooty locks. By now his bonnet was halfway to Calais.

On the forecastle of the St Moluag stood Aymer, ruler of his private dominion, riding the decks amid the storms and serpents of the high and rolling seas. Born in the sylvan heart of England, as a lad he fished the Avon in a coracle or darted among the minnows, so perfectly at ease in water that Hal's ducking – which might have killed a lesser man – had caused no more than an icy shock before he flitted away, skirting the river's wicked boulders with strong and supple strokes. By night, when Aymer didn't sleep, he'd envision himself as the Mer King, no less, dragging down ships by the anchor and spearing sailors with a trident. But the youth had never seen salt water until he gazed out from Lindisfarne Abbey; never so much as dipped his toe in the ocean. Now, at last, he was borne upon its breast, with endless reaches before him and forty fathoms beneath, intoxicated by the slewing sea.

Behind, a more prosaic sight. A row of buttocks bedecked the rail; men doubled over and heaving. Upwind of the sufferers Loic swayed, shouting pleasantries over the obscene rumpus, his lips plastered with sodden, gilded curls.

Somewhere out west was solid ground. The master of the St Moluag scanned the coast and scudded in to shore, approaching the familiar town of Hartlepool from an unfamiliar angle. Down went the boom chain and they eased between the towers, tailed into the harbour by de Vere's craft and Beaumont's, in good order. The town hurried out to greet them. Shortly they were swaggering along the quay like conquering heroes while the ground bobbed, unnervingly, beneath their feet.

Soon the Wyverns' progress was impeded by a gaggle of young women, those befriended on the flight from Thirsk. Several were boasting smooth curves beneath the girdle; like walking calendars, each of them at the six month mark. Findern's arm encircled one of these blossoming girls, a wide grin across his ill favoured face, looking about to ensure his fellows had seen the likely signs; slowing to show her off, most particularly – it seemed – to Richie.

The next morning they were blown away by a roaring northerly that pressed the ships so hard that the skim from the North Country to the south coast was accomplished in rare time. Reginald Grey prayed, ostentatiously, amidships, taking all the credit as the sails above him swelled with the billow of God's breath. Getting away cleanly in the teeth of a contrary wind would be more of a challenge; in due course, perhaps, the priest would cast about to explain the reversal of fortune. But this was a sinuous man, infinitely adaptable; the very opposite of his master.

* * *

Loys presented the jewel on the night of his return, sombre and unsmiling, as was his way, fixing it about his lady's throat with lingering hands. She too was silent. The sight of the emerald called to mind a tumultuous time too lately lived and not yet lost through layers of memory to come to rest, mute, in the depths; a gentle shipwreck.

The emerald threatened to recall Edmond; the shock of joy on first meeting her husband. And on Edmond she could not allow herself to dwell; not for a moment. When she held their small son, she and Ned were the only two, and when she looked into Ned's face, it was a mirror only to his mother. This child – to whom three men might have stood father – now had none.

The jewel was the strangest of gifts. If she knew Simon better now, she barely understood him. Alice might wonder as to the *why*; she did not wonder as to the *how*: *how* he'd come to know the existence of the lost stone. She'd long felt the dark forces at work within the castle. The small chamber perched above them contained, surely, among its imagined array of wondrous horrors, some all-seeing eye. Simon had but to peer into the instrument and he knew, at once, the devices and desires of men's hearts.

213

The other gifts caused barely less discomfort.

Blanche received a girdle that would have fitted neatly a year ago. Either Sir Hugh was showing a wanton lack of tact, or he was making a point. She wept stormy tears at him, mourning her spoiled figure and the beastliness of men, who were – it turned out – all alike; all of them, given the chance. And of course the disappointment came hard on the heels of an earlier unmasking: Loic Moncler's treasured gift was – it also turned out – but one of a job-lot; the filigree crosses churned out as cheaply as those Wyvern badges, passing between man and master, to be scattered where needed.

No doubt Sir Loic deserved much of the gentlewoman's scorn, but not in this regard, for there was only ever one pair of those pearled crosses – just as expensive as they looked, although, of course, Moncler did not foot the bill.

Meanwhile, the ribbons were welcomed with noisy delight, at once giving rise to a sour suspicion among the witnesses. Elyn was rifled for an explanation, and she did not help herself. "He caught me as I was passing near the small chamber, Lady Alice, and asked me to name a present. I'd been waiting and waiting for someone to remark the terrible state of my ribbons, but nobody came to my aid except Sir Simon. I thought we settled only on lilac or pink, which he said best suited my prettiness, but now he has given me a vast wardrobe of choice. And he remembered all about the knots and the lengths. A very loving and thoughtful brother-in-law; I see it now."

"It was kind of you to treat my poor half-sister to a gift." This was early morning, two days after the return from York. His wife's voice was like ice and his heart thrilled. "But she is not quick, and will misunderstand; or, more to the point, others will misunderstand, which is humiliating for me."

"What is there to misunderstand? The girl said her ribbons were draggled. If she's ill presented, it does not reflect well on me. A subject unduly petty when I have rather more important matters to contemplate."

"And it is not jealousy! You should not think such a thing, if that is what you are thinking. It is my duty to safeguard Elyn." She was close to tears. They were all of them in his power, and it was appalling if harm should come also from this quarter.

He kissed her hair. "Jealousy is the most futile of emotions; one should stifle it always. Come. I don't want to get up yet. Prayers can wait." He led her back to the bed and pushed her down.

"I am as far from jealous as it is possible to be. Your ceaseless appetite is hard to bear, and you'd hear no protest from me if you satisfied yourself elsewhere. But not among my gentlewomen."

"If a wife is warm, a husband has no need to look elsewhere. It's you who fail in your duty by the coldness you display, despite my many kindnesses."

"Not that I would encourage you into sin, of course. I should not have invited you to look elsewhere. You are right to keep yourself in check. Assuming you do keep yourself in check."

Loys had wrung all he wished from Elyn and would draw this to a close; he couldn't bring himself to pursue the idiot, even to provoke so delicious a reaction in his wife.

He would have been less complacent had he known quite how greatly the resentment had pent up. Unknown to him, Alice had learned the truth: that Robert had not ridden heedless away, abandoning the heir of Lancaster. Somehow he had learned of Simon's presence at Dyffryn. When Robert rode north from Monmouthshire it was because he knew the babe was lost to him. It was only Alice whom he had abandoned.

* * *

Eventually, the little convoy slid into the wide haven of Southampton. It was blindingly bright; much too warm for March, when snow scarts clung still in the lee hollows of the North Country. At the pinnacle of the mainmast they'd hauled down the Castle of Edinburgh and run up the Stag's Head of Hartlepool – not that anyone noticed, for it was Sunday morning and the good natives were at church. There were many craft rocking, peaceful, at anchor, but the harbour was not the target. Past the stout stone walls and north to the beach, where a number of hulks could be seen, mastless, lying up in slips on the foreshore.

This was the small fleet intended for Brittany: ships being fitted out to carry English archers to the defence of Nantes and Rennes against the French. King James of Scotland – keen, green and self-appointed ally of France – was eager to stop that force embarking; it was for this purpose that he'd tipped his English guests out of Edinburgh. So here was Clifford, allowing himself to be used by his new patron, as he'd been used for years by Charles of Burgundy, but this time the purpose chimed beautifully with his own.

"I dreamed of this." Clifford found himself beside George at the bow, as the first of the little boats pushed out from the St Moluag and slipped towards the shore. "The captain of the Breton expedition is Anthony Woodville, York's brother-in-law: these are his ships, or his hirelings. In the dream we caught him hard at work, hammering the keels with his lily-white hands."

"Did you dice him up, Uncle?"

"I diced him up."

"And piss on the pieces?"

"Ah, I did."

"How I wish we'd find him here! The Queen's own brother, all sweaty and stripped to the waist!"

Clifford's grin faded. "Don't call him the *Queen's* brother!"

"Dumbfoundling," muttered the priest.

"Your pardon, my lord! You know … what I meant."

"It can be hard to remember, I suppose," Bellingham interjected, swiftly. "Especially if you've grown up in John Neville's household."

A voice from behind: "It can be hard to remember *if you're thick*."

But when George spun around, he saw only a crowd of impassive faces and Guy wasn't even among them.

* * *

The fourth gift was presented on the walls of the castle. Leo Brini had invited Mistress Joanna to address the question of whether it was or was or was not possible to glimpse the sea from such a vantage.

216

Joanna had sharp eyesight – sharper than Master Brini's – but she could make out no more than a faint smudge across the horizon which she suspected, correctly, to be the shadow of cloud on heather. Her eyes were watering from the wind.

"Oh well. Let us imagine it is the sea, for that is a lovelier notion. If you climb to Sir Simon's workroom, your keen eyes might make out the water. In fact, I think so, Signorina Joanna, given the angle and the distance." His fingers trembled; he longed to invest her with the vast sweeps of his mind: the movement of the stars; the curvature of the earth; resisting, with difficulty, the urge to foist triangulation on the girl.

"Oh. But I am not sure..." Confusion reigned, as well it might, for surely no trespasser would emerge unscathed from such a place.

"No. Mio signor keeps the key close. We cannot enter."

She nodded, relieved.

"I'm glad to have you a moment alone, though, signorina, for when we visited York, I was passing a goldsmith's shop, and I spied a pretty little trinket. It is a veritable nothing, but I thought perhaps it would look sweet against your auburn hair."

He sidled near and shyly produced the present; holding it at hip height where he could comfortably focus, for he had left his eyeglasses behind. Humbly, she took up the little box and peeped in, smiling and smiling. The gold ornament possessed a fragile simplicity: a dove with eyes of sapphire. He wanted emerald and could have had it, but that colour was spoken for by his master. They both longed to pin it into place but he hesitated to touch her and she feared to seem forward. The wind trumpeted and she almost dropped the little thing. She returned it to the box.

"Shall we go down, signorina? It's very breezy and I think you are growing cold."

* * *

Anthony Woodville was not hammering keels upon the foreshore. No one was stripped to the waist; no one was working. Crouched around a brazier in the sand were four men and a boy, who sprang to their feet and ran off, appalled. The little cries faded out, and the fugitives reappeared among the waves, furiously rowing downstream to raise the alarm. The men in the Scotch ships were watching, and tried a volley, but the skiff was beyond bow-range.

By now six boatloads of the exiles had leaped onto the sands and were milling about while a small handful set alight every ship in Woodville's fleet. The hulls and spars were dry or dry enough; down here it must have been sunny for days, for they succumbed to the flames without protest. Soon there were lazy whorls of smoke arching overhead, and nothing further to do. So they purloined the watchmen's breakfast – nicely roasted – and rowed away.

When the men had clambered aboard and the boats were stowed, they slewed about and tacked as best they could into the draining tide. Entering deeper water, the three ships were gusted, suddenly, towards the walls, almost running down the skiff with its tattletale crew. From their overbearing vantage, the Scots archers silenced the tale-bearers. Oarless, the little craft joggled and spun until it ran aground and the seagulls gathered.

They may as well have let them live: already, faces were appearing all along the west wall of the harbour. The alarm was going up. Those disingenuous merchant banners fluttered in vain. At any moment, the town would disgorge enemies like a stream of frenzied wasps. But the breeze was still in the same quarter; when the exiles gave the ships their head, they cleared the Isle of Wight, driven before the squally wind, straight towards Brittany.

* * *

The boys were romping in the river when Piers came to join them, as he'd done several times in this unseasonably warm spring. He swam inelegantly, bellying and spouting like a whale.

Gregory scrambled from the water at once, twitching for the towel, as always when there came a witness to his infirmity. Then he'd lie against a tree, shrouded from the waist, and strum the lute and sing over the splashes, making songs for girls who would never notice him.

Some time later they were joined by Sir Mark Rohips. After Master Brixhemar's unappealing description, the knight was not as Hal envisaged, but tall and lean and hale, with regular features and a vigorous stride. Only his face betrayed his age: it fissured when he smiled. He was indeed a difficult character, though his darts were aimed exclusively at his nephew. Hal glanced sideways at poor Brixhemar: a moment ago, the quintessence of merriment. In Hal's imagining he was now peppered with barbs, like St Sebastian.

Rohips polished his wit an idle while and then, instead of relieving them of his presence, chose to strip and join the younger men in the water. Diving with tidy poise into the river, he challenged Stephen Clifford to a race. "My nephew's too short and fat to bother with, and this young giant here would outpace us both with ease. But I reckon you and I are well-matched, Master Clifford."

Although Stephen won the contest, it was not by any large margin. Rohips had the frame of a much younger man. "If I'm as strong at your age I'll be well content, Sir Mark."

"I'll outlive you all, I don't doubt, with a young wife to keep me keen. That's all that's needful: a bonny wife and plenty of youngsters around my ankles. While I'm here at Crawshay I mean to take a good look at your sisters, Master Clifford. They say Idonia bids fair to grow as tall and lovely as the celebrated Beatrice. Triston won't deny me; I'll take her without a dowry."

Brixhemar turned away. If his uncle would but drop this creaky jest and acknowledge him as heir, he might, himself, make headway with Sir Triston. Already Brixhemar had sought Idonia's hand, and been rebuffed. Twice.

* * *

The coast of England faded from view. The wind had swung north west. They could not make it back to Scotland; not now; not in the teeth of these gusts, and so they aimed for the Cotentin Peninsula, safely over the Breton border into Normandy, and the three ships were tight together as the sun set. But by morning, the Wyverns were alone.

"We're a little farther west than I was expecting, my lord." The captain squinted at the distant coast of France, the cliffs a thin, wavering line. His bonnet was a damp rag in his fist. "My deepest apologies."

Their loneliness was relieved when another ship hove into a view: a smallish merchant vessel, skimming the shoreline, furtive. "Can you make out its colours?" said Clifford.

"No, my lord. Certainly French, though, I'm sure of it."

"Burgundian! Monseigneur, I see it."

"Flemings, eh? What do you say, my son?" Clifford clapped a hand on Aymer's shoulder.

Aymer grinned. "Should we, Father?" Wherever Hal was hiding, in that moment Aymer pitied him. "I think we should."

"I think we must!"

The captain eyed his cargo with bitterness. He'd no wish to carry these English devils; he'd been leant on and lied to, and now this. "My lord? I'm sure you've noticed that our fo'c's'le is somewhat low for a cog of this size and not in the best of repair …"

"Odd, because in Leith, you were boasting of the strength of your vessel. Your forecastle is higher than theirs, is it not? And we have the weather gage. On, then!"

Swiftly they closed on the smaller craft. Now they could make out its name – De Roos – and the Flemings upon its decks: helmeted, by this time, and fumbling into their padded jacks, mute and jittering as the St Moluag bore down upon them, all dull grey gleams and prickling with weaponry. The Scots ship was still flying an English flag, but its prey drew no comfort from that.

George jostled to his proper place beside his uncle, and reached for a grappling iron in the same instant that Aymer's fingers closed on it. It was much heavier than it looked, an awkward and clumsy shape and for a moment George paused, irresolute, as the weight swung between them. Here was his rival, steady at his side, that want of inches giving Aymer a clear and unwavering advantage on that pitching deck. But then George pictured his cousin aiming, and missing:

a delightfully public mishap. He let go. As Aymer weighed the device in his hands, they closed with the other vessel. The bows crashed and sprang apart and crashed again with the teeth-jarring screech of shearing timber. The St Moluag plunged as De Roos rose. Feet firmly planted, Aymer braced himself and whirled the iron hook towards the other forecastle. It sailed straight and true, snaring the Flemish bow and a Flemish seaman along with it, pinioned by the twanging, wrenching rope, skipping in a mad and horrid dance, his shrieks splitting the air.

As the two vessels surged and shuddered, the Wyverns were knocked about in their unsteady turret and the youngsters, clinging only to each other, sprawled over like puppies. Then many hands were on the cable, and – all along the sides – another cable, and another, dragging the foreign ship into an uncouth embrace until they had her by the hip. Crossbow bolts sailed, harmless, over English heads. Swarming about, the Flemings sawed at the dragging ropes, but it was too late for that. A number surrendered, cleanly, to arrows and a larger number toppled into the whetstone breach between the ships and were ground away.

Then Clifford leapt from his ship as the other forecastle rushed up to meet him, stumbling as his knee hit the deck. Head-down, a Fleming charged in with a dagger, collapsed beneath a mace blow and rolled down the steps, tripping his fellows. Clifford extended a solicitous arm to steady Loic, who had slipped past Aymer, the first to follow.

"Enough!" cried the captain of De Roos. "That's enough! Fall back."

Clifford strode forward and ripped the fellow's sword from his grasp. At once the enemy flung their weapons from their hands as though the steel were scorching. Conversing amiably in Flemish, the Wyverns set about securing the captives.

"Ah," Clifford turned and grinned into Walter Findern's craggy face. "News takes weeks to reach Edinburgh. Let's hope France and Burgundy haven't made peace."

* * *

At last Loys's household moved south towards the sun.

From her place behind her husband, Alice watched Joanna leaning from the rear of the carriage, bestowing her little smiles on Master Brini, who was gesticulating widely. Delighting her with geometry, no doubt.

It was like a blow to the chest: the forcible remembrance of another carriage journey, eons ago; a man bending to laugh with her, as she perched, just so, looking shyly into his face; a time when her fortunes were bent upon an upward trajectory, and the sky had not fallen in.

"It's going slowly but well, don't you agree? Friend Brini is a cautious fellow, but he shall have her in the end."

"Have her?" repeated Alice, sharply.

"Have her in marriage, you fool. Who are her family? Can she expect anything when she weds? I'd rather not supply the deficit, but if I must, then, for Brini's sake, I shall."

"Joanna's family hails from Essex, like my own. She has been my constant companion since we were little maidens at Wivenhoe and Hedingham, and came north when I was sent to live with the Earl of Warwick at Middleham. She is orphaned, but a niece to Sir John Ames of Blakeney."

"And does this Ames have an heir?"

"Yes, sir: a daughter of his own. Sir John may probably assist Joanna, but only if he approves the match, which I'm confident he will not."

"How rude! Brini is my best friend – by which I mean that he's the only creature whose company I can tolerate. That should be recommendation enough. Leo is clever and steady and hard-working."

"None of which would commend him to Sir John, I'm sure: a friend of my father, a veteran of the French wars and a proud Englishman. Master Brini is a poor man, a servant, a foreigner and – forgive me, sir, but I think – of low birth? Would you be glad to give your daughter to him?"

"Of course not. I would not inflict Catharine on any man I esteemed. Poor Brini has had a hard road of it and I should like to see him well settled. Is that too much to ask? Christ, but England is a backward country. In Venice, or Florence, or in Milan, a man may rise by wits alone, How much pleasanter it was to live where learning is prized more highly than bigotry and brute force."

"Did you spend long away from England, sir? I think you contrived to miss Towton and, indeed, every other fierce battle of that time."

He dropped the reins in surprise and craned around, trying to inspect her. "Christ! Now you add cowardice to my tally of virtues? My absence was an accident, you vixen, and nothing more. Three years I was abroad, or so. As it happens, I fell in with John, Earl of Worcester, your father's nemesis, who was also travelling on his studies. Now, he was a clever and cultured man. I was primed to join his council on our return to England, and would have done, had Warwick not been clamouring for my service. John of Worcester was another of those few men I have admired."

"How *could* you?" she muttered.

Loys raised his stinging tones. "He was certainly a finer man than your brother Aubrey, whom he beheaded with such dramatic and impartial justice."

Behind his back, Alice made a small mewl of outrage, but he ploughed on. "Aubrey de Vere was an arrogant fool who believed his puerile charm and good looks would save him from the consequences of plotting against King Edward. And he dragged your dolt of a father down with him."

Her hands had gripped his belt. He looked down on white knuckles. "And – as if your family had learned no lesson at all – what did the de Veres do but embroil themselves in this latest attempt to put Henry the halfwit back on the throne? Your brother Jack, who'd never lifted a finger in the cause of Lancaster, riding Aubrey's reputation to insinuate himself with the Lancastrian lords. Thank God all that's behind us. Your brother is reaping a just reward for the treachery to King Edward, who showed your family nothing but mercy, bestowing the earldom of Oxford on Jack when your father and Aubrey were attainted as traitors. I'm sick of the subject now. Loosen your grip. You're giving me colic."

* * *

"This is Perteuil, isn't it, Lord Robert? It is! We set out from Perteuil in '63." Bellingham turned his cheery looks on Loic. "And, by Christmas, we were safe and sound in Skipton. Many a good omen, this time round!"

"For God's sake," muttered Patrick Nield.

"Ah, Bell… and lost Skipton again before Shrovetide!" Clifford was lying on his back in the little cabin as Loic peeled his master's chilly, sodden hose.

"Let's hope we can put up at the same inn. Decent food. What was it called?"

"La Clef D'Argent," said Castor.

"La Clef D'Argent. That's right. What was the fellow's name? Big local man."

"Etienne Ste-Croix."

"Ste-Croix. He was a pleasantish fellow, I seem to recall."

"Ah, when we dock, Bell, you find Ste-Croix and bring him to me. Take Patrick." He flicked his fingers at Nield. "Just look at old thunder-face! He's irking me again. You too, Arthur; you're very green. If you've the urge to hurl, don't do it here. Not you, mon petit: I want you at work on my knee. It's paining me."

Loic lowered himself to the damp and reeking floor.

"Keep us tethered to the *De Roos* and tell the Flemings to stop making such a racket."

"One of them's still pinned to the guard-rail, Lord Robert. I'd cut him free, but that will start the bleeding again. I reckon he'll need an amputation."

"Not very chivalrous of you, Bell! Put the fellow out of his misery at once."

They had, indeed, chanced upon Perteuil. Their old friend Etienne Ste-Croix, by now the mayor of this little port, hastened down to the harbour to greet the illustrious visitor. Ste-Croix knew better than to demand sight of their safe-conduct from King Louis: there was none. Even before he left his inn, he'd dispatched a courier to Pierre du Chastel at Beauvais, where, he trusted, the royal agent would be found in attendance on the King.

The visit to the ship served no use but to flatter the exile's vanity. Now Ste-Croix was in a hurry to exit: moist to the ankles, and there was a queasy smell in the cabin. Lord Clifford hadn't troubled to rise from his cot – naked from the waist down, feet a yard apart.

The mayor's gaze was drawn, time and again, to Clifford's obtrusive crotch. "Since you last honoured my inn with your presence, Milor' de Clifford, my daughter Melisande has grown to womanhood, and I have married again. May I make so bold as to request …" He ran a hand through his thinning locks. "Such a number of young men about you, and we know what young men can be …"

"Have no fear on that score, Etienne. I'll castrate any man of mine who touches a Ste-Croix woman."

An unfortunate choice of words, when the scene was dominated – eclipsed – by the mound of sprawling privates.

On this first night, Clifford dined with the mayor, his wife and daughter at the family townhouse adjoining La Clef D'Argent.

Madame Renée Ste-Croix could never be mistaken for Melisande's mother: slim, very dark, hers were ruby lips, sharp cheekbones and a grave manner, where Melisande was blushing-fair with great bluebell eyes; with dimples at every pretty, peeking curve. But a brood heifer: come the childbearing years, she'd drop with fatness – not a look Clifford admired. He turned back to Ste-Croix's wife. A still woman, not happy; beautiful in her way. The breath ruffled in his throat.

A high wall, pierced by a little door, divided the hostelry from the sunlit garden of the private dwelling and cast the inn yard in perpetual shadow. Madame Renée had the keeping of the key to the garden door, as she had the keeping of every key to the place. Watching Lord Clifford watch his wife, Ste-Croix wondered if the key were safer in his own hands. But Renée was a woman both virtuous and wise; she was older than Lord Clifford and she was, with a very proper froideur, evading his eyes. *Eye.* Not so Melisande: gawking at their guest, the disgust rather too marked across her comely face.

Next door, the men were making themselves at home, elbowing out the few paying guests, who retreated swiftly to La Petite Clef, Ste-Croix's smaller hostelry: a safe distance.

* * *

That night, the party rested at an inn at Pontefract, for religious houses also gave Sir Simon colic. He avoided their hospitality where he could.

Under the hubbub, Alice pulled her gentlewoman aside. "I wish to speak to you, Joanna. Follow me upstairs, if you please."

Sir Simon exchanged glances with Brini.

Alice closed the door to her chamber, gestured Joanna to the bed and walked to the window, looking down on the peaceful street. "Master Brini seems to pay you some attention, Joanna. I think you are encouraging it. That pin in your hair can only have come from him."

"Oh! But I'm not behaving improperly, I hope! Signor Brini means nothing dishonourable. Does Sir Simon disapprove? I have very little, of course, unless Sir John Ames will help me."

"You like him, then?"

"So very much! He's kind and clever. And handsome, to my eyes. Suitable, do you not think?"

"No, I do not think him at all suitable!"

There was a look of desperate disappointment.

"His birth is not good, he's a foreigner and Sir Hugh says he lost his last position under suspicion of murder. And worse – worst of all – he and Sir Simon are ungodly men, with those unchristian goings-on in the small chamber at Avonby." She had but a dim conception of what might be involved. Certainly burning. "Nor will it stop when we reach Sevenhill. Sir Simon is boasting of a larger and better equipped apartment laid out for their use in the new house. This should give all devout women a disgust of them."

"I'm sure there is nothing unchristian afoot! Signor Brini would attend prayers more often if I asked him, I'm sure. And both gentlemen are too interested in the material world – mathematics and the movement of the stars and so forth – to spend their time on the occult."

"Your desire for him has clouded your judgment. You are more worthy than this, Joanna. When we're settled in Essex I shall look about for an honourable husband for you. One with birth and virtue on offer, rather than a pert smile."

It was the first mutiny of her life. "Why so unfair to me? I have never had an admirer. No man ever sought my favour. Not once. Freckles, and a brown face and so forth. But I've watched my friends enjoy male company wherever we go. It's not fair to deny me this man, when he looks at me, and likes me and means no dishonour. He is chamberlain to a landed knight, and I am gentlewoman to that knight's lady. There is no reason for me to give him up. Everyone about me has been behaving in a way that's not the slightest bit maidenly, while I'm singled out for criticism when I think only of marriage!"

Freckles? Not freckles: moles. Very, very many moles. Alice shook her head, staring out into the fading light, unwilling to engage with what was fast becoming a jumble of overheated accusation.

"It's true! Lady Blanche misbehaved herself with Sir Loic before she took Sir Hugh, and you have closed your eyes to it. Sir Loic kissed Cecily and asked her to wait for him. Constance was chased by Bede and Richie FitzClifford and poor Sir Leonard Tailboys – not that she's interested. Elyn is always looking at men, and men are always looking at Elyn and we all know why, and Guy and George FitzClifford were competing openly for her. And you – you more than any of them!"

"*Me?*" The moles were forgotten. "How *dare* you?"

"Duke Edmond and Lord Clifford brawled in the street over you, and it was talked of everywhere. Even then you judged it right to leave your husband and flee with Lord Clifford, riding in his lap. We all saw the tantrum of jealousy when Master Hal called you by name and took you in his arms! Aymer FitzClifford followed you everywhere; he couldn't take his eyes off you. All of this you know, Lady Alice; you know it full well. And yet, in spite of everything, you are prized beyond measure! No wife could be more beloved of her husband. There is nothing Sir Simon would not do for you. He is besotted."

"I wouldn't go that far, Mistress Joanna," said Loys from the threshold, where he'd been lounging, apparently a while. "*Besotted* suggests a deficiency of reason, and I trust no one could accuse me of that. But seems to me, Lady Alice, that Joanna is, in large measure, correct. You've not managed to safeguard either your gentlewomen or, indeed, yourself to a degree that would give anyone confidence in your judgment. Fortunately, Joanna's fate doesn't lie in those unsteady hands. Your opinion counts for nothing. *I* give my consent."

* * *

"What are you doing here, Monsieur du Chastel? Ah, waiting for me, no doubt."

"No, Milor' de Clifford. I am not waiting for you. My master has greater matters afoot than you and your adventuring." The mournful circumlocution of old was gone: Pierre du Chastel's voice was direct and withering.

"You startle me!" Clifford reclined until he was virtually supine. "I thought King Louis designated you as my personal agent. I thought you were following me around, trying to pay my pension. It's in arrears, by the way."

Etienne Ste-Croix had been hovering, uncertain, within the doorway of his own little day room. Now he bowed to the two protagonists and backed out. Never had he heard Pierre du Chastel addressed in such a manner, at once familiar and dismissive; when Ste-Croix looked on the agent he saw not the twisted old sage before him, but King Louis himself: a plump, bulbous-nosed dolphin, threshing with energy; terrifying.

"War is coming."

"Don't I know it! I struck the first blow! I burned York's ships – every last one – massing at Southampton for the defence of Brittany. I fought off Anthony Woodville's prize soldiery, and slaughtered the lot of them – though we were vastly outnumbered, as usual." Lounging, still, in the mayor's chair, Clifford waved du Chastel to the low window. "Look! I bring Burgundian tribute to your master." But the window gave out on an alley. "Go to the harbour. Take a look at the tribute."

"I've just come from the harbour. Was it not sufficient to slay their sailors at sea? I hear you were still murdering them after you'd put into port. Provocative, Milor', to say the least. The surviving Flemings must be sent home with their ship. Ste-Croix should have done that at once."

On the far side of the door, Ste-Croix winced. At such a moment, any course would have proved the wrong course; there was no handbook for this.

"And I shall write in the king's name to Duke Charles of Burgundy," continued du Chastel, "and blame you for the outrage. Scuttle back to Scotland, Milor', and quickly, before the Duke sends an armada to look for you."

"I haven't the wherewithal to get back to Scotland. Pay the allowance and I might just manage it. Otherwise, I dawdle about in the narrow sea, running down shipping. French shipping, possibly. I'm bound to grow careless."

"You are making this more difficult than it needs to be. I do have instructions to come to an arrangement with you, Milor', *after* you've turned your attention to harassing England, and not before. But Ste-Croix tells me your friends have landed further up the coast at Honfleur; I go from here to speak with the Earl and his friend, Milor' de Beaumont. I trust these noblemen will prove more amenable to sense."

"Beaumont and de Vere are puppies who trot at my heels. Don't go, my friend." The thrumming voice turned confidential. "I've a plan I'd like to share with you. You want Edward of York to turn his attention from Brittany. How would it be if I assaulted Calais?"

Ste-Croix stumbled back from the door. *Calais?* Last English toehold in France; a bristling hedgehog of a city. *Calais?* That needed time. Time to plan and fund and muster. The Englishman would be taking his ease yet awhile in Perteuil before leading his men away to a splendid and noisy suicide.

At the foot of the stairs Ste-Croix found his wife delighting her stepdaughter with the rudiments of housewifery. On and on droned the voice, sweet and low; Renée's finger pointing here in the ledger; pointing there. Melisande's eyes had long since slipped to the window with its oblique view of the lane. Over the last hour, several of the FitzCliffords had discovered matters to occupy them in the alley outside; making their meandering way, chancing to glance through the casement as they passed. While the girl leaned over the accounts, a slow hand was sliding about beneath her neckline, fingers rootling to pluck and hoist. By now her breasts were on coy display, smooth and proud as two eggs.

The husband gave his wife a swift précis. "Speak to Patrick Nield. You can manage everything through him; the steward's a decent man. Ensure the bill is settled in full and in advance. He'll ask for credit; don't give it, for there'll be no return visit." Off went the mayor to the market hall, leaving the younger of his clerks. Fabien spoke an approximate form of English, the only one who did.

While she considered how best to tackle the steward, there were more mundane matters of housekeeping: a broken window in the best chamber. Renée tweaked her stepdaughter's chemise to vanquish the bosom then led little Fabien through the garden gate and into the precincts of the inn. With a sharp look out for the dangerous one, she mounted the stairs to an upper floor of the house, where two chambers adjoined the stairwell.

Both doors stood open. The best room, Lord Clifford's own, lay empty. But something worse than a broken window was amiss. For the grand bed – her mother's prized bed, principal part of her dowry – had gone. In its place stood the workaday frame from next door: larger and less ornate. Renée backed out of that room and into the next. There, on the wrong bed, her mother's bed, in their dirty boots, lounged two of Lord Clifford's sons, playing at cards. They scrambled up.

The slighter boy, that poor mute, made a mumble that was no proper greeting in any tongue. The other – a great, unsightly hulk – stepped forward and presented himself in hobnail French. After the briefest return of courtesy, she blasted them with a torrent. Fabien raised pleading hands.

"Oh – the bed!" At last Richie understood. "Your pardon, Madame. My father's a very long man and could not squeeze himself into the one he was given; his feet hung out the end. So my brothers and I spared you the trouble by changing them over."

While Fabien did his work, Richie waited, then blenched before her raging. "I did not think it valuable! Your pardon! There was woodworm; some of the dovetails came apart, but I reckon I banged the joints up well enough." He gave it an exploratory shake. The tester lurched ominously.

More storming; a pained translation from Fabien.

"Well, no – my father would not take this chamber, for it's small and dark and he likes his view toward England. Your pardon. Jesu, Madame, your pardon! I'll not rest my boots on the foot, I swear, and nor shall Will. The frame's too short for me, anyway." His own pallet was shorter by far, but then, they always were. "My brothers share this bed by night; the twins are men of more common height."

Forgetful of the reason for her visit, Renée shrugged a wrathful shoulder and descended the stairway, driving Fabien before her.

Richie threw himself back on the bed, scuffing mud into the carvings. "You knocked it about as much as I did! Why the fuck is it always my fault?" He sighed. "What a woman, though. A warm wench for a cold night, eh? Reckon she likes me." He raised a hand. "Not that I mean to do anything about it."

Will laughed.

Renée turned the corner and there was the devil himself, a throng of men below him. At once the herd backed out of view.

"What can it be, Madame Ste-Croix?" A sleeve grazed her ear as he lounged against the wall, keeping her from moving on. "You are distressed." The voice thrummed at her chest; the very foundations rumbled. By the barest movement of his head Lord Clifford motioned the clerk away.

Fabien the Spineless. She'd have him beaten for this. Already they were alone.

"Excuse me, Milor' de Clifford, if you please!" An impatient motion, to no avail when she was imprisoned by his arm: dark velvet, rich and warm. Her ceiling was the collar of his shirt; she could not bring herself to contemplate that vile countenance. The man whose father killed her own.

"If my men have done aught to offend you, I must know of it. I made your husband a promise."

So she'd been assured by Etienne. A defective vow, when the promisor was excluded from its ambit. She could not evade him now except by remounting the stairs which, swiftly, she did, but he was swifter, at once alongside, fingers catching her elbow.

"Very well, Milor' de Clifford. There is one matter, of trifling importance, no doubt."

They had reached the threshold. Rain pattered; the narrow chamber was dim and gloomy. Lord Clifford must have gestured to his boys – back on the bed in their filthy boots – for they hastened away, cringing. Now he was behind her, blocking the exit.

With grave attention he heard out the stilted complaint and answered in his faultless French. "Forgive my sons. Their zeal for my comfort has led them astray. They would have taken more care, if they only understood you as I do. So … this life is comfortable, as far as worldly goods go, and Ste-Croix is a good man. But marriage came late in life; you fear you'll bear no children of your own. Your step-daughter's an idiot who'll make some merchant an incompetent wife, though you do your best by her. I watch you in church: your chief solace is your devotion to Our Lady, through whom you see your lost mother. Am I right? And this bed kindles her presence as nothing else can."

It was a recitation of taunts; a litany, not a conversation. She giddied. One hand swam out to find the cool solidity of the wall.

"The damage is all the harder to bear when you warned your husband against lodging a crowd of renegade Englishmen, though you'll not tell him of the insult to your property, for he would not understand how deeply it has pierced you. But I understand. I understand you in every particular."

Self-control had forsaken her, scoured clear on a queasy gust of outrage. She trembled in its wake. "Well! Nigh on the full tally: all those petty laments. You missed only my father's death at the hands of the English rabble in Pontoise."

That shut him up. The tyrant gaze dropped from her and, after a moment, he lowered himself to the bed. Crumpling a sheet, Clifford began, with methodical inattention, to polish the tracery. Thinking on his father, no doubt – that marauding abomination.

When breathing had stilled, he raised his head – soft words at the ready – to find himself alone. Careless of his boots, Clifford lay back to consider the sharp angles of Renée Ste-Croix.

* * *

By the time they reached Cambridge, a measure of Master Brini's confidence had ebbed away. While Sir Simon supposed there to be no further difficulty, Leo was developing a rebellious scepticism over his master's judgment. But he must know where he stood. That evening he induced Joanna to slip away for a moment. They wandered down to the river below the fine colleges.

"Mistress Joanna, just imagine what it must be to study at this seat of learning, as Sir Simon did. It honed his brilliance, he says."

"I'm sure you'd profit from it, were it possible, Signor Brini. We cannot always have what we want, unfortunately."

"Oh. But perseverance may achieve much."

"Sometimes."

They walked on. The buildings were finer from a distance; close to, the river was smelly and there was refuse in abundance.

With one accord they turned to each other, and as he took her hand, she shook her head.

"Please –"

"I cannot."

"You know what it is that I wish: nothing a man should be ashamed to ask a woman. I was married, once, at a young age. One month of joy before I lost my dear one to the Great Death. My heart has been bleeding ever since, and you have healed it."

"It cannot be. I could not oppose Lady Alice's wishes, even if you were a prince. I have shown terrible ingratitude, when I owe everything to her and her family."

He studied her face, flowing with tears. "I understand. I want nothing that would make you unhappy. Only, say it is not the end."

"Unless my mistress changes her mind, it is the end."

* * *

They were close now; very close to home. The carriage was filled with the drone of Blanche. "I simply cannot credit it. Just when I begin to think I might be returning to my right size … now this! I must have fallen within two months of little Simon's birth. I cannot imagine how it is even possible."

There was silence while everyone tried to ward off the possible.

"Sir Hugh's appetites are beyond anything endurable. Let this be a lesson to you maidens: set down strictures from the first, or a husband will think he may …"

"Sir Simon!" called Alice from the window at the rear. "May I ride with you? I want to see Sevenhill as soon as it comes into view."

Within the hour, they crested the last wooded knoll, and there it was, familiar yet unfamiliar; broad and magnificent, the stones crisp-edged, the grass dusty and trampled. Far too much of it was on view.

"Where is the tree?"

"What tree?"

"The great oak that shelters the house so well! What has happened?"

"Oh, that. I cut it down. It blocked the view from my brother's land, and that would never do. Sir Nicholas must be able to see Sevenhill in every season. You do understand that?"

"No, I do not! My brothers used to climb that tree. Aubrey made a swing in its branches. Jack fell and was stunned; my father wouldn't permit the sport after that, so they set up another, out of sight. I cannot bear that it is gone."

"I ground away the stump and not a trace remains. Do try to keep your mind on the present. For someone so young, you are remarkably maudlin."

The cutting of the tree was an impulse of malice, but it was not directed at her. She looked about. "What is happening at that barrow?"

"What do think is happening at the barrow? There is said to be treasure within, so Petronilla tells me, though you unaccountably failed to mention it. If it's there, I shall find it. I shall melt it down."

"Warriors sleep within these hills! If you wake them, they will walk. We'll have no peace if you destroy their graves."

"No, you foolish child, they will not walk. They are dead a thousand years. I am not destroying the hill; I am digging a shaft. Now, if you cannot say anything complimentary, then hold your tongue." Taking his wife's hand, Sir Simon guided her about with evident pride. The ground floor was tiled in blue and gold, illuminated by large windows; a sumptuous effect. But the building disconcerted her; some parts as she remembered, some wholly new, built on an imposing scale. Here was her bedchamber, with its adjoining bath, fed by water that moved uphill. It looked like sorcery, but when he explained the workings, she saw that it owed more to the application of mathematics, and stopped listening.

Within the jewel box of a chapel, proud badges stood in glistening glass: the pale star of the de Veres, its pure and silver streams gleaming down on the Loys insignia, the industrious bee. The glassblower's art had faltered there; the insect was far from lively, flattened against the pane, target of one too many swipes.

The craftsman had sought to honour his patron also in a vast and vivid depiction of the martyrdom of his namesake, St Simon. Alice took some steps back from the altar to study the image. Again, something amiss. Was the saint not an elderly man at the time of his crucifixion? Yet here was a strapping youth, black locks tousling his brow, gazing down on his tormentors with pale eyes and a nasty smile. And all but naked! About the hips floated a tiny loincloth. No fold or clasp secured the linen; the merest breath of wind would flutter it away.

"What an obscene waste of money," said Sir Simon in her ear, making her jump. "I've a good mind to take it down. Why should the fellow grin so inanely? The only men who smile at their own execution are those who've lost their reason, like your first husband. Attending mass is painful enough, I can't be looking at a madman into the bargain."

"I wish you would stop repeating this. My husband was *not* a madman." Here was Edmond, at last, before her inner eye, in a thousand fleeting images. Unhappy, not insane. Most probably he greeted the axe with glad relief, like an old friend.

"I watched him mount the scaffold; you didn't. But have it your own way, if it soothes your conscience." Sir Simon smirked. "Now tell me: did you ever mean to share the secret of the hidden staircase, or were you planning to use it for your own purposes?

"Oh, the staircase!" She turned with relief. "I would not have told you, of course. It is too good a joke. The masons found it, I suppose?"

"Is there any other hiding place within the house?"

When she shook her head, he wondered: deceit or ignorance? The workmen had discovered a further chamber opening from that concealed stairway. Built by the Earls of Oxford for the purpose, probably, of secreting their gold. He would use it likewise – if and when there were ever gold in surplus. *Ignorance*, he decided: Alice knew nothing of the room's existence.

* * *

The first wife of Etienne Ste-Croix had been a woman of unsteady temper and unbridled avarice, one who needed careful watching; his second was her perfect counterpoise. Once he'd tasked Madame Renée with the presentation of the bill, he left her to it.

Renée wouldn't venture again to the hostelry. When she summoned Lord Clifford's steward to her house, Nield brought Loic along, uninvited, trusting to the Frenchman's accustomed wizardry. But they found her implacable. Her courteous request was a rude assault on their time-honoured custom – which was to spin out the term, evade the debt and, at a later date, flit off.

Nield shook his head. "I can't oblige you directly, Madame. I suppose I must head over to Honfleur and see if I can borrow the money from the Earl of Oxford or Lord Beaumont. We're particularly skint, just at present, for the King of Scotland is rather hard-up himself, it seems, and can spare us little." His mournful looks told the unhappy truth: their new patron, King James, in whom such hopes resided, had spared them not a penny.

She nodded, merciless, and allowed her gaze to stray to the young chamberlain. The kingdom of France possessed other Monclers, perhaps – lesser creatures, whom Charlemagne had snubbed. If so, Renée did not know of them. Loic's every part – peacock bearing, finespun features and a dulcet voice – proclaimed the true Moncler lineage, ancient and splendid. At first, her concern had been to keep Melisande from the lure. Now the resolve was faltering. She opened her mouth, closed it, and dared to delve in. "I hear your noble cousin of Moncler is an elderly man, sir. And they say … childless … since he lost his only son just lately, campaigning in Artois."

Silence fell. The young man looked anything but glad of her news.

Now there was a rosy flush creeping on her cheeks, unexpectedly girlish. "Forgive me, sir. I spoke out of turn."

236

"There's nothing to forgive, Madame. But I put that life behind me, long since. I would never, *never* leave Monseigneur, not for all the riches in France. I am his man; I am an English knight."

She bowed her head as though she understood. The Monclers were past their peak, as far as power and riches went. Yet in all of France, there was no name more venerable. What could lead a man to turn his back on such eminence and follow a wicked English rebel?

Once the pair passed through the garden door and the key had clicked behind them, Nield cuffed his young colleague on the back of the head, a violence he'd not done in many a year. "Could you not have played along, you dunderhead? All that stuff: the woman was thinking of her daughter, wasn't she?"

Loic blinked. "Monseigneur would not approve any pretence on that score. I'm a Moncler. An inn-keep's grub is no fit wife for me."

"Are you, now? I thought you were an English knight. So we're stuck with a muckle great bill and no means to pay it. This stupid plan to assault Calais will fair clean us out. If he has any more wild notions for wasting money we don't have, give him a great kicking from me, will you?"

"I have an idea on that."

* * *

If Loys were surprised when Alice challenged his mastery, he did not allow it to deflect him. Soon after their arrival in Essex, he wrote to Sir John Ames, who was entirely a stranger to him, and invited the man to visit.

"I can force Lady Alice to recant and give her approval, Leo; have no doubt on that score."

"Please do no such thing, mio signor. Mistress Joanna would know at once how her ladyship was brought to it. That would help me not at all."

"Which is why I've handled my wife with the usual forbearance. And so Mistress Joanna's uncle is our best hope. You see, my friend, what I would not suffer for your sake? I know just what this Sir John will be. My wife calls him a *proud Englishman*: I can think of few beasts less amenable. But let him come to me and I will most probably succeed with him. We desire only his blessing; we do not, ultimately, require his money. If the old bore should accept you as a nephew, Lady Alice will have no further excuse for obstinacy.

Alas for Leo Brini and his hopes. Sir John replied promptly, declining the invitation. He and his lady were not presently going out among the world, for they had suffered a dolorous blow. Their daughter – their only child – had sickened and, within the last week, was gone from them. The letter delivered a further shock. As Sir John had now no living offspring, he desired Joanna to come to live at Blakeney Hall: she was now his heiress.

Leo lowered his eyeglasses and handed the letter back to his master. For a while there was silence. Sir Simon gestured Brini into a chair, but he did not sit. "She must go to them, of course," said Loys. "There's no way to prevent it. I'll take the girl myself; Blakeney lies towards a number of my new manors; I should inspect them, and there are men out that way whose acquaintance I must renew. I suspect the case is lost but still, I shall do what I can."

"The case is lost. No, mio signor: even if you could work sorcery on Sir John, and bully your wife into submission, Mistress Joanna must not sacrifice her position in such a way. It would cause her misery, and her misery would bring misery on me in its turn."

After some further moments, Sir Simon stood and walked to the window, diverted, as ever, by the long sweep of his lands before him. "No doubt you'll think me precipitous, my friend, but remember there are other gentlewomen whose position is quite different. If your eye were to fall on Constance, or even Elyn – God forbid – there would be no difficulty. Baseborn, and wholly dependent on me.

"What are you saying? Certainly I cannot think on this now, when I've lost my heart's companion."

"And I thought I was companion enough for you! If it must be female company, go to Colchester and sample the oysters. Cheaper and more peaceable than matrimony. So I'm told."

When Brini was gone, Sir Simon summoned Joanna. "So, you see, your fortunes have altered quite significantly."

The girl sat, a long time, and he did not disturb her. Eventually she raised her eyes.

"You may tell me the truth, Mistress Joanna: if Lady Alice and Sir John were content – unlikely as that may be – would you take Brini?"

She tried to picture Leo Brini as master of Blakeney Hall. The image slipped about like a bubble in oil; she couldn't grasp it. Slowly she shook her head. "Signor Brini would never be accepted by the gentry of the county, and that would soon lead to his unhappiness, and mine."

"You are right, and it grieves me."

When the party set out a day later, Brini was at the door to see them off. Joanna, who'd been evading him with a cowardice that was as reasonable as it was reprehensible, lifted tearful eyes. Smiling back, he caught her hand amid the flurry of departure and pressed it to his heart. "May God bless you, always."

The door slammed and a hush fell. Alice and the chamberlain faced each other across the entrance.

* * *

It was the feast of St Germanus, patron of Perteuil.

The foreigners whose arrival caused such a stir about the place were ready to demonstrate their good intentions: Lord Clifford let it be known that the conduits would run with his wine. Once there was an Englishman who wrought great destruction in these parts, but that was half a lifetime ago. Most of the townsfolk welcomed his son's reparations; a few longed, perhaps, to cross him in some dark and ungallant alley – but that was only to be expected.

Like so many that day, the Wyverns started early. They'd occupied a tavern, penning the locals up the far end. Now they were debating in hushed voices. A keen observer might have scented mischief, but it was a holiday and the natives' wits were somewhat dulled.

Clifford was brooding on a more ancient mischief; on the siege of Pontoise; on finding echoes of his father in so far a place. At this offbeat moment Lord Thomas flooded his thoughts, a grim hero, bones forlorn and untended in the Abbey of St Alban. His heart spun.

"Under six foot?" Findern said, puncturing his musings. "Under six foot, and a man will generally pass unnoticed. That's where we draw the line, I think."

"Agreed," said George, looking down his nose on the twins. Only an inch or two taller, he had to tilt his head backwards to do so. "No one notices dwarves."

Bede nodded. "Dwarves. Little folk."

"You really *are* thick," observed Guy. "He said *under* six foot."

"That won't do," Nield growled. "Bell and Jolly and I are too old for crawling about in the dark. And all the others are too slight; we need some heft." Now everyone was looking at the twins.

"We are *not* under six foot."

"Right." Clifford settled it. "Six foot and under. And practise walking like Frenchmen."

The fair was in full swing. Every second house was brewing. Across on the quayside, a huge ox smoked and sputtered into the embers. The men emerged from the tavern into the tipsy air. Head and shoulders above the crowd, Clifford was casting about for his quarry when he spotted the butts beside the custom house. Archery was a particular delight: of all the exiles, he alone had brought his bow all the way from Skipton: a vast thing; an unwieldy inconvenience. "Run back to the inn and fetch it, Jem. Let's show these foreigners how it's done." He might have brought up Agincourt, but caught Loïc's eye and didn't.

Clifford strolled over, taking his time, searching in vain among his audience. He measured the distance, and motioned for the target to be moved back, then back again. The crowd swelled, thronging in.

"No other man in Christendom can bend my bow."

That old fib. Many of the Wyverns and most of the FitzCliffords could handle it.

"Hal's as fine an archer, and he's pinched that bow often enough."

"The rest of us can do a fair job, I think you'll find." Aymer's drawl was inaudible to Clifford – unlike George's booming undertone.

"You can't! You'd have to stand on a box."

At last, Etienne Ste-Croix emerged from the custom house, descending the external stairway, his womenfolk a step behind. Clifford gazed at Renée until she lifted her eyes. He bent the bow and fumbled his shot, the arrow veering wide, splashing far into the harbour. Lifting a hand to silence the jeers, he took a deep and conspicuous breath before drawing the string once more and skewering the distant bullseye. His gaze hadn't left her.

"That miss was deliberate."

Castor turned to find Aymer close behind. "Yes: a neat trick, and well-practised. Of course, if you're half-blind it's not much odds whether you're looking or not."

Richie cocked his head. "You only need one eye to aim, so he's no worse off than the rest of us."

George sniggered. Castor shook his head in disgust. "Have you paid me no heed? All those hours of training; I might as well talk to myself! Find your stronger eye, use it, but don't close the other, for God's sake!"

"Archery's a churl's pastime. Don't trouble yourself." Richie stalked off.

"No wonder he can't hit a barn door," said Findern. Richie was absolutely as skilled as the rest.

"Christ on the cross!" bellowed Nield, and they all swivelled. Richie's accomplishments were no longer at issue: the steward had just watched Lord Clifford accept the winner's purse, only to hand it straight back, to noisy acclaim. "He is testing me to the very limit!" He scowled at Renée, who was applauding with the rest.

"Soft, my friend." Loic had idled up. "Come twilight, we'll repair our fortunes."

* * *

"Cecily, fetch your cloak, and mine; I see Master Nicholas and Mistress Petronilla at the side gate." Alice raised a hand. "No, Elyn; I told you already.

You cannot come. There isn't the space for you at Petronilla's aunt's house. You *won't* be alone, silly! There are plenty of folk about. Blanche is here. Mitten is here, and Master Brini also. And mind you keep him at arm's length."

The departure was rudely hurried and – if they cared to turn – there she was, glowering at the window, hand-on-hip. When she'd drained Mitten, she'd bedevil Master Brini – who was nowhere on her yardstick – but Elyn was a girl who preferred any company to her own.

Petronilla glanced over her shoulder. "I'd have strangled her after an hour. I don't know how you tolerate it."

"She is my sister," came the small voice.

Free and easy, the small party entered Colchester and divided itself further: Nicholas and his few attendants went about their business, while Petronilla led Alice and Cecily along the shops and stalls of the High Street, tailed by a manservant. "I must speak with the apothecary about my headaches." Progress was slow. "God in Heaven, Alice! There's not such a crowd thronging to greet you when Simon is about." At last Petronilla disengaged her sister-in-law from the abounding well-wishers and tugged her down an alley to a low-browed window like a winking eye. There was no array opening on the street, only the rusty, swinging sign. In they went. Petronilla shut the door in the servant's face.

Inside, Master Farrimond saw to their comfort. "I have the honour to serve Sir Simon in my own small way, my lady, with those elements I can source for his illustrious work."

Alice twitched her cloak about her.

"Nothing I may do for you today, Lady Alice?" Bowing, he uncoupled Petronilla from this stranger who gilded his room like a resplendent Madonna, and led the older woman deeper into the dim cave. A door creaked and entombed them. He pressed Petronilla down on a hard, three-legged stool. "Headaches, mistress?" She hadn't told him of her trouble. "I warned you the powder may have unwanted effects."

The grey man settled before her, bald velvet brushing the floor. Taking a hand, he caressed the pads of her palm, his breath dampening her fingers, his head lowered in close contemplation, though his eyes were overcast and the room in three-quarter darkness. Iron hair swept back from hollow temples, from a pensive face, the nose beginning to hook, the mouth beginning to sink. Over his shoulder she could make out the narrow bed, and closed her eyes. Slow moments passed. Upturned in his clasp was her rosy wrist; she sensed her own pulse; she heard it. Her frame shivered and began, softly at first, to throb. A finger touched her lips. When they parted, he probed within, skin perfumed with mead, tasting of dust, and parchment dry; it blotted the moisture from her tongue.

Once the pounding eased, she opened her eyes. Master Farrimond was now a wholesome distance, gazing on her with the sad, sweet patience of an old dog. "The drug has been at work, Mistress Petronilla, after its own fashion. You fired the ardour of a man who could not bring himself to it before. It may or may not have been the man you seek; that's not for me to say. His seed blossoms within you. You are with child."

* * *

Darkness fell early, for the wind had whipped up, driving in leaden cloud and a chilly shower. By then the Wyverns were back in the tavern, along with a mass of townsfolk. Under cover of the hubbub they parted, the taller men mingling with the drinkers while those of more regular height hooded themselves and turned out into the wet and blustery street. They weren't hurrying. They ambled past the dead fire with its blackened spit, the dogs squabbling over strips of charred hide. They passed the little market square: the archery butts were gone; the gullies of wine sluiced clear by rainwater. They passed the customs house, dark and empty, and paused to retrieve, from beneath its staircase, a wheelbarrow that Loic had deposited at first light. Then they trundled it on to Etienne Ste-Croix's stone warehouse.

The dwellings were becoming poorer here beneath the cliff, and all was quiet, the residents sleeping or spinning out the festivities elsewhere. The men made a swift circuit of the building. All the windows stood at the upper level, as expected; the great wooden door its only weak spot. At first there seemed to be no guard at all – a strange state of affairs – until two bodies were found slumbering on the seaward side. One of the men was unrousable. Bellingham gagged him and he slept on.

The other opened his eyes to smile into Loic's face. "Hey, pretty girl!" He stroked the chamberlain's stubble. "Rub a dub dub, pretty girl. I'm so stiff. God alone knows how I came to be here."

"Let's get you out of those wet clothes; I'll rub away to your heart's content."

Loic set about stripping the fellow and, once he'd done so, Lewis Jolly put him back to sleep with the hilt of his sword. Patrick Nield was kneeling nearby, prising the base of the door with a chisel; it wasn't sharp enough to serve as a jemmy, splintering rather than levering. At Skipton, there was an array of burgling tools, of course, but they couldn't bring everything and they'd chosen badly. When there was a degree of give, Nield stepped back, motioning Guy and Aymer to lie down. The twins wrapped their boots in the watchman's sodden garb. With a series of heavy, muffled kicks, they failed to break through the loosened boards. They righted themselves, and everyone took an impatient turn with the chisel. Then the pair lay down and started again with the clobbering. Once they'd burrowed inside, they demolished the door from within.

Nield lit a solitary lantern and vast shadows sprang up. The warehouse was well-kept, with bales and sacks in orderly rows. In such poor light it took a long, weary time to find anything practical to steal. Much of the contents was bulky stuff – linen or leather – of no use to them, but among it all, some small, weighty wooden boxes containing tiny silver ingots – an illegal export – together with a chest of pepper, a huge lopsided pearl and a hoard of reddish, uncut stones that they wished very much to be ruby but guessed, correctly, to be beryl.

So as to cover their tracks, the men collected a random assortment of the lighter sacks, loaded them on to the wheelbarrow and tipped them over the sea wall. At the last moment, one bale was found to contain some wonderful sable pelts, glossy and sleek, so they unloaded that one and brought it back up, then returned to the warehouse to look for more, but when they couldn't find any, they secreted their booty and pitched the wheelbarrow into the waves.

Then the burglars slipped to join their taller fellows in the tavern, where Clifford was creating a conspicuous alibi, diverting the drinkers with a rendition of North Country ballads; sweet gibberish. Never had the burghers of Perteuil been so greatly flattered by a nobleman; the incomprehensible treat was talked of for weeks.

Still the singer looked about him, searching among the crowd. For all the ever-present homesickness, he'd forgotten that this was not England, and respectable Frenchwomen did not frequent taverns.

* * *

"Respectable Frenchwomen do not frequent taverns. Nor do the Flemish ladies. Duke Edmond had been so long abroad that he forgot England was different; he was shocked when my brother took Lady Margaret and me to dine at his favourite!"

"The Tabard?" interrupted Nicholas. "I spent many a happy evening with Lord Jack in that hidey-hole. Well – whenever I was in London, which wasn't often. I've never even been out of England. You're fortunate, Alice, to be so well-travelled."

She drained her cup. "Not so fortunate. Ah, my life has been hard and unsteady."

Nicholas smiled into her lovely eyes, glossy in the candlelight. Simon, too, would be shocked to learn of today's jaunt; shocked and furious. "Have you enjoyed yourself? You called on the priest of St Giles, I hear. He would have been flattered by your visit, especially as you didn't call on the Abbot. The two are daggers-drawn, as it were. But most men hereabouts are well-disposed to the de Veres, of course." She'd been seen by everyone, spoken with most and the outing would be the talk of the town, in just the way his brother would deplore.

"Everyone was so pleasant and respectful. I think Sir Simon's presence intimidates the good folk. He glowers at them."

"And you spent a merry time wandering the shops and stalls, I don't doubt. Have you bought much? I'm sure my brother would wish you to please yourself."

"I tried on a girdle. I didn't take it, for he likes to choose my things himself. We found ribbons for Elyn in the colours she doesn't have. And Petronilla went to the apothecary. I didn't like him. The shop was dirty and I'm certain the man trades in the occult."

"I've been plagued with headaches, Nicholas, but Master Farrimond could not help me. There's nothing amiss," she added, when her husband didn't ask. "Nothing that time won't cure."

Nicholas was smiling, still, at Alice. His fancy had made her a frail rose beneath Simon's heavy heel. Now, in her presence, he tingled with her tiny thorns. "If Farrimond makes a few pennies selling amulets and whatnot to the credulous, they won't do any harm. He's a clever man, most learned in transmutation. Simon and Brini haunt the place."

Alice tilted her chin. "So I hear. And people wonder that I won't permit Joanna to marry that outlander!" She nodded to herself. "In Venice, Brini was suspected of sorcery – so says Sir Hugh – and lost his position over it. And now he works his evil among us!"

Nicholas was frowning now, above the smile. "It's true Simon rescued the man when he was destitute. The usual jealousy and finger-pointing among servants."

She would strew the riches of her experience. "To my mind, no smoke without fire. Where there is talk, there is, generally, truth."

Husband and wife were blinking down on her like owls.

Behind them, in the doorway, the tavern-keeper ducked and wove, tackling a small commotion of townsmen intent on accosting the noble guest. When Nicholas beckoned, they gushed for a while, a little the worse for drink, backing away at last, their bonnets busy. Petronilla was fanning her cheeks with her hand, pink in the firelight.

"Your pardon, Lady Loys! The tavern-keeper bobbed at her elbow. "This is becoming a nuisance." They should have been ensconced with Petronilla's aunt by now – awaiting the incense of the de Vere presence.

Nicholas waved the man away. "If Brini's casting spells, he's doing it on the quiet. There's none my brother despises so much as a fool who believes in magic."

"A fool who believes in magic?" echoed Alice. "But, Nicholas, we speak of a man who furnishes a chamber solely for the casting of spells!"

Nicholas gave a startled laugh, and broke off just as quickly. "My brother, a necromancer? How odd, that you could know him so little! He's an apostate and a blasphemer, no doubt, but it's only his own soul he's imperilling. The trials that he and Brini labour over are grounded in learned arts and his insatiable lust for gold. Simon is an alchemist."

"Alchemy?" said she in a doubtful tone. "Seeking to change base metal into gold: is that not a form of sorcery?" The all-seeing eye was raised, and dismissed with incredulity – by both of them, now.

"Simon's an inquisitive man, and clever one. But Alice! A magical device that allows him to look into your mind? I think you'll find he is listening at doors, for he has no scruples."

"Very well," said Alice, rather stiffly. "Perhaps I am mistaken. In fact, I see that I am. Let nothing further be said of this, I beg you. Especially to him."

* * *

The next morning, Clifford was out in the inn yard, training with the men. "Impressive! My brother would have been proud of you, George. I only wish John could have seen you at Barnet." Wherever Hal might be, his father's comments were, as so often, aimed only at him, as though his son hovered, invisible, within earshot. But George beamed and puffed his chest. To undo the damage, Clifford elbowed Findern aside and charged in, shoulder down. George flew backward like a rag doll. "That is just how you will be unmanned, you mawk! Attend!"

"He's right, of course," murmured Findern as he heaved George to his feet. "Beware the enemy who mourns your father: it is a ruse."

Etienne Ste-Croix had entered through the garden door and stood awhile, observing the Englishmen at their perpetual pastime. This was their life now; all they were good for.

Clifford noticed him at last. His hand was warm on the man's shoulder. "How do you go, my friend? A rough head after yesterday? I know I have."

"Not really, Milor'. Not too bad. I have suffered a blow though. Last night my warehouse was broken."

"Your warehouse? Who could have done such a thing?"

"I have a shrewd idea, Milor'."

"Do you?"

Ste-Croix turned, more drab than usual, to frown up into his guest's face. "The goods were not … there's no sense in it, save to spite me. The robbers took up a sample of each type, and threw them into the sea. Two bales of linen washed up this morning, still labelled, and the spars of a wheelbarrow. The owner's mark is carved into it."

"Is it, now? Then you have the culprit, it seems."

"So I believe. Of course, he says it was stolen from him during the festivity."

"He would, though, wouldn't he? Who is it?"

"Portiers. Jean Portiers. An old friend; Melisande is intended for his son. But lately, my rival for the mayoralty. We quarrelled, and now he is giving me a warning, perhaps. They say Portiers was in the tavern with you and your men last night, Milor', when you condescended to sing for the company. Your pardon, but may I ask if you saw anything amiss? Any comings and goings among the men?"

"Plenty. But there were whores everywhere, plying their trade. My own men were in and out, as it were. Speak to my chaplain. Probably he was overseer; he usually is."

As if there were not enough pleasure to be had on the previous night, George was now idling before the entrance to the yard, advertising his intentions to any who might wish to partake. "Peter, you must come with us to the tavern. You're of an age now, and your French will come in handy." George was firmly rooted in his native tongue; discourse with outsiders passed through the mouths of other men, and all the better for it. "If you don't come, fellows will say you have strange inclinations."

"Who will say that?" Over time the boy's submissive manner had ebbed away and then pivoted, aggressively, into reverse. "Benet has not touched a girl, so they say; Sir Arthur Castor sits it out; Edwin never goes unless Father twists his arm; Aymer won't consort with whores. Yet no one says anything about their inclinations."

"There is something wrong with Aymer, as I've told you before, my lad. Don't look to him as your pattern."

"Aymer is much as other men, George, only cleverer, a finer soldier," Peter made sure to pierce the thick hide, "and a better tutor. There's nothing amiss. He has a sweetheart, is all; he means to stay true to her."

"*Aymer?*" doubted Bede and George, together.

"For sure. Her keepsake never leaves his person. A costly emerald, befitting a great lady. Sometimes I see him take it out and handle it, but always he keeps it close, for all that it's worth a pretty penny, and us so poor."

* * *

Having left Joanna, subdued and dutiful, with Sir John and Lady Ames, Loys made his rounds with his steward. If the manors were a little smaller than expected, they were, at least, well-ordered. Cross-questioning the under-bailiffs, he was satisfied for the most part, dismissing one where he could not wring straight answers, and one where the ledgers would not yield up their secrets.

Then on to Pearmain, to his half-sister Jane. The gentlewoman welcomed Loys with her customary coolness. Her husband, Sir Gilbert, was considerably warmer; it was indiscriminate though, his ruddy face ever beaming: good natured and bluff. There, Loys discovered that his nephew Hugo was, in the near future, to wed Triston Clifford's daughter.

"No one mentioned it to me."

Jane shrugged. "It slipped my mind. Come if you must."

Sheringham puffed in. "My apologies, Simon. Naturally you're welcome; we long to meet the new Lady Loys, of course." He looked at his wife. "I don't believe there's room at Pearmain for any more guests, but Triston will house you, of that I'm certain."

"He's stayed at Avonby before now; I don't expect his manners to be deficient."

Before he left Pearmain, Loys shucked off another female: Catharine was left to her Uncle and Aunt Sheringham for a prolonged sojourn. Welcome news to bring back to Alice.

It was late afternoon when Loys led his party towards Crawshay Hall. With one accord the men pulled up as the vista opened before them. "Sevenhill is larger, of course, and better placed, but Crawshay is, undeniably, a perfect little gem. When last I was here, years ago now, there was no moat. I wonder how he diverted the river. An awkward undertaking."

Had Brini been beside him, they would have begun disputing it. As it was, Loys embraced Triston Clifford and at once enquired after the source of the water. Sir Triston chuckled. "You haven't changed, Simon! I suppose you'll give me no peace, so the gentlewomen shall go within, dinner can wait, and I'll show you how we managed it. The boys are probably swimming in the river, but we'll go and surprise them. Piers Brixhemar is about, somewhere."

Gregory saw them first: his father beside a horseman leading a tail of men. At once he put aside the lute. "Stephen! Stephen!" he called, with soft urgency, but the others were swimming and did not hear.

Piers floated past, giving the newcomers a lazy wave.

"Is that you, Brixhemar?" came the rider's cold voice. "What an ungainly sight." Still ahorse, Loys watched as Stephen stumbled from the shallows, plucking up a towel. The lad bowed, but Loys was no longer looking, distracted by a great shape coasting beneath the surface.

Hal knew nothing until Piers smacked him on the back of the head. He surfaced abruptly, nose and eyes streaming, to find himself thigh-deep in muddy water, blinking and naked before Sir Simon Loys.

The knight's wintry eyes travelled down his body, taking it in.

Triston beckoned Stephen forward. "I daresay my sons have grown out of all recognition. And everyone knows Piers, of course. Out of the water, Piers, there's a good fellow; it's dinner time. And this strapping and somewhat immodest young man before us is my nephew and steward, Hal FitzClifford."

Hal bowed, deeply enough, though rather slow. Loys hadn't moved. "Ah, I've met Sir Simon before, Uncle. His son is a page at Alnwick, where I was under-steward to the Earl."

Loys sneered openly. "I haven't the slightest recollection."

As Hal combed fingers through his dripping hair, great bands of muscle coursed in his arms. Then he was hands-on-hips, feet widely planted. His appearance was a weapon; his form more impressive this way; more intimidating, and he thirsted to threaten. Hostility crackled and surged. What an improbable notion – that he would serve this man. He wouldn't serve this man; he would kill this man.

Piers sculled slowly backwards, eyeing the scene with interest.

"Hal," prompted Sir Triston, eventually. "A towel, if you please."

* * *

While the bathers donned their clothes, Sir Triston was gesturing and expounding – something about watercourses and angles. Loys had dismounted and was pacing about. He seemed to have forgotten the presence of a rival.

Alice. Alice, within the house. Hal couldn't focus, could barely hear above the shouting in his head. He pictured himself slamming the cur against a tree; he lingered over the cleave to the throat; the twitching pulses of liquid heat. Then, in his mind's eye, he was striding down to her, buck-naked, running with blood; crimson droplets shivering off him like rubies. At this most inopportune moment he was becoming aroused, and had to shuffle briskly into his hose, bent double.

After a moment or two, he'd mastered himself sufficient to stand. Turning to assist Gregory, Hal found himself face-to-face with Hugh Dacre and Andrew Chowne. The arms folded themselves and up came the chin. As he

251

glared down at them from a commanding height, the older men shrank away. There was an absurd desire to roar in their faces; he was grossly overexcited, he realised, and lowered his arms. "How are you, Sir Hugh, old friend?"

Sir Hugh glanced across at Chowne. "Not so bad, Master FitzClifford, I thank you."

"And Mistress Carbery?"

"Oh, well, we are married now. Lady Blanche has given me a son already, and another child on the way."

"Can it be so long as that? It seems only yesterday when the Wyverns rode out from Dyffryn, leaving the Duchess Alice in your care."

Sir Hugh cast about miserably for a means of escape.

"And you, Sir Andrew? Sir Hugh's presence doesn't in the least surprise me, but your appearance is unexpected."

"Hal," Stephen interrupted. "Would you help me with Gregory, please?"

"It shouldn't be. I would never abandon Lady Alice."

"I suppose you should be commended for that!" said Hal, taking the comment as a sly sting, though probably not meant as such; Sir Andrew was a plain-speaking man.

"But your presence is also a surprise, Master FitzClifford. You've left your father, then?"

"I have, Sir Andrew. It's a long story."

"Hal – the chair has rolled off down the slope again."

* * *

When the men reached the house, Grace was hovering at the entrance. She caught Hal's eye as he hurried past, and shook her head. He slumped, the wide mouth setting to a sulky line. It seemed the lady was not within.

On any standard day, Hal would dine with his uncle at the table. But Sir Simon was a grand enough guest that the steward must be relegated to servile status, waiting on the gentlemen in the parlour. The women were seated apart. He looked them over and caught sight of Constance. Warmth shone forth.

Constance was shocked; most troubled to see the man there, alone. It was common knowledge – the bad blood between Robert and Triston Clifford. She could only conclude that Hal had left his father for good. And then she was wondering if she, herself, were the cause of the rift and that brought to mind the nasty ordeal in the stables of Dyffryn, to which, as a rule, she paid very little heed.

Attending on Loys was beyond him. Hal manoeuvred about, forcing Boulter and Petyfer to serve the knight. All the while his gaze was drawn, inexorably, to the great ruby at the man's thumb. Hal stared down at the ring as Sir Simon watched in his turn, cold as a corpse, unsmiling and abstemious. Then his head was lowered also; inclining in to Triston, interrogating him. Still the eyes were trailing Hal, blatant, not bothering to hide the enmity; parading it, rather.

He hates me. The youth rejoiced. But all the while, his mind was open like a book, and Loys was leafing through.

Later, Grace pulled Hal aside. "You go on like this, some accident will overtake you. That is hardly a man to be trifled with. You see how his men fear him? Not a happy sign."

He removed her hand from his sleeve and squeezed it. "Sir Hugh fears everyone. It's how we know he's alive."

"Please don't jest. Sir Simon is watching you like a hawk. Have you said any word about his wife? He seems to know."

Hal patted her shoulder and took himself off to bed, wakeful a long while, envisaging Constance arriving at Sevenhill on the morrow, bursting in upon the beloved, full of the news. He saw her dawning joy.

* * *

"Hal. *Hal.* Is it likely I didn't mark the stone upon his hand? My own father's ring? I questioned him on it at once. Robert gave it freely to Lady Alice, and so it has passed into Simon's keeping."

Though Hal had fallen asleep to thoughts of Alice, it was the ruby that filled his dreams. "That is an utter lie." He was speaking through his teeth. "I

253

was there when my father gave it to the lady. They were in the herb garden at Dyffryn Hall, planning their future."

Triston eyed his nephew thoughtfully.

"It was a pledge only," Hal continued, "for her to hold until his return."

"But that is the nub of it, eh? He never returned, so Simon tells me. If you're not prepared to pay the price, you should keep your pledges. That is Robert all over: reckless, even with such a treasure."

Hal scrubbed at his hair. "Ah, I begged him to go back for her. When we heard of the marriage, I *begged* him." His voice was quite wretched; time had done too little to stifle the howling grievance. "He had cried two days and a night, but still his pride would not permit it." The volume doubled. "And meanwhile that stunted little prick – your pardon, Uncle – had weaselled himself in there …"

"By God! Get a grip on yourself! I have known Loys a long time; a sharp fellow and not a man to cross. The Clifford ruby is lost, and I feel that loss more than you. It is your father's doing, as ever. Do not lay the blame on others."

Hal slouched off to look for Brixhemar, and found him stretched out beside Stephen in the garden, singing to the girls in just the way Hal mustn't. Beatrice was beside her brother. Bess and Idonia, two of the younger ones, were bright-eyed, tapping along, paying insufficient heed to the lyrics, which were warping away from the well-known words and skirting into treason. *He's making it up as he goes along*, thought Hal, in wonder. Some of the wilder slanders on the Queen's family were beyond his cousins' understanding, but Stephen looked like he was stifling panic, and Beatrice raised a dubious brow as Hal lowered himself to the grass.

"The window to my uncle's day room lies open, Piers," murmured Hal. "You can be heard within."

The verses veered back to their familiar path. As the notes died away, Brixhemar nudged Stephen. "Just my little joke, Master Clifford. No one pays me any heed." He leaned back, hands clasped expectantly. "So, what do we make of Simon Loys? Mistress Idonia: your view please."

Idonia would only defer, as usual, to Beatrice, who turned on Piers with a small smile. "A well-formed man. Rather conscious of his own consequence."

"A consequence insufficient to bear the enormous weight that's been placed on it. He must be buttressed by some invisible force. What can have given him such power, one wonders. Oh! I have it! A little lady with a grand name. How I look forward to re-acquainting myself with the charming sister of our exiled Earl."

Hal was pointing at the open casement above. "Shall we walk?"

"I do so enjoy watching the man!" pronounced Brixhemar, when they had barely moved away from the house. "So deliciously affected; so unnaturally self-conscious. Now, that was a most amusing scene by the river yesterday. Loys gave you a good looking-over, Hal, and you seemed keen to invite his appraisal. Why should he favour you with his cold stares, when he barely bothered to insult me? Let's muse over the myriad possibilities until we hit upon the right one."

"Let's not."

"Could it be that you bullied his son at Alnwick? Your father beat young Humphrey Loys senseless when they were both Northumberland's squires; the obliging Sir Hugh told me all about it. That's why Simon didn't squire at Alnwick himself. Has history repeated itself?"

"Of course not, Piers! Kit Loys was a mere infant when I left Alnwick. If Sir Simon doesn't like me, I can't guess the reason."

"So we must riddle it the other way round."

"Ah, must we?"

Why do you so dislike our self-important knight? Let's see. He is wearing your father's ring: rather rude. He filched the Lady Alice from your father: very rude. But then, you have fallen out with your father also; I can't imagine you burning with vengeance on *his* account. Unless ..."

"Unless what, Piers?"

"Unless ... well." He turned to broadcast a wink to the others. "We shall see."

A young man approached on horseback. Brixhemar groaned. "Master Brixhemar, sir," called the messenger. "Sir Mark bids me ask if you are ever planning to return to Roliford. You said you'd be away a night, sir, and it has been four already. Sir Mark says you promised to accompany him to Colchester yesterday. He insists that you return home at once so that he is not thwarted again."

Brixhemar rolled his eyes. "Alas. Oysters."

"To Colchester for the oysters, eh, Piers? Lucky you."

"Indeed, Hal: to Colchester for the oysters. It's been a long while, and Uncle Rohips lured me into a false sense of security. If the old goat has his appetite back it doesn't bode well for my inheritance."

PART III

WOUNDED CREATURES

It was not joy that was uppermost in anyone's mind the next afternoon when Loys returned to Sevenhill. Alice watched the party from a window. When the gentlewomen were helped from the carriage, one among their number was absent, and that was a source of sorrow. When she noticed the other absence, cheer briefly returned.

Sir Simon had no intention of allowing Constance to burst in upon his beloved with the news. The unwelcome development had already occupied far too much of his attention on the road home, with Sir Andrew to one side of him and Sir Hugh to the other, casting their dim and flickering light upon the obstacle.

Loys learned that Hugh Dacre had known Hal FitzClifford some ten years, and now, with the immediacy of the menace removed, it turned out he did not dislike the youth nearly as much as he should, describing a shrewd and dependable young man, respected by all; an image squabbling violently with Loys's construction of the fellow: reprobate, brawler, rakehell.

"He may look like his father, Simon – Sir Simon, rather – but they're not so alike, in truth. Actually young FitzClifford's a decent-enough fellow."

"Apart from the obvious," added Chowne. "I mean – he looks like Clifford apart from the obvious."

"*What* is obvious, Andrew?"

"Well, Robert Clifford is a one-eyed man, Sir Simon. A black leathern patch across his face."

"Has he now? Christ. When I knew him, the beast was hideous enough; how could any woman bear him beside her? My horse has more discrimination." He swung down before the groom could reach him. "I wish to be alone with my wife. I'll not be disturbed."

He tugged Alice to the bedchamber; she had to scuttle to keep up. By now his nerves were wretchedly near the surface, barely concealed beneath the sheerest of skins; half-raw. Alice would be forewarned soon enough by Constance, and forewarned was forearmed. He must speak of the matter directly, whether he wished to or not – and he did not. The one and only time he'd bared the soft underbelly, she raked him with her claws. The anguish boiled up again, ghastly, acid and resentful.

Slipping from her shoes, Alice lowered herself, presenting her back so that he could unbutton her gown.

"What are you doing? I said I wish to speak to you."

Pink-cheeked, she straightened, staring fixedly through the window.

He knelt between her stockinged feet, his face very close. "So: let me tell you what has passed. I've delivered Mistress Joanna safe to her uncle. I quite charmed Sir John Ames, though I say so myself. The old bore would agree that black is white if I told him so. Too late for your poor gentlewoman, of course, whose chance at happiness you so inexplicably dashed. Anyway, it is done. I've deposited Catharine with her Aunt Jane for some indeterminate period, but may it be long protracted. It turns out they're preparing for a marriage at Pearmain. Hugo, the eldest of my half-sister, will, within the month, wed the daughter of Triston Clifford. *Look at me when I speak to you.* We'll attend the wedding, though Jane won't have me at Pearmain any longer than she must. So we'll stay at Crawshay, Triston Clifford's house. I visited the man on my return."

Still the face was quite immobile. She was commending herself – prematurely.

"Triston has acquired a new steward." The enviable physique obtruded itself in all its gratuitous detail. "A strutting young ruffian. I wonder if you can guess his name."

No, she could not. From not more than six inches, Loys studied her eyes, primed.

"He calls himself *FitzClifford*. Hal FitzClifford."

A tremor. Her lips parted. She tried to avert her face.

He almost groaned aloud, his hand hurtful at her chin. "The boy looks just like his father, doesn't he? *Doesn't he?* Except for that missing eye. Christ! What ails you, woman? You picture Clifford before he was twisted by all that torture and murder and rape? Is that it?" He shook her, really quite hard. "You'd have to look a long way back for that. At fourteen, Clifford beat and kicked my poor brother to the doors of death; he was already a devil by then. His bastard will not have escaped the taint, but you cannot help yourself. You disgust me."

He was spitting in her face. Dazed and aghast, she had begun to weep.

* * *

Still Madame Renée waited for Nield to pay the bill. Nield couldn't pay the bill until he'd sold the goods stolen from her husband's warehouse. Meanwhile, in Honfleur, Jack de Vere and William Beaumont were awaiting, rather impatiently, a visit from Robert Clifford. It was his place to come to them; the man was, after all, of an inferior rank – even if his title were beyond dispute, which it wasn't.

But Clifford had, always, an eccentric view of his own standing on earth and exile was robbing him of the last vestiges of decorum. For several weeks, he confidently expected the Earl and Viscount to arrive in Perteuil and report to their leader. There was the assault on Calais to plan and, though he no longer spoke much with his steward, it was clear that money was running short.

Bellingham paved the way, since Nield wouldn't.

"Well then, Bell, you may pay them a visit. It's not for me to do so." Clifford shifted on the bed, motioning Loic to rub his knee. "Tell them we captured the Flemish ship single-handed. Find out if they've seen Pierre du

Chastel; if they've had money off him. And if they have, why haven't I? Du Chastel's not pulling his weight: he promised me a fleet and a force of men for the assault."

"It might perhaps be wise to make the journey yourself, Lord Robert."

"I'm not going! Aymer can go in my stead; my eldest son. And since he's baseborn, I'm not paying them too much of a compliment. Tell Nield to obey Aymer as he would me."

"He won't." Reginald Grey was concluding his customary hour at the prie-dieu. Prayer was a pounding treadmill; a hefty contrivance, powering their every endeavour.

"Then I'll dismiss him."

The priest heaved his gaunt frame upright. His knees cracked like burning logs. "No, Lord Robert. You will not do that."

* * *

"In London you said I was guiltless, and now this!" Her eyelids were lilac-tinged and swollen. "Neither Hal FitzClifford nor his father has ever laid so much as a finger on me. I never harboured any such thoughts. Your mind is a gutter."

One hand was already at her chin; the other, at her shoulder. A trifling adjustment and they had closed around her throat. She began bleating. The temptation to throttle was almost overwhelming and, for the briefest moment, it did overwhelm him. And then, just as quickly, the hands dropped from her. Loys pushed himself up and walked to the window, drinking in the view of his lands. When the rise and fall of his breathing had sobered, he turned and left the room.

Eleanor Percy's warning tolled, again, like a solemn bell. Easing herself back on the pillow, Alice pondered the lady's words, that tangle of dubious claims. Was Simon a wife-murderer? She could not hope to sift the truth.

And then Constance did indeed burst in upon her mistress with the news, to find a siren voice had got there before her. "He has mistreated you, hasn't

260

he? He's been in a filthy temper since he encountered Master Hal; spoiling for a fight."

"Why would that be?" whispered Alice. "I cannot understand it. There is nothing there to rile him. I've spoken no more than a dozen words to Master FitzClifford. And now I've heard what he's capable of, I wouldn't let him near me. And nor must you."

"Oh, I've spoken to Master Hal already. At Sir Triston's house. And told him how glad I was to see him. I was trying to find out how he came to be there, when some fat gentlewoman came up and dragged him away."

"You must not speak to him again, Constance. Not after what Lady Eleanor told us." Her voice was full of hiccoughs.

"Nonsense," said her niece, with cheerful disrespect. "Master Hal is a truer knight than most who bear the dignity for real, and would never blackmail a lady. Eleanor Percy may be an earl's daughter, but she's also a great whore who accuses others to cover her insatiable lusts. Why should you be always seeking to absolve Lord Clifford, yet damn his son on so flimsy a charge?"

Alice pushed herself against the bedhead, knees drawn to her chest. She was recalling the Wyverns' departure from Dyffryn Hall: Constance and Hal beneath her window; the inaudible exchange. "You say I should not believe Lady Eleanor, but you have no reason to trust him either; he has done us no good turn and shown his father no loyalty. That man has beguiled you, Constance. I've never heard you speak like this."

A verdict both peevish and mistrustful. Constance, too, had found herself whisked away to Dyffryn; an unpleasant sensation. "No such thing! Anyway, the important point is to ensure no accusation of blackmail reaches Sir Simon's ears."

* * *

The next morning, Bellingham and Nield were bustling in the yard, making all ready. Clifford and Loic were still abed, as were the FitzCliffords, none of whom was invited along. Nor was Aymer anywhere to be seen until some time after the appointed hour, when he strolled in, late and conspicuous – emulating Lord Clifford, no doubt. He vaulted on to his horse and led the men out of the yard at a trot. As they passed beneath the arch, Aymer glanced up to see Guy and Richie gazing down from their chamber window. He raised a hand; they didn't.

With chortling joy, Aymer relived that first trip to Bolton Abbey to pray at the tomb of Lord John. Or, rather, relived his feelings on watching Hal and George head off, for on the former occasion it was he who was excluded. Now, alone at the head of the party, he could barely stop from writhing with delight. How he wished that Hal were there to see it! He was wishing for Hal's presence so often these days it might be supposed that he missed the man.

The household wasn't keen to engage, so he'd leisure enough to muse on his place in the firmament. After a while – as was his habit – Aymer began a silent and lopsided conversation with his twin. He might have welcomed Guy's thoughts on the task that lay ahead, but his imaginary comrade was mute. Sulking, no doubt.

After a while the triumph waned. After a further while, the familiar fear was creeping upon him. He found he'd slunk to the raw place in his mind; the wound inflicted by Marjorie Verrier – that unlikely nemesis. He resumed his picking at the sore. At last he succumbed entirely and, dropping back in despair, manoeuvred Castor's horse away from the group. "I was wondering, Sir Arthur – for everyone says you've an exceptional memory..."

"Mmm. Your mother, is it?"

"*What?*"

"Have you asked Lord Robert about her? No, I suppose not. Why put questions in his mind, eh? Why set him thinking? You don't want to risk your position."

The eyes showed genuine shock. A rapid blinking, the pupils huge, swimming and starkly black. Though Castor's heart twisted with pity, he was keen to stifle it. This handsome wretch had vexed him time enough, putting those little insights to mischievous work. Aymer richly deserved to be worked over – just a little; a gentle riposte. So Castor rode on in silence.

At last, Aymer managed a thin chuckle. "Truly, you're a marvel! I was going to ask about my mother, as it happens. It's a long time ago, but I wondered …"

"As it happens, I do. Rather a memorable night." For all the wrong reasons; another episode to consign to oblivion – had he the choice. "Kenilworth, Christmastide, twenty years back; but you know that, obviously. So we're there, staying in the guesthouse of St Mary's Abbey." Aymer would be sorry he asked, but Castor wouldn't trouble to warn him. "Everyone was watching this dark-haired girl – a really beautiful girl – much too young for a washerwoman. Never a happy sign, that, meaning there's no one to care for her. So, we're only looking, at first, and crude talk. Oh, you needn't give me that look! Yes, I had girls aplenty in those years. Plenty, when I didn't know which way was up, and probably the happier for it. Anyway: later, we're all drunk, of course. Someone's seen where she's gone: a tiny hovel near the ford below the castle. By the time we get there, it's pitch black and roaring with rain and a good half of us have slipped over in the mud. I think it's John Dormer who falls in the water and floats off. The hut's pretty well secured. Walter shreds his hand trying to force the shutters; they're lined with pot shards. Of course there are taverns in town with fires to dry off and girls to be had for less effort, but by then John Clifford has the bit between his teeth – you know how he was. Well, you don't, but that's how he was."

Aymer was staring at his hands. Well – he'd earned this.

Castor pressed on. "So we're pounding the door and howling around to give her a good scare. Then up on the roof, beating our feet, jumping about. The thatch gives way, of course. The wretched little thing is crouched in a corner with a knife, threatening us, threatening herself. Lord Robert wants to leave her be …" He'd only just remembered that detail, and smiled. "He's afflicted with pity, of course; and after the pity, guilt. It's the undoing of him."

"*Pity? Guilt?* Oh, for sure!" Aymer's voice was derisive. "Edmund of Rutland had a lucky escape, there!"

"Rutland? The ugly work of Wakefield had Lord John's fingermarks all over it. And *Randall* was there, of course, urging them on." It was Castor's turn to give Aymer a look of long significance as the name thrummed in the silence. "Anyway. Let me finish the story…"

"The whole household knows, don't they? Laughing behind my back."

"Knows what, Aymer? Don't be so thin-skinned! They're not even speculating; why should they? Anyway – Lord Thomas was still alive then, so none of the older men were even with us, that night at the hut. They were of his household at that time, serving him. You boys probably see the Wyverns as a single troop, but we never were. Cuthbert Bellingham, Patrick Nield, Reginald Grey, Jolly, Bigod, Tailboys and so forth: they were all Lord Thomas's men. Us youngsters – John Clifford's henchmen – we were always the ruffians; the brawlers. The greybeards repressed us where they could. I suppose we've become the greybeards, now. Anyway," continued Castor, "Lord John grabs the knife from the girl but sends the rest of us off, so only those three – the Clifford brothers and Randall, I mean – will profit, which happened often enough when the rest of us had done the grunt work."

"So the three of them had my mother?" The voice was desperately bleak.

"How should I know? Lord Robert's the only one left. He believes he's your father. From the first, he acknowledged you. He favours you. He's made you his ambassador on this mission, hasn't he?"

"He doesn't know or care. He never remembers which of us are his or John Clifford's get."

"Oh, his memory's not so bad as he pretends. It's an affectation." An irritating one, at that. "But no, he probably doesn't care too much, so long as there's Clifford blood in there somewhere. *Let him not revert to it*, prayed Castor. Had they been alone, he would have taken Aymer into his arms by now, for this arrogant young buck had dwindled to something much more wieldy: fresh, untried and lovely.

"Sir Arthur? Tell me of Miles Randall."

"Oh, *Aymer*." Another great sigh. He gathered himself. "Well. There was an air – an allure, you might say – about Miles; he drew men in, even when they should know better." Castor, who'd loved Randall so well, cast about to find anything worthy. "A gifted soldier…"

"A brave man?"

"Bold as a lion."

"Tell me of his looks. Tell me." *Let me know the worst.*

Castor glanced across, then away. Inwardly he groaned. At last, the coup de grâce: "Black locks; eyes of palest blue; not so tall but most … striking."

A tremor in those lilac-hued lips. "There we are, then. There is nothing more to say."

"But …"

"But what? But *what*, Sir Arthur?"

"You forget, my friend: those were also your mother's looks."

* * *

"Must we attend the Duke's wedding? Or rather, you must, of course, but must I? I'm so very tired, Sir Simon. You've carried me hither and thither these last months when you know I'm not strong and Ned's birth almost killed me. Could that not excuse my absence? No, I read the answer in your face! Your daughter says you did not care when your other wives died and I see for once she is right." She peeped at him, waiting for the guilt to show itself.

"Not so tired that you couldn't make a vulgar show of yourself at Colchester. Christ, woman, if this is how you revenge yourself after a little mild chastisement, I begin to wish I had finished the job."

That settled it, surely. No murderer would joke of his crimes in so careless a fashion.

"What sort of wife does not welcome such honour for her husband?" he continued. "Not for me the outer darkness: I'm invited to attend the Duke's dressing and escort him from his mother's house to the Abbey. I'm to dine beside the foremost in the kingdom."

"In the third chamber? Out of four?"

There was a short silence. His voice iced over. "Evidently you've spent too long in Petronilla's company; the sarcasm is contagious. It does not befit any female to sharpen her tongue on a man. Go to your room, now, to consider your conduct. Remain there until I come to you."

A second exile to the bedchamber, though not, she trusted, as long as the last one; after the outing to Colchester, she'd been caged for days. An hour later, the kitchen sent up a somewhat meagre dinner. Possibly the food was laced with poison; probably it was not.

All through the soft and peaceful evening, Alice lounged on the generous feather bed with the prayer book beneath her hand, gazing though the glass framed by imaginary fingers of the well-beloved oak, the oak that was once the vastest tree in all the county. Where did its timbers lie now?

She would have been surprised to learn that the timbers had been sold to a middleman and flogged on – unseasoned and unsuitable and twice the price – to Anthony Woodville's shoddy shipwright. Three months later, the tree had risen again: the mainmast, keel and cross-spars of a large vessel meant to bear English archers to Brittany. Had this purpose come about, it would, no doubt, have warped and split and taken on water. Its final end was to be more rapid and no less ignominious, fired like kindling on the foreshore at Southampton by a handful of the Wyverns' junior men. But Alice had ceased to wonder what had become of the tree. Her thoughts were – as so often – elsewhere.

* * *

Aymer's party lingered a good long while in Honfleur. No doubt he was bringing all those notorious gifts to bear; relishing his mission, the first time he'd acted the eldest son. And, possibly, Nield and Bellingham were finding it hard to raise the cash.

If there were trouble brewing among the merchant class of Perteuil, Clifford neither knew nor cared. He knew only that the haul from the warehouse was so mean and haphazard that Ste-Croix thought the motive not burglary but sabotage. Aside from a stolen wheelbarrow, there was no clue to link Jean Portiers with the crime, and Ste-Croix was too prudent to challenge the man without proof. So he replaced the warehouse door with one braced with iron, and replaced the watchmen also. He could do no more.

While many of the Wyverns were absent in Honfleur, Ste-Croix was absent also. His business took him here and took him there; this time, to Caen, leaving Madame Renée solitary and unguarded.

Since the fête in Perteuil, the attractions had moved on. The boys had to pay for their drink once more. A sad state of affairs, when the church was a keener hunting-ground than the tavern. Into the old wooden edifice, so very dark and close, the FitzCliffords would attend Lord Robert. They watched Melisande with a concentrated hunger; her fame had grown out of all proportion to her allure.

At the close of every mass, Clifford strode forward, ready to escort his hostess to her house, and Madame Renée would smile serenely, answer pleasantly and stare directly ahead, chin raised, acting in so unnatural a manner that her neighbours – who didn't like her – fabulated tales about the pair. But she never asked him in, and he never followed her.

By night, when Loic had undressed him and the boys were off roistering, he would cross the landing to the little chamber with its southward view. There, he leaned upon the sill, gazing out over the moonlit yard, across the blackness that was the garden beyond and into the windows of the silent house. In several chambers, candles burned. At the second floor, through the boughs of a great chestnut, a faint skeleton of light marked out the shutters in the widest window. There she was, alone. When a soft breeze stirred his naked flesh, Clifford shivered with an amorous chill and wondered, again, how he would come to possess her.

* * *

On the morning of Gloucester's wedding, Loys was to be found in the midst of the intimates, sharing breakfast, assisting in the dressing, praying beside the Duke – or appearing to do so; he never prayed. There were other knights in attendance and a great crowd of esquires, but when Loys looked about, he reckoned himself foremost, by influence if not by birth.

The next moment he dropped a degree, for Sir John Howard banged in, ruddy-faced; a flamboyant bow; beetle eyes tripping, restless, across the crowd. "Loys! We must speak, heh? Later we'll speak. Don't slink away."

Sir Simon shrugged off the clout to the shoulder. "Howard." One man he didn't wish to see; a man he particularly wished not to see.

"*Lord* Howard!" Half a dozen voices corrected him, Gloucester, reedy, among them.

"Your pardon." Loys bowed smoothly. "I did not hear of your elevation." *Now he will be worse. Insufferable man.*

Lord Lovell had slipped in behind their backs. Richard of Gloucester embraced his childhood friend with warmth. "Francis! Come and sit beside me. Now the day is complete."

"Greetings, Lord Francis." Loys obtruded himself before Francis Lovell, bowing low.

"Simon. I haven't seen you since I left Middleham. Or since you left Middleham – which may have happened first." The young man hurried on, with a faint flush. "Stuck out in Suffolk now, I don't meet anyone. A trip to court is a treat for me. We came past Sevenhill on our way to London. Actually we detoured just to see it. It's very fine; I congratulate you."

"The finest house that debt could buy," interjected Howard. "And worth every penny, I'm sure. Though I've had no invitation as yet, which is somewhat strange under the circumstances."

Gloucester laughed and pushed John Howard out of the way, leaning so he could see Loys's face. "Before you leave London, Simon, go to the church of St Clement Danes and retrieve your wife's sister-in-law. The King has expressed a wish for our cousin Margaret to be welcomed into the bosom of your family."

Loys glanced around him. Each of the lesser men shifted a touch, as if to say, " – *don't mind me.*" "Is this wise, my lord? Margaret de Vere is not some abandoned nobody; she's Warwick's sister and the Earl of Oxford's wife."

"Don't call him *Earl of Oxford.*"

Loys spun on his heel.

"Oh, *Simon* – I'm teasing! Smile, will you? It's my wedding day."

"As I was saying, my lord, I've not been long in Essex, but already it's clear to me that the county is seething."

Gloucester clicked his tongue. "Even now? The commission turned over every stone."

"They were thorough enough with the petty men; a hundred dangling from the gallows. All the significant troublemakers were allowed to buy their way out, of course."

"Well. The King is somewhat short of the readies."

"I understand."

Howard interjected. "Good of you to *understand*. Your own brother was among the purchasers, was he not?"

"Nick is a dreamer, my lord." He was answering Gloucester rather than Howard. "There are others who do more than dream. I repeat: Margaret de Vere should be constrained elsewhere, out of reach. I'll dispatch her to Avonby, shall I? Truly in the middle of nowhere; that will break her spirit, if anything could."

"But that is not the intention, Simon. Take my cousin home to comfort at Sevenhill. Better her gratitude than her enmity. Meanwhile, keep watch. Sometimes one must let out a little rope before the noose pulls tight. Now, who is this arriving in such a bustle? My lord of Buckingham! A walking manifesto to the joys of matrimony, come to give me his tips."

"My God, Lord Richard, you need no help from me. Some fellows have all the luck. Noble; heiress; virgin, too, so they say."

"Henry Stafford, the boldest lion at court." Gloucester kissed him on both cheeks. "How does your lovely Woodville duchess, my friend?"

"It's weeks since I saw the vinegar-faced whore. So – well-rested for the wedding night?"

"Why? Do you suppose my bride means to wear me out? Perhaps she does, Henry; perhaps she does. A merry ending after those sad travails!"

Loys was still planted in the centre of the group, slow-nodding to draw attention to his connection with Gloucester. He raised his voice. "Travails indeed, my lord! Our brides of Lancaster have suffered much, and now have much to be thankful for." Anne of Warwick's fortunes were about to change, as his own wife's had changed, greatly for the better. His mind was wandering to the recent disagreement with Alice. He rubbed his mouth. If she were tired and wan, there could, perhaps, be good news in store. Only that morning, the girl was tense and tender beneath his touch.

Loys was still thinking of her breasts when he noticed the Duke of Buckingham looking at him as if he'd said something foolish. Then Buckingham turned his back. "I should think the Lady Anne would be eager for marriage, after all she's endured! Where was it George concealed her? The largest pie in London? That's what I'm hearing. Crouched beneath the crust of a great savoury pasty. You scooped her from the gravy with a ladle, so they say, before carrying her off. I hope you licked her first."

A brief silence, then the three noblemen sniggered, and others took up the knowing laughter. Loys stared at the wall. He had no idea what they were talking about.

"Of course George didn't hide my bride in a cookshop." At last Gloucester deigned to enlighten Francis Lovell, who was free with his confusion. "We put it about just to rile my brother. And it has, greatly. George is absolutely furious. But since he made no secret of his anger at my marriage, no one credits his denials – though the story grows sillier by the day."

Finally Loys could join in the laughter, which by was now petering out.

* * *

The change in Anne's appearance was startling. Gone was the straggled hair, the slack and unbecoming attire. Someone had taken her in hand; someone with a good eye and benevolent intent. It wasn't her sister.

Alice watched the harum-scarum friend of her childhood move, decorous, through the ceremony; sit, decorous, through the feast; move, decorous, through the dancing. Beside his bride, Duke Richard chattered away, a hand at his mouth so none should trespass between them.

Everyone was remarking George of Clarence's demeanour, a subject as incontrovertible as the weather. The young man made no attempt to hide his chagrin as he watched half the Neville estates give themselves away at the altar. Why had he come? His duchess had forced him to it, clearly; not that one could tell; not by looking: Lady Isabel was a faultless counterbalance, all soft smiles and gracious contentment.

Anne did not speak to Alice – not once – and acknowledged her obeisance with a distant inclination of the head. Edward of York was swift to make amends: a wet kiss; fondling Alice awhile in an alcove, as he fondled many a young woman, not liking to leave anyone out. Lately she'd taken to calling him *King Edward* – a pragmatic surrender – but after the manhandling, he was demoted again. When her discomfited eyes darted off, she found Simon at some distance, waylaid by the Duke of Norfolk's cousin, and her own: John Howard was pinching her husband's sleeve between his fingers, his other hand aloft as he chopped the air for emphasis. Simon's face was marble.

It was very late that night when the couple could go their rest. They had returned to the same inn in Pudding Lane, a short distance from Baynard's Castle where the nuptial feast was now unwinding.

The noon following, Loys and Alice dined alone, barely a word passing between them. Today he was dressed in a doublet of vivid mustard. Yesterday it was puce, the shoulders crusted with a double row of seed pearls. Outings to London would produce new outfits, always, as a holiday season. There was a touch of ostentation in his make up; more than a touch. But like many a dark man, he looked his best in a plain white shirt.

Alice rose when her husband rose, and wandered after him to the head of the narrow, twisting staircase lit by leaded panes. He had passed on before her voice caught him; her soft reproach. "You haven't spoken in hours, husband. Are you angry again? I could not help the … King's conduct. There was nothing I could do. What could I do?" She glanced behind her, but all was quiet.

"I'm not angry. Or not with you, little wife," came the reply. His face re-appeared at the angle of the stair.

She nodded. "Are you engaged today? Perhaps you'd care to join me in a game of chess? I know the rules quite well. John Neville taught me."

"Did he? Then your strategy will be marred by muddled thinking and end in the abandonment of your king. We already know how it plays out, so the game is pointless. Besides, I am engaged, at Westminster. Francis Lovell has challenged me to a tennis match."

Francis Lovell: these last cruel years had not roughened that one's hide or sharpened his teeth. She nodded again. "Lord Lovell is a sweet youth."

He shrugged. "And Gloucester's best friend."

She had descended until there were but two steps between them. Loys laid his hands at her waist and slid a palm over her belly. "So, Alice. Are you with child, do you think?"

After quite a moment, she whispered, "Why do you ask me that?"

"I know the signs. But it is too early, perhaps. We'll talk again when you miss another flux."

A vivid blush in the shadows. "Please hush!"

"I've been meaning to speak to you on another matter. You've lost one of your maidens and the others will doubtless follow her away into the world. How would it be if I bestowed a new companion? One dear to you, who will not leave you."

"Who might that be?" All change was troubling by now. And then she thought of Elizabeth Ullerton and her heart hammered within her.

"A lady I've long intended to welcome into the bosom of my family. Your sister-in-law, Margaret de Vere." There was the tiny pop as her mouth fell open. Loys endured the joyful outpourings no more than a moment, turned on his heel and vanished.

* * *

"How dare you make such racket outside Monseigneur's chamber? He has only just quieted, you imbéciles, and now you've roused him again." It was an unusual intrusion. All the boys knew better.

Will and Guy, in the doorway to their own room; beyond them, Richie, craning from the window. "There's a fire – in Ste-Croix's house! A fire, Sir Loic. It's on fire!"

Monseigneur's first sleep was always the deepest. He was infuriatingly hard to wake. By the time the two men emerged, clad only in shirt and hose, the three lads were gone. Down the deserted stairway they sprinted, and across the moonlit yard. A small crowd fretted at the garden gate. Loic strode forward, in his hand, the key. Ignoring Clifford's look of incredulity, he let them all through, and they ran into the orchard.

No one craned at the windows: they lay sleeping, or they lay dead. Forcing himself to the fore, Clifford smashed through. While the back door was innocuous, there was an inferno within. Someone fetched water. He upended a pail over his head before sousing everything in sight. When he rounded the corner, the stairs were gone in a hanging firestorm. Clifford turned about him. Richie was close behind. They nodded at each other and headed off in search of something to climb. Working in wordless tandem, the pair bundled a kitchen table through the doorways and set it beneath the yawning stairwell. Many, now, were dashing in, but these were shorter men. Richie shouted for water and they dowsed themselves again. Then they leaped on the table. When Clifford tested the floor above, it came away in a blazing shower, singeing his face and his shirt. Yelping, he tumbled from the table and fell back.

Loic appeared with more of the boys, manhandling a fruit ladder from the orchard, a squat, steady thing, built into a frame. Once more, they dowsed everything. Clifford wound his hands in bandages torn from his disintegrating shirt.

Melisande had been roused by now, Fabien, the little clerk, dragging her to the first floor window, but the girl screamed and cried and wouldn't make the leap. The chamberwoman had already catapulted into Bede's arms. Richie was guided by the clamour; Clifford thundered on. The upper stairway was blazing in places; still passable.

Above them, Renée opened her chamber door and shut it at once, opened her shutters and the casement, then slammed those also, when the beam above the door was swallowed by flames.

Already the air was dense and bitter. Dropping to her knees, she tried not to suck too greedily. No ladder would reach this window and beyond the door was hell on earth. She rolled onto her back and the nightcap fell from her hair, black curls streaked with grey. Closing her eyes, Renée crossed herself and crossed her wrists at her breast. She murmured her prayers. She would choke before she burned.

Of a sudden, the door crashed open and the room roared with heat and red light. In strode the devil himself, huge, dark and glistering with sweat. "Renée!"

She tried to raise her head.

"Do you live?" Hot lips covered hers and he blew smoke. At that, a great wrack of coughing enveloped her, wringing her chest in its terrifying grip. Hands clawed helplessly. Bubbling from her mouth was an ashy slime streaked with soot.

She was up, and cradled in his arms. Then they were away, swift through the rush of the dragon's breath, banging past falling timbers and down the collapsing stairway. Tongues of flame shot out: they scorched her ankles. Clifford lost the trailing folds of her bedgown and, in an instant, the linen flared. He set her on her feet, fell to his knees and, yelping, tore at the burning cloth, slapping the burns in his own hose; the singed hair.

"Up! Quickly. There."

Eyes tight shut, she pressed her face to the pungent flesh of his shoulder; the quick, vital scent of the hero.

A menacing growl, and the ceiling began to bow and then to seep and spew into their path, gliding like warm honey. He was still a moment, panting, until the curtain of flame dropped and he strode on, head bent, shielding Renée. When they reached the yawning pit where the lower staircase had stood, he halted again, measuring the distance: a perilous drop through a ragged, smouldering hole. It was a grim effort to keep his balance as he half-fell, half-clambered onto the steaming, swaying ladder and bore her out, but, somehow, he found he had managed it. George and Guy and Findern swarmed in, pulling the woman in different directions. Clifford batted them away; no knight would surrender his lady at such a moment.

The garden was exquisitely cold. Icy air speared the lungs, thin and sweet. Clifford staggered away. Time flowed on, until, at length, came a terrible tearing from the house; a rumbustious gust of smutty and sweltering air. Renée came to herself, wheezing, propped against a tangle of roots beneath the great chestnut. Beside her, Robert Clifford was face down on the ground, filthy hair straggling into her lap, a heavy arm pinning her thighs. It seemed churlish to leave him, but the garden was filling with townsfolk and the man was next-to-naked and she must see to Melisande, whose wailing soared above the roar of the flames. There, in the flickering light, was the girl, supine beneath the north wall. The bedgown had rucked around Melisande's knees; she looked to be holding that huge English boy hard against her in the act of love, but that could not be right, there, before a great throng of onlookers. Renée willed herself to rise. Nothing happened.

Loic Moncler was darting about, crying blindly for his Monseigneur. The man at her side made no move; he seemed to have passed out. When the chamberlain caught sight of Renée, he swerved, hurling himself down beside his master; heaving him over; snowing the charcoal face with kisses. "Some said you were within. But then I saw her …"

Lord Clifford spluttered and struck Moncler with very little force, like a kitten. Staggering to her feet, Renée stumbled away. The fire was on the turn now, dying back. All the eastern range had collapsed, neatly, within its own footprint. The rest of the building looked mild enough from outside, but the black windows gaped their horrid truth. Burned houses were treacherous. This one must be pulled down.

As she plodded towards her stepdaughter she was circled by an eager revelry of neighbours, exclaiming at her appalling appearance; the thrilling rescues; the prohibitive cost of rebuilding. There were insistent offers of shelter, though they stood within feet of her own inn. So she set her jaw and elbowed though to where the great English oaf had propped Melisande into a sitting position and was binding her left hand, three fingers of which jutted at a nauseating angle.

"What are you doing, Master FitzClifford? Can't you see they're broken? What are you doing?" Her voice growled oddly, sticky and quivering with phlegm.

"Yes, Madame, of course I can!" Richie was all tender care and didn't want assistance. "She'll not let me put them back, so I'm sparing her further harm." But his answer was a babble.

With great weariness, Renée sank to one knee and leaned in. Gently she took the hand and, with a smart crack, thrust the fingers into place. Melisande's mouth opened like a vast tunnel but, mercifully, Renée could hear not a sound and then the garden shimmered somewhat and she lowered herself, by unsteady stages, to the ground.

* * *

For some reason best known to himself, Sir Simon did not go in person to break the glad news, but dispatched his wife to the inmate of St Clement Danes. Alice found Lady Margaret outside the bounds of sanctuary, in the mean parlour of the priest's house, attended only by one Rohaise Locke, the daughter of Jack's marshal and a maiden they'd both known from childhood. Alice burst in upon her brother's wife, heart overflooding.

"So," Margaret dropped her darning to the floor and pushed to her feet, "you've come at last! It has taken you long enough. I know you've been in London, Alice – and with whom."

"My Margaret!" Alice tried to throw her arms around the lady's neck and half-managed it. At last the tale could come tumbling out, mostly backwards. She made no attempt at concealment, but told it all, tidying Lord Clifford's role just a little, for good order. "So, at last," she finished, "Sir Simon bids you come to live with us at Sevenhill, and I have wished it so much, Margaret. I am so happy."

"Sevenhill? The jewel in my own dower! Settled on me by Jack on our wedding day! It was no man's to give away. Stolen by a coarse little upstart who wishes for my company no more than I for his. Mark my words: his arm has been twisted to this by the same men who come week-in, week-out, warning me to throw myself on Richard of Gloucester's mercy. They all thought they'd wear me down, but the Earl of Warwick's sister is made of sterner stuff. And now I hear that Loys has joined Gloucester's affinity. Those two deserve each other."

"You don't know Sir Simon, if you think the Duke could force him to offer you a home. My husband is a man who goes his own way, always. He has determined on this only for my sake. I've been begging him since last summer. Sometimes he likes to do things to please me, especially now …" Alice was about to share to her hopes for the future, and swerved, just in time.

"I know Simon Loys only too well; better than you, it seems. A less well-intentioned, less principled man I've yet to meet. Loys has changed allegiance several times over, and only to suit his overweening ambition. But you are a little child, Alice, who understands nothing of life, and must cleave to whomever seems strongest."

A swirl of words whisked up and tangled in her throat. "He is my husband, whether I chose him or not, and whatever my private loyalties. I didn't choose him, of course, but I told you that already. Surely you should be thinking of Jack? In the midst of all his troubles, it must put his mind at ease to hear that his wife is well-cared for. Margaret – please."

"You may tell your *husband* to come and beg on his own account. Tell him to stop hiding behind his wife's skirts."

Alice left the precincts of the church very much out of charity with her sister-in-law and bristling on her husband's behalf. When Sir Simon came to her that night, she was still taking indignant turns about the bedchamber. He watched her progress. "What a termagant Lady Margaret is. Perhaps I shall change my mind. The thought of having my ears chewed by that lady, day-in and day-out, is not appealing."

"She's not showing the proper gratitude for your kindness. I can only think that without Jack, she is lost and unhappy."

"She must be used to it by now. De Vere has a history of shrugging off his wife at the first opportunity, and I can't say I blame him." Waving Constance and Elyn away, Loys undressed his wife with his own hands and pressed her down in the bed.

"Husband!" said she. Her tones were prim. "If you will not forbear for the sake of the Church, at least do so for the sake of the babe. These are early days, when you may shake the child loose."

Loys grinned and laid himself beside her, lips in her hair, stroking the smooth belly with a warm palm.

After a few moments, she said, "Did you support the house of York from the beginning?"

He had long expected – then ceased to expect – the question. "I know where this has come from: Lady Margaret has impugned my honour, hasn't she? Of course I did not support the house of York from the beginning! You know my father was of Northumberland's affinity in the days of the present Earl's grandfather. And you know my brother Humphrey squired at Alnwick. You know the old Earl fell at St Albans in '55 fighting for Henry of Lancaster. At least, I hope you know it. Your ignorance is fathomless, of course."

"Then you fought for Lancaster at St Albans?"

"Naturally! And was knighted there, beside Humphrey, on the eve of our first battle." He pictured himself at the rear of that snaking, shuffling file of excited youths, some long distance behind Robert Clifford, who towered at the front like an ogre, blocking his view of King Henry. *Don't call him King Henry.*

She jarred him from the reminiscence, ingenuous and silly: "You fought for Lancaster! You! Margaret did hint as much. When did your allegiance change? Was it when you returned from your wanderings and found York had already triumphed?"

He rolled onto his back. "Christ, woman, you make me sound positively rudderless." It was during those *wanderings* that he'd probed the mysteries of the most hallowed and ancient seats of learning. "When I returned from my wanderings, as you put it, King Edward was easy on the throne; my little liegelord, Harry Percy, was a prisoner and Warwick was ruling the country. I did what any wise men would do – even Humphrey, who was braver than he was wise: we joined the Nevilles in ridding the North Country of the last of the Lancastrian rebels. At Hedgely Moor and Hexham we were fighting under John Neville's command."

Hexham. Still it was no easier, though seven years divided him from the pain. A loyal subject of King Edward by then; he and Robert Clifford at open enmity, which felt more comfortable, given his loathing for the man. Not that he risked an encounter in the flesh, for Clifford was easy to spot on the field and easy to avoid. It was a most satisfactory day, until that closing hour, when the Loys brothers split in their pursuit of the foe. When Simon next saw Humphrey, he was shrunk to a limp and trampled corpse, a quiet tragedy amid the triumph.

Alice was reflecting on his words, surprised, perhaps, to find in him a seasoned warrior. "So you joined the Earl of Warwick's affinity and later betrayed him?"

"Be careful. I left him, yes. Richard of Warwick had a gift for appearing sane and sober when he was well-nigh crazed with ambition. Others were sucked in; I wasn't. But you know all about his descent into treason: you were part of it, not that your presence will ever grace the chronicles. The name of de Vere has sunk without trace, along with Lancaster and Beaufort and Clifford, never more to rise."

A further silence fell. Loys was thinking, still, of Humphrey, that fine and gallant youth. He wasn't thinking of the Wheel of Fortune; he wasn't drawing lessons from the times through which he'd lived. But the Wheel of Fortune is just that: a wheel. If those illustrious names were sunk to the depths it was, in all likelihood, a fleeting decline. "What lessons do you draw from all this? None, I should imagine. Consider, Alice: I am the man who rescued you from the consequences of your own folly, and wiped away the stain on your honour. I have brought up your son as my own. I have given you a magnificent home. Where is the gratitude? All this time, your heart has belonged to another."

Still she lay silent. She had fallen asleep.

* * *

279

A messenger rode for Caen, missed Etienne Ste-Croix – who'd moved on to Falaise – raced after him, and brought him back, eventually, to what was left of his home. That took a week, during which Madame Renée and her household settled into La Clef D'or. The manager of the arrangements was, nominally, her stepdaughter, whose spirits rebounded with admirable speed. When the missing half of Monseigneur's household should return from Honfleur, the family must relocate themselves to La Petite Clef, so Loic gave notice of quittance to the guests at the smaller hostelry. Meanwhile, he evicted the boys from the chamber abutting his own, to lay Madame Renée in her mother's bed, sharing with Melisande: there, he could keep an eye on the ins and outs, and ensure Monseigneur's vow was upheld.

Renée spent one day resting and, on the next, she was up and taking the reins.

Clifford was not so quick to recover. A great singe-mark striped his face where a timber had struck, unnoticed at the time. He'd lost most of his brow and all of his lashes. And though Loic bathed and bathed the face – disturbing his sleep and desiccating his skin – still, the one eye glowered red, rimed with soot, giving him the look of an enraged miner. Awake or asleep, every breath was a struggle.

On the third morning, Clifford woke to find his hostess perched at the end of the bed in a pool of peaceful light. In her lap, a little bowl. "This is salve to calm the skin; I made it myself. Sir Loic, I've asked you already to stop washing Milor's face. The inflammation is worse than yesterday."

"Then you must heal him yourself, Madame, since you know best." Loic should be glad of a new bird to nest in Monseigneur's heart. Anything to supplant the Queen of Heaven. But his voice was sulky nonetheless.

With thistledown fingers she touched the beast. Silent in a corner, her chamberwoman hunkered over the stitching. Time and again, Loic glanced at his master, then glanced away. The floor creaked heavily as Findern and George tiptoed up, peered in and tiptoed off. All the while, Renée was holding her breath – less from nerves than because her patient reeked of charred crackling; his lungs were heaving up acrid gusts, laced with a sulphurous whiff. She wondered if he would die.

When Renée was done, he took her cool hand in his blistered one and clasped it. Then he closed his terrible eye and she stole away.

* * *

The distant silhouette of Sevenhill appeared against the morning sun; the snakepit of the court lay far behind. Margaret de Vere had not accompanied the party home to Essex, though Sir Simon had bestirred himself to visit the lady and do his best, which turned out to be not nearly enough.

"Lady Margaret will come around, though, Sir Simon?" A question, not a promise.

Loys turned his head a little. He'd been reluctant to take Alice up on the saddle. When she carried Edmond Beaufort's child, there was no such concern.

"Especially now the King has promised an annuity if she leaves sanctuary. She told me she was greatly troubled with her living expenses. Only two servants remain to her."

He gave a humourless laugh. "Even the annuity was thrown in my face. She accused me of chasing her for the gold. As though anyone would bother! If the King pays more than the first instalment it will be a miracle."

"She'll be grateful once she has thought further, and then she will surrender her will to yours." Alice leaned her cheek a moment against her husband's shoulder. He stroked her fingers, directing them into his lap.

It was most necessary that Margaret de Vere surrender – and quickly – or Gloucester would be demanding an explanation. Naturally there were means to free him of the burden, later, if it became insupportable. In point of fact, he carried the means near at hand. Elixir of Ichor was the substance of choice: a most uncommon exotic, closely sealed and snugly wedged in Brini's saddlebag, sourced at no small cost from an ancient, dark-skinned apothecary who skulked the lanes south of Fleet Street. Poison was not its purpose; merely a useful ancillary.

Alice sat up, shaking Loys off. "What is this? A *second* barrow! Oh, Sir Simon, you ordered the digging to commence in my absence; I know it! How could you be so rash? It is calling down a curse upon our house."

"Hold your tongue, you foolish child. Believe me, the want of gold is more pressing a spur than these delusions of yours." He drew the hands downwards.

* * *

The night of the return to Sevenhill was marked by a tremendous storm. Sturdy as it was, the house was shaken to its roots.

"Listen!"

She lay in the dubious comfort of his arms, unable to do otherwise. The wedding night was yet too raw; the night this chilly man became a monster against just such a thunderous backdrop. She turned away from the memory and ground her face in the pillow.

"Stop that. There! We see the lightning before we hear it. Now, why might that be? Think before you answer."

Slumber beckoned at once, seductive. From somewhere he was droning: the world was a ball, again, or something equally unlikely; the thunder had to skirt its curve. She couldn't follow, and what she could follow, she couldn't accept.

"… So, that is why: in short, our eyes are stronger than our ears, but in daily life the difference is too small to be apparent."

What nonsense. If she were less sleepy, she would counter him. She'd only just drifted away when there came a truly tremendous crash that froze her, breathless, against the sheets. Panicked hands clutched for Simon, but the bed was smooth and cold. Alice reached for the bedgown – she was forbidden to wear it in bed – lit her candle from the hanging lantern and prepared for the climb to the workroom, where she'd startle her husband and, doubtless, vex him.

As she robed herself, tapping about for her slippers, she was pondering his habit of rising at night. He'd not done so in London, nor all the time at Avonby: this wakefulness was a recent development, hinting at fresh worries; the troubles that must be pressing upon him – concerning her brother, perhaps. Alice sent up an urgent entreaty for Jack's safety, wherever he might be, and she hoped most earnestly that it was Scotland. Dear William

Beaumont, too, was remembered in her prayers and, by then, it seemed churlish to exclude Robert Clifford. After a pause, there was a perfunctory prayer, also, for the wellbeing of Sir Simon, accompanied by a growing sense that each such plea must be mutually exclusive; irreconcilable; that even God could not hope to address them all.

Alice paused before the window, gazing at the sky. There was no torrent; not yet. Indeed, there was no rain threatening at all, for with that final reverberation the storm had sailed away; the moon presiding, vast and milky in the blue-black. As she turned to the door, her eye was caught by a movement beneath the trees. The breath stopped in her throat. The second barrow – latest to be despoiled – was yielding up a man to the night: a thickset man in full harness, visor down. She caught him in the very act of emerging, like a wasp writhing from a peach. With a heavy heave, he swung his knees onto solid ground and pushed to his feet, brushing soil from his gauntlets. Then down the slope. On he came, striding toward the house; toward her; the naked blade of an axe gleaming across his shoulder, in the way that only a young man, and a raw one, would tend to bear a weapon. He reached a pool of shadow and then in an instant vanished, like the pinching of a candle flame.

Alice staggered backward. Her own candle tumbled over and went out. There was no prospect, now, of leaving her chamber for the dark and echoing ranges of the house. Somehow, on trembling legs, she gained the bed, headfirst beneath the sheets, whimpering for her husband.

She awoke with a horrid start, and still the bed was empty. But Simon's solid presence soothed the dread: he was lounging in his gown before the window, holding a letter to the morning light. When Alice sat up he put aside the parchment and came, smiling, to her side. "You're dishevelled, child." The plait had come undone and he tucked a creamy lock behind her ear. "There is a nest on your head." Then he was dragged into a desperate embrace and the ominous tale tumbled out against his throat.

"I told you this would happen, Simon – did I not warn you? You have woken the warrior and he rises from the barrow to take his revenge, as I said he would!"

He was back in the bed by now, hard against her. "No, you little fool. Like the first, it is empty of bones as it is empty of treasure." On the previous day he'd stood watch as the bones were emptied; as the warrior was reburied, discreetly, some distance off, at the edge of his lands, by the stream in Scop Wood. This was unhallowed ground, which unsettled the workmen, but they did as Loys ordered, for he held the purse strings. The only treasure yielded up by the earth was a rusted iron helmet of peculiar design. The piece was, in fact, inlaid with bears and boars most skilfully rendered in silver, but by the time the labourers had rolled it in the mud, the precious detail had been lost and the helmet followed its owner, tossed, an afterthought, into the shallow and hastily-dug pit. "I've been beside you all night long. You did not rise from the bed, and I did not leave the room. It is a dream. Now hush."

She watched his hands roam her nakedness. There lay her bedgown, at the head of the bed as usual, though she was wearing it when she fled from the vision. He was right: it could only have been a dream.

* * *

Madame Renée could not bring herself to leave the inn, not even for church; not with the meddlers in holiday mood. And so Sir Reginald obliged her with a domestic mass. This first occasion, he led the devotions from his prie-dieu beside Lord Clifford's bed, in the largest chamber. Even with so many absent, the train of worshippers extended through the doorway, filled the boys' adjoining chamber and straggled down the stairs, where most could not hope to hear, murmuring the words to themselves or, for the most part, chatting openly.

Richie had squeezed himself nearly to the top of the stairs. From this vantage he watched Melisande. Prayers were concluding, Grey gave the congregation his frosty blessing and the benediction passed to those below. As she waited for the crush to disperse, Melisande was gazing past Richie, into his own bedchamber, where others of the FitzCliffords had gathered. He couldn't see the object of her interest – George, or one of his coterie – but, plainly, that object was not himself. Not that he fancied her. Small breasts were lovely, but only on small women, while this was a somewhat fleshy girl, as he'd discovered in hauling her from the fire. The breasts were not in proportion, and that was something intolerable to his tastes. He decided not to tolerate it and, when she smiled, he looked away.

Divine service hadn't been a success, and wasn't repeated. From then on, only a chosen few were present; the rest had to take their solace from the church of St Germanus.

These were tranquil days, a short-lived lull, before Ste-Croix would return to begin the pulling down and the raising up; and with it, the inquisition and the anxieties. For now, Renée was often to be found seated in a cushioned chair beside Lord Clifford's bed. He was decently garbed in nightcap and nightshirt, contrary to his usual practice – engaging him in quiet conversation on decorous subjects or reading aloud, while he sat, propped against his pillows, meek as a lamb. The writings of the Church fathers were the customary choice; sometimes the lives of the saints. Hermits were preferable to martyrs, of course, for the latter might prove too exciting for Melisande, who was lolling in the background, sighing audibly, neglecting her stitching, peeping at Loic Moncler – the only bright spot in the room. But the light of his countenance wouldn't shine upon her or, if would shine upon her, it was marred by the look of bad-tempered disdain.

For two hours each morning, Melisande was absent, walked to her tutor by the chamberwoman, for Renée was anxious lest the girl's reading and writing, which were progressing steadily, should drop off. The arithmetic could hardly have dropped any further; she had squandered her money there.

A few days on, when Clifford, Renée and Loic were left alone, Renée slipped out her prized possession – survivor of the fire – a text that Ste-Croix thought too forward for his daughter's ears. Clifford took up the book and grinned. It was Christine de Pisan. He was intimately acquainted with the author from his years in Babette Delaurin's company. Many a night he'd lingered in the City of Ladies.

"Truly, Milor' de Clifford," Renée exclaimed, when he quoted a favourite line. "You didn't strike me as a defender of women! I thought you one of those who'd dismiss the female sex; a soldier must tend to view us as weak and helpless. Or so I thought."

By now he was strong enough to pull her in; to pin her to the bed; to render her weak and helpless but, like the wolf in the tale, he lay sly in his nightcap, sheet tucked to his chin, growing more dangerous by the moment. "You know little of me, Madame, or of my life. No man could think such things who was raised by Lady Clifford, or followed Queen Margaret at the head of an army. So many of my friends are strong women, making a livelihood as a widow, or managing their own lands. Once a lady rode through the night to arrest me!" He hadn't thought of Eleanor in quite some time, and smiled at the memory. "Wearing a breastplate and wielding a sword. I liked her not the less for it. In truth, I'm Christine de Pisan's most ardent scholar."

Renée gave a delighted laugh. "You are full of surprises!"

"Are you sickening, mon petit?" said Clifford, without troubling to look at Loic. "You seem poorly; go and take the air. Madame Ste-Croix will see to me."

She stood. "I should go also, Milor' de Clifford. You need your rest. I'm tiring you with these tales of intrepid ladies."

"Nonsense. I could never tire of ladies and I can't be left alone; I'm too weak. Go, Loic!"

By the time Loic banged the door behind him, she was at the window, as far from the bed as could be.

"The sea is my consolation," said he, softly. "I look out and imagine the coast of England. How I miss my lands and those I've left behind!" Now was the moment to conquer her with Farewell, but his lungs weren't up to the task.

"I am sorry." She turned, and hesitated. Her voice, too, had softened. "Did you leave behind a wife, Milor' de Clifford? No? Were you never married?"

"I never had the good fortune. My life has been hard and unsteady. When the lady I loved had plighted me her troth, she married another. Twice."

"Two women? Oh, that is ill luck indeed!"

He was wishing he'd never begun; there must be easier ways. "The same one."

"Your pardon, Milor'. I did not catch that."

He cleared his throat, a painful growl. "No – it was the same woman. The same one, twice over."

Clearly, she didn't know what to say; too kind to laugh. "Would it ease your pain to speak of it?"

It would not. Nevertheless, he told it all, tidying his role just a little, for good order. At last, lost in the tale, he forgot Renée's presence entirely; forgot his stratagem, his subterfuge, his lickerish lust. The pain, so well-repressed, hit him, full-force, and he was pierced with a sudden, sharp longing for Alice. Only to see her; to speak with her; to ask her *why*. He knew, then, that he could not live like this. Sooner or later, he must go to her.

"Milor' de Clifford?" The silence had stretched on. Head averted, he was coiled in on himself. She raised a hand to his shoulder, filled with feeling for this poor, wounded creature. But Loic, whose footsteps had led him nowhere, now stood – arms folded, chin raised – across the bed, warding her off.

* * *

That morning, as the household gathered in the parlour, Leo Brini was supervising the laying of the fire, and spoke up in the silence. "That's the fourth time you've yawned, Mistress Constance – did you realise? You must have slept badly, as I did. Venice has spectacular storms, where the sky turns green, but they're not common here and I've grown unused them. I did not fall asleep for several hours and, as soon as I did, Sir Simon woke me. I had my revenge, though. My head was so heavy and dull I was of no help at all."

Alice turned stiffly to stare at her husband, and then rose without a word and quit the room.

Sir Simon rolled his eyes. "I thank you, Leo," he said, puzzling them all, then rose also and followed his wife to their chamber, where he found her beside the window, as expected, looking out towards the barrows.

"Very well! So I was absent for a time. I didn't want to frighten you by seeming to confirm this fancy of yours. It proves nothing."

"Did you undress me? When I returned to bed I was wearing my gown, but in the morning it was back on the head of the bed."

"Of course not. How would I have done that without waking you?" There was nothing easier; he could do as he wished when she was dead to the world, and often did.

She had turned back to the window, emanating mistrust.

He lowered himself to the bed. "So what was he like, this warrior of yours? Was he armed?"

"He bore a naked poleaxe over his shoulder."

"Not well-trained, then! We had no master-at-arms at Avonby, but my father would have given me a thick ear for carrying a weapon like that. What was he wearing?"

"Harness, of course! That's how I know he is the warrior."

"Full harness? Plate armour, like my own?"

She nodded.

"That proves it was a dream. Those barrows were raised many centuries ago. Even in the reign of the last King Edward, a knight would have looked strange to your eyes, with a great, pointed bascinet like a snout; how could you fail to notice the effigies in our own parish church? A hundred years before that, there was no plate at all; he would be clad all in mail, bearing a shield. And your warrior, if he existed, would have sported a curious helmet with a nose-piece and hinged cheek-guards. You would not recognise him."

He waited for her to pounce on his odd acquaintance with thousand year old helmets, but she only bit her lip and frowned on. What seemed a slowness of wits might be a simple desire for reassurance, but Loys was not a charitable man. "So I suggest you don't frighten my daughter and the other idiots with this tale. Alice?"

His wife had grasped for the chair and sank slowly to her knees.

Loys sprang to his feet in alarm. "What is it? Child – what is it?" He helped her up and lifted her on to the bed. His hand came away smeared with blood.

* * *

One of the grooms had entered the chamber to give Clifford a few hours' warning of the others' return.

Renée shut the book with a snap. "A good omen. You are well enough to get up, Milor' de Clifford. It's doing your lungs more harm than good to lie flat. Training, as you like to do so often: that is healthful. Better, I would say, is swimming. There's a fine spot beneath the cliffs a little to the east of the town. Fabien can show you."

"What does the physician say, Madame Ste-Croix? Have you asked him, or are these your own insights? The sea is cold at this time of year. We cannot risk Monseigneur's health; a chill might carry him off."

Clifford chortled, a spectator at their joust.

"I have asked him, Sir Loic. He says – *by all means.*"

Since her removal to La Petite Clef, Renée had resumed the daily round: church, instructing her step-daughter, keeping her accounts, stitching, attending to her husband – and visiting the invalid. The townsfolk watched her go. She didn't stay long, but she was punctilious in observance. Now he was strong again, and the inn would throng with Wyverns reunited, and she would come no more.

Once Clifford understood that the visits were at an end, he discarded the nightcap, pulled on an old shirt and gave Findern a belting in the yard. He was a little slower, a lot stiffer, a belly laugh was perilous, but all would be well.

That afternoon, the others returned from Honfleur. On their way in, they passed the black bones of Ste-Croix's house, but they must disgorge their news before they could hear the story. Clifford was leaving his chamber as he caught the fanfare of arrival, and turned back so that they should come to him and not the other way around. When the household men were assembled, he threw himself on the bed, the usual manner of receiving a report. "Well?"

"It's good news, Lord Robert. We sold our booty; we got a fair price, I think …"

"Never mind that."

Castor took up the account. "The attack is set for a month from now, give-or-take. The French forces will put into Perteuil and we'll sail together, via Honfleur, for Calais. We've hammered out a plan for the assault."

Clifford didn't like the plan: it wasn't his plan. He raised objections, some shrewd, some petty. Plainly, there was nothing to be done, now, so the men didn't bother to counter him.

"Your eldest acquitted himself very well indeed. Master Aymer charmed the Earl and Viscount Beaumont and, to more effect, Pierre du Chastel. We have half the pension with us, Lord Robert, in cold, hard coin."

"Half? Where's the rest?"

After a moment, Castor replied. "You shall have it, Lord Robert. In due course, says du Chastel. If the assault succeeds."

"By which time there'll be more owing! One cannot trust Frenchmen. Not any of them. My father knew it, and tried to rid the world of these vermin. Go now. All of you. Send Aymer to me."

Not long afterwards, his son reappeared downstairs in the doorway of the hall.

Nield banged down his wine cup and eyed Aymer in disgust. "Sent you off with your tail between your legs, has he? God in Heaven. This has gone beyond ingratitude; it's assailing my honour."

Aymer quirked a brow at him – a warning of sorts, but much too late – and turned his head. "So, Father: which tavern do you favour? Allow me a moment to fetch the cards. I should warn you: I feel lucky, just at present."

*　*　*

Shortly after dawn on a sunlit and chilly morning, a cavalcade left Sevenhill heading north-eastwards to Crawshay and thence to Pearmain for the wedding of Beatrice Clifford to Hugo Sheringham. Nicholas and Petronilla and their few attendants added to the train. Alice drowsed awhile in the carriage, her eyes lingering over Petronilla's face – not so beautiful as usual; pearled and waxen as a warm cheese.

"Yes," murmured the woman eventually. "I am with child."

"Oh! I'm so very glad for you."

"Quite a way along. First headaches, now sickness. Alice, I would have told you sooner, but you were grieving over your own loss. Other people's good news has a way of making misfortune heavier. But you are both of you healthy and fertile; there'll be a brood of little ones before long."

Objections raised themselves, though Alice would not speak of the curse that lay over Sevenhill; it felt far-distant and toothless on that mellow morning. And besides, Petronilla was as likely to tease her as Simon.

The gentlewoman continued, "He told me of your fears, but surely you must know these for what they are: mere figments."

"I see you've been laughing together behind my back!"

"Far from it. He believes the terror of the dream brought on the miscarriage." She sighed at Alice's sullen face. "Simon blames himself. Judge him by his actions rather than his words, and you will know him better."

Over the next hour, as they trundled on, Petronilla's pallor shifted slowly from greyish-yellow to yellowish-green, prompting in her companion recollections of other uneasy journeys. Alice was forever pursued by recollections in one form or another, so that she was sometimes barely present; looking on the world, as it were, with one eye closed.

Fresh air was now urgently wanted, and the two wives dismounted to ride pillion behind their husbands, who were side-by-side in silence at the head. The sunlight was caged and glistering in the great ruby at Loys's thumb, catching the eye of his sister-in-law.

"Sir Triston will surely remark the Clifford ring, Simon."

"He has remarked it already, displaying as much offence as the fellow can permit himself, though he's never what you'd call menacing. By the way, Alice, when I visited Triston, I raised the idea of a match between Catharine and his eldest son." He felt his wife shift in the saddle. "I won't pretend he jumped at the chance. Triston swears Buckingham made some promise to push his aunt in the boy's direction. But then Triston also admitted he's been prompting the Duke for a year already and nothing has yet come of it."

"The Duke of Buckingham's aunt?" said Alice. "Would she not be much older than young Master Clifford?"

"Probably. As long as there's a chance of catching so great a prize, he won't consider another bride for his eldest. The man had the temerity to suggest Catharine weds his younger son, who stands to inherit some beggarly manor or other, and a cripple into the bargain. I soon put him right."

Petronilla stifled a yawn. "They say he's having trouble finding a wife for the younger boy, who has no feet, I seem to recall. An unappealing prospect. Not that Elizabeth Stafford would top anyone's list."

"Elizabeth Stafford." Alice breathed the name, searching her memory.

"Elizabeth Stafford. You must know the story," said Petronilla, "though it's a while back now."

"I know very little, if there is a scandal. The Countess of Warwick forbade the servants from gossiping with the maidens. Sometimes I caught a snippet of news, but rarely."

"Extraordinary," said Loys. "If you cannot learn from the mistakes of others, you are doomed to make them for yourself and we all know where that has led you. Elizabeth Stafford is the youngest daughter of the old Duke. When the Duke dawdled in finding her a husband, he woke to every father's nightmare: she'd found one for herself among his household. An under-steward or some such. Just like the Pastons, though you probably didn't hear of that either."

"I know the Paston family," interrupted Alice. "Good folk, steadfast for the de Veres. Why, what has befallen them?"

"Exactly the same; a misalliance with the bailiff, on that occasion. Marry them off early; I quite agree with Triston on this point. Elizabeth Stafford might be widowed, but she'll not be choosing a second husband for herself. Not after exercising such poor judgment the first time."

"Not the only widow to suffer a denial of choice!" Petronilla arched a brow at her brother-in-law.

"Must you make jokes of such stifling obviousness? It's truly tedious."

"Are you out of sorts, Simon?" Nicholas spoke for the first time. "You seem more than usually morose."

"Not particularly. Anticipating the many impending hours in the bosom of my family."

His sister-in-law bit her lip, tilting her head sidewards, but he would not look across. Simon was out of sorts; very. He'd confided in Petronilla – to a point, though it was well-nigh impossible to speak openly of Hal FitzClifford, even to her. Those fears and doubts were pitiable and, worse, nonsensical. An overheated imagination; the trait one would least expect to find.

Now, an hour from Crawshay, Alice lost the power of speech, the coming ordeal occupying all her energies. The two brothers were unforthcoming, Petronilla could not sustain a conversation alone and silence descended.

As so often in the last weeks, Alice found herself wondering on Hal FitzClifford and how he came to Crawshay. The bad blood between Robert and his youngest brother was common knowledge; she could only conclude that Hal had left his father for good. And then she was wondering if she, herself, were the cause of the rift, and that brought to mind the heart-stopping moment before the gates of Goodrich when Hal swept her into his arms and the ground shook with Robert's rage.

As they approached the park, her thoughts were ambushed by a more immediate prospect: the beauty before her. Sevenhill was very fine – resplendent even – but her first glimpse of Crawshay was so enchanting – despite the flimsy battlements and cock-eyed symmetry – that for a time the sight banished all else. And then it struck her: the house evoked those floating chateaux strung along the route from Angers to Paris, past which she and Robert had travelled, a thousand years ago, on their journey to Flanders.

She was still lost in history when Triston's son Stephen emerged to greet the party. Lofty, of course, and dark, with regular features, the boy put her instantly in mind of one of the FitzCliffords – which particular one, she could not immediately say – and such musings didn't help to pierce the reverie or recall her to the present.

When the dismounting and the milling about was done, Master Stephen led the party to the house and ushered them within. There, in the parlour, Alice was presented to Honor Clifford. They had exchanged only a few words before the gentlewoman drew her attention to a tall stranger at her side. Alice recognised the man at once by certain resemblances.

"Oh, Sir Triston! I feel I would know you anywhere!"

He smiled, frowned and smiled again. "Truly? I have not my brother's great size, my lady, nor, I trust, his fearsome looks." And his voice had none of Robert's swagger; it lacked the power and the rumbling note.

"I do not find Lord Robert so very fearsome. Always such evil is spoken of him – undeserved, I think." She could hear Simon some way off and her voice was low.

He answered her gently: "Then you must, in truth, know little of my brother, and I am glad of that." Triston gazed at her with earnest attention, as though troubled by pity.

She had thought to please him. Her face was reddening. *This man is nothing like Robert*, she thought. *Nothing at all; measured and mild.* "Forgive me," she murmured at the floor, "for I spoke out of turn."

"But there is nothing to forgive. Lady Alice, may I present my second son, Gregory? He cannot stand to greet you. And you may recall my nephew, Hal FitzClifford. I believe he escorted you for a time before your marriage to Sir Simon." Triston was picking his path with great delicacy.

She dared not raise her head. There, before her, were Hal's boots; so few men had feet so large. Her reluctant gaze slid up his legs, traversing the heavy cambers of muscle. Vaulting the codpiece, her eyes came to rest at his chin, and then she had to step back so that he could make his bow.

"Lady Alice." *There* was Robert's voice, at last. "It does my heart good to see you."

Finally she submitted her face to his inspection. The words were pleasantries, but there was no smile. Hal's eyes were boring in to her.

"*Wife.*" Sir Simon's hand was at her shoulder, his tones calm and light. "You've not yet greeted the bride. Triston – may I speak with you a moment alone?"

From across the parlour, Grace watched them go. When she turned to Hal, he was still staring, heedless and hopeless, after that small, pale sprite.

Furtive, Grace looked her fill. Not so very beautiful, in truth – a solemn, watchful face with tilted eyes and a pointed chin. Beatrice was prettier by far. Grace crossed to her friend's side. "While you've been gawking at Lady Alice," she murmured at his chest, "Sir Simon has taken Sir Triston off. And what do think he is saying?"

"How should I know?"

"*'Your nephew is in love with my wife,'* he is saying. *'I want the man gone.'*"

"No, Mistress Grace. He is not saying that."

"I should think he is."

"He is not saying that. Men do not say such things to each other. To expose his weakness; to show himself fearful and foolish? Perhaps he would like to say that, but he will not."

* * *

Loys followed Triston up to the day room, ruminating as he went. How he longed to say it: *your nephew is in love with my wife; I want the man gone.* But he would not, of course, say it. Instead of stabbing the servant where all would see the knife, he'd find a way to stab him in the back.

They settled themselves across the table and Loys dismissed Hal FitzClifford from his mind. "So here's a glad occasion: your daughter to marry the Sheringham boy – my half-nephew, if that's the correct term. Let's double the joy: your heir and my daughter? You've given no answer as yet. Gilbert Sheringham may have done well for himself, but I shall do better. Already, Gloucester takes my advice in all things; he wants me constantly at his side."

"I don't know, Simon. I still have hopes of the Duke of Buckingham. His aunt's youngish; she must marry someone. He'll want to see her safely disposed before she takes matters into her own hands again. And to speak frankly, I hear you have problems of your own. It's said that Sevenhill has broken you and you are living beyond your means. John Howard has you in his fist, they say. And a number of the London merchants, likewise. It will all end in the Fleet prison, they say."

"Who says? There is mischief afoot. Brixhemar, is it?"

"Everyone says, Simon. I hear you've been selling timber on your more distant manors. You cannot do that on the sly: men read it for what it is."

"And what is it?" Loys was angry now, though his voice grew quieter. "I have more timber than I can use, so I sell. There is nothing in it."

"My friend, there may be nothing in it. But we all know it causes talk. And because it causes talk, a man does not do it unless he has to. And so our neighbours say that you are desperate and have no other remedy."

"And the Duke of Suffolk? Has he no other remedy? Suffolk has been selling timber from his estates; so much that he's disrupted the market and the price has tumbled. Yet men do not say that Suffolk shall end his days in the Fleet."

Triston only shook his head. "How old is your daughter?"

"What? I don't know. Marriageable age, by the look of her."

"You don't know?"

"She was born ... she was a little maiden when I went abroad. So she must be less than twenty years now. Sixteen years, I'd say, or thereabouts. The right age for your eldest."

"The right age – if that's what she is. I tell you what I'll do. I'll go to London, see the Duke of Buckingham and press him for an answer one way or another concerning his aunt, the Lady Elizabeth. If there is a *no* from that quarter, you and I will speak again. But I warn you: I would expect a decent dowry with Catharine, in coin and up front. And meanwhile, you shall think on it and decide whether coin might or might not be forthcoming at the present time. I am not a rich man, but I am a prudent man, and I have no truck with debt.

* * *

When the two friends returned to the parlour for dinner, Hal found himself attending to Sir Simon with alacrity, for this time the knight's lady was among them. Loys had himself well in hand. The meats were served to him, and he did not heed the server. The salt was brought up, and he did not heed the bearer. Petronilla nodded her approval. He rewarded her with a blank stare.

Alice was evading Hal's gaze, and Loys certainly heeded that, although on this occasion the all-seeing eye had failed him and he came nowhere near reading her thoughts. He would have been shaken if he had. For his lady's mind was ensnared in a vision of Hal FitzClifford and an earl's daughter engaged in a practice that would damn them both to hell and, despite her very proper disgust, she could not quite banish it.

After dinner, the evening was chilly and darkening, so the party crowded about the fire. When Sir Triston called for music, Hal was tuning the lute before anyone else had the chance to offer.

"Christ," groaned Loys in Petronilla's ear. "How is it I know *exactly* what's coming?"

She turned, whispering into his mouth. "You are beginning to bore me, Simon; something I never thought possible."

Though his voice was a murmur, the sneer broadcast his rancour to the room. "You've always shunned the peculiarly female flaw of jealousy. Take care: you haven't enough good qualities to risk losing that one."

"Come – this is much better! The hypocrisy, at least, is interesting." She removed herself and slid in beside her husband.

Loys's instinct was correct. So was his wife's and, though she intended otherwise, Alice was gazing at the youth when he struck up the first heart-stirring notes.

"That is a most beautiful song, Hal," pronounced Triston, as the melancholy tones died away. "Well done!"

Hal examined his boots with a prim smile.

* * *

The next morning the party set out to Pearmain for the nuptials of Triston's eldest daughter, Beatrice. Alice was borne in his carriage, where she spent the journey soothing the nerves of the bride, trying to engage her with a game of cards. What a pretty girl Beatrice was, tall and voluptuous. This was how a daughter of Robert's would look, no doubt. And then Alice recalled that Robert had, in fact, a daughter; one at least: a little maiden abandoned in Bruges along with Babette Delaurin. Her name was Marie.

That morning Hal had barely a glimpse of Alice. The night just past, he'd crept, restless, from his bed to the door of the guest chamber below. There might have been a murmuring within. Soon he was catching his name, then again and again. He loitered a while longer, but it was only his fancy, and he knew it. What would his father do? Strangle Loys with his bare hands, no doubt, and usurp the warm bed. The satisfaction would be all the richer if those two events occurred in reverse order, preferably with a lengthy intervening delay. He crawled back to the consolation of his blankets.

Never mind, thought Hal, as he laughed and joked with his cousins; there would be a chance at the wedding. There would be dancing, and dancing meant touching. Soon he and Stephen were singing together, in high spirits, competing in turns. *Tamlin of Carterhaugh* was Hal's opening barrage; the powerful voice resonated through the convoy and Alice fumbled her playing cards.

Pearmain was not many miles distant and, even before they came upon the house, the bridegroom and his father had ridden out to meet them. Hugo Sheringham was a few years younger than Beatrice and few inches shorter, pink, stocky and beaming. A light rain began to fall and the party hurried the last two miles, forded a stream, rounded a copse – and there was Pearmain. At once, Triston's complacent looks blew up to consternation, bordering on panic. "Oh sweet Jesu!"

Surrounding the house, and just in the moment of arrival, was a great cavalcade, richly caparisoned. The clamour could be heard from a good distance.

"Why was I given no warning?" gasped Triston. "Oh sweet Jesu." He signalled the party to pull up, in urgent conference with Gilbert Sheringham. The other gentlemen pressed in.

"Never fear, Triston; my wife will manage! We're well-supplied. He must sleep here at Pearmain; he may have the bridal chamber. We will manage!"

"No, no, Gilbert, that will never do!" Horror and delight were chasing each other across Triston's features. "My lord of Buckingham is come expressly to honour me, of course; I am his man. The Duke must sleep at Crawshay. We have to get rid of Loys." He turned to find Loys at his shoulder, one brow raised in a belligerent quirk.

"Oh. Hal? *Hal*! As soon as we've deposited the gentlewomen, take the carriage and go full speed to Colchester for provisions. Spend at will on my credit. Take Boulter and Petyfer."

"I don't need them, Uncle. Let them enjoy the feast. Master Cardingham and I will manage all between us, never fear."

"Bless you, my boy. What would I do without you?"

"Uncle, our carriage is rather small. Perhaps I might borrow another?"

"For sure." Triston had turned back to Loys. "May we, Simon? You'll have it back before long, of course."

"Certainly not! Christ. You have left us with nowhere to sleep. You shall not leave us without conveyance."

"One of my men to follow after with ours?" suggested Gilbert Sheringham.

Hal's thoughts were brisker than his uncle's. "Moppet! As soon as the carriages are emptied, you and Sir Gilbert's man will drive after me to Colchester to collect the provisions I've purchased, for I shall be back at home by then. Barnaby – quick now: home to Crawshay! Rouse Master Cardingham! Away with you."

Hal trotted up to Hugo Sheringham, wrung the boy's hand then leaned to kiss the brow of his cousin Beatrice, giving her cheek a little pat – his affectionate farewell. And then, bowing to the company in general, he turned and galloped away, not altogether sorry to leave Alice frowning after him.

* * *

In the early days, the fire had done Clifford a great favour, melting the ice. He saw Renée but rarely now and, when he did see her, she was beside her husband. So he was surprised when she appeared one morning and asked for speech with him alone.

He gestured her up the stairs, following behind; close behind. As she turned the last corner, Guy entered the stairwell, stopped, stared in surprise and retreated with a knowing smirk. He didn't shut his door.

Renée placed herself, once more, at the chamber window, looking out to sea. Clifford would have liked to throw himself on the bed, but suspected she would run; she was quivering like a hare. "This is a rare pleasure, these days! I almost wish I were ill again, just to be assured of your company."

With a resolute step she crossed the space. "Milor' de Clifford, forgive me, but ... forgive me. I must speak to you in relation to our bill. The bill, here, at the inn. It has not been met."

He'd been lounging in the little cushioned chair beside the pillow, legs stretched before him and comfortably crossed at the ankle. Now he stood, and his size dwindled her. "Madame Ste-Croix!" The voice was low and stern and thrummed with reproof. "Life has been cruel; it would be idle to pretend otherwise. But do not allow yourself to forget that I am a baron of England, descendent of kings. It is not for a Clifford to lower himself to such matters." This was grubby. "Go to my steward, if you please." When she covered her mouth with her hands, his voice gentled. "Ste-Croix sent you to me." He nodded to himself and took her wrists.

"No, Milor' – it's not that," she murmured. "I should not be here, God knows, but I wanted to tell you that I asked Monsieur Ste-Croix to forgive the debt and he would not."

"Forgive the debt?"

"You saved the life of his wife and child. I would not press for the rent after that. But he's bidden me do so, for we've lost our house and the cost of rebuilding will be a great weight. So I must go to your steward, and you will think ill of me. I had to tell you."

"I, think ill of you?" It was the first time he'd sensed weakness. He was holding her, still, as if he'd forgotten. Now he raised her hands to draw her in. "When it was my own father who led the English *rabble* at Pontoise?"

"I know that. It was unjust of me to ... you are not responsible for my father's death."

Still she did not shake him off, and went on gazing into his face with a look of such troubled candour that he felt himself falter within. But that appalling impulse of mercy had wreaked enough damage already; he would not submit. The war was going his way when Loic entered – without the courtesy of a knock, a cough or a warning footfall – and greeted Madame Renée in a smooth voice, as if he hadn't just caught the pair, handfast, before the bed. Either the woman was truly guileless, or she was a practised dissembler: she welcomed Loic with placid goodwill; she didn't snatch back her hands. More likely she was neither, only older and wiser.

Clifford released her and sank into the chair. "Do you know what, mon petit? You've forgotten the swimming expedition that Madame Ste-Croix advised." Loic couldn't swim. "We'll go tomorrow. See to it."

"What was Honfleur like, Aymer? Better than Perteuil?"

The three of them turned toward the boys' chamber, where Richie could be heard, loud and unclear. His mouth was stuffed as usual.

"No better. Though I finally got to meet a selkie woman."

Clifford raised a brow – the scabbed and puckered flesh where a brow once was – and gestured Loic to push the door wide.

"You saw a mermaid? In Honfleur?"

"I did. A fisherman had caught her in his net and brought her ashore. Now he's sold his boat and makes a living showing her up and down the coast. He has this little tent. In you go, and she's lying on a pallet. It cost me a penny."

"A penny just to look?"

"Well, the same as a penny. Castor's worked out all the foreign coin and carries the rates of exchange in his head."

"Did you fuck her?"

"No, that was tuppence. Besides, there was no way in that I could see. Not that it was a proper tail. More like two legs that melted. She was just in the moment of turning into a woman as the fisherman pulled her from the waves."

Head cocked, Clifford was translating in a whispered scurry, one finger raised to silence Renée. Bursts of breathy laughter farted through his nose. Loic eyed them crossly. This was bound to bring on another spasm.

"Who'd credit the tales of a showman?" scoffed Guy's voice. "He saw you coming, didn't he? Odds are she's a common whore, born that way."

"It's a strange thing, whatever," said Richie. "I once saw half a man at the fair in York; they have all the good ones there. Was she beautiful?"

"What? No, not really." Judging by Aymer's tone, the selkie was a terrible disappointment. "She was quite rough."

Richie continued, "Our first time in Southwark there was a girl with two heads – do you remember? Only it was thruppence just to get in, so we didn't. And that one was particular. She wouldn't be fucked at all."

Now Renée, too, was laughing, though not at the exchange next door. Clifford wheezed and squeaked like a bagpipe, motioning Loic to take up the translation, but the Frenchman was soon hopping about, beating him on the back, for by now Clifford was, indeed, doubled over in a paroxysm of coughing that spattered the sheets with dark stains.

Renée nodded. "It's good: keep laughing! Bring it all up!"

But he was desperate to stifle the disgusting eruption. He wiped his eye and winced.

* * *

The wedding of Hugo Sheringham and Beatrice Clifford passed off smoothly enough, despite the alarm to the couple's parents. Henry, Duke of Buckingham had come alone to Pearmain: that is to say he brought an inconveniently large entourage but no family. His detested Woodville wife was, as usual, at court beside her sister the Queen, and his aunt – the interesting Elizabeth Stafford – had not been brought along for inspection.

But as that lady's prospective bridegroom was present, the Duke inspected young Stephen Clifford for all he was worth. Buckingham was head of the house of Stafford, but he was only a fledgling, and the exercise of each dynastic duty was not, as yet, a dreary chore but a solemn charge. As it fell out, the two young men soon discovered a shared passion for falconry that would form the footing of an enduring friendship. After a lively discussion of an hour's duration, still Buckingham had not moved on, talking and joking at Stephen's side, his hand on the youth's sleeve. Triston had stopped pretending to listen to his neighbours and was openly observing the pair, his breast swelling. When he glanced around to share the pleasure with his wife, he found that she was watching not the eldest, but their younger boy.

Without his father or Stephen or Hal to care for him, Gregory might have sat forlorn in a corner, but he'd acquired a companion: Joanna Ames was seated beside him, unusually animated, her gaze wandering the youth's slim, dark face, his high cheekbones and curling lashes. And then Triston forgot Buckingham for a moment and raised thoughtful eyes to Sir John Ames.

Alice was watching the pair also, with high satisfaction – knowing that she alone had preserved the girl for a proper fate. Now Joanna's uncle had risen and, smiling, Sir John Ames seated himself beside the wheeled chair, questioning Gregory, so gentle and engaging. After a moment, Joanna excused herself and returned to the side of her former mistress.

"So, Joanna – Master Gregory is a pleasant youth, I think. How do you like him?"

"Oh, Lady Alice!" she whispered. "He is simply perfect; the handsomest young man I ever saw. He puts me in mind of Bedivere FitzClifford – they are cousins, of course."

Bede FitzClifford? No, no – it was Sir Triston's elder son Stephen who more closely resembled Master Bede. Now Alice called him to mind, though Bede's name had escaped her on the previous day. Quickly she chanted over the FitzCliffords like rosary beads; none of them must slip away, nor any detail of those days in the forest. Lose that and she might forget who she was – and that would never do. She glanced back to Gregory. "He is much darker than Master Bede. I think he looks more like young Tom FitzClifford."

Joanna was indignant. Certainly not Tom FitzClifford, with his frame of an ox and his terrible skin!

The disagreement was deferred when Petronilla passed before them, stiff, with a ghostly pallor. Alice hurried to help her into the air, pursued by Joanna and Constance. The women were seated together in a little arbour when

Nicholas appeared. He was arm-in-arm with a shorter man – distantly familiar – who looked at Alice with interest, raising great hooped brows. When he bowed, he managed by some contortion to keep her in view.

"Alice," said Nicholas, "this is my good friend Piers Brixhemar, another of your brother's retinue in days past." Nicholas was paying his wife no heed, despite her wretched appearance.

"Lady Alice! Do you recognise me? I see you do. For I knew you in Essex when you were a little maiden. And we met last year at your brother's house in London. That is to say, we didn't quite meet, because your attention was entirely consumed by Robert Clifford and he's not a man I would shoulder-barge."

Yes! She knew the fellow now; she remembered. That night at Jack's house last spring, when she was the bearer of such sad news for Robert – the death of a little daughter – there had been an intrusive stranger at her elbow, joking with the Earl of Devon but leaning in as Lord Clifford murmured his pleas for pity; it was one of his *wounded and wretched* speeches. Alice opened her mouth and closed it again, pierced by a sudden, sharp longing for Robert. Only to see him; to speak with him; to ask him *why*.

"I was trotting after you all the evening, hoping to pay my humble respects; I even followed you out when you departed. My last chance, but what's this? Robert Clifford again! On a mission of some importance, it seems, for there was a letter you must give him. The poor fellow looked most unusually meek and pensive, but you were kind enough to comfort him. The Duke wasn't quite so glad, I seem to recall. If ever I am married, my wife may take any fellow by the hand – no matter how atrocious his reputation – and I shall think nothing of it. In fact, I shall hang a sign about her neck, giving my permission in advance. That would save a deal of jealousy, wouldn't you agree? I'm sure you would agree: from what I gather, your second husband is showing all the same tendencies."

There was a circle of open mouths. Nicholas was now trying not to look at Alice. "Control your tongue, Piers, for God's sake! Alice, I beg your pardon for inflicting this silly fellow on you. He makes it up as he goes along; a poor, harmless fool."

Brixhemar nodded earnestly. "Just my little joke, Lady Alice. No one pays me any heed. Please don't doubt my devotion to the house of de Vere: I was brought up with your brother Jack. I'd follow him to the ends of the earth."

Constance pounced with her usual acerbity. "Then what are you doing here, Master Brixhemar, taking your ease among us? The ends of the earth are just where the Earl is presently located."

"Perhaps he is and perhaps he isn't, Mistress Constance. Perhaps he's a great deal closer than that; somewhere a little warmer and a lot more civilised. But I am following him in spirit – as it were – even when I can't be beside him in person." Brixhemar patted his doublet, which rustled suggestively. He made a move as if to draw out its crumpled contents.

"Have you lost your wits?" A low snarl from Nicholas, his knuckles sharp at his friend's nape.

"As you're so quick, Mistress Constance," continued Brixhemar, quite unabashed, "pray unravel a mystery for me: what would be the cause of the bad blood between Sir Simon Loys and young Hal FitzClifford? Come, there's no call to look to Lady Alice; her blushes are pretty, but they don't answer the question. Or perhaps they do! What an enticing tangle. And here we have Mistress Ames." The bow did not interrupt the excruciation. "She who now stands to inherit Blakeney Hall. Gregory Clifford will be a landed man one day, mark my words; Triston's troubles are at an end. Oh, very well, Nick! Don't hiss at me, for I'm taking myself off: Simon is in one of his sneering fits, and I mean to tickle him if I can. No, I insist you stay here. Your wife looks very poorly indeed. A tiring journey for a gentlewoman in her condition."

* * *

The happier grew Triston's looks, the sourer Loys became. He glowered at Hugh Dacre for a time – not that the man noticed. Any decent steward would have addressed himself at once to the question of accommodation, but there was Hugh, the embodiment of worthlessness, settling himself with Chowne and John Twelvetrees and a jug of wine. As usual, Leo Brini was the man excluded. It was starting to dawn on Loys that Dacre's incompetence was more sham than sincere. In truth, the steward's control of the estate was perfectly satisfactory; his memory was excellent; he'd any number of valuable London connections from those years in Warwick's household. Yet demand of him any task requiring courage or initiative and he became smugly, defiantly useless. Then again, the man Hugh had replaced, Peter Considine, had limitations of his own; shortcomings in intelligence and demeanour both. Hailing from the humbler merchant class of Ripon, Considine added nothing to Loys's prestige. So he'd been left to stew in Avonby – his master's ears and eyes in the North Country – and not one useful report had come south.

Loys returned to the nuisance of the night's accommodation, eyeing Triston with resentment, the man who had caused their predicament and then failed to proffer an alternative, now strutting about like a cockerel, dropping Buckingham's name at every opportunity. Setting his teeth, Loys backed away from Piers Brixhemar.

"Simon! I cannot stop fretting about you. Where – *where* – do you sleep tonight? Do you have any friends in Essex? Any friends in England? How mortifying, to be dropped so publicly by your host!"

Loys simply looked at him, resisting the urge to shiver. Talking with Brixhemar was like being explored by wasps.

"There's always St Radegund's Priory. In the wrong direction and the food is terrible, but beggars can't choose." Piers continued to twinkle at him, his eyes flicking to his uncle, who'd approached from the garden door and was now standing at Loys's elbow.

"Hold your tongue, Piers. I told you Loys will stay with us at Roliford."

Loys bowed to Mark Rohips. He knew they would end up at Roliford; it was just the arranging of it that was so unbearable.

The older man continued, "I've been speaking with your wife, Simon; a most charming and gracious reminder of the lost and lamented de Veres. Our missing Earl is a finer man by far than the greedy imp of Gloucester who purloined his lands."

306

Loys looked around hopefully to see if anyone was eavesdropping – the Duke of Buckingham, for instance. No doubt Sir Mark thought himself a venerable wiseacre, beyond the reach of the headsman. On went Rohips with the proud parade of treason. "It's a rare pleasure to speak with one of the family. Of course, I soldiered with her father, Earl John, many a time. A great pity I had to disappoint young Lord Jack last year; knees not up to it now. But Piers here fought for Oxford at Barnet, didn't you, Piers? You and Simon's little brother Nick. Glazed with pride over your shiny new knighthoods." The man's smile was gleaming malevolently. "Alas, eh, nephew? Oxford scuttles off to Scotland and leaves you two wringing your hands before Edward of York, lucky to lose only those new honours. Easy come, easy go."

Sir Simon's gaze darted up to Rohips's face. The man had said it, and said it deliberately, in a room full of ears: *Edward of York.*

By now, someone was eavesdropping, but it was only Nicholas. He strolled over, exchanging a steady look with his friend Brixhemar. "I watched you playing at quoits the other day, Mark. Knees didn't seem to bother you then."

Rohips brayed. "Knees work when I need them to! Now tell me: who's the dark wench yonder, flirting with Buckingham's man?"

"If you mean Mistress Elyn, she's a baseborn daughter of your old friend John de Vere. She attends my wife," said Loys. There was no need to warn off Mark Rohips. Elyn wouldn't look twice at the fellow.

"Is she now?" A broad grin split the knight's face. "Your sister-in-law, then. A beauty and no mistake! Mistress Elyn staying with us at Roliford tonight? Good. Good."

Loys changed his mind. "Spare the girl your gallantries, Sir Mark, or you'll offend Lady Loys."

He cackled. "Nothing of that sort!"

But when the dancing commenced, Sir Mark led the way. If the knees were protesting, they went unheeded as he caught Elyn's hand and led her into the circle. The girl turned about her, trying for a means of escape. When she could not loose the gauntlet grip, Elyn gave in with good grace, smiling at her captor. Sir John Ames had the other hand; another man old enough to know better.

*   *   *

Three hundred miles north and on the same day that Beatrice Clifford wed Hugo Sheringham, Harry Percy wed Lady Maud Herbert. The marriage had thrown Alnwick into commotion, requiring as it did a great deal of preparation, much of the labour falling on Eleanor's shoulders. In this, the lady was most ably assisted by Sir Gabriel Appledore, whose health improved markedly when he had an almighty distraction to occupy his mind. Appledore became almost cheerful, and the lady found the new under-steward notably more obsequious and considerably more amenable than his predecessor. And the one before that.

Both before and after the ceremony there was jousting and feasting and dancing and hunting; not since the Earl returned to his patrimony had Alnwick seen such display. Many of the nobles north of the Trent were present and a great number of knights and gentlemen also.

Waryn FitzClifford was in attendance: a landed gentleman, now, enjoying his rightful place among the guests. Mistress Anna did not accompany her husband, for she was heavy with child and had taken to her bed in the chamber at Belforth; the chamber in which the unfortunate James Thwaite had so recently departed this world. Amongst Waryn's little retinue was Sir James's son Lyall, who had, at last, reappeared, after months at sea in recovering from his fright and planning his revenge on the Cliffords. But the ominous plotting left no discernable mark, and Lyall attended his uncle with every appearance of grateful deference.

Also present was Sir Roger Clifford and – steering well clear – Sir Lancelot Threlkeld. Sir Roger was sending his fellow knight glances of the purest venom. Between these two houses seethed a most notorious and venerable feud, as everyone knew: a breach predating the ambush on the Wyverns at Thirsk; predating the bonfire Robert Clifford had made of Gawain

Threlkeld's house: it was years since the disappearance of Lord John Clifford's heir. Like everyone else, Sir Lancelot had noticed the black looks cast in his direction. What he could not know was that the young FitzClifford he left for dead on the streets of Thirsk was, in fact, Sir Roger's bastard son. He could not know that Sir Roger had but to look in his direction to see again the first words of that calamitous letter –

'It grieves me to inform you, Brother, of a most dolorous occurrence …'

– the letter purporting to come from Lord Robert, in fact composed by Aymer and corrected, sealed and dispatched by Loic – for Robert himself had not troubled to glance at it.

King Edward wasn't present at the wedding, of course; he'd never been so far north, not even for warmongering. George of Clarence promised to attend and hadn't, and Richard of Gloucester made his excuses well in advance. Simon Loys had been mulling the journey, but when he heard from Gloucester he resolved instead to grace the more humble nuptials of his nephew Hugo Sheringham, together with the unlooked-for Duke of Buckingham.

Despite an utter dearth of the higher nobility, Eleanor intended to dazzle the North Country and, more than this, she intended to dazzle her new and most unwelcome sister-in-law. Naturally enough, the trespasser bore not the slightest resemblance to the woman of Eleanor's imaginings. Maud was not prim, or stiff or sour. Instead, she was short and very dark, with a comfortable bosom and lively black eyes, a deep, sweet voice and an abundance of cheerful good sense. It was clear, even to her rival, that the lady would make an excellent countess and chatelaine. Harry Percy was delighted with his consort, and Maud seemed equally satisfied in her turn. Their alliance was so natural, so instinctive, the friendship of such long duration, that poor Eleanor was quite wrong-footed and instead of cowing her sister-in-law from the start, she found herself behaving with restrained good manners and a quiet dignity that greatly pleased her brother.

* * *

It was a trying evening at Roliford. It could not be otherwise, with the party so thoroughly at Brixhemar's mercy.

Before they parted for the night, Loys snatched a moment alone with Petronilla. "What's the matter? A corpse has more life in it."

She sighed, heavy-lidded. "I think the child is determined to kill me. I've never felt so wretched."

"I thought you yearned for this?"

She gave him her sourest look.

"I *said* you need only be patient, woman." He pinched her chin and dragged it upwards, their lips an inch apart. "I said you need only shut your mouth, open your legs and stop thirsting after a man who has himself well in hand and means never to touch you." Loys was much too close for a man who meant never to touch; one who touched all the time; little touches, brimming with devilry.

When the slap came, he was too quick, as ever, trapping her wrist.

"Don't you mock me!" She breathed and steadied and, after a moment, continued. "Nick's in a temper with Piers, who more or less announced Jack de Vere's movements to the world, and a temper with me, because he thinks I'll tell you."

Loys gave a quiet laugh. "Oh, we've a shrewd idea where de Vere is hiding and who else he's drawn into the cesspit. Christ, they're a slapdash lot. I doubt there's anyone left in Essex who doesn't know they're plotting. I'll discuss it with Richard of Gloucester."

"Discuss what? There's no proof. Not yet. You'd only make yourself look foolish."

"That would certainly be undesirable. Keep me informed." He pressed a fingertip to her dimple. "Now go up before he misses you. Your face is repulsive."

Early next morning, Loys's party was on the road. Sir Simon had much on his mind; it was something of a relief to admit a more trivial matter. Immediately on the return to Sevenhill, Alice found herself seated in the magnificent day room, to which she was so seldom invited. The formality of the interview was designed to crush; she saw it at once. It was clear she'd made a misstep of some sort; Hal FitzClifford at the root of it, perhaps. She set her face.

"Do you care for my brother? Don't look like that! I'm not trying to trap you, you stupid girl; I've seen the way your tastes run, and it's not in that direction. What I mean is, do you care what befalls Nick?"

Confused protestations.

"Be silent. By now you may have some glimmer of understanding concerning Jack de Vere's whereabouts and his intentions. Let me make myself perfectly clear." He was speaking very slowly and distinctly. "If anything comes to your ears, you are to tell me at once. If you receive any communication, from de Vere; from another concerning him – Brixhemar, for example – you are to tell me at once. If anyone attempts to draw you into conspiracy, you are to tell me at once."

Alice simply blinked at him. Until he mentioned it, the glimmer was just that: indistinct and blurry. Now she was sifting Piers Brixhemar's hints with urgency, when yesterday she'd tried to escape them.

"My brother is a fool, and yours is worse. You do no good to either man by keeping their secrets to yourself; it will lead to your death as well as theirs. I expect your entire obedience, Alice. We'll leave the matter there." On to another matter on which he predicted rampant disobedience. "Sit down and hear me out; I didn't give you leave to go. So: before we left Roliford this morning, I took a walk with Sir Mark, as you saw."

She didn't see; she'd been hiding from Master Brixhemar.

"Rohips had a proposal for me. The man's a widower, of course, and childless, and probably half-way to the grave, but apparently hasn't given up hope of an heir. It's your half-sister Elyn on whom his choice has fallen. A splendid match, for her, at least. I trust you'll not attempt to thwart the girl's happiness as you so unaccountably thwarted that of Mistress Ames." Alice had risen, in spite of his direction, hands clasped and lips parted. He readied the withering retort.

"I cannot believe this news! This is far more than I hoped for her. Thank you, sir! You are doing very well by my poor sister."

"Oh! I'm glad to find you sensible on this matter, at least."

"But the dowry, Sir Simon? Elyn is baseborn, and ... not clever, and the de Veres sunk so low. Surely he will be asking much of you in return?"

"If Rohips were holding out for intelligence, Brixhemar would certainly inherit Roliford. Clever women are like dragons: everyone knows a man who's seen one, but when it comes to it, the proof is always lacking. No, the girl is young and pretty and the daughter of your father, who was Rohips's companion-in-arms and an earl to boot. The old fool is smitten. She goes to him without a penny."

"Truly? May I tell her, Sir Simon? May I tell her now?"

"Please do. The last few days have been particularly trying. I cannot face a further onslaught." How his wife's sister met the news was a matter of indifference. Elyn had, in fact, told him of a sweetheart, but he could not be expected to remember, for the FitzCliffords were of interest only in their bearing on his wife. Loys congratulated himself, once more undeservedly, on his diplomatic skills, and dismissed the matter from his mind, returning to the trouble entangling his family like bindweed.

Alice was not so sanguine. At once she sought the help of Blanche and together, they summoned Elyn to the parlour. How well Alice recalled the moment when Jack broke the news of Lord Clifford's courtship. Her brother had been tactless, to say the least; brutal. She smiled. "My dear, I have some very interesting news for you. I have spoken, just now, with Sir Simon, who's been busy on your behalf. He has arranged a marriage for you, my love; a very proud marriage. You shall be a happy bride."

Elyn sat up, eyes wide. Could it be that *he* had come at last, to seek her in the proper manner? To be *his* wife: it was beyond anything good.

"Yes! Sir Mark Rohips is eager to wed you."

A mile off, in Scop Wood, the rooks had gathered to taunt a fox. Tiring of the game, they rose together and flocked towards the house in a tumultuous stridency. Elyn flung back her head and drowned them out.

* * *

Brini was pouring the substance one viscous drop at a time into a tiny glass spoon when the uproar began. He flinched, spilling the contents of the vial into the flames. They puffed up, sea-green and acrid. "Gesù! Mille scuse, mio signor."

Seated before his papers, Loys had not moved. "What? You've spilled it? How careless, when Elixir of Ichor can't be had in Colchester. Next time we're in London, buy a double quantity if you plan to throw it about with such abandon. Now make a full note of the effect on the flames or the expense is wasted."

There was fresh round of shrieking and the slamming of a door before he looked up and found Brini eyeing him with some alarm. "It's only the half-wit. Mistress Elyn is another gentlewoman who's gone beyond you, Leo. She greets the news of her marriage with some excitement, it seems. But let us not be distracted; we'll learn the absurd particulars soon enough."

* * *

On the ride to the bathing place, the Wyverns passed Ste-Croix's warehouse, its new door bright against the weather-beaten stone. There was a flurry of quips and jests. Little Fabien, the clerk, cast around the faces of the men, his English too slow and stiff for their banter.

"So, what are you teaching Melisande?" There, at Richie's shoulder, was Guy's lazy smirk. Buried in the ragging tone was a sharper note. "Any time a fellow comes near, you clam up."

"If you troubled yourself with a bit of French, you'd know, wouldn't you?"

"Must be something filthy, you scapegrace. I've a good mind to tell her mam. *Don't let him walk her back from church, Madame Ste-Croix. He's no hero, just a grubby lad out to cop a good feel.*"

Richie sighed. "I copped a feel already and you know it. A big arse and weazen titties. Not to my taste. Anyway, she likes a pretty boy. She likes Bede. Satisfied?" At least it wasn't George. George would be hard to bear.

"Donkey, eh? There's gratitude for you! And just when you'd started cleaning your teeth. Never mind, perhaps you'll catch yourself a selkie if you look sharp." He laughed. "More like some rough shyster stinking of fish."

Those within earshot turned to Aymer, who shrugged. From behind, a *miaow*. Probably Findern; it usually was.

Reginald Grey spurred forward to partner Aymer. "Never permit the bitterness of others to deflect you. Lord Robert tells me you've committed yourself to the path of righteousness. You now shun meat, so he says. This is very good. Remind me later and I will take your vow on that matter."

Aymer wound the reins absently in his fingers. Of late, each succulent morsel of flesh would turn sour on his tongue, his belly bucking and heaving until he leaned aside to spit and shudder. Red meat was poison. "That would give me great comfort, Sir Reginald. At the same time, I'll forswear women. I can better serve my father if I put all temptations from me."

It was the priest's turn to frown; to examine his hands. Their horses were jostled by an interested crowd, George among them, for by now he'd drifted back from the head of the column, where Loic was scolding Lord Robert with reckless enthusiasm.

"What about your lady-love, eh? You can't disappoint a lady, Aymer. Not one so generous with her gifts. Go on then! Let's see this famous gem."

Aymer's hand clutched, convulsively, for his purse, even as his head twitched up. On George's face, the usual grin, honest and stupid. Richie and Will exchanged a wary glance. Peter was hot scarlet.

Before Aymer's snarl could find voice, the priest gave his verdict. "No vow of celibacy is warranted in this household. In due course, Lord Robert expects his sons to marry. Moreover, a bachelor need not strive particularly to avoid women. St Augustine himself regarded chastity as a mutable thing."

Behind Grey's back, the Wyverns were shaking their heads at the old joke; soundless chuckling. St Augustine should have been more careful in his pronouncement. That man had a lot to answer for.

* * *

So here was another hound refusing to come to heel. By the time Loys and Brini descended, Elyn had been hauled to her chamber over Dacre's shoulder, sobbing and elbowing him in the head. The household enjoyed a good dinner; Elyn did not.

In the low sun, Loys strolled across the lawn. He lowered himself to a bench amid the springing heads of lavender and closed his eyes; nocturnal labours were taking their toll. In due course, the sheaf of parchment fanned from his hand. He lay back, assailed, once more, by those pressing predicaments: the debt that shadowed his heels like a slinking dog and, more dangerous yet, his brother's self-destructive urges.

Among the women, all minds were on Elyn and her base ingratitude, but the talk was interrupted by the object herself, raging and storming above them in a most unmaidenly fashion; eventually driving them outside, where Alice crossed, dutiful, to join her husband. Silent, she took a seat by the supine figure – in just the way she'd done, a year before, on another evening, in another garden of tranquil sunshine, with another man altogether.

This man took her hand. He'd never content himself with so chaste a touch. As the fingers travelled on their way, the gentlewomen exchanged glances. Simon Loys was getting an unfortunate reputation as a man who couldn't believe his luck; a man who'd never let his luck alone; perpetually fiddling. They turned their backs and set out a game of bowls.

"Well, little wife? So you've locked the poor simpleton away. Dacre says he's to starve her into submission. By tomorrow you'll be beating her, I predict; chasing her round the room with Twelvetrees's staff. And there was I, supposing you'd curse me for giving your sister to an old lecher!" Loys slipped an arm about her waist and pulled Alice in until she was cradled comfortably against his chest.

There was a faint wheeze and a crackle beneath her ear; a legacy, perhaps, of his weakling youth, but she was full of umbrage and didn't hear it. "How could you think I would not delight in such a match? How strange – that you could know me so little!"

Everywhere and every day, unwelcome marriages were urged on the reluctant. But to find, in her, that particular combination of the prosaic and the ruthless: it was unexpected.

Alice continued stiffly, "You're remembering my reluctance over our own marriage, I suppose. That was an entirely different circumstance, with grave matters at stake. I'll not have Elyn throw away her chance on a hopeless passion for some shabby fugitive."

Which made him laugh aloud.

* * *

The emerald was not, in fact, burning a hole in Aymer's purse, but lying tranquil beneath the floorboards of his spartan chamber, so it was safe to discard doublet and hose and dive among the welcoming waves. For days he'd been coming to these spangly sands in the little bay beneath the cliffs, alone and joyous.

Reginald Grey settled himself beside Loic on a broad, warm rock, his dignity quarrelling with his desire to swim. Aymer was now a distant speck, due north, springing like a salmon to the spawning grounds, as if he never meant to return. Below them, Robert Clifford strode into the water, a figure from a danse macabre, great bands of naked muscle clenching and flowing at each splashy stride, skin shredding like a leper. Loic hopped to his feet. "A good rub-down with wet sand, I think. That should serve." He was speaking to himself.

"Leave him be! Leave him be. Hectoring and sulking and pawing at the man will not bind him any more closely, as I've told you often enough." The tone softened. "Love, in all its forms, Loic, is Our Father's perfect gift. It's not finite. It's not rationed. Share him, and there'll be no less to go around." Sometimes the reprimands were more eloquent than the sermons.

"She's a sly one!"

"She is *not*. A worthy and upstanding woman. God knows, he needs a little comfort and companionship until he can reclaim Alice de Vere."

Beside him, Loic gave a tiny jolt.

"Oh, the Lady Alice will be his. A covenant with God."

And now, the small, dejected sag.

"Come, now! You didn't welcome Babette Delaurin either, I seem to recall. By the end, you two were inseparable."

The young man took a peek, seeking the twinkle buried deep in the priest's eye, where most would miss it. Grey stood and briskly stripped. "Guard my clothes, will you?"

Loic watched him go, their fine shepherd, compassionate and undervalued. Before him, some of the boys had taken to football on the sands; the sea was bobbing with men. Then he forgot all else. Far out east he'd sighted first one mast, then another, rounding the headland towards Perteuil. Loic bounded up the tumbled stairway of boulders until the harbour came into view. He shielded his eyes. The ships were turning in. Surely this was Pierre du Chastel's promised force, come to bear them away to adventure. Loic turned and looked down on the cove. He whistled through his fingers.

Amid the excited chatter, every man scrambled to dry and to garb himself, to mount, to canter back towards the inn. All but Reginald Grey, a thunder-browed Lady Godiva, naked beneath the borrowed cloak, for his clothes had unaccountably disappeared.

* * *

"Sir Simon, may I have a moment of your time?" Constance was hovering as the knight and his chamberlain climbed to their apartment.

He gave a brief nod, but when she made to follow him, he waved her back. "No, Mistress Constance. Into my day room, if you please. I cannot admit a woman to the workroom; you'd be trying to peep into the all-seeing eye, no doubt, or steal my broomstick."

She chuckled, loudly, to show she'd never been a believer, and took herself off to await the master. Two chairs faced his throne across the broad table. Settling in one, she contemplated the chest occupying the other. The key lay in the lock. She looked away and then, after a moment, she looked back.

Here I am! it nudged her. Its bands and hinges formed themselves into a smirk.

Within the strongbox lay files of parchment; tallies of figures. Heading the pages, the names of prominent London merchants and, on many of them, the signature of Lord John Howard. Just in time, Constance closed the lid. Loys seated himself and regarded her in silence.

"Lady Alice is mishandling Elyn." It was blurted out, rather, to cover her confusion.

He groaned, and placed his hands on the arms of the chair as if he would rise again.

"There are better ways to achieve your aim, sir."

The hands remained as they were. "My aim? You mean putting Brixhemar's nose out of joint? I can think of few better ways than this marriage. If you've come to rescue Mistress Elyn from my wife, you need not have bothered."

"That isn't it. But perhaps I should not have bothered, Sir Simon. I'll go now."

"Since you have bothered, though, you may as well continue."

"I can talk Elyn around easily enough, sir, but I want something in return."

"Oh yes?"

"You seem in the mood for marriages, sir. I want it known that I have no wish to wed. I intend to remain beside Lady Alice. I need your promise that you'll do nothing to impose a husband on me."

"Another matter in which I have little interest. Except in this respect: your friend Joanna Ames has brought my friend Brini very low. To the extent that I care for anyone's happiness, I care for his. If you don't wish to leave my household, then why not stay within it and take my chamberlain? That way, you may bear children, enjoy the pleasures of the flesh and yet remain always beside your aunt." He was picking at his teeth, which were narrow and somewhat greyish. "In fact, I don't know why Leo didn't approach you rather than Mistress Ames. You're certainly more desirable."

"He had no encouragement. Nor will he. I don't wish to bear children. I've no interest in the pleasures of the flesh, as you call it."

"That's only because you've never been touched. Once a man has handled you, you'll learn to like it."

Leonard Tailboys had grunted something similar as he ground his crotch against her, but that had failed to do the trick. Her mouth twisted.

"I'm not suggesting myself!" Loys misread her face. "My wife is sufficient for my wants. I don't tend to stray."

With perfect timing, there came a thunder of banging and breaking glass. Constance was growing impatient, even if Loys wasn't; here was a man who liked the sound of his own voice. "If you'll write your pledge and sign it, Sir Simon, I'll go and restore peace."

"You shall have it in writing if you succeed. Go to the imbecile and work your magic. Why not borrow my wand?"

* * *

Hal was in the maidens' chamber, where he certainly shouldn't have been after his previous error. Here was a man who never would learn a lesson, thought Grace, tailing him in, her only care to protect the poor fool. This time there was no gallivanting. Hal was at the casement, behind Idonia and her younger sisters, all of them craning towards the west lawn. Grace approached and insinuated herself until she was close against him, inhaling the familiar fragrance: leather, bay, camphor, pine needles – and sweat. Though the essential perfume was delicious, Hal was never quite as fresh as he might be.

Peering beneath his arm, where the scent was strongest, she espied the object of their interest: Joanna Ames, manhandling Gregory's wheeled chair across the grass. The moles had been busy in the breast of the earth and the conveyance jerked and jolted over their hummocks, embarrassing its occupant. Joanna paused and mopped her brow.

Well out of earshot, Gregory was saying, "Please sit beside me, Mistress Joanna, if the grass is dry enough. It must be uncomfortable work over this rough ground."

At once she complied, wrapping her arms around her knees and looking shyly into his bright face.

"You know why you've been brought to Crawshay, I suppose? Sir John has told you, I'm sure."

"He has, sir."

"It's not every maiden who'd take a cripple for a husband."

"Oh! But I would, Master Gregory. Gladly."

"That makes me very happy. I want you to understand something, though. I don't know whether you have given it any thought. Surely you have. It is a customary thing to think about, isn't it, when a young couple becomes betrothed? I think it must be customary, even if it's not proper to say the words aloud. So you shall excuse me when I speak, for it's only to reassure you." The preamble had got away from him, assuming a life of its own. "Surely you must be wondering about it, for all that you're too maidenly to ask. Of course you are. So I will put your mind at rest, if you will forgive me for mentioning it." He was cursing himself by now.

A bemused shake of her head.

"I can do it! I can do it. And I have done it; you may be sure of that. But only the once. I wouldn't again, not with another, not now. It was in Southwark, of course; my cousin Hal arranged it, for he's a man of the world. That's all I need say on the matter. It's just that: I can do it, you see. A man needs only his knees, you see. They're damn good knees."

She had turned a painful hue, trying to cover the flush with her hands.

"Oh – oh. Your pardon. You had not wondered about it, after all. Why would you? Oh God." He passed a hand across his eyes, and then came a miserable little laugh.

She swallowed and peeped and laughed a little also. Then she caught his eye, and the laughter blossomed until it enveloped them both in mortified delight. The young man was seen to throw back his head – heaving and twitching – and a commotion sprang up among the watchers at the window.

Hal raised a hand. "Hush! There's nothing amiss. Look at Mistress Joanna."

The girl was on her knees, her hands in his, and then Gregory had scooped her up and she tumbled into his lap. An outbreak of clapping and crooning from his sisters. Hal turned, seeking his friend, a broad grin across his rough-hewn features, but Grace had fled the room.

* * *

A little later, Alice was disturbed at her grim needlework by the two kinswomen. Elyn shuffled in, hands clasped, and, awkward and sulky, made her submission.

Alice embraced her with graciousness. "This is very good, Elyn. I do not require enthusiasm, but I do demand obedience."

When Constance had seen the matter completed, she went once more to that quarter of the house where the men were sequestered. Leo Brini opened at her knock, raised a finger, then gently closed the door. He reappeared, smiling, with the key to the day room.

Another hurried rifle in the chest. Here was a reference to a ship – *God's Gift* – with a description of its tunnage and dimensions. Other than that, she found nothing meaningful.

Once more he faced her across the hefty table, a chit of parchment in his fingers.

"Elyn is content, sir, and Lady Alice is content. Is that the promise I requested?"

"How Lady Alice can suspect me of necromancy, when there is a miracle-worker among us … !" He must find the joke most particularly amusing, for he would keep reverting to it.

"Is that the promise I requested, Sir Simon?"

"Here is your promise, with my autograph upon it. You are safe from the taint of men, though I do suggest you listen when Leo asks, as he doubtless will; witnessing my happiness has spurred him to matrimony. So tell me: the half-wit did not exact any onerous condition?"

"None at all." She extended a hand.

He waved the parchment idly in his fingers. "Since you're here, you might as well tell me what you said."

Now it was her turn to eye him in silence. "You may not approve. Since our flight from Little Malvern, Elyn has fancied herself in love with Lord Clifford's baseborn son – one Guy FitzClifford."

"Don't call him *Lord* Clifford. Yes, I recall something of this. That one has a twin, does he not? Men of surpassing beauty, if my memory serves. They cannot have got their looks from their father. Changelings, the pair of them."

"A twin, yes: Aymer FitzClifford is the other. Anyway, Elyn is still waiting for Guy to come for her, absurd as that is. I simply had to point out that Roliford is much nearer the coast and, as mistress in her own house, she'll be less closely watched. After that, she dried her tears."

He gave a bark of laughter. "Well, well, Mistress Constance. Very neatly done, but mind Lady Alice doesn't learn how you achieved it! My wife is settled now; I would not have you spark those old longings for freedom."

"I wouldn't have said it if there were any possibility of it coming to pass."

Loys, who knew that the exiles were close at hand, was less sanguine than his young friend. "So, you don't think the charming twins harbour a tenderness for the women of my household?"

"Certainly not. Those men are rapists and brutes of the worst kind."

He handed over the slip of parchment.

Before dinner, Loys was towed into the gardens by his wife. She began to boast of her triumph then learned, to her puzzlement, that Constance had got there before her. When Alice reflected further, she found it wasn't the first time the girl had made an unlikely and private alliance.

* * *

When the steeple of baggage toppled into the sad sag of the mattress, it dragged the unsuspecting Notch down with it. There lay the twins' manservant, head-first in the puzzling trough, until he hit upon the cause of his tumble. The culprit was Master Will, who never could resist a wager, bounding from the far end of his father's chamber and across his own without once touching the floor. It was the boy's final flying leap that won the gamble and cracked the bed's load-bearing brace.

As the servant staggered, over-burdened, from the room, Aymer glanced up from the corner where he was squatting, palm flat on a floorboard. "Notch is not your man." He pushed to his feet, rolling a twist of rag between his fingers, and opened his purse. "You two shall bear your own bags. Go after him."

Richie opened his mouth.

"Or summon Pleydell."

Will and Richie trailed Notch downstairs at a disobliging distance and passed out into the yard, arms unencumbered.

Lounging by the casement, Guy brooded sourly on his twin, who was still fidgeting with his wicked prize. "It's only a matter of time before George or Donkey says something to Father, and then …"

"He'll wallow in my guts?"

Guy closed his eyes. There was blank silence until Notch panted back into the room. "Masters, *time to go*, says Sir Patrick."

Broad smiles at the head of the column that wended down the steep and narrow streets. Clifford nodded this way and that, acknowledging well-wishers. The cheering was probably ironic. Ste-Croix rode beside his departing guest, for the bill had, finally, been paid and the landlord was all keen attention.

"Pass my farewells to your wife, my friend. I'd hoped to thank Madame Ste-Croix in person."

Ste-Croix caught the unvoiced question and picked at his nails. It was uncivil of Renée to absent herself. By now, no doubt, she'd reached the little chamber at the top of the house, itching to inspect that wretched bed.

The bed could wait. All this while, his wife was watching from the best chamber. When the cavalcade vanished, briefly, behind the buildings on the waterfront, she hastened to bring up the low chair from its usual place and settle at the casement. Then, finding that she'd no view but the window sill, she rose to fetch Milor's pillow, meaning to perch upon it. At once his scent assailed her, powerful and unambiguous. She carried the pillow back to the bed and laid it carefully in place.

Soon Clifford and his men were aboard, milling on the decks while the luggage was stowed. The vessels weren't French and the crew wasn't either: Hansards from Hamburg and Bremen, when Clifford was all but promised an army of France at his command. This is what came of sending a boy to do a man's job; Hal's job. Hal would have dragged King Louis's ships along by the anchor. Clifford turned to scowl at Aymer, but Aymer was presiding over the forecastle of the next ship, so he scowled, instead, at Nield and Nield – he could have sworn – scowled back. He loosed his temper, instead, over the captain, though the man was none the wiser, for their interpreter was a charlatan, tagging along for the ride, his English a string of obscenities, his Flemish bad and his French worse. Bertrand Jansen would have translated without difficulty, but Jansen had run away.

At the quayside, the crowd was changing in character: younger townsmen and ragged boys. No one saw the stone. George cried aloud as blood sprang out on his cheek and spilled through his fingers.

Choking down outrage, Clifford forced the words through his teeth; he couldn't be heard across the deck, though the roar filled George's ear: "Get below!" Some of the FitzCliffords began at their clamouring. With a furious motion he silenced them and strode across to lean on the guard rail, ostentatiously visible but out of missile range, while the men-at-arms made a casual parade of their crossbows.

With a few of his men, Ste-Croix dismounted and plunged into the throng. There was a pushing and a shoving and a sing of knives.

Sails unfurled and the ships slipped away.

* * *

There lay Percy, drowsing at his ease in a bed of heavy magnificence, legs tangled with hers. The act he'd judged so trying, so hedged about with false expectation and exuberant excess had proved, with Maud, quite the opposite: serene and pleasurable.

"Your poor sister," mused his bride. "I'm afraid you've been remiss, my lord, in not finding the lady a husband. Robert Clifford! Those tales reached even to my ears, in the Welsh Marches."

Percy shifted a little, seeking, always, after flawless comfort. "Her head is filled with silly notions," he conceded. "They would have wed, had King Edward not returned. After that, I couldn't wean her off him."

"Her loyalty does her credit – though not, perhaps, her wisdom. It could be worse. We've seen what happens when the menfolk don't find husbands for excitable maidens: they look for partners among the household, like poor Elizabeth Stafford. At least Robert Clifford is noble by birth. We should be grateful your sister had no liaison with an under-steward or the like."

"God, no. Eleanor has more sense than that. And Clifford laid not a finger on her, of course. When he carried her off to Lindisfarne, I mean. To safeguard her honour, a man of mine spent the night in full harness outside her chamber."

"Of course, Harry. It's just the appearance of the thing that's so against her. I fear your sister has suffered some slight in the eyes of the world. The foremost in the land may be beyond her now."

They were silent awhile, thinking of Eleanor; thinking of her silly notions and the riotous damage they had wrought.

"It's rather unsatisfactory," murmured Maud. "That hair. She's too old to wear it loose – unwed or otherwise. Of course, all the gentlewomen follow suit. And her gowns: they cling so. I wonder, Harry. My father was considering the Earl of Arundel, at one time, for me. William FitzAlan's a widower. He's been a widower a long time."

"FitzAlan? He's ancient. You don't know Eleanor. She wouldn't stand for it."

"We shall see."

* * *

Loys was away towards Suffolk, tallying his manors, making the circuit, as he'd done many times since taking possession. Few of his neighbours were so assiduous. "There goes Simon Loys, again," they said, probably. "Checking it's all still there. Some men can't credit their luck."

He journeyed back by way of Pearmain, his sister's place. The groom had cantered on to warn her, but when Loys rode up there was no stirrup cup to greet him. Jane Sheringham was concealed in the rose garden, kneeling on a cushion, fiercely snipping. A pair of hounds reclined nearby, rumbling at him.

He stood awhile in silence, contemplating the woman's narrow back, wondering. Their own brother was the beating, vital heart of the conspiracy – which made Gilbert Sheringham some sclerotic artery. Loys's thoughts drifted, again, to Mark Rohips, a man of traitorous impudence and brazen dissent. Soon he and Sir Mark would be linked by marriage. Then it struck, all of a sudden, that a bystander might guess Loys, himself, to be the centre of the web. He gave an involuntary bark of laughter and his sister straightened.

"Simon. You've come to fetch Catharine, at last." Jane looked around her, sharp nose pointing. "That girl stalks my steps til the very moment she's wanted. It's most disagreeable. Well?" she tossed over her shoulder, returning to the roses, "What news, with you?"

"Nothing to speak of. Mistress Elyn is to wed Sir Mark, as you heard, no doubt. I've been made a Justice of the Peace, and Collector of the customs at Norreys …"

"Rohips should have taken your daughter. A good enough match for Catharine. Why waste Roliford on a baseborn chit?"

"Rohips? I can do better than him. William FitzAlan is weighing my proposal as we speak."

Jane pushed herself up, lip curled in purposeful contempt. "Oh yes? And I'll dance naked at the wedding! My niece, the next Countess of Arundel? I shall tell every gentlewoman in Essex. You'll be besieged for particulars. And so, before long, will he." She laughed in his face.

"Perhaps. More likely I'll choose the Howards. John Howard is very much the rising man at court. His heir is a good wager, in the long run."

"Has he the habit of welcoming his debtors' children to his hearth? But you and Howard are Gloucester's creatures; you should stick together. Spare the rest of us from the taint."

"In truth," he lied, "I did come here to fetch Catharine away. But I find I can't deprive you of the girl's company. Keep your memento of me." He doffed his bonnet and stalked back to the hall, prising Dacre loose. Rather than ride straight for home, the party detoured to Colchester.

"Summon Farrimond to the inn. I can't face that dingy hole of his," said Loys to his steward, lowering himself to a creaking chair. "But first, pour me wine. My sister gives me toothache."

Garit Farrimond was already tucked in his narrow cot, reading by the light of a candle stump, when Sir Hugh hammered on the door. As it cracked open, Dacre folded his arms and stared away down the alley, lest the mysteries within contaminate his eyes. Slipping past his fellow servant, Brini greeted the apothecary with gentle respect, packing his bag while the older man retreated to the shadows to dress.

"You acquired the Ichor, then, Master Farrimond?" Brini remarked, to the man's back. "Sir Simon will be pleased."

"Only a tiny quantity, I'm afraid, and the supply's not certain, but you'll be in London before you run through it, I daresay. Now –" he turned. The Venetian was examining the bottle. "Gloves! Gloves, Master Brini, please! What are you thinking?"

"Oh, I never use them. I'd be more likely to fumble it." Brini flushed in the gloom.

"Waxed gloves, Master Brini. *Always*. You've not seen the ruin Elixir of Ichor will make of the body's innards."

True enough, though Sir Simon's description had been sufficiently vivid. "Waxed gloves?" Brini murmured, with a rueful shrug. "I might as well grip the vial with my feet."

Farrimond took up his staff. With Dacre following, they hurried through the dark streets – for Sir Simon did so hate to be kept waiting – and, at once, Sir Hugh was banished to the tap room below, where Chowne and Twelvetrees were already ensconced.

The Ichor was received with gladness; since Brini's careless slip, a most promising direction of travel had been closed to them. In a comfortable upstairs chamber, the three men fell to animated discussion, Loys leaning in the chair, Brini and Farrimond lounging on the bed. In his eagerness, Brini rose and took a few turns about the room. The cups were emptied and filled.

When silence fell, at last, Master Farrimond was fidgeting as though he had more to say. Absently he took up the hazardous vessel in his stiff glove, swirling its slow, oily iridescence: now midnight blue, now verdigris; mutable as shot silk. He looked up. "Did I mention that your lady graced my humble shop, Sir Simon, during her recent visit to the town?" The difference in rank, dwindling in the warm firelight, now loomed like an outsize shadow.

"So I heard. You left no very favourable impression." Alice was not the object, and Loys knew it. Petronilla: Farrimond was blighted by the need to speak of her.

"Alas, sir. That grieves me." A laden pause. "I was honoured, again, by your sister-in-law, Mistress Petronilla, who rejoices in glad news, so I'm told."

Loys cocked his head. "*So you're told?*" He gave his most sardonic smile. "Now, who could have told you that? Your circle is not wide, or well-informed."

"Your pardon, Sir Simon. Perhaps I guessed it."

"Then perhaps you strayed a little too close."

The implication was terrifying. "Oh no, sir! Never that! I did know, I confess. It was done by way of a drug of my own devising. A means to tame a man," he blurted out, defenceless; a myopic shrew beneath the falcon's gaze. He must scramble to explain himself; to explain himself away. "She was so unhappy! I did what I could to help her: I mixed the powder with mead and she drank. The aim is to change the imbiber's essence; her scent, if you will, and thereby attract the object of her passion. And it can be done, Sir Simon, as I have shown! It's no love potion. I would not beguile her with such foolery."

"It is you who is beguiled, Farrimond, if you think your drug has answered the woman's prayers. Someone has got her with child, certainly. And if not you, it can only have been her husband. No wonder she looks so sour."

* * *

328

Clifford wouldn't go ashore at Honfleur, of course, though Aymer disembarked, unbidden, to welcome Jack de Vere and William Beaumont on board. Spying Clifford from afar, Jack waved his bonnet in the empty air then, after a moment, turned on his heel.

The force sailed on to Boulogne and came quietly ashore. Though Pierre du Chastel was nowhere to be seen, the party was clearly expected: a cautious reception and a modest revictualling. After a sober night in town, the men girded up, formed themselves into a column and set off the twenty miles to Calais. Front and central was Clifford – Reginald Grey beside him like a shield, flouting conventions of rank – dividing Jack from Beaumont and interrupting with grunts when they spoke across him.

Clifford might have been merrier, for this was the sort of raid he enjoyed, back home, in the good old days: the noble pleasures of arson and burglary. Calais was one more naughty neighbour who'd got above himself.

It was dim and misty as they crossed from France into the unmarked marshy sink. A hundred years of war, and this was all they had to show for it: this tiny, scrappy clod they still called England.

"My father bore King Henry's standard at Agincourt."

Bellingham looked surprised to find he'd spoken aloud, but William Beaumont turned on him with some relief, for conversation had been limping. "Did he? How splendid! Then you, sir, shall be the talisman for our triumph."

"Talisman for our confusion," murmured Castor in Findern's ear. "We've just marched through France to attack England."

When Beaumont and de Vere made ready to lead off the Hansards, Clifford barked at them. "Not so fast! You're not taking all the archers! Who said you could take all the archers?"

"Your son, as it goes," retorted Jack. "We worked it out with Aymer. If you can't be bothered to join the parley, Robert, you shouldn't complain about the plan."

"The garrison will come for me the moment they see fires. What am I supposed to meet them with? Curses?"

"Charge them quick enough; they'll fall back."

"That's the answer, is it? Charge? You did that at Barnet, de Vere, and it didn't end well. A rout among our own men. When you'd enough of charging one way, you turned about and charged the other. Warwick died because you wouldn't stop charging. Mother of God! I take no lessons from you."

Any number of tart retorts might, justifiably, have been offered, but now was not the moment. Beaumont motioned a dozen archers over to Clifford and fluttered his fingers in Jack's affronted face. Then the two noblemen stood off, stony-faced, at the opening to a rutted ditch that ran in the direction of the walled city, with its strong battlements and its rampant garrison; landless sons, swaggering, belligerent and having the time of their lives. There was no prospect of taking it, of course, but that was never the intention. The exiles couldn't make war, they could only make mischief.

Clifford led his men past the town for the settlements outside its walls. By the time they reached the first hovel, the inhabitants had sprinted into the distance. No doubt there were caches of coin concealed somewhere but they hadn't the leisure to look. They fired the first and then the next. Beside the fifth door they paused. Inside, someone was scurrying about. A young man emerged from the gloom, hands aloft, and addressed himself to Clifford, his English laced with a French accent. "In the name of God, I beg you to pass us by!" Gazing around at the circle of impassive faces, he tried French, with an English accent. "Grandfather is within, my lord. He's gravely ill."

"Are you English or are you French? Come on! English or French: which is it to be?"

After a moment, the young man ventured a guess. "English, my lord."

Clifford bellowed with laughter, gusting him backwards. "Wrong answer! I never shirk the killing of Englishmen, and the French are my friends!" He brought his sword down at the junction of neck and shoulder. The blow looked no more than a mild cuff, a rebuke, so the result was something of a surprise. Clifford nodded at his manservant. "The blade's nicely honed, Jem. You're improving."

Guy was rummaging the single chamber. As the flames caught the windows, he strolled out. "Grandfather seems to have expired."

"This is a bit off," said Bellingham, in a low voice, to Findern. He pursed his lips like a fish. "Bit off, if you ask me. We've changed sides without noticing."

Castor glanced over Sir Cuthbert's shoulder. "Lord Robert!" he cried. Now he was pointing with his sword; bad form, in a master-at-arms. "Here they come."

Clifford measured the phalanx of men streaming from the citadel. Then his gaze was drawn northwards, toward England; to the sky above England. The clouds had turned a peculiar shade, an unnatural rosy green. Below, the sea was pale as a queasy face.

"My nephew's in the garrison," Jolly remarked.

"Would that be Anne's son?" said Bellingham. "I always had a fancy for Anne. Mind you, she must be fifty, now, if she's a day."

"My God, there are hundreds," murmured Peter, gazing at the swiftly moving column. "I'd no idea they were so strong."

Aymer was at his shoulder. "Keep close, lad," he said. "I've trained you for this."

The boy nodded, sheathing his sword, and passed the mace back and forth.

Jolly squinted, too, at the approaching soldiery then turned back to the marshal. "No, Bell, not Anne's boy. My nephew by marriage."

"Didn't she marry one of Dormer's brothers? John – didn't Anne Jolly wed your brother?"

"No," said John Dormer. "There was some thought of it, at one time. No, and a good thing for her: Edward's on his fourth or fifth wife. I can't imagine …" He dropped his visor and the rest was lost.

Clifford strode to the fore. "Let's give them something to chew on in London." He lowered his head and charged.

* * *

Constance had been sent away, already, by Loys, his voice muffled behind the chamber door. An hour later, the girl returned to an unedifying sight: her aunt, seated by the pillow in her bedgown, with Sir Simon in his, combing out the luxuriant locks. Worse, Alice wasn't wearing the appropriate expression of distaste; between the couple flickered a frisson of complicity.

In lowering silence, Constance laid out the chemise and gown and filled the bowl from a pitcher. "May I help you now, Lady Alice? The morning's already old."

The bed creaked. "Well, Constance, hear this news: we believe I am with child!"

Loys nodded, and the bed creaked again. Constance kissed her aunt's cheek. "I'm so glad! And this time, I trust nothing will be allowed to disturb you. Sir Simon, when you're ready, you may wish to summon your daughter. Mistress Catharine arrived yesterday evening, after you and Lady Alice retired for the night. She was attended only by a manservant, sir. They'd ridden from Pearmain. No carriage!"

"Why should I wish to see her? When I deposit an object, I expect it to stay put. Warn her, rather, to keep out of my way. I was in good humour this morning and now it's dissipating."

These days Alice was less ready with her counsel; Constance suffered no such constraint. "I judge it was not Mistress Catharine's doing, sir. Your sister probably found fault on your account. Shall I tell the manservant to await your message before he sets off?"

"Certainly not. That's just what Jane desires." He paused. "On second thoughts, do catch the man before he leaves. Ask if he'd be willing to wed the girl. I doubt anyone else will oblige."

Constance tied the sleeves of the gown without troubling to reply. When all was done, Alice turned to her husband, swaying her skirts, waiting his approval; another performance to set one's teeth on edge. But Constance found her teeth never would lie quiet – not in that house – protesting, little and often.

"Perhaps she should go with Elyn. That's it!" He drummed his hands on his knees, grinning with gleeful spite. "She'll go with Elyn to Roliford. Rohips, Elyn, Brixhemar and Catharine. The merriest household imaginable. *Christ*."

* * *

Charging was, in the end, all they knew.

The last-minute addition of archers had little effect. Only Englishmen handled a longbow with skill; the Hansards should have stuck with crossbows, a weapon more suited to incompetence.

At the first blow, Clifford's ill humour lifted. The garrison was well-drilled and that made it more of a pleasure. He slayed his way across the field, following Loic, who was prancing about in the usual style. Behind them, several of the grooms succumbed to arrows, but that was always happening; they could be replaced. The FitzCliffords advanced steadily, Peter remembering his lessons and learning a few along the way. George and Bede were leading, attended by their manservant, as ever, assisting his masters with slaughter as he assisted them with dressing.

Then came a terrible shock. In the midst of the struggle, as bodies began to pulp underfoot, a ball bowled against George's legs and he half lost his footing. When he glanced down, there was Taffy, gaping back. Weak-kneed, George slithered. A bolus of vomit bounded neatly from his mouth like an owl pellet. Then something struck his arm with brutal force, crushing gauntlet against vambrace so that the broken wrist, which had mended well, gave way and the mace jumped from his hand. He couldn't go on. Hunched over in the melee, he lurched his way to the rear.

"George!" panted Bede, who'd followed him out. "Are you wounded?"

George looked up, mouth hanging. "Taffy has fallen. His head's off. Oh, Bede."

"Jesus, George! You can't just stop." Bede noticed the state of his cousin's harness; blood was coursing from his fingers. "Fight left-handed, then. Come on!" He plunged back in and disappeared.

Not far off, Patrick Nield had paused to draw breath. One hand was gripping a sword, the other, a severed forearm. He tossed it away. The victim writhed like a landed fish, thrashing out with his cuff, drenching Nield and those busy around him.

Nield caught sight of George some distance to the rear, and raised his visor. "What are you about, you great dunderhead?" he cried, though his words were swallowed by the din. "Get in there at once." He turned back to the combat. An arc of black needles pierced the anemone clouds; many arrows, gliding in. Very slow, it seemed to George; so very slow that Nield had ample time to drop his visor, but he did not drop his visor. As George stood, transfixed, the stocky figure stumbled to his knees. Quick as thought, a garrison man was on him, probing with a dagger, and Nield collapsed onto his side. Then George found himself launching upon the assailant, crushing the man's helm; in his clumsy left hand, a flail. He didn't even know he had a flail. He'd no idea how it got there.

The Wyverns were far outnumbered and losing ground, pressed backwards by a wave of force. George was knocked down in its ripples; he scrambled up; slipped again. By now he was so dazed and bloodied that when he staggered off, it was in the wrong direction; a hundred yards before he turned, focused and saw smoke above the city. By then it was over. Jack de Vere and William Beaumont had been shooting, hurling and dropping their incendiaries over the walls to fire those warehouses filled with precious English wool. The garrison were quick to the rescue, for Calais was a city built on fleece; not the firmest of foundations.

Gathering themselves, the Wyverns pursued the raring foe at an exhausted distance, veering off with open relief towards Jack and the others, who waited at the same ditch where they'd parted an hour or so before. Within the walls, storerooms smouldered. Several houses flared, briefly. Flames fingered the castle, then dwindled away.

Glum and weary, many of the exiles had slumped to the ground. George leaned into Bede's neck, tears darkening the collar of his arming doublet. Findern was on all fours, scrubbing his face with ditchwater, and Bellingham was doubled-over, coughing, wretching. After a time, all the men pushed to their feet. The garrison seemed to have forgotten them and it was a long march back to Boulogne.

Clifford glanced over his shoulder. The last of the smoke whirled above the walls. He folded his arms, lifted his chin, and cast around at the men. A speech was forming. The usual theme: courage in the face of adversity; God's purpose; the distant promise of home. "Where's Patrick?" he said.

* * *

Hal leaned from the casement of his chamber, presiding over the loveliness. Little puffy clouds, going nowhere, their reflections basking in the moat. Beyond, the fishpond, with its waving weed and lazy ripples; the hedge with its feet in the marigold beds; the cone-roofed dovecote, capped by a weathervane. None of the grandeur of Northumberland: the silent sweep of the hills, the cold tones and racing winds. Times had been tranquil, too, at Alnwick – waiting for life to begin – but the anticipation was sufficient excitement when he knew no better. Now he looked out over this prim pleasantness and felt it as the calm of death. His life was over.

After a time, Hal's attention was drawn by a lone horseman approaching from the north. The rider must have come down through the woods, leaping the river at its lowest point. He vanished into the angle of the house, shouting for a groom. Such casual entry: it could only be Brixhemar. As so often, Hal had no particular duties that morning. Taking up his bonnet, he trotted down to meet his fellow steward. Something was wrong.

"Walk with me, Hal. I can't stand still."

In silence they passed across the moat and wandered back the way Brixhemar had come, until they left the precincts of the house. "You're heavy with news, Piers?" When Brixhemar raised his dejected brows, Hal was assailed by the usual impudent thought: *if I were Piers I'd school myself never to move those black, comic arcs – and I'd pluck them.*

"Such news, Hal. My uncle is to marry. It's the end of all my hopes."

"Has he a gentlewoman in mind, or is he just talking again?"

"Oh, worse: his suit has been accepted! And, since he's giving himself and Roliford away without a sniff of dowry, it's all been settled with the least possible delay, as you can well imagine."

"My God. Who?"

"A baseborn sister of the Earl. The Earl of Oxford," he added, impatiently.

Hal halted. "De Vere's baseborn sister. Can you mean Mistress Elyn, Alice's gentlewoman?"

"*Alice* to you, is she?" said Brixhemar, listless. "Yes, Lady Alice's gentlewoman. I blame Simon Loys, of course. Was ever a man so blameworthy? May God preserve him for a most hideous death."

Hal's thoughts flitted off, coasting over Alice and Elyn; over Guy and George and Aymer; then Tailboys; Constance; back to Alice. He reined himself in. "I'm truly sorry, Piers. That is a blow."

"Yes it is." All the life had gone out of him. "A new Lady Rohips: a possibility I dimly believed I could frustrate, perhaps for long enough. Not only have I lost Roliford at a stroke, probably, but with it my own prospects of marriage. Triston turned me down already, but if Sir Mark had only died as he ought to, I might have been in time."

"Idonia, you mean?"

"He's giving her away, isn't he? Triston's giving her away to someone else. Fulk Demayne, so I heard."

"You could be right," said Hal. He was right. "There's always young Bess."

"That pudding? You don't understand. Anyway. I'm a servant. A servant is all I shall ever be, now. Idonia is perfection in womanhood. She's been too long in Beatrice's shadow."

"No she hasn't. Everyone says she's prettier; I've heard it a hundred times. And much less interesting."

"She favours me, I know it. Always the certain sidelong look …" Before Hal's eyes, with masterful mimicry, Piers *became* Idonia; the neat visage, like a shadow, overlaying his outsized features. The expression spoke less of admiration and more of unease. "Oh God. What am I to do?"

"Have you considered murder?" At once, Hal regretted the flippancy.

"I couldn't. He took me in when I was orphaned. He paid for my schooling and the pardon after Barnet. And besides, everyone would know. Sir Mark hasn't any true friend, but he has no real enemy either. All fingers would point to me." Brixhemar looked about as if they were being tailed. "Look, Hal – how far may I trust you?" They had wandered to the shade of the woods. He threw himself on the ground.

"What? Utterly, of course." Hal lowered himself beside his friend.

"You fought for us at Barnet," said Brixhemar, as though he were King Henry himself, returned to life. "Why abandon us now? Why are you serving Triston, when you should be following your father and Jack de Vere?"

Hal made himself comfortable. "What's all this, Piers?" *You first.*

"My loyalties have never changed. I'm Jack de Vere's man to my core. I should have followed him into exile. I know it now. I was thinking of Roliford; always Roliford, with me. A moment's hesitation and it was too late. I watched them gallop away. Now I mean to right that wrong. Our Jack has a grave purpose: to overthrow Edward of York. And I mean to help him. I've pledged as much; I've put my name to the bond. To be honest, I've little left to lose. But there are many of us who feel the same; the whole county is seething. And you?"

"Well, I'll be honest too: I'm not that bothered. I grew up with Percys and Nevilles both. Unlike my father, I don't really care who rules in London. What difference can any of that make? It's your kin and your friends who matter, and I'm missing mine. Badly. All the time. Look at me: I was made for warfare and adventure. I can't just sink into a backwater. This life is slowly drowning me."

"Just so! Warfare and adventure will surely be yours if you join us. There will be danger; there will be bloodshed, but if that's what you thirst for, then that's what you'll have. And after we've triumphed, riches and glory. So, are you with us? Say you're with us, Hal! Say you'll join in this enterprise!"

Fortune hadn't so much tapped his shoulder as closed its hands around his throat. For a moment he eyed Brixhemar in silence, then drew a deep breath, stretched on the grass and grinned. "Ah, why not?" It was only later that Hal realised he'd omitted to ask any number of pertinent questions.

"But that's wonderful! The best news I could wish for. See, you've quite cheered me up!" He seemed buoyed; no less brittle. "When we're victorious I'll buy a dozen Rolifords with my small change. Now then, Hal. Answer my question: why did you leave Lord Clifford?"

"Why did I leave Lord Clifford? In truth, I'd no wish to leave him. From the first I was his favourite. Then my father turned against me. He loves Alice de Vere and so do I. That didn't help." Hal waved down his friend, who'd bounded to his knees. "But things started to go wrong before that. It was when he decided to wed the Earl of Northumberland's sister. There can only be one cause, I reckon: somehow he'd made a chance discovery."

Brixhemar was still now – ears whirring, as it were.

"You see, Eleanor Percy had been sucking my cock for months."

"Oh!" Almost as soon as Piers was laughing, he was crying.

* * *

Once there was a ship that set a course for home, black sails unfurled. The grim appearance was unwarranted, an oversight on that merry vessel, grieving for no one. But at its distant approach, a watcher, one who'd craved the ship's return, sighted the mournful omen and leaped from the cliffs in despair.

The return of Theseus, Loic thought. Wasn't it? This splinter of antiquity had been pricking him, insistent, for days – which was odd, given the Wyverns journeyed under circumstances so precisely the opposite. Their sails were the common, grubby shade, specked with flies; there was a corpse, already, on board – only one, for Taffy and the rest were interred at Boulogne; the darkest veil of mourning hung over the ship and, most poignantly, no one was watching, for they weren't going home. The corpse was going home.

And now they were back at the Blackfriars as if nothing had happened. Davy Nield snatched his brother away and buried him somewhere out west, under sheets of blustery rain. They didn't follow. The fallen grooms weren't replaced. Pleydell was serving Bede again and the twins found themselves sharing Notch with George.

After a few weeks in Edinburgh, shrill agony dulled to a sick ache, as it always would, and they resumed the daily round: worship, training, drinking and gaming. Beneath the surface, each was, to some degree, crippled, like a lame swan.

The post of steward went unfilled. Arthur Castor was endorsed already in the minds of most; there were few among the household with hopes of their own.

"He'll not give it to me," muttered George to Bede, as they filed out of chapel one morning, after a particularly fervent bout of prayers. Rumour had it a nomination was imminent. "I know that. Not now, after Calais. But …" The lads gaggled past Lord Clifford's chamber. The door opened. Loic beckoned Aymer within. George was closed out and turned to Bede, aghast.

The pair could not loaf about indefinitely. At midday they dined – somewhere cheap and iffy – and sipped, slowly, all afternoon, one mug of ale between them, like dipping birds. By sundown there was no coin left. "They might be out searching for you now, to give you news. And you, sat here, glooming," said the unhelpful Bede, and George's heart jumped, painfully, anew.

When they made their way back, the day room was thronged with those who might have been out searching, were there cause to do so. Castor and Aymer were at the thick of it in an exaggerated pageant of swordplay like a stately dance. There was wine on the floor.

"Here he is! Here's old man George." Findern was propped against the wall, half cut. "You've missed the frolic."

"Who is it?" George demanded.

"Arthur, of course. Who else?"

"So you're to be master-at-arms?"

"Me? No, I thank you! Butler suits me well enough. A master-at-arms should be young and springy."

Loic reached up to tug George's shoulder, tethering him. "Aymer is master-at-arms." *Bear it like a man*, he wanted to add, taking no pleasure in the slaughter of innocents.

But George had slipped the anchor, cresting to his cousin's side. "I wish you well, Aymer!" he cried. "I was once master-at-arms to the Earl of Northumberland, you know. It's your turn now."

Aymer patted at him. Then the door banged. In strode Clifford, flanked by Reginald Grey and a grave-faced Bellingham. The revellers made their bows in hasty silence.

"Don't let me stop you, lads. Raise a cup! Here, in my hand, is a letter from Jack de Vere. He's been in parley with King Louis, yes, and shown him a bond signed by a score of his gentry, pledging to rise if he invades England."

"God bless them them for the rash fools they are!" whispered Findern, very loudly.

Clifford laughed. "Right enough, Walter." He snorted again. "And, friends, there's still the small matter of which king we're fighting for. But we'll not quibble just now. Louis of France sees George of Clarence's seal on the bond, and that is enough for him. He promises gold. He promises ships. Let's make a pilgrimage to Essex!"

He was thinking of her, of course; the spoils of war. Across the room, Aymer tapped his purse and weighed its precious cargo. Everyone was looking at Lord Robert; reading his face. No one read Aymer. Guy would have read Aymer, but Guy was long gone. That morning, when Aymer ascended to heaven to sit at the right hand of the father, his twin had stalked off, seeking some dark hole to writhe in; as anguished as George and even less adept at masking it.

Pages circled with brimming jugs and the talk sprang up again. Loic watched Arthur Castor sidle to his master, those fresh cheeks a rosy-pink. His nose was pink. A bashful flush, thought Loic, with liquored insight. Poor Arthur was shy, suddenly, to find himself raised to the pinnacle; proud and contrite, all at once, when the honour came from Nield's dead hand. He tripped across. "It's what Patrick would have wanted," Loic whispered into the bewildered ear. Clearly it was not what Patrick would have wanted; not by the end. Nothing less than a mass mutiny would have satisfied him.

Castor was frowning at Loic. Loic blessed him with a smile of wide benevolence: his co-emperor, joint ruler of the household; their little realm. How he loved Arthur! Not quite so well as Arthur would have wished, perhaps, but never mind that. He turned. "Did the letter mention Henry Tudor, Monseigneur?"

Clifford pressed the parchment on him. "Of course not. The Tudors are still in Breton hands, and like to remain so, for now: safe and sound. Let George of Clarence fund the rising and take the risk. He thinks he'll be king; he'll never be king. I'll dice up Edward of York as I diced up his brother Rutland, and when I've diced up York, I'll dice up Clarence into the bargain."

"We mustn't neglect Richard of Gloucester, Father," murmured Aymer. "Collect the four brothers of York, and you shall have a knave of every suit."

"Well said! Well said, indeed! I am Vengeance, am I not? Unhurried and inexorable. They shall not escape me; not any of them."

* * *

In a little house on the edge of Alnwick, beneath the shadow of the woods, Waryn was sitting at his grandfather's side on a pallet before a small fire. It was the same drafty, smoky hovel in which a twelve year old Robert Clifford had courted Janet Prynne, all those years ago; the same bed in which Waryn, and Hal, were begotten and born; the bed in which Janet died.

The old man's claw lay within the great warm clasp. Master Prynne gave a faint cough. Gently the younger man raised the elder and wetted his lips with fine wine, purloined from the castle. "It's a good thing I was staying with the Earl, Grandfather. If you fall again, send for the physician. You know I'll pay the bill."

A soft swish-swishing behind him. Sweeping the floor was Dorcas, Hal's poor discarded drab. The broom prodded a small boy squatting by the hearth, daubed with jam and prickly with sweepings.

341

"Where is Hal?" The old man's quavering voice broke in on his thoughts.

Waryn sighed.

"I'm not wandering. Have you heard from him?"

Waryn shrugged. "Still in Essex, as far as I know. No reason for him to be elsewhere."

"He could rejoin your father. Those two are peas in a pod. I'm surprised they ever parted. You are a good boy, Waryn; Hal is not. It's a shame Hal is his father's heir."

Waryn was staring into the fire.

"I said: Hal is his father's heir."

"I heard you, Grandfather. Not really, he isn't. There's no title, no lands and Hal was gotten in shame, as you know full well."

The old man's voice was a little louder, with a querulous note. "Hear me out! Robert Clifford wed my Janet and you two are his trueborn sons. I'll be dead before long; might as well tell it."

Waryn slouched, crossly.

"Oh yes, Waryn. I'm a silly old man, isn't that so? Attend to me, if you'd be so good, for this is how it stands: I come home one winter evening twenty-odd years back, and find the two of them buck-naked in the bed, your father bearing a cocky grin from ear to ear. '*While you've been a-trapping rabbits, friend Prynne, I have married your daughter,*' says he, '*and got a child on her, I don't doubt.*' '*Well then, young Master,*' says I, '*let's call in the neighbours to drink a mug of ale and toast the happy couple.*' But Janet looks into his face and tells me to wait awhile. And she goes on telling me to wait awhile until it's too late."

Waryn was frowning at him, flummoxed. "Is this …? This is what you wish had happened, Grandfather."

"No! Listen to what I'm telling you. '*Janet,*' I keep saying, '*you've all but lost your chance. Let us tell it at once, or how shall any believe it? Let us travel to Skipton, to Lord Thomas Clifford, and lay it before him. He may take it better than you think, for you are a good girl and Master Robert is only a younger son.*' But all this time, your father is fast growing into a man, and the foolish girl is growing in love for him. And then he has outgrown his squireship and off he skips to his father's lands away down south. And all the while, my only child pining until the sickness takes her, wasting away before my eyes."

Waryn blinked rapidly. There was silence for a moment. A still silence, for the sweeping had stopped.

"At last Robert Clifford is back at Alnwick, the winter of '59, and comes a-calling, but Janet is already gone from us, a bare month since, leaving me alone with you two boys and no way to care for you. '*Sir Robert,*' says I – for he is knighted by then – '*these are your trueborn sons.*' '*Not so, old friend*', says he. '*There was never no marriage that I recall, and if you're a wise man you'll not cross me.*' So Robert Clifford takes you two up to the castle and shows you off to the old Earl as his baseborn sons, and I hold my tongue, for your father is a man of ill repute by then, and I fear him. And the Earl of Northumberland – God rest his soul – takes you in."

Waryn was no easy man to shock; nevertheless he was, by now, very greatly shaken. "But if this is so, Grandfather, why would my mother not have spared her shame by proclaiming the marriage from the rooftops?"

Master Prynne bridled. "Every time I dare to raise the matter, he rages and threatens to come no more; if she calls him *husband*, he walks out the door. She would rather have a trace of him than none at all, I suppose. For certain she suffers at his cruelty, when she loves him with all her might and cannot bear to have him long apart from her. A headstrong girl who never would listen to her father, and this is the result."

Waryn took his distracted leave of Master Prynne and cantered back to the castle, scattering townsfolk, leaving his dignity on the highroad. He said not a word to Mayhew, putting a finger to his lips every time the manservant threatened to speak. It was lucky his wife was left at Belforth; he would not have silenced her so easily.

Rifling a chest, he found a half-ream of parchment and began to scribe rapidly, capturing his grandfather's colloquial manner, while the covering note fell far below his usual measured style. At last, when he could draw breath, Waryn read back the account, a tale so sadly commonplace, and was

343

confounded, again, at its bewildering significance. For a longish while – a long, prudential while – he sat there in deliberating silence. There were no lands, now, for Hal to inherit, and their father had trampled the title. Waryn splayed his fingers across the scrap of parchment, strongly inclined to crumple it in his palm.

But a man must be guided by truth, for God is his witness. Waryn directed Mayhew to find a courier and dispatch the letter to Crawshay Hall in Essex. He sat another spell in stillness, then lowered his face into his hands.

THE END

LIST OF CHARACTERS

The principal characters, as they appear in relation to each other at the opening of the book in 1471 (fictional characters appear in italics):

ROBERT CLIFFORD'S FAMILY AND CONNECTIONS

Robert, 'Lord' Clifford

Second of the four sons of Lord Thomas Clifford (killed by the Yorkists, 1455) and younger brother of Lord John Clifford (killed by the Yorkists 1461). Brought up in the household of the Percy Earls of Northumberland. Self-proclaimed baron and successor to his older brother John. Diehard supporter of the house of Lancaster

Sir Roger Clifford

Third son of Lord Thomas Clifford and younger brother of Robert Clifford. Residing in the North Country

Sir Triston Clifford[1]

Fourth son of Lord Thomas Clifford and youngest brother of Robert Clifford. The only Clifford to support the house of York. Residing at Crawshay in Essex

Lady Honor Clifford

Wife of Triston Clifford

Stephen Clifford

Elder son of Triston Clifford

Gregory Clifford

Younger son of Triston Clifford

Beatrice Clifford

Eldest daughter of Triston Clifford

Idonia Clifford

Second daughter of Triston Clifford

Master Prynne

Father of Janet Prynne (Robert Clifford's secret wife (d.1459) and the mother to his sons Hal and Waryn FitzClifford). Residing in Alnwick

---

[1] Known to history as Sir Robert Clifford

Dorcas Formerly Hal FitzClifford's mistress. Mother of his sons. Residing in Alnwick

The FitzCliffords

George Son of Lord John Clifford. Brought up in the household of Harry Percy, Earl of Northumberland. Gentleman in the household of Robert Clifford

Henry ('Hal') Son of the clandestine marriage of Robert Clifford and his late wife, Janet Prynne. Brought up in the Percy household in Alnwick. Gentleman in the household of Robert Clifford

Waryn Son of the clandestine marriage of Robert Clifford and his late wife, Janet Prynne. Brought up in the Percy household in Alnwick and now the Earl's understeward

Aymer Son of Robert Clifford. Twin to Guy. Brought up in Roger Clifford's household. Gentleman in the household of Robert Clifford

Guy Son of Robert Clifford. Twin to Aymer. Brought up in Roger Clifford's household. Gentleman in the household of Robert Clifford

Richie Son of Robert Clifford. Brought up in the household of Lady Clifford. Gentleman in the household of Robert Clifford

Bedivere ('Bede') Son of Robert Clifford. Brought up in Lady Clifford's household. Gentleman in the household of Robert Clifford

Edwin Son of Robert Clifford. Brought up a lay brother at Fountains Abbey. Gentleman in the household of Robert Clifford

346

LIST OF CHARACTERS

Oliver	Son of John Clifford. Brought up by his mother's brother in the North Country. Gentleman in the household of Robert Clifford
Robbie	Son of Robert Clifford. Brought up in Roger Clifford's household. Gentleman in the household of Robert Clifford
Peter	Son of Robert Clifford. Residing in Roger Clifford's household
Jean	Son of Robert Clifford. Residing with his mother, Babette Delaurin (formerly Robert Clifford's mistress), in Bruges
Marie	Daughter of Robert Clifford. Residing with her mother, Babette Delaurin

VARIOUS MEN AMONG ROBERT CLIFFORD'S HOUSEHOLD (THE 'WYVERNS')

Sir Patrick Nield	Steward
Sir Cuthbert Bellingham ('Bell')	Marshal
Sir Loic Moncler	Chamberlain
Sir Arthur Castor	Master-at-Arms
Sir Walter Findern	Butler
Sir Reginald Grey	Chaplain
Sir Walter Grey	Almoner. Reginald Grey's brother
Sir Lewis Jolly	Gentleman

Bertrand Jansen	Dane, former mercenary
Sir Edward Bigod	Gentleman
Sir John Dormer	Gentleman
Jem Bodrugan	Manservant to Robert Clifford
Benet Penwardine	Manservant to Loic Moncler
Taffy	Manservant to George FitzClifford
Moppet	Manservant to Hal FitzClifford
Notch	Manservant to Aymer and Guy FitzClifford
Pleydell	Manservant to the younger FitzCliffords

ALICE DE VERE'S FAMILY AND INTIMATES

Alice de Vere	Only sister of Jack de Vere, brought up in the household of Richard Neville, Earl of Warwick, at Middleham in the North Country. Pregnant and newly widowed after the execution of her husband, Edmond Beaufort, Duke of Somerset
John ('Jack') de Vere 13th Earl of Oxford	Second son of John de Vere, 12th Earl of Oxford (executed by the Yorkists 1462) and younger brother of Aubrey de Vere (also executed 1462). Fled after defeat by the Yorkists at the battle of Barnet; his whereabouts unknown
Margaret de Vere, Countess of Oxford	Wife of Jack de Vere and sister of Richard Neville, Earl of Warwick. In sanctuary in London
William, Viscount Beaumont	Close friend of Jack de Vere. Fled after defeat by the Yorkists at the battle of Barnet; his whereabouts unknown

Blanche Carbery	Senior gentlewoman to Alice de Vere
Joanna Ames	Gentlewoman to Alice de Vere
Elyn	Natural daughter of John de Vere, 12th Earl of Oxford. Gentlewoman and half-sister to Alice de Vere
Constance	Natural daughter of Aubrey de Vere. Gentlewoman and niece of Alice de Vere
Cecily Welford	Daughter of Laurence Welford of Dyffryn Hall. Attendant on Alice de Vere
Mitten	Chamberwoman to Alice de Vere

LANCASTRIANS: NOBLES, SYMPATHISERS AND ADHERENTS

King Henry (known to the Yorkists as 'Henry of Lancaster')	Henry VI, Lancastrian king of England. Overthrown by Edward of York in 1461. Briefly retook the throne in 1470. Recently imprisoned again by Edward of York
Queen Margaret	Daughter of the Duke of Anjou. Wife of Henry VI and mother to Edward of Lancaster, Prince of Wales (recently killed at the battle of Tewkesbury)
Jasper Tudor, Earl of Pembroke	Half-brother of Henry VI. Holding Chepstow Castle for King Henry
Henry Tudor, Earl of Richmond	Young nephew of King Henry and of Jasper Tudor
King Louis	Louis XI, King of France. Cousin of Queen Margaret and supporter of the house of Lancaster
Pierre du Chastel	Agent of King Louis, acting as his intermediary with Robert Clifford

Yorkists: Nobles, Sympathisers and Adherents

Edward of York (recognised by the Yorkists as 'King Edward')	Edward IV, Yorkist king of England. Overthrew the Lancastrian dynasty and seized the throne in 1461 with the help of his cousin Richard Neville, Earl of Warwick. Briefly lost the throne during Warwick's rebellion and recently regained it following the battles of Barnet and Tewkesbury
Elizabeth (née Woodville)	Edward of York's wife; Queen of England
George, Duke of Clarence	Younger brother of Edward of York, brought up in the household of the Earl of Warwick. Aided Warwick's rebellion in the hope of taking the throne himself. Married to Warwick's daughter Isabel. Recently reconciled with Edward of York
Isabel, Duchess of Clarence	Elder daughter of Richard Neville, Earl of Warwick. Married to George, Duke of Clarence
Richard, Duke of Gloucester	Youngest brother of Edward of York, brought up in the household of the Earl of Warwick
Anne Neville	Younger daughter of Richard Neville, Earl of Warwick. Widow of Prince Edward of Lancaster. Residing with her sister, Isabel, and brother-in-law, George, Duke of Clarence
Henry Stafford, Duke of Buckingham	Married to Catherine Woodville, sister of Elizabeth Woodville
Francis, Viscount Lovell	Childhood friend of Richard, Duke of Gloucester, brought up in Warwick's household at Middleham
Sir John Howard	Cousin to Alice de Vere and to the Duke of Norfolk
Sir Simon Loys	Previously an adherent of the Earl of Warwick. Fought for Edward of York at the recent battle of Tewkesbury

LIST OF CHARACTERS

Catharine Loys   Simon Loys' daughter. Residing at Avonby Castle in the North Country

Leo Brini   Chamberlain to Simon Loys

John Twelvetrees   Marshal to Simon Loys

Peter Considine   Steward to Simon Loys

Sir Roger Vaughan   Yorkist adherent. A prisoner in Chepstow Castle

Sir Lancelot Threlkeld   Formerly of the retinue of Lord John Clifford. Now the second husband of John Clifford's widow Margaret. Residing in the North Country

THE PERCYS AND THEIR ADHERENTS

Harry Percy, Earl of Northumberland   Scion of one of the foremost Lancastrian families. Spent his youth in captivity; recently restored to his earldom by Edward of York. Residing at Alnwick Castle, Northumberland

Lady Eleanor Percy   Sister of Harry Percy. Previously the intended bride of Robert Clifford. Residing at Alnwick

Marjorie Verrier   Senior gentlewoman to Eleanor Percy

Kit Loys   Son of Simon Loys. Page to Harry Percy

Mayhew   Manservant to Waryn FitzClifford

Sir James Thwaite   Adherent of Harry Percy, brought up in the Percy household. Residing at his fortress of Belforth, Northumberland

Lyall   Natural son of James Thwaite

Anna Murrow (nee Thwaite)   Sister to James Thwaite. Recently widowed

351

VARIOUS INHABITANTS OF LONDON

Richenda Tilney	A resident of Southwark
Leaping Abel	A money-changer
Richard Carling	Master of God's Gift, a trading ship
Barnaby	A groom

VARIOUS INHABITANTS OF ESSEX

Nicholas Loys	Half-brother of Simon Loys. Adherent of Jack de Vere, fighting under him at the battle of Barnet. Residing at Danehill in Essex
Petronilla Loys	Wife to Nicholas Loys
Sir Mark Rohips	A childless widower. Old companion-in-arms to John de Vere, 12th Earl of Oxford. Residing at Roliford in Essex
Piers Brixhemar	Nephew and steward to Mark Rohips. Brought up with Jack de Vere in Essex and fought under him at the battle of Barnet
Jane Sheringham	Half-sister of Simon Loys. Residing at Pearmain in Essex
Sir Gilbert Sheringham	Husband to Jane Sheringham. Fought under Jack de Vere at the battle of Barnet
Hugo Sheringham	Son of Gilbert Sheringham
John Cardingham	Steward to Triston Clifford
Clement Petyfer	Chamberlain to Triston Clifford
Adam Boulter	Marshal to Triston Clifford

LIST OF CHARACTERS

Dove   Manservant to Triston Clifford

Mistress Sibel   Gentlewoman to Honor Clifford

Mistress Grace   Gentlewoman to Honor Clifford

Garit Farrimond   Apothecary at Colchester

MASTERLESS MEN

Sir Hugh Dacre   Formerly a knight in the household of the Earl of
                                Warwick, subsequently an unwilling adherent of
                                Robert Clifford

Sir Gabriel Appledore   Formerly steward to Edmond Beaufort, Duke of
                                Somerset

Sir Andrew Chowne   Formerly chamberlain to Edmond Beaufort, Duke of
                                Somerset

Sir Lawrence Welford   Old companion-in-arms to Robert Clifford. Residing
                                at Dyffryn Hall, Monmouthshire

CASTING A SHADOW

Edmund, Earl of Rutland   Younger brother of Edward of York. Murdered by
                                John and Robert Clifford after the battle of Wakefield,
                                1460

Edmond Beaufort, Duke   Leader of the Lancastrian faction. Husband of Alice de
of Somerset   Vere and father of her unborn child. Recently executed
                                following his defeat by Edward of York at the battle of
                                Tewkesbury

Sir Leonard Tailboys   Gentleman in the household of Robert Clifford. Killed
                                by Hal FitzClifford in the stables at Dyffryn

Sir Miles Randall	Formerly chamberlain to Lord John and Robert Clifford. Missing, presumed dead
Henry Clifford	Son of Margaret Clifford and, possibly, her first husband Lord John Clifford. Missing, presumed dead

Acknowledgements

I read very widely in researching this series, but I'm particularly grateful for the work of the wonderful historians Charles Ross, Helen Castor, Susan Rose, Richard Almond and James Ross.

I would also like to thank Mark Ecob at Mecob, for his excellent cover and ideas for the rest of the series and Dean Fetzer at GunBoss Books for his great design of the interior.

Sophy Boyle
London, 2017

About the Author

Sophy Boyle studied History at Oxford University and then worked in the City for many years. She gave up her legal career to write the *Wyvern and Star* series. She lives in South London.

Wyvern and Star is a series of novels following the exploits of Robert Clifford, Alice de Vere and their circles. Robert and Alice are fictional characters, and their immediate families have been trimmed and shaped to accommodate them. The historical background has been left, where at all possible, untouched.

The next book, *A River Filled With Teeth*, will follow in 2019.

To keep up to date with the Wyvern and Star series and to be notified when the next book is coming out, visit

www.wyvernandstar.com

Printed in Great Britain
by Amazon